Michelle Smart's love affair with books started when she was a baby and would cuddle them in her cot. A voracious reader of all genres, she found her love of romance established when she stumbled across her first Mills & Boon book at the age of twelve. She's been reading them—and writing them—ever since. Michelle lives in Northamptonshire, England, with her husband and two young Smarties.

Clare Connelly was raised in small-town Australia among a family of avid readers. She spent much of her childhood up a tree, Mills & Boon book in hand. Clare is married to her own real-life hero, and they live in a bungalow near the sea with their two children. She is frequently found staring into space—a surefire sign that she's in the world of her characters. She has a penchant for French food and ice-cold champagne, and Mills & Boon novels continue to be her favourite ever books. Writing for Modern is a long-held dream. Clare can be contacted via clareconnelly.com or at her Facebook page.

CHRISTMAS BABY WITH HER ULTRA-RICH BOSS

MICHELLE SMART

TWELVE NIGHTS IN THE PRINCE'S BED

CLARE CONNELLY

MILLS & BOON

First published in Great Britain 2023
by Mills & Boon, an imprint of HarperCollins*Publishers* Ltd,
1 London Bridge Street, London, SE1 9GF

www.harpercollins.co.uk

HarperCollins*Publishers*, Macken House, 39/40 Mayor Street Upper, Dublin 1, D01 C9W8, Ireland

Christmas Baby with Her Ultra-Rich Boss © 2023 Michelle Smart

Twelve Nights in the Prince's Bed © 2023 Clare Connelly

ISBN: 978-0-263-30696-5

10/23

This book is produced from independently certified FSC™ paper to ensure responsible forest management.
For more information visit: www.harpercollins.co.uk/green.

Printed and Bound in the UK using 100% Renewable Electricity at CPI Group (UK) Ltd, Croydon, CR0 4YY

CHRISTMAS BABY WITH HER ULTRA-RICH BOSS

MICHELLE SMART

MILLS & BOON

CHAPTER ONE

TWO HUNDRED AND ten kilometres north of the Arctic Circle, adjacent to the Torne River, the main lodge of the Siopis Ice Hotel was filled with chattering staff. The wooden lodge, which served as the reception and administrative offices, and the cosy chalets surrounding it, were open all year round for guests to enjoy the changing of the seasons, but it was when November arrived and the river froze enough for the craftsmen and women to get to work, that the magic really happened. In the four years Lena Weir had worked there, she'd never failed to be awed by the talent and creativity and sheer hard work that went into creating what was known as The Igloo out of nothing but blocks of ice and snow; never failed, either, to sigh wistfully when spring arrived and the magical creation melted back into the river from which it was formed.

Today though, spring felt a world away. It was nearly 2 p.m. It could be midnight. The sun had made its last brief appearance three days ago. Lena, along with the rest of the staff and their guests, had stood outside and basked under its weak rays for the full twenty-six minutes it had graced them. It wouldn't show its face again other than as a brief glimmer on the horizon for another three weeks.

The lack of sun had never bothered her during her previous winters here in Sweden. She enjoyed them, liked experiencing what her mother had lived through for the first twenty years of her life. She struggled far more in the summer months when the opposite happened and the stars rarely came out and the sun never slept.

In three days the first guests of the winter season would arrive. Those adventurous enough and rich enough would spend a night in The Igloo itself. The activity happening in the lodge was the final staff meeting before the official winter opening of The Igloo. Welcoming the first guests through its doors was always a thrill. The exterior of the design was always the same, basically a giant igloo, but the interior was always different. The only constant was the sparkle of the ice, translucent through the carefully woven lights.

As the staff layered themselves for the biting outdoors, the reception phone rang. Sven being the closest picked it up, and in perfect English said, 'Siopis Ice Hotel, how can I help you?'

If he hadn't immediately looked at her, Lena would have missed the flicker of panic that crossed Sven's face as he listened to the caller. He nodded vigorously and ended the call saying, 'Of course. I will get the housekeeping team on it immediately.'

'What's wrong?' Lena asked. Everything at the Ice Hotel ran so smoothly that it was rare to see any of the staff flustered. Had one of the cabins' coffee machines stopped working? A guest greeted with an unmade bed? It couldn't be anything more serious than that if the housekeeping team was being called into action.

Turned out it could be.

'That was Magda. The six-month inspection has been brought forward.'

She raised an eyebrow but was unperturbed. Lena had nothing to hide. She'd privately thought scheduling the inspection for three days before Christmas was bonkers timing. Bringing it forward made a heap of sense.

But Sven hadn't finished. 'Mr Siopis is coming himself to do it.'

Lena actually felt the blood drain from her head down to her toes in a whoosh.

Gripping hard to the reception desk, she forced air into her lungs and managed to croak, 'When?'

Konstantinos Siopis only ever made one visit a year to the Ice Hotel and that was in the summer. He wasn't due back for another seven months.

Unsurprised at her reaction—no doubt Sven thought it entirely reasonable—he said, 'He will be here in four hours.'

Fighting her body's determination to drop into a ball and rock back and forth, Lena tightened her grip on the reception desk and did her best to keep the panic from her voice. 'You are going to tell housekeeping to sort a cabin out for him?'

Sven nodded.

'Okay. I will arrange for the car to collect him from the airport.' Sending their guests favourite mode of transport—the huskies and sledges—to collect him was out of the question. 'Did Magda say how long he will be here for?'

'No.'

She wouldn't chide Sven for not asking. Magda was as terrifying a PA as it was possible for the owner of a luxury hotel chain and investor in cutting-edge technology to get. She was almost as terrifying as her boss. Who also happened to be Lena's boss, too, and the ultimate boss of every member of staff there.

He also happened to be father of the secret baby growing inside her.

Konstantinos looked out at the unpitying darkness. Some people got a thrill out of endless nights and relentless cold but he wasn't one of them. Sun-drenched islands like his birthplace Kos were his natural habitat. He never felt the need to escape to colder climates, and generally worked his annual diary so he would always be somewhere the sun beat down.

Where his pilot was currently preparing to land, almost as north of Sweden as it was possible to get, the only illumination came from a smattering of lit-up homes and research centres and small tourist areas. The sun wouldn't show itself for weeks.

The landing went smoothly but the biting cold hit him the moment the cabin crew opened the door. A short walk later and he was in the back of a heated car and shaking his hat off. He supposed he should be grateful it wasn't snowing. Konstantinos's dark olive skin did not appreciate wet ice landing directly on it. His legs didn't appreciate having to spend extra time walking through it. The rest of him didn't appreciate having to wear layers of unstylish clothing to protect him from it.

As a child he'd watched Christmas movies with picture-perfect white settings and envied the children in them and the fun they had making snowballs and snowmen and sledging. His first personal experience of snow was aged twenty-one when he'd taken Cassia to New York for a long weekend. It had taken him all of five minutes to despise it. By the time he'd returned to Kos, he'd vowed to avoid the cold and snow for the rest of his life.

So why had he made the impulsive decision to delay his scheduled trip to Australia and instead head to a part of the world that currently provided none of the comforts he thought essential, namely sunshine?

It was standard practice in his organisation for each of his hospitality businesses to be inspected twice a year. Konstantinos's aversion to the cold meant he entrusted all his cold-climate northern hemisphere winter inspections to his specialist team. Early that morning he'd been woken by a call informing him that Nicos, director of said inspection team, had been admitted to hospital with gallstones and was likely to be off work for six weeks. Nicos was scheduled to inspect the Ice Hotel three days before Christmas, less than a month away.

The Siopis Ice Hotel was the jewel in Konstantinos's crown, a hotel complex that never failed to deliver year-round rave reviews. Each winter people from around the world flocked to stay the night in The Igloo, a magnificent structure built anew each autumn from ice and snow. Since its opening eight years ago, Konstantinos had deliberately timed his annual visits to the summer months when The Igloo had long melted in the spring thaw, and the permanent year-round log cabins were visited by wealthy adventurers seeking wilderness tours and rafting experiences.

Nicos's being out of action and the rest of the inspection team's schedules being full meant the Ice Hotel's inspection would have to be delayed. This wouldn't be a significant issue if Konstantinos hadn't five months earlier entrusted the running of it to Lena Weir, the youngest and least qualified candidate to apply for the general manager's role. Lena's weekly reports were as succinct and thorough as he'd come to expect from the individual managers of his hotels, the reviews as glowing as he'd come to expect, too, but only a thorough inspection could determine if things were as shiny internally as were projected externally. He would have to suck up his loathing of the cold and dark, and make the inspection himself. Thinking quickly, he'd determined that as it was his turn to spend Christmas with his family in Kos, the timings of the scheduled inspection would be cutting things too fine, especially if unexpected issues were revealed, so had made the decision to undertake the inspection immediately.

It was an impulsive decision he'd regretted as soon as he'd made it.

He'd never visited one of his businesses with such a tightness in his chest before, and for that he blamed himself and his stupidity of five months ago.

Since striking out on his own, Konstantinos had conducted a version of what his own father had done whenever hiring a new member of staff for the family restaurant, namely sharing a meal with the new recruit, the simple breaking of bread a gesture of welcome. As Konstantinos now hired thousands of people around the world, it had long been unfeasible for him to continue it, but the tradition held in its own way, those responsible for hiring anywhere within his organisation expected to take new staff members out for a meal, the expenses taken care of by the Siopis Group. As the most senior appointments were made by Konstantinos himself, he continued the tradition with staff appointed directly by him. Which was how he'd ended up sharing a meal with Lena Weir after promoting her to manager of his Ice Hotel.

Although the location was as remote as remote could be, there were a range of high-class eateries dotted around the site, including the hotel's very own Michelin-starred restaurant, which is where they'd dined. They'd made their way through the whole tasting menu, pairing each course with the recommended wine, and somehow managed to get through three bottles between them. It had seemed like the most natural thing in the world to walk her to her cabin, even more natural to accept her invitation of a coffee.

They'd been exceedingly polite to each other the next morning and he'd left Sweden reasonably certain it wouldn't affect their working relationship. He'd been given no reason to think otherwise since.

Lena Weir was no fool. She was a woman who did her homework—her tenacity in all things was one of the reasons he'd entrusted the job to her—and she would know a man didn't reach the age of thirty-seven without settling down or having any notable relationships unless that was exactly how he wanted it.

Shapes emerged through the car's headlights. They'd almost reached the hotel complex.

His chest tightened into a pin.

Konstantinos had never gotten drunk with an employee before. He'd certainly never slept with one.

It had been a mistake. They'd both agreed that the next morning.

It had been a mistake that would never be spoken of or alluded to again.

When the huge all-terrain car pulled up at the front of the all-year reception lodge, Lena avoided Sven's attempt to meet her gaze. She knew the fear she'd find in his stare would only feed the rancid panic gnawing in her stomach.

But her panic was not the same as Sven's or the other staff who, when told the owner was making a surprise visit, had started racing around like headless chickens. It was their reaction that had pulled her together, even if only superficially, and she'd clapped her hands together to get their attention.

'We all do our jobs to the high standard he expects of us so what is there to worry about?' she'd said, before pausing and adding with a half smile, 'Although, if anyone feels they might have cut some corners in some way, now would be a good time to rectify it.' A few members of staff had sheepishly scuttled out.

Lena knew whatever corners those staff had cut, they had been minor. Her staff worked hard, for their guests and each other. They were a solid team and had each other's backs. Konstantinos Siopis would not find anything here that did not meet his exacting standards. At least, she prayed he didn't. He paid his staff extremely well and was generous with the benefits written into their contracts, but in exchange he demanded perfection. A bad review demanded a thorough investigation, and any staff found to have been negligent in their duties could consider themselves lucky to get away with a written warning for a first offence. There were no second chances. In the five months Lena had been manager she'd only had to deal with three incidents of neglectful staff. Luckily, those minor infringements hadn't made it onto any review sites and she'd failed to put those infringements in writing on the staff's individual records. But there was no way Konstantinos could know this…could he? That would be grounds for him to dismiss her.

She swallowed the bile rising up her throat and watched Konstantinos unfold his long, rangy frame out of the back of the car. An abundance of strategically placed LED lights gave enough illumination for anyone to find their way around safely outside, the glow reminding her of the fairy lights her father used to drape around their garden at Christmas when she was a child.

Wrapped in a long lambswool coat that, even with the collar turned up, would give little protection against the cold, he trod his way over the compacted white snow towards the lodge door. Each step closer made the beat of Lena's heart heavier, and she had to stop her hands moving to protect her belly. Apart from the hotel's on-site doctor who was bound to confidentiality, no one knew she was pregnant. It was a secret she hugged fearfully to herself, a maternal instinct that had unfurled when the test had proved positive.

Lena could not afford to lose her job. Without it, she had no way to provide for her baby. Nowhere to live outside this remote corner of the world. Her parents' home in England would always be open to her but there was no room for her and a baby there, not with her tiny childhood bedroom now a makeshift pharmacy and medical equipment storage room for her sister. She had no savings other than what she'd squirrelled away since the pregnancy test had come up positive. Whatever savings her parents had amassed had been quickly depleted after the terrible accident Lena had walked away unscathed from but which had left Heidi needing twenty-four-hour care.

The man she should have been able to turn to, the father of her child, was almost at the door. Her weighty heart almost became stuck in her throat.

While Sven darted forward to open the door for him, Lena grabbed the thick folder she'd prepared and placed it in front of her belly, then sent a silent prayer that Konstantinos didn't pay too close attention to her figure. The heating inside the lodge was so good that most of the staff usually just wore their uniform polo shirts but in the past couple of weeks, Lena had taken to wearing the smart thick black sweater dress with an inbuilt collar the female customer-facing staff was provided with. Only the most eagle-eyed person would notice that beneath it were signs of a neat but developing bump. To play safe, she'd helped herself to an oversized sweater dress, which so far had been a successful means of disguising it.

Konstantinos stamped the snow stuck to the soles of his boots off at the mat before the door and stepped inside.

His gaze fixed straight onto the woman he'd spent the night with the last time he'd been here. Her large, dark brown eyes met his. A beat passed between them before a welcoming smile lit her face and she strode over to him, a folder clasped in one hand over her stomach, the other outstretched.

'Mr Siopis, this is an unexpected pleasure.'

'I'm sure,' he replied sardonically, clasping his fingers around hers in a businesslike fashion. A flash of warmth darted over and through his skin, and his hold on her tightened reflexively. Immediately, he released the hold and also released his stare to cast his gaze around the immaculate reception room, taking in the traditionally Swedish Christmas decorations and beautifully decorated fir adorning it. The scents of tinsel, cinnamon and orange permeated the air.

Even though the whole non-ice sections and cabins of the Ice Hotel were heated by geothermal means, the main lodge reception had an open log fire roaring, a welcome feature to the freezing cold guests on their arrival. He stepped over and placed his hands before it.

After a moment to gather himself, he turned his face back to Lena. He detected an apprehension that could almost be confused with fear. Both emotions were understandable. He, too, had felt an apprehension at seeing her again. At least, he thought it had been apprehension that had tied his stomach in knots and made his chest feel tight from the moment he'd made his decision to come here. A committed short-term monogamist since Theo and Cassia's betrayal, Konstantinos had never been a man for one-night stands. The few he'd enjoyed had been hookups with strangers, women he never expected to see again. Women he'd never had to see again. Women he'd never wanted to see again. None of them had lingered in his memories.

Lena had. Lingered, that is. Another reason why breaching professional boundaries was a bad idea. Konstantinos owned twenty-three hotels and invested in numerous other businesses. Since their night together, his heart had skipped a beat that was both unprofessional and inexplicable whenever her name pinged into his inbox. Her emails, always concise and professional, were the only emails he found himself reading twice. Her weekly reports were the only reports he read with more than a scan for the pertinent information.

Never again, he told himself grimly, again. Mixing business with pleasure was a recipe for disaster he'd learned the hard way. To have lapsed as he had, even with the excuse of alcohol thrown into the mix, was a mistake he was forced to regret every time Lena's name diverted his attention from whatever work he had in hand. And now she stood before him in the flesh, her dark brown hair with the glimmer of russet tones loose around her shoulders, one side tucked behind a small pixie-like ear, framing an oval face that any man would look twice at. Large, velvet brown eyes. Pretty, straight nose. Wide, generous lips. All atop a slender frame with breasts far more generous than the clothes she wore would...

He cut his thoughts off. He should not still be able to feel the weight of Lena's breasts on the palm of his hand.

'Has a cabin been made ready for me?' he asked curtly. Here, in the middle of nowhere, there was a rule that a cabin should always be kept free in case of emergency.

'It has,' she confirmed. 'I have the accounts for the last quarter ready if—'

'The business side will be dealt with later,' he interrupted. 'My first priority is to tour The Igloo.' Get that part over with and then he could spend the rest of his short stay here out of the damned cold.

She nodded and gave another of her bright smiles and indicated the tall Scandinavian manning the reception desk with a young Spanish woman. 'Perhaps Sven can—'

'No. You're the manager. It is for you to show me around it.'

Her lips twitched and another flash of apprehension flickered in her eyes but Lena's smile didn't waver. 'Of course. I only suggested Sven because his father was the lead architect and Sven was involved in creating one of the art rooms.'

'Do you not have the same knowledge of its creation?' he challenged.

'I do, as do all the staff.'

'Good. Sven can show me to my cabin. Meet me back here in thirty minutes and we can get started.'

'Do you want to walk or ski to The Igloo? Or go by

snowmobile?' Lena's preferred way of getting around the complex was with skis. It didn't actually involve any real skiing in the hurling down a mountain sense; it was just an easier way of getting around in these conditions than walking.

'We will walk,' he answered, without any hesitation.

'As you wish.'

He met her eyes, gave a sharp nod, and set off through the reception room with Sven in tow to the back of the lodge and to the most direct route to the cabins.

As soon as the door closed behind him, Lena expelled a long breath and closed her eyes.

Well, that had to rank in the top two most excruciating moments of her life. She couldn't decide if it trumped the morning after the night before.

She'd gazed at Konstantinos sleeping in her bed with her heart thumping wildly, then climbed out, sniffed his discarded shirt as she'd put it on, and thrown open the blackout curtains. The bright summer sun had kissed skin still marked with the passion of Konstantinos's mouth, and she had whipped around to face him, joyous laughter bubbling up her throat, legs already preparing to spring back to the bed and wake him with a kiss when she'd found his eyes open. The expression in them had made the laughter die in her throat.

'Last night was a mistake.'

Those five words had pierced her. In less time than it took to blink, the joy she'd been full to the brim with had seeped out of the hole his piercing words had made.

She'd hugged his shirt tighter around herself and nodded. 'Yes.'

He'd thrown the sheets off and climbed off the bed.

'It is not a habit of mine to sleep with the staff. Rest assured it will not happen again.'

Pride made her say, 'Let's just put it down to too much wine and forget about it.'

Green eyes more piercing than his tongue fixed on her again. 'You can do that?'

'I'm an adult and quite capable of separating my personal life from my professional one. Last night was a slip made when I was off duty and one I doubt either of us would have made if we'd been sober. How about we both chalk it down to experience and never speak of it again?'

She'd forced herself to take the weight of his stare as he sized her up, judging the value of her words. Eventually, he'd given a short nod. 'As long as we are both of the same mind.'

'Totally.' She'd mimed zipping her lips.

He'd almost smiled.

CHAPTER TWO

ONCE LENA HAD added a few extra layers over her work clothes, she carried her all-in-one snowsuit from the storeroom to the reception to wait for Konstantinos, only to find he was already there, back turned to her, grilling Sven.

Her heart quivered and jumped painfully, and she closed her eyes and breathed deeply through her nose, just for a moment, just long enough to catch her emotions before they spilled over.

She hadn't expected that seeing Konstantinos in the flesh again would feel so emotional. Pregnancy hormones, she supposed, although it pained her to suspect that she would still be reacting in the same way if she hadn't conceived.

Lena hadn't expected to fall into bed with him. Until he'd walked her back to her cabin and her heart had suddenly lurched to know their evening together was over, she hadn't considered him the slightest bit attractive. The uncharitable would go so far as to call Konstantinos Siopis ugly, what with his angular features, his long, sharp, prominent nose that bent at an angle, bowed lips always fixed in a straight line, and deep-set eyes ringed in dark shadows and topped with bushy black eyebrows. He wore his thick, curly hair cropped short and clad his long, rangy figure in varying shades of black. That he rarely smiled only enhanced the impression of brooding, almost vampiric unattractive menace. That his fang teeth were a teensy bit longer than the rest only added to this. If he were an actor, he'd be typecast as the baddie, every time.

But he'd smiled that evening *and* without his face cracking. His eyes—a gorgeous clear green she'd not even noticed until sitting opposite him in the restaurant—had lost their coldness and, if not softened, warmed. Possibly it had been the wine goggles she'd ended up wearing but the longer their meal went on, the more fascinating she'd found his face and the deep olive of his skin, which always looked in need of a shave, and the more fascinating she'd found the deep, gravelly voice she'd always thought faintly terrifying. Konstantinos's English was so precise and his Greek accent so heavy that to her ears he'd always sounded as if he was barely concealing impatience. That evening his tone, like his eyes, had warmed. By the time they'd reached her cabin her whole body thrummed, hot, dizzying awareness rocketing through.

It hurt to look at him now. It hurt to hear his voice.

Her body had come alive for him. It had sung to him. She'd gazed at his sleeping face the next morning with a heart clambering to break free and then climbed out of her bed and practically bounced to the window like a spring lamb to throw the curtains open.

Inexplicably, it had been the single happiest moment of her life in six long years.

And then he'd woken and delivered those awful words that had punctured her inexplicable joy.

As she walked apprehensively in her three pairs of socks over the thick carpet to him, she wondered for the umpteenth time how she'd gone from finding Konstantinos completely unattractive to incredibly sexy in the space of one evening.

Noticing her approach, he gave a short nod of acknowledgement and continued his grilling of Sven, forcing Lena to stand around like a hovering lemon and do her best not to let her eyes keep falling on him. He'd removed the dark suit and long overcoat he'd arrived in, his lean frame now wrapped in black jeans and a thick black sweater. She hoped he had thermal layers on beneath it. Layers were the key to survival here. Multiple layers. She wouldn't ask him, though. Konstantinos was not a man who encouraged unsolicited advice.

She wished she didn't care if he'd layered up. She doubted he cared if she had. She doubted he'd given her a second thought since he'd left her cabin five months ago.

'You're ready?' he asked a short while later, finally fixing his attention on her.

'I just need to put my snowsuit and boots on.'

He nodded and strode to one of the armchairs by the open fire where a black thermal snowsuit had been draped over it. Snatching it up, he sat down to put his feet into the legs and then stood back up to pull it to his waist, past calves and thighs far more muscular than would be believed when clothed.

From the other side of the room, Lena did the same with her too-large staff-issue blue-and-white thermal suit, trying not to watch him, trying not to let her mind remember the strength in his arms as he slid them into his suit's sleeves, or think about the defined muscularity of his abdomen and chest, or the thick black hair that covered it as he zipped it up to his chin. When he sat back down and forced his huge feet into the all-weather boots that would allow him to tread on the ice without danger of slipping, a sliver of fear crawled up her spine.

Lena had toured the latest incarnation of The Igloo just three days ago. Her own boots were as sturdy and ice resistant as Konstantinos's, but she'd had a real terror of losing her footing and landing on her backside. It wasn't fear of hurting her bottom that had frightened her but fear of hurting her baby. She knew there was little danger of slipping in the Ice Hotel, but knowing something intellectually was a lot different than feeling it emotionally. Today she had the added danger of touring it with her baby's father, the one person she so desperately needed to keep her pregnancy secret from. Konstantinos's discovering she was pregnant was the single biggest danger to her baby. She couldn't risk him finding out yet. She just couldn't. She hadn't saved enough money yet to support herself for longer than a fortnight and had none of the supplies a newborn baby needed.

She hated that she had to keep it from him, but the coldness emanating in waves from him was unnerving enough to convince her that she'd made the right decision. There was little chance of him accepting the baby as his without a paternity test and every chance he would sack her on the spot.

Both fully suited and booted, thick hats rammed on their heads and thick scarves wound around their necks and half their faces—Lena always felt claustrophobic with a balaclava on and only wore one in blizzards—they lifted their hoods over their heads and stepped out into the bracing cold.

The vast complex that constituted the Siopis Ice Hotel was dominated by two main sections. One was the year-round area centred by the main lodge reception. Dotted around it were the guest log cabins, restaurants, boutiques, spa, the buildings that housed the snowmobiles and ski hire, and all the other facilities that enabled them to cater to their guests' every adventurous or more sedate desires. To its left was the path that led to the second section, commonly known as The Igloo.

A ten-minute walk from the all-year reception, the path to The Igloo was lit by the same magical quality lights used to guide guests and staff to the lodge and cabins. The only sounds as they made their way to it were the low throb of music from one of the occupied cabins and their own breaths, each exhale accompanied by a white cloud of expelled air.

'How long are you planning to stay here?' Lena asked as they passed the ice rink and snow-covered permanent cabin used as The Igloo's reception and the huge, cleverly lit dome of The Igloo itself emerged fully from the darkness, and she could bear the tension tautening her every sinew no more.

'One night,' he said with a clipped tone of voice that suggested it was more than enough time.

'One night too long?' she queried wryly while inwardly heaving a giant sigh of relief. That meant he expected the inspection to be wrapped up by the end of day tomorrow.

One night was manageable. With any luck, he'd leave Sweden none the wiser about the child growing in her belly.

When she did tell him, he would be furious. The green eyes that had flared with such hunger would fill with loathing; the mouth that had kissed her so passionately would curve in disgust. There would not be an ounce of warmth in his voice.

She wished she could blame him but she couldn't.

'At this time of year, one hour is too long to spend here.'

'Not a fan of the cold?'

'No,' he answered shortly.

The entry to The Igloo was a permanent structure. The sensor doors slid quickly open and they entered a world of sparkling white. Before them lay the welcome room adorned with long chairs and low tables made entirely of clear ice, and with a fireplace carved into the wall that gave the illusion of white flames flickering in it. It was a sight replicated year after year that never failed to bring a gasp of awe to their guests' mouths. It was an awe that only increased when they were led through the rest of it.

The cold of the Ice Hotel's interior sucked the air from Konstantinos's lungs. He knew it was warmer inside—if you could call minus five degrees warm—than outside but being plunged into an ice-white surround played tricks on the mind. The immediate plunge into silence didn't help with the mind tricks. He tightened his hood and kept his gaze on the giant dome he'd stepped into rather than the woman he'd entered it with.

He was in half a mind to leave when the tour of this icebox was done with. He could fly to his hotel in the south of Spain where the weather was currently balmy, stay there for the night, and then fly as planned to Australia to deal with his many southern hemisphere business interests until Christmas. Have Nicos complete the full inspection when he was back to full health.

To leave Sweden immediately, though, would be a sign of defeat, not just of the cold but of Lena. He would not be pushed out of his own hotel because of the tightness that pulled sharply at his stomach every time he looked at her. She was a beautiful woman. That was a fact he'd registered on a superficial level at their first meeting much in the same way he noted the colour of a person's clothing. Until that damned celebratory dinner, she was just another employee. Just another face. Another name.

That was all she was to him now, he reminded himself firmly. Just another employee. These strange feelings currently gripping him and making his insides feel hot and cold at the same time were solely because this was a novel situation he found himself in. A situation he wouldn't be in if he hadn't been so damned stupid as to sleep with her.

Clenching his teeth, he inhaled the frigid air into his tight lungs and forced his attention back to where it should be. On the jewel of his crown, the giant Igloo.

Off the vast main dome were the warrens of iced tunnels that led to the dozens of individual rooms, and they set off into the nearest one. The tunnels were higher than he remembered, the walls thicker.

The rooms they toured were each individually crafted and therefore unique, the majority containing nothing but a large bed made of ice and topped with a thick mattress that itself was topped with reindeer hide.

'Have you spent a night here?' he asked when they went down yet more ice steps and into a room carved into a forest scene with pine trees and reindeers, the bed having the effect of rising off the forest floor. The customer-facing staff was encouraged to sleep in the hotel during the window between completion—not that it was ever completed. Ongoing maintenance was needed for such a huge, complex structure—and the first guests' arrival, but this was not mandatory.

'Once. My first winter here.'

'And?'

'I found it too claustrophobic to want to do it again.'

Surprised, he gazed up at the high forest scene above

his head then back at her with an expression that demanded explanation.

She shook her head. 'When the lights are turned off...'

'Explain,' he commanded.

'It's the darkness,' she said with a shrug.

'It is always dark this time of year.' As dark as it was cold.

'Not like it is in here. It's a completely different experience. In here, the walls are so thick that nothing penetrates it, no light or sound...you must hear it now, the absolute silence. And I stayed in a room with a door.' Most of the ice rooms had fur curtains for doors, which let slivers of light in from the tunnel corridor LEDs that were kept on at all times for safety reasons, but a handful had real doors designed to cope with subzero temperatures. Those rooms were the largest and most spectacular of them all and guests paid a premium for them. Lena had hardly believed her luck when she'd been appointed one for the night. That was until the door closed, her room's lights went off, and she'd been pitched into absolute blackness.

'Outside there is always some form of light, whether from the moon and the stars or, if you're *really* lucky, from the aurora borealis, but in here...' She rubbed her arms and shivered. 'It's like sleeping in a tomb.'

'Be sure not to tell our guests that,' he said sharply.

'Of course I won't,' she said, stung at his tone. The vast majority of their guests loved the experience. 'But you asked me to explain and I explained because that's how it felt to me at the time, and it does say on all our literature and online information that staying in The Igloo isn't suitable for claustrophobic guests. Those who suffer from it stay in the cabins.'

'So why did you stay in it if you suffer from claustrophobia?'

'I didn't know I did until that night.' Not until she'd been lying in the pitch-black and found herself thrown back to that terrible night when she'd been trapped in the dark with her sister, praying for Heidi to wake up, praying for help to come quickly. She'd imagined she could still smell her sister's blood.

He contemplated her for another moment then indicated the fur-lined ice door. 'I have seen enough of the rooms. Take me to the bar.'

The bar was to the back of The Igloo, close to the ice tunnel that took their guests to the permanent non-ice heated changing rooms, and reached by climbing a number of wide steps. Lena sat on a fur-lined ice booth and kept quiet while Konstantinos took it all in. She had the distinct feeling her confession of claustrophobia had irritated him. No doubt he wasn't scared of anything at all.

In her opinion, the creator of the bar had surpassed himself this year. The craftsmanship and artistry were incredible. It was like being in a swish wine bar with wooden panelling and optics and pumps, except one made entirely of ice. Witty pictures hung on the walls; each table had beer mats carved into them…there was even a coat stand with coats hanging on it. All carved from ice. The only things in the bar that weren't illusions were the fur lining on the chairs to prevent frostbite and the drinks they served. While Lena would never wish to spend another night in The Igloo, that didn't stop her revelling in the sheer spectacle of it.

She watched Konstantinos examine a shot glass made of ice, real fascination in his expression.

'Drink?' he surprised her by asking.

She shook her head.

The semi-frozen vodka poured thickly and when the ice glass was filled, he drank the shot in one go. He gave an exaggerated blink as it slid down his throat then screwed the lid back on the bottle. 'Too cold for my tastes. Let's return to the lodge.'

Konstantinos's arrogant assumption that he'd be able to conduct the tour with his business head on had proven a fallacy he rued darkly once they were back on the path to the main lodge. The longer they'd spent in The Igloo, the greater his awareness had grown that by his side was the woman who'd lingered in his head when she should have evaporated from it, and the greater his resentment. Whether his resentment was aimed at Lena or himself or both of them, he couldn't say. He'd disliked watching her tentative movements in The Igloo and the way she'd touched the walls with every step she took, her movements much as if the ice beneath her feet scared her, which it couldn't, not with her being a seasoned pro on it. Disliked it because there had been a vulnerability to her movements, which had disturbed him to even notice, but not half as disturbing as the compulsion to offer his hand for support, which in itself wasn't half as disturbing as the extra ice that had slivered in his veins when she'd described her claustrophobia, and an image of Lena herself entombed had flashed in his mind.

He should have opted to take the snowmobiles. If he had, they'd be back at the lodge by now and the crowding memories of the night they'd spent together would already be dimming amidst the noise of other people.

'How are you finding your role here?' he asked abruptly. The way he was currently feeling, the idea of shutting himself away with Lena in her office was intolerable. Get the questions he wanted answered by her done now and over with, spend the night going through the books—alone—and then get out of this place.

'Good, thanks.'

'What about the workload? You find it manageable?' He should not be hoping she would confess to finding it too hard and resign on the spot.

'It's nothing I didn't expect when I applied for the role,' she answered.

'And the responsibility? It is a big step going from duty manager to general manager.' It was a responsibility not everyone was cut out for. Hopefully, she would admit to being one of those people.

'It is,' she agreed, 'but I have a great team around me. Everyone pulls their weight.'

'Anything you have concerns about or feel needs my attention?'

'Nothing that's occurred since my last weekly report.'

They'd reached the lodge. Stopping to stamp the snow stuck to their boots, he asked, 'You haven't held anything back from me?'

If he hadn't glanced at her he would have missed the flicker in her eyes.

She gave a quick shake of her head and said equally quickly, 'I report everything that needs reporting.'

Narrowing his eyes, Konstantinos wondered if the colour in her cheeks was purely a side effect of the cold, or down to her having just told a blatant lie. He was well aware his managers sanitised their reports for his reading, failing to include minor incidents that he should, by rights and by contract, be kept apprised of. He let them go. He couldn't micromanage every aspect—that was what he paid the managers to do for him and he had to trust their judgement on what was deemed serious enough to notify him about. Occasionally though, he would learn of incidents that had no place being swept under the carpet. The question was whether Lena was covering up for something minor or something more serious. Her reaction made him suspect the latter.

They stepped inside. Konstantinos pulled his hat off, unzipped his snowsuit, and appraised her flushed face one last time. 'I believe your shift has finished. Leave your office unlocked for me. There are members of staff I wish to speak to.'

She'd made no attempt to remove any of her own clothing, and now he detected a noticeable flicker of fear in her dark brown eyes. 'About me?'

By now convinced she was hiding or covering up something, he smiled tightly. 'Everything appears to be in order but I take nothing at face value. I will call you in if I discover anything that needs your attention or explaining. Enjoy your personal time.'

Long past midnight, stripping off in the privacy of a log cabin far more luxurious than the last cabin he'd slept in whilst there, Konstantinos was unsure if he was relieved or disappointed that the only misdemeanours Lena had failed to notify him of were so minor it would have annoyed him if she'd added them to a report. He'd been disgruntled to find that all the reasons he'd promoted her a good few years sooner than he would anyone else in her position had proven sound and that Lena was an exemplary manager. She had the respect and loyalty of her whole staff and, in some cases, adoration.

Glass of Scotch in hand, he climbed into the rolltop bath he'd run to warm his frozen bones, sank under the hot water, and tried not to mentally plot the route to Lena's cabin. She would have upgraded since their night together, staff accommodation being consummate to position. Only staff with a managerial title had a cabin to themselves. The general manager was granted the largest of them all.

After a large sip, he leaned his head back, closed his eyes, and tried to breathe out the tightness in his chest and the heavy ache in his loins.

He should have taken that woman in California up on her offer the other week. He'd attended a tech investment conference—Konstantinos's businesses were varied—and her interest in him had been obvious from the moment she'd read his name tag. It never ceased to amaze him how his sex appeal grew once his name was recognised. Beautiful women who barely gave him a second glance when he was anonymous suddenly switched into beguiling flirt mode. A cynic would think it was his money they were after. A cynic, if in the mood, would take them up on their unspoken offers and enjoy a night of no-strings sex. If he'd accepted the Californian woman's offer of a nightcap in her room, an offer made as she fingered the length of his tie, he could have purged himself. Five months of celibacy wasn't healthy. He'd never gone this long between lovers before, which only brought his thoughts back to Lena, the last woman he'd been with.

Konstantinos threw the rest of his Scotch down his throat and swallowed it in one gulp.

Come the morning and he wouldn't hang around. He'd keep appearances up, congratulate Lena on running a tight ship, and then get the hell out of this godforsaken place until the summer.

CHAPTER THREE

LENA DABBED CONCEALER under her eyes to hide the dark circles that had formed after her terrible night's lack of sleep. Many more nights like that and her circles would be as dark as Konstantinos's.

A smear of balm over her lips and then she donned her snowsuit over her work clothes and set off on the short journey to the lodge. Apprehension and fear had compressed into knots in her stomach. She'd spent the whole night on tenterhooks waiting for her phone to ring and for Konstantinos's unemotional, gravelly voice to invite her back to the lodge so he could sack her.

She'd been convinced she was going to lose her job, certain he'd discover the incident of the missing petty cash—whoever had taken it had replaced the money the next day—and the drunken scuffle between two members of staff that hadn't been witnessed by any of the guests but which had resulted in broken furniture in the staff lounge. That, too, had been resolved the very next morning with a brisk hungover handshake, a bear hug, and a lot of glue.

After hanging up her snowsuit and checking her small bump was still hidden beneath the oversized sweater, Lena headed to her office.

Konstantinos was already there, sat at her desk, unshaven but dressed in a shirt and tie and black sweater, looking at something on her computer. Her knotted stomach lurched and her heart made that same quivering jump from yesterday.

He must have turned the heating up. The air in her usually balmy office currently felt more like the air in the sauna.

Somehow, she managed to inject a form of brightness into her tone. 'Good morning. Is everything okay?'

He glanced up from the screen and gave a short nod. 'You have an email from one of the grocery suppliers. They will be late with their delivery today.'

'You're going through my emails?'

'Your work emails,' he corrected. 'And I wasn't going through them. The notification popped up on the screen two minutes ago. Would you have a problem with me looking at them?'

It was the narrowed scrutiny of his green eyes that made her cheeks burn, but she kept her frame and tone steady. 'Not at all. How's the inspection going?' If she was about to lose her job then get it over with. The wait for feedback had become more than she could endure.

'I'm done.'

'Already?'

He leaned back on the seat. *Her* seat. Those deep-set green eyes bore into her. 'I congratulate you. You delegate well. The place is spotless. The guests are happy. The staff are happy. You run a tight ship.'

Her relief was such that she blew out the air she'd been holding and laughed. 'Phew.'

'You sound surprised.'

She pulled at the ends of her hair, which she'd left

loose. 'I was under no illusion that my perspective of how I run things might differ from your perspective.'

'If your perspective is that you run things to a high standard then we are in agreement.' He looked at his watch and rose to his feet. 'Time for me to leave.'

Instead of jubilation that he was leaving so soon, there was another, stronger lurch in her stomach, more like a plummet, and a definite tremor in her voice as she politely asked, 'Where are you heading to next?'

'Australia.'

'The climate more to your liking?'

His lips twitched before he grunted his agreement and thrust his hand across the desk to her.

The beats of her heart increasing in weight and tempo, she stretched her arm out. The instant his long, warm fingers wrapped around hers, all the organs in her body contracted then released with a burst.

'Until the summer,' he said briskly.

The compulsion to throw herself into his arms and confess that they were having a baby and beg him to stay and share her joy and be a father to it was so strong and so sudden she almost staggered under the weight of it.

His eyes crinkled with concern. 'Is something the matter?'

Releasing her hand from his, she swallowed and shook her head. 'Just a bit warm in here,' she whispered. It wasn't a lie. The room was sweltering.

And what wasn't a lie, either, was that she didn't want him to go. As terrifying as the whole situation was, as terrifying as Konstantinos's being here was, and the inherent danger that came with his discovering the pregnancy when he had so much power over her fate...in that moment the thought of him leaving was close to unbearable.

He stared at her a beat longer then gave one of his sharp nods and stepped around her desk.

Another beat later and he was gone from her office. All that remained were the remnants of his citrusy cologne.

Konstantinos's car hadn't left the complex when he realised he'd left his phone by the computer in Lena's office.

Telling his driver to give him two minutes, self-recrimination roiled in his guts. If he hadn't been so keen to get away from her he wouldn't have forgotten the damned thing and now he had to go back in there and see her one more time. With any luck, she'd have left the office to run an errand somewhere and he wouldn't have to look into those large brown eyes and be transported back to the night he'd lost himself in her.

All these months he'd done his best to forget. Time should have put enough distance to make it nothing but a vague memory, but seeing her again had made it all slam back into his consciousness and it was no longer just the weight of her breasts against the palms of his hands he could still feel, but the silkiness of Lena's skin compressed against his and the exquisite bliss of being buried so deeply inside her. When she'd walked into the office, his tongue had suddenly tingled to remember the taste of her, a deep jolt of heat in his loins to recall the scent that had lingered in the air after they had collapsed in each other's arms.

He could still see, vividly, the way her eyes had widened when he'd first entered her, hear the intake of breath that had turned into a moan that had fed his desire for her in a way that had blown away every sexual experience he'd ever had before her.

Was it any wonder he'd felt it so necessary to leave her office?

He would not linger. He would grab his phone and get the hell out and stay the hell out.

Nodding at Anya, one of the women working the reception desk, and at the bundled-up couple checking in, he strode to the office.

Lena was opening the window, her back to him. She'd removed her sweater to reveal a fitted plain white long-sleeved top that enhanced the silhouette of her trim figure over her tight-fit black trousers. She'd put a little weight on since their night together, he observed dimly.

She turned her head and visibly jumped with shock to see him.

'I left my phone behind,' he explained tersely, grabbing his phone and shoving it into his back pocket.

She didn't say a word, just stared at him with a look that reminded him strongly of a deer trapped in the glare of headlights.

He left the office as quickly as he'd entered it. His hand was on the door that connected to the reception when his feet brought him to a halt.

Something, some sixth sense, was thumping for attention in the back of his brain. The thumping extended to the rest of him.

Mouth suddenly dry, he turned slowly and strode with leaden feet back to the office.

He pushed the door open.

Lena's arms were in the sleeves of her sweater and she was in the process of pulling it over her head. There was a frantic quality in her movements, and when she tugged it down over her protruding belly and spotted him standing there, she no longer looked like a trapped deer. She looked like a *guilty* trapped deer.

For the longest passage of time her terrified eyes remained glued to his.

Blood pumped hard through him. Getting air into his lungs became impossible.

'Lift your sweater,' he commanded hoarsely.

Her face crumpled and she folded her arms protectively beneath her breasts and over her stomach.

He breathed deeply and lifted his chin. 'Do not make me repeat myself again, Lena. Lift your sweater up.'

It was hearing Konstantinos say her name for the first time since he'd arrived back in Sweden that broke Lena. The iciness in his voice. Her nightmare was coming to life but in this one there was no way of waking herself before the worst happened.

The tears she'd been holding back all these months broke free and rolled down her cheeks. With shaking hands, she gripped the hem of her sweater and pulled it up over her pregnant belly.

While he stared without blinking at her stomach, her baby moved inside her. She didn't know if he saw the movement but the impassivity on his face changed and he staggered back and fell into the visitor chair, the colour leeching from his olive skin.

Hands gripping his knees, he bowed his head. His shoulders rose and fell in almost exaggerated movements before he slowly lifted his face back up to meet her eyes. 'Is it mine?'

She tried to nod but her body was shaking too hard and all she could manage was a whispered, 'Yes.'

His face contorted into a frightening mix of rage and

comprehension and, fury etched in his every sinew, he shot back to his feet. 'You lying, deceitful, poisonous—'

Only by the skin of his teeth did Konstantinos stop himself from uttering the cruel curse he wanted to throw at her. White-hot, rabid fury had infected every part of him, an anger so strong that he turned on his heel and stormed out of the office lest the poison consuming him erupted.

Uncaring that the snow had started to fall, he flung the emergency exit door open and stamped out onto the treated path at the rear of the reception lodge. On either side of the path snow was piled as high as his knees, and he scooped a load into his hands, packed it into as tight a ball as he could manage, and hurled it through the air with a roar. And then scooped more snow.

By the time he'd worked the worst of his fury out of him, he was soaked to the skin, his lungs were burning, and his hands frozen. Making a real effort to control his breathing and the rage still boiling in his veins, he went back inside.

Lena, her eyes red and her face blotchy from crying, was sitting on the visitor chair with a tissue clutched in her hand.

'Get your snowsuit on and come with me,' he snarled.

'Come where?' she croaked.

'My cabin, where we can speak without being disturbed...' A thought penetrated the fury in his brain. 'I assume no one else has been given it yet?'

She shook her head.

He stuck his head out the door and tersely shouted, 'Anya, keep my cabin reserved for me until further notice and call Sven in—he's in charge until further notice, too.' Then he looked again at the deceitful face of the woman who'd deliberately kept that she'd conceived his child a secret from him. 'Snowsuit.'

Feeling as sick as she'd ever been in her life, Lena obeyed, scuttling out to the staff storeroom and hurriedly donning a snowsuit, hat, scarf, and boots.

'Are you not going to change, too?' she tentatively asked when she returned to the office.

'What's the point?' he said bitterly. 'I'm already half-way to frostbite.'

The look on his face told her not to bother arguing with him.

They left through the same rear door Konstantinos had used to work his fury into the snow. The usually pristine mound of snow lining the path had had gouges taken out of it from where he'd made his furious snow-balls. She'd watched with her hand over her mouth from the window, her heart aching and her head reeling at his raging anguish.

She welcomed the cold air she breathed in through the falling snow and by the time they reached his cabin, her mind felt clearer and sharper. She wished the rest of her felt clearer, too, but guilt and apprehension lay too heavily inside her for that. But there was a smidgen of relief mingled in her churning emotions. Konstantinos knew.

His learning of the pregnancy was the only thing she no longer had to fear. The rest of her worries and night-mares could still come to pass.

Inside the luxury cabin that was at least ten times the size of her own, Lena stripped down to her work uniform while Konstantinos hung up his sodden coat in the heated cupboard by the entry door, and removed his soaked shoes and socks. Her heart twisted to see the snowflakes glistening on his black hair. Despite the warmth of the cabin, he must be freezing.

'You should have a bath to get warm,' she said quietly.

'Do not feign concern for my well-being,' he snapped, then yanked his sweater off, ripped his tie from around his neck, undid the top three buttons of his shirt, and whipped that off, too. The wet clothes all landed like puddles on the floor.

The last Lena saw of him was his ramrod straight back as he stormed into the bathroom and slammed the door shut behind him. A short moment later came the sound of running water.

Needing to keep herself occupied for fear of driving herself crazy with her fearful thoughts, she gathered Konstantinos's discarded clothes, intending to place them in the laundry box situated by the main door to stop sodden clothes from damaging the wooden flooring. For reasons she couldn't begin to comprehend, she pressed her nose into the bundle. The scent of his cologne made fresh tears swim in her eyes and, feeling choked and sicker than ever, she dropped the bundle into the box.

Each cabin came equipped with its own drinks station. Knowing Konstantinos took his coffee black, she slotted an espresso pod into the machine then made herself a hot chocolate. Once both drinks were done, she hesitated before helping herself to a miniature Scotch from the mini-bar and pouring it into his coffee. She knew she could have done with a stiff drink herself when she'd first discovered she really was pregnant.

At the bathroom door, she hesitated again before gently knocking on it. 'I've made you a hot drink,' she called, and wished she didn't sound so tremulous.

The door swung open. A cloud of warm, citrusy steam escaped.

Konstantinos, phone in hand, wearing only a towel around his snake hips, glowered down at her.

At five foot five, Lena wasn't particularly short but in that moment she felt tiny. Almost a foot taller than her, it was only when Konstantinos was undressed that his full strength and muscularity became apparent. Clothed, his masculinity was almost threatening in its intensity. She'd never known anyone so rampantly *male*. Undressed, there was a raw, rugged beauty to his physique that had stolen her breath the first time she'd seen him naked and now brought her close to spilling hot coffee over herself.

His gaze dropped accusingly to her hand.

She swallowed the moisture that had filled her throat and mouth and whispered, 'It'll help warm you.'

A pulse throbbed on his jaw. His chest rose and then, fingers brushing against hers, took the cup from her hand, gave a sound that could be interpreted as grudging gratitude, and closed the door.

Lena blew air out of her mouth and pressed a hand to her chest, the other to her swelling bump. She would take it as a positive sign that he'd accepted the drink.

Miserably, she sat on one of the armchairs and thought back to a time when looking for the tiniest positive sign was all that had kept her sane. The blinks that showed Heidi understood what was being said to her. The first smile. The first attempt at speaking. The first successful attempt at speaking. And then the knowledge had come that this was as good as it was going to get, that her sister had reached the limit in her recovery. There would be no more new positives.

How could Heidi not have resented Lena for her health,

resented that Lena had walked away physically whole while Heidi was condemned to a life of paralysis? It made her want to weep to think of the life Heidi should be leading. She *had* wept. Oceans of tears. But those tears didn't change anything. Heidi would never be a mother and have the family of her own she'd craved since they were little girls. Lena hadn't given two thoughts to having children until she'd missed her period. She was only twenty-five. Children and family had been years away... until they weren't.

Feeling more movement in her belly, she closed her eyes and rubbed it, wondering again how Heidi would take the news she was going to be an aunt when Lena told her family on her leave next month. She imagined the shocked but delighted smile but—

The bathroom door opened.

Lena's eyes snapped open and her thoughts scuttled away.

Dressed only in a complementary grey Siopis robe that was too short for his tall frame and yet still managed to look as if it had been designed with Konstantinos in mind, he carried his cup to the coffee machine and slid another pod into it. 'Can I get you anything?'

The offer brought a lump to her throat. 'No, thank you.'

As she'd done, he poured a miniature Scotch into his coffee then carried it to the armchair beside hers, straightened his robe, and sat down.

Although outwardly calmer, she could feel the tension vibrating through his frame, sensed he was holding on to his anger by a whisker, and when he finally fixed his green eyes on her, the coldness in them made her quail.

'How certain are you the child is mine?'

'Completely certain.'

His top lip curved. 'Be very careful, Lena. I am aware of the amount of bed hopping that takes place amongst the staff here. Are you positive no other man could be the father?'

'One hundred per cent positive. You're the only man I've been with in six years.'

Something dark sparked in his eyes. The pulse in his clenched jaw set off again. 'You expect me to believe I am the only man you have been intimate with in six years?'

'It's the truth.'

His cold gaze didn't leave hers. He was weighing her up, she realised. Judging whether or not to believe her.

All she could do was stare back and hope he recognised the truth in her eyes. If he chose not to believe her...

Her whole body trembled. She knew what the consequences would be if he decided her claims of his paternity were a lie. Destitution until the baby was born and she could force a paternity test.

Still staring intently at her, he took a long drink of his coffee before placing the china cup on the small round table to the side of his chair. 'If you are telling the truth then answer me this,' he said in a low growl. 'If I am the father of your child what in hell gave you the right to hide it from me?'

CHAPTER FOUR

THE STRICKEN EXPRESSION on Lena's face made no impression on Konstantinos. If anything, it disgusted him. He'd done the maths. She had to be five months pregnant. She must have known for four of those months; three months if he was being generous. At least three months in which she'd kept the secret of the life they'd supposedly conceived together from him.

To expect him to believe he was the only man she'd been with in six years when she'd been the one to instigate their lovemaking? Did she take him for a fool?

He'd known when he accepted her offer of a coffee in her cabin that he was making a mistake, but for the first time in his life he'd ignored his own internal warnings, too caught up in the intoxication of the woman whose spell he'd slowly fallen under the longer the night had gone on to think of resisting.

Her cabin had been cosy, only a small sofa in the living space at the foot of the bed. She'd produced a bottle of vodka and two shot glasses. Her hands had trembled as she'd poured them both a slug of it. They'd downed the shots in unison and then taken their coffees to the sofa.

He'd sat facing the small television, the beats of his heart as weighty as he'd ever known them. He couldn't remember ever feeling such awareness, his body a tuning fork vibrating to the music of the woman curled beside him, her knees barely a centimetre from his thigh. The danger he'd been heading towards had rung loudly in his head. 'I should go,' he'd said. But instead of making the effort to move away from her, he'd twisted to face her.

Her head was rested against the back of the sofa, dark brown eyes on his. 'Already?' she'd sighed.

Under the soft lighting of the cabin he'd seen for the first time what beautiful smooth skin she had. His fingers had tingled to stroke her face. The warning in his head to leave immediately had grown louder.

But then she'd stroked *his* face. Just a gentle brush of the back of a finger across his jaw. His breath had caught in his throat. The vibrations of his body had thickened. Her face had inched closer to his. The backs of her fingers had then brushed down the exposed part of his neck, trailing fire over his skin. The desire in her eyes had been stark but there had been a hint of bewilderment in her stare, too, as if she was as confused as he at the thickness of the electricity crackling between them and at what her fingers were doing.

At the first whisper of her lips against his, all the warnings in his head had been drowned in the flood of heat that had consumed him.

He severed the memories with a sharp blink.

To expect him to believe he was the only man Lena had seduced or had allowed to seduce her in the four years she'd worked here was beyond the realms of credulity. The Siopis Ice Hotel was so remote that all the staff lived in, the vast majority in special staff quarters. It was the only one of his hotels where he turned a blind eye to his staff's licentious behaviour. So long as it didn't affect their work then who was he to judge how they passed the long, dark nights when they were off shift?

He'd despised himself for those fleeting moments since their night together when his guts had coiled to imagine who the latest employee Lena had invited into her bed could be. They'd coiled to imagine *anyone* sharing her bed. Touching her. Breathing in her soft, feminine scent. Tasting her.

'I asked you a question,' he said through clenched teeth. 'If you expect me to believe I'm the father of your child, why hide it from me?' Konstantinos had amassed a fortune so vast he was regularly named as one of the top three richest Greeks. Just as believing Lena had lived like a born-again virgin for six years was beyond credulity, so, too, was believing that she wouldn't have thought she'd hit the jackpot if she'd been certain he was the father. Conceiving his child would be a lottery win for any woman, and he wasn't deluded enough not to know that greed had been the most potent mix in his lovers' desire for him.

He hadn't seen that greed in Lena's eyes, he suddenly realised, but pushed the thought away as quickly as it had formed.

Konstantinos had known since his brother's betrayal that he would never marry or settle with a permanent partner, and if he wouldn't marry or settle then he wouldn't have children. Protection against pregnancy had always been paramount when embarking on an affair…or had been until he'd been naked with a woman whose every kiss and touch had fed his hunger, and he'd realised he had no protection at hand.

'It's okay,' she'd whispered as her tongue traced the rim of his ear. 'I'm on the pill.'

Hating the thrill that ran through him at the memory, he snarled, 'You told me you were on the pill,' before she could answer his previous question.

'I was,' she replied tearfully, her eyes filling up again.

'Save your tears,' he snapped, angry with the both of them. How could he have been so stupendously stupid as to disregard the need for proper protection because in the heat of the moment he'd thought he might die if he didn't take possession of her?

But he wouldn't have died. Penetrative sex wasn't the only way to reach satisfaction. If she hadn't told him she was on the pill they would have used other means to bring each other to...

He grabbed his skull and dug his fingers into it as hard as he could. He had to stop thinking about that night.

Wiping her eyes, she leaned forward, arms wrapped around the belly within which a baby was growing. 'Konstantinos, I'm sorry,' she said. 'You have every right to be angry with me. I was on the pill, I swear, but it was the mini-pill and you're supposed to take it at the same time every day and I was sloppy about taking it because I only used it to regulate my periods and not for protection, and at the time it didn't even cross my mind that my sloppiness would result in this, but it was entirely my fault and I am so, so sorry for that, and I'm sorry for not telling you as soon as I took the test but I was terrified of how you'd react and what you'd do, and I thought—rightly or wrongly—that it was best to wait until the baby was born before telling you because I knew you'd want a paternity test before you acknowledged our baby as yours.'

'You mean you made assumptions.'

'Of course they were assumptions but I had to do what I thought was best for me and the baby.'

'How the hell did you think you would make it to the birth without me finding out?' She wasn't obviously pregnant yet but the loose clothing she'd disguised her bump behind wouldn't hide it for much longer.

A loud rap on the door put a halt to the most excruciating conversation of Lena's life.

Konstantinos opened it. A blast of frigid air entered the cabin in the seconds it took for him to bring his luggage inside and close the door.

'I can't believe I have to stay longer in this godforsaken place,' he muttered darkly as he slung it all on the bed. He opened the larger case and glared accusingly at her. 'I'm supposed to be on my way to Australia. Magda's having to postpone all my appointments and meetings indefinitely until this mess is sorted.'

A flare of temper sneaked up on her. Lena had known he would blame her but being on the receiving end of anger that was colder than the weather outside was harder to bear than she'd imagined. 'Have you got her to put out the word for my replacement yet?'

'Don't give me ideas,' he growled before rummaging through the case.

'I'm surprised you haven't officially sacked me already. After all, you've already put Sven in charge.'

'Someone has to be in overall charge and you can't be if we're in here sorting out the mess *you've* created.'

'The mess *I* created but which you were a very willing and active participant in,' she reminded him bitterly. 'We both know you're going to sack me so why not get it over with or are you getting a kick out of prolonging my misery?'

He pulled out a pair of black, snug-fitting briefs and stepped into them. Pulling them up his legs, he bestowed her with another glare. 'So not only did you make assumptions about how I would take the news of your pregnancy, you've made assumptions that I'm going to sack you?'

'Well, that's what you did to my predecessor's predecessor.'

'*What?*' He untied the sash of his robe and irritably shrugged it off.

Suddenly confronted with his practically naked body, Lena quickly averted her eyes. 'You sacked Annika for being pregnant.'

'I did not.'

From the periphery of her vision she saw him pull on a pair of black jeans and, breaths and heartbeat quickening, had to make a concerted effort not to stare at him, hating that she *had* to make a concerted effort not to stare. How was it possible that she could be so physically aware of him when her whole life was on the cusp of being destroyed *by* him?

'I was told all about it. You called her into her office. She thought you were going to discuss her maternity leave but you sacked her on the spot for no reason.' It was Annika's dismissal that had seen Thom promoted to the general manager role and one of the receptionists promoted to Thom's role of duty manager, which in turn had created the receptionist vacancy Lena had filled. Konstantinos Siopis's sacking of the popular Annika had been a nugget of information she'd learned shortly after her arrival at the Ice Hotel and stored in the back of her mind, practically forgotten until she'd taken the pregnancy test.

'Then you were told wrong.' He dragged a black, long-sleeved top over his head and pulled it down over his muscular, thickly haired chest and abdomen. 'I sacked

Annika because she allowed the lodge reception to be unmanned for two night shifts. No duty manager, no receptionist, not even a member of the housekeeping team. During one of those unmanned shifts a guest was taken ill.'

Lena's mouth dropped open in shock. 'Are you being serious?'

'Have you known me to be lauded for my jests?'

There was no reason on earth, not under the current circumstances, why this should remind her how surprised she'd been when Konstantinos had, over the course of their meal, revealed himself to actually have a sense of humour. It was a subtle, dry humour but as soon as she'd caught on to it she'd felt like a schoolgirl given the results of an incredibly hard test and learning she'd come top of the class.

It had been while grinning at something he'd said and catching the glimmer of humour in his green eyes that something had shifted in her. In practically the blink of an eye the unattractive face had taken on an endearing quality. By the end of their meal endearing had morphed into fascinating. Beauty was in the eye of the beholder and to Lena's eyes Konstantinos had become mesmerising.

It pained her that if she wasn't extremely careful, she could easily find herself mesmerised by his vampiric unattractiveness all over again.

'What happened to the guest?' she asked. It had been drilled into Lena during her induction just how important it was that both the lodge reception and The Igloo's reception always be manned. In this remote, dangerous corner of the world, anything could happen and someone needed to be available to assist in those 'anythings' at all times. The reception was always the first port of call. Everything flowed from there.

'He tripped and suffered a serious head wound walking back to his cabin at night. His wife went to the lodge for help but there was no one there.'

Her eyes widened in horror. 'No one at all?' This should not be possible.

'Now you understand why I had to dismiss her? The guest lay on the path for thirty minutes before help reached him. This was in April. The temperature was below freezing. He was lucky not to have got hypothermia.'

'I knew nothing of this.'

'I wouldn't have done either if the gentleman hadn't threatened to sue us for negligence. I paid him off and I paid Annika to go quietly, too.'

'You paid her off when she'd been grossly negligent?' If Konstantinos was telling the truth then paying Annika off made no sense. There was no reason on earth the lodge should be unmanned. There was always a duty manager and receptionist on duty at all times, plus a doctor on call and numerous other staff on hand to pitch in if needed. They were deliberately overstaffed here to stop anything like an unmanned reception ever occurring.

'I paid her off because she was pregnant.' He sat back on the armchair and locked his eyes back on her while he rolled thick socks onto his long feet. 'I didn't have to give her anything and there is not an employment judge in Europe who would have disagreed, but her baby didn't deserve to be born into hardship because of its mother's negligence, and now I would like you to explain to me how you thought you could make it to the birth without me finding out.'

It took Lena's brain a few moments to catch up with the swerve from Annika back to herself. She shook her head. 'I don't know. I was going to work as long as I could and hope you didn't get wind of it before I left.'

Socks on, he dug his elbows into his thighs and continued looking at her with the gaze of an enemy interrogator. 'You must have made some form of plan. Were you planning to leave without working your notice? Take maternity entitlement? What?'

'I wasn't stupid enough to think I could arrange maternity leave without you finding out.' Konstantinos would have to personally approve whoever was appointed to cover for her, which meant he would have definitely learned about the pregnancy before she was ready for him to know.

'Then what were you going to do? Give birth in the staff room and then demand the immediate paternity test you spoke of?'

'I don't *know*,' she repeated, her voice rising and quickening in response to his icy sarcasm. 'I just knew I needed to work for as long as I could and save as much money as I could before the baby comes because I have nothing. I have no savings, no home of my own—'

'So you want my money?'

'Absolutely.'

For a moment his expression morphed into surprise before his top lip curved in distaste. 'You admit it?'

She would not feel shamed into wanting what was best for her baby. 'My child is entitled to support from its father, and let's face it, you're not short of a bob or two.'

'Is that what this is all about? A way to extort money from me?'

'God, *no!*'

'You told me you were on the pill.'

'I told you—'

'Excuse me if I treat what you say with cynicism when you've spent months hiding the child you claim is mine. How very convenient that you fell pregnant after one night together.'

The implication that she'd either deliberately connived to get pregnant by him or was deliberately conniving to make him believe he was the father winded her.

She gazed into his cold green eyes and begged the fresh tears burning her retinas not to fall.

Were all her memories of the night they'd shared false? Had she spent months imagining the passion that had consumed them both in a whirling vortex of sensation that had left no room for thought or rationality? Had she *imagined* the depth of the shared intensity? Why else would he even consider that she'd approached their lovemaking with calculation if that passion and intensity hadn't been shared?

Somehow, that hurt far more than his scepticism of his paternity. All these months she'd comforted herself by thinking that whatever the future held for her child, at least it had been conceived with genuine passion. That she could be here now and still feel that same burning awareness for Konstantinos only made it worse.

'See?' she said shakily. 'This is why I didn't want you to know until the baby was born. You're so cynical about everything that I knew you wouldn't take my word for it being yours.'

His eyes glittered. 'Don't forget your assumption that I would sack you for it.'

'Can you blame me?'

'Yes, I can and I do, and I blame myself, too, for falling for your seduction.'

'*My* seduction?' She threw her hands in the air and shook her head with disbelief. 'So now you're rewriting history? We'd both had too much to drink, and yes, I made the first move but at least I hold my hands up and accept my responsibility for what happened but it takes two to tango, so don't even think about portraying me as some money-grabbing seductress who deliberately set out to get pregnant because if you think I ever wanted to be in the position of being a single mother with sod all money and limited emotional support then you are raving.

'All I've been trying to do these past months is build a nest egg to carry me and the baby through the birth until a paternity test confirms what I'm telling you.'

'And then what?' he sneered. 'You must have thought about what comes after. What would you like to happen? A large transfer of cash into your bank account?'

'Well, that would be nice,' she said tartly, refusing to let him see how badly his coldness was hurting her. His reaction was nothing she hadn't anticipated but living it was much worse than she'd imagined.

The pulse set off on his jaw again. 'I won't marry you,' he warned.

She reared back. 'I don't want *that*.'

Marriage hadn't even crossed her mind. Never minding that they'd spent the grand total of one night together, what woman in her right mind would want to tie herself to a man like *him*?

'I mean it, Lena. While I accept there is a strong probability that I'm the father, I will never marry you, so put the idea from your mind.'

'I just said I don't want to marry you, so get off your

ego trip. You might be as rich as Midas but you're not the catch you think you are.' Jumping to her feet—she had a feeling she wouldn't be this sprightly for much longer—she folded her arms over her belly. 'Are you going to sack me?'

Now he was the one to be thrown at her swerve in the conversation. 'No, but—'

'You can stop at the *but*. If you're not going to sack me then I'm going back to work.'

'You're not going anywhere. We're talking.'

'You call going round in circles and taking verbal lumps out of each other talking?' She sucked her cheeks in as she tried even harder to keep the tears at bay, but when she continued she could hear the choke in her voice. 'We can talk tomorrow when we should both be calmer, and see if we can at least start finding common ground, but if you're not prepared to accept you're the father without a paternity test and keep coming at me as if I'm some kind of bad-faith agent then there's no point in us even doing that, and you might as well just fly off to Australia like you'd planned and we can talk properly when the baby's born.'

The way Konstantinos's elbows were digging into his thighs she thought they might bore holes into them. But he didn't say anything to stop her leaving. Not verbally. The dark tightness on his face told its own story.

CHAPTER FIVE

AN HOUR AFTER Lena left his cabin, Konstantinos was still sat on the same armchair having barely moved a muscle, replaying every word they'd exchanged. Replaying Lena's hurt.

Either she was the best actress in the world or she was telling the truth and the baby was his.

Finally, he shifted position and rested his head back. Gazing up at the pitch-dark pine ceiling, he thought back twelve years to when he'd last been with Cassia. She'd looked him in the eye and told him that *of course* she still loved him and that nothing was wrong.

Deep in his guts he'd known she was lying but had chosen to believe her. Their wedding day had been fast approaching. They'd even chosen the rings and given them to Theo for safekeeping. Konstantinos had long stopped wondering if Theo wore the larger ring on his own wedding finger. Time had blurred much of the pain but not the betrayal. That still felt as fresh as the day it had happened.

There was nothing in his gut telling him Lena was lying. If he was being truthful, his gut was telling him the opposite.

But there was an ache, too. It had been pulsing deeper even than his guts since Lena had lifted her sweater to reluctantly show him her neat, barely noticeable bump. It was a strange ache unlike the ache that always formed when he thought of her and which heated his veins just to breathe the same air as her, and it warned him more than anything of the danger of taking her word at face value.

He knew better than to take anything or anyone at face value.

Stretching his back, he got to his feet, removed his laptop from its bag, opened it, and got searching.

His eyes were gritty when he finally closed the lid.

Lena's social media presence was far more discreet than most people in their twenties. She had all the usual accounts but her privacy settings meant he couldn't access them, and so he'd searched the other staff here at the Ice Hotel and found a number for whom privacy must be an alien concept. As luck would have it, those were the staff who liked to document every aspect of their social lives and, as Konstantinos already knew, the staff here was an actively sociable crew who liked to drink and party the dark nights away when not on duty; there were many photos to go through. Lena's face was a rarity amongst them.

Pushing his laptop to one side, Konstantinos dragged his fingers through his hair. He had two choices. Hold on to his cynicism until the baby was born and then make arrangements with Lena after a paternity test confirmed what his gut was telling him. Or he could accept she was carrying his child now.

The ache deeper than his guts throbbed.

Gossip spread at the Ice Hotel quicker than the wildest wildfire but even Lena was taken aback at the avid, curious glances she kept catching from the staff. It was patently obvious the entire workforce knew Konstantinos had whisked her off to his cabin for two hours. She could guess what they thought they'd been doing.

Resolutely ignoring their curiosity, she tried her best to concentrate on her work but it was hopeless. Her head was too full of Konstantinos.

She still felt winded. More than that, felt like she'd been run over by a truck. Her insides were so squished they'd liquidised and fallen into her churning belly, and it made her burning brain swim to imagine that right this minute he could be on his way to the airport.

The thought of being on the other side of the world to him should bring relief. She'd been entirely unprepared for Konstantinos discovering the pregnancy at this point, had had no time to fortify herself against the cold opprobrium she'd known would be fired at her. She'd expected it but the reality of it hurt far more than she'd believed it could.

What if he *had* gone already? But what if he'd stayed? She didn't know which outcome she feared the most. Or which outcome she wanted the most. It frightened her that her emotions were so heightened at the thought of either.

It made her feel wretched that she might have gotten him wrong when it came to his treatment of Annika because it was this treatment that had solidified Lena's fear of Konstantinos's reaction to her pregnancy, that he would not only deny paternity but sack her, too.

Reaching the point where she was afraid her brain would explode from the circles it was going in, she snatched her phone off her desk and made a call.

'Lena!' Thom said when he answered. 'This is a pleasant surprise.' In the background, a baby was crying. It was a sound that made her heart ache.

'Sorry to disturb you,' Lena said.

'Not at all! It's great to hear from you! How are you getting on?'

'Great, thanks,' she lied. 'How's Noomi?' she asked, referring to the crying baby whose conception had prompted Thom and his wife, Freja, to quit their jobs at the remote Ice Hotel and move to Stockholm.

After a few minutes of catching up, Lena finally found the opportunity to ask the question that had prompted her call. 'You remember Annika?'

'Sure. Why do you ask?'

'I was just wondering if you remember why she was sacked. It was before my time and all I've heard are rumours—I figured you'd know the truth.'

'She was sacked for gross negligence.' Thom proceeded to relate the exact same story Konstantinos had told her. 'What were you told?'

'I'd heard she was sacked for being pregnant.'

He snorted. 'Total rubbish but I get why people might have believed it—Mr Siopis ordered the circumstances of her sacking be kept quiet for reputational purposes. I was only told because I got her job but as far as I know, I'm the only one and I never shared it with anyone.' A strange note entered his voice. 'This is all history. Why is it concerning you now?'

'Curiosity. Anyway, thanks for satisfying it. I'll let you get on.'

There was a moment of silence before he said. 'Freja and I have a spare room if you need it. Anything you need, call us, okay?'

It was the compassion she heard in his voice and the realisation that she wasn't quite as alone here as she'd believed that had the tears spilling down her cheeks before she'd put her phone back on her desk. Burying her face in her hands, Lena let it all out.

Her tears were cathartic and once they were all purged, she felt a little better in herself.

The worst was over. Konstantinos knew about the baby. She had no control over what he would do next and to tie herself in knots about it achieved nothing. She still had a job to do and unless she wanted to give him an actual valid reason to sack her, it was best she got on with it.

Rummaging in her bag for a tissue to blow her nose in and for her emergency makeup bag, she masked the blotchiness of her cheeks as best she could with foundation and blusher, and added fresh mascara and the fawn lipstick she favoured. Reasonably happy that she no longer completely resembled the bride of Frankenstein, she woke her computer from the sleep it had fallen into and got to work.

It was 8 p.m. by the time Lena finished. Exhausted in all senses of the word, she trudged on her skis through the falling snow to her cabin at the far end of the complex where all the staff accommodation and facilities were located, set far enough from the guest cabins to make it a private—if much less plush—complex within the complex. As she passed the fir trees the guest cabins were dotted amongst, she made sure to keep her gaze fixed ahead and not peer through the trees to the super-posh cabins. She didn't know if she could bear seeing the light on in Konstantinos's. Or bear seeing it switched off.

Finally safe inside the warm confines of her cosy cabin, she thought briefly of food. She'd hardly eaten anything all day. Having no appetite, she decided to shower first and then decide if she had the energy to trundle to the staff canteen, but once she was clean and dry, fleece pyjamas on and her thick cream robe wrapped around her, she stared unenthusiastically at the ready meals stuffed in her tiny freezer. Before she could decide whether to stick macaroni cheese or spaghetti meatballs in the microwave, a sharp rap on the door made her freeze and the hairs on the nape of her neck rise.

When the door remained unopened, Konstantinos knocked again. He knew she was inside.

The handle turned, the door opened a crack, and Lena's face appeared.

His heart caught in his throat. 'Can I come in?'

She hesitated before stepping back to admit him.

Standing with her back to the wall, her dark eyes watched him warily while he went through the usual rigmarole of removing his outdoor clothing. Maybe it was because she'd clearly just showered and was dressed for bed in the un-sexiest nightwear he'd ever seen, but there was a vulnerability to her, a fragility he would never have associated with his firm-but-fair Ice Hotel general manager, as if one more blow could shatter her.

As angry as he still was with her, it sat badly with him that he was the cause of this fragility.

She waited until he'd stored his outdoor clothing in her heated cupboard before tucking her damp hair behind her ear and quietly asking, 'Does your being here mean you believe me?'

Konstantinos held her stare. *Did* he believe her? Did he genuinely believe the child in her stomach was his?

He gave a sharp nod, and immediately that he'd made the gesture, the weight that had been lodged deep inside him lifted free.

He did believe her. He did believe he was the father of Lena's child. He'd known it in his guts from the moment she'd lifted her sweater to reveal the small bump.

Her eyes closed and her shoulders slumped as if her own weight had been released. Then she straightened and, blinking rapidly, turned her face away and took the few steps to the inbuilt freezer all the staff cabins were supplied with. 'Have you eaten?'

Thrown at the question it took a moment to answer. 'No.'

Lena opened the freezer door. Her hands were shaking again. Her whole body was trembling. Konstantinos believed her. He was here. He believed her. The burst of relief had been dizzying but with it had come another welling of tears—she wouldn't have believed she had any left after the bucketload she'd cried earlier—and suddenly it had become necessary to *do* something, to keep her trembling body busy while it absorbed the shock of his unspoken admission. 'Do you want to eat with me?'

'Lena, we need to—'

'Talk,' she finished for him while keeping her gaze rooted to the meagre contents of her freezer. 'I know. And we will. Just give me a few minutes to compose myself, okay?'

'I...' He sighed but it didn't sound like an irritated sigh, more of an accepting one. 'Sure.'

'Thank you.' Blinking back more tears, she blew out a puff of air. 'Macaroni cheese or spaghetti meatballs?'

At his silence, she glanced up at him. The look he was giving her made her give a choked laugh and lightened her thumping heart a fraction. 'Not a fan of ready meals?'

He raised an eyebrow. 'I'm Greek. Ready meals are illegal there.'

She nearly asked if he was being serious but then she recognised the dryness in his voice and the glint in his eyes, and her heart lightened a little more. Whatever anger he still felt towards her, he was trying to contain it and, for the first time since she'd taken the pregnancy test, a tendril of hope unfurled that her baby's father would want to be involved in its life.

Konstantinos had watched the stress lining Lena's beautiful features melt away at his admittance of paternity and, with no makeup covering the shadows beneath her eyes, had seen the exhaustion lining them. But it was the way she'd stared into that freezer visibly trying to keep her composure that had set the wave of emotion rolling through him. And now it was the expression in her shining eyes that set another wave rolling. Such a mixture of emotions contained in them.

Lena was carrying his child. She was going to have his baby. Whether the conception had been deliberate or not he needed to accept things as they were and park his recriminations and anger.

He took a long, deep breath through his nose but it didn't help quell anything, not when it filled his lungs with the soft floral scents emanating from Lena's skin. They weren't the scents of perfume—he couldn't remember noticing her wear perfume—just the simple scents of showered cleanliness. The memories they triggered, the heat and scent of her skin underlying those scents...

He was standing far too close to her. Much closer and the swell of her breasts would brush against him.

Gritting his teeth, Konstantinos leaned back against her tiny food area to increase the gap between them.

'Go and sit down,' he ordered 'You have had two long days and you're exhausted. I'll have food delivered to us.'

Her forehead creased with confusion. Immediately, his thumbs tingled to press against the smooth skin and massage the lines away. 'We don't do cabin service for staff,' she said blankly.

He jammed his hands into his back pockets. 'We do for me.'

Lena tapped her forehead in disbelief at her own brain fade. 'Sorry,' she muttered. 'I wasn't thinking.'

Not with her brain. Konstantinos had gotten so close to her that her brain had become quite scrambled.

'Go on, sit,' he insisted. 'Take the weight off your feet. What would you like to eat?'

'Anything. You choose. I'm not fussy... But no shell-fish. I'm not allowed to eat that. Bad for the baby.' While she babbled, the limited floorspace meant she had to practically shimmy past him to reach the sofa. No sooner had she slumped gratefully on it when it hit her that her lack of other seating meant Konstantinos would have to share the sofa with her. It was either that or plonk himself on the teeny bit of flooring that didn't actually have any furniture on it. If he stretched out on his side and chopped his legs off from midthigh, he might just squash into that sliver of space.

She would not allow herself to think of him sitting on her bed.

'Can you eat Arctic char?'

She turned her head back to him. He had his phone to his ear but was looking at her.

As she stuck her thumb up at him, she felt movement inside her. Her baby was awake.

While he finished giving his instructions, Lena pulled her robe open so she could rub her belly. This had become her favourite time of the day. It was as if her baby knew

Mummy had finished work and woke up specially to say hello. Every day her baby's movements grew stronger.

The silence of the cabin suddenly felt very stark. Turning her head back to Konstantinos she found him staring at her stomach.

Slowly, his gaze drifted back to her face. Her heart squeezed at his expression and the longing contained in it, squeezing again to understand that this was a longing from a father to his unborn child.

Instinctively, she held a hand out to him. 'He or she's awake. Come and feel.'

He took a visible deep breath. 'You are sure?'

She nodded. Feeling her baby move inside her was the greatest blessing Lena had ever experienced in her life, and she'd often had to stop herself from imagining Konstantinos's hand on her belly marvelling at what was happening beneath the surface, sharing this most wonderful joy with him. She'd had to stop herself because her own longing had always hit the hardest then.

His throat moved before he stepped to her.

Instead of sitting beside her, he knelt before her, jaw clenched, breathing heavily.

The thuds of her heart pounded in her ears, awareness prickling her skin, but she smothered the effects as best she could.

'It doesn't bite,' she said softly when he made no effort to put his hands on her stomach or drop his gaze back to it, and then it came to her that his hesitation could be rooted in him not wanting to touch *her*.

A spasm of pain washed through her, harder to smother than the thickening awareness of him kneeling so close, his body so long his eyes were level with hers, but she smothered it enough to lift her pyjama top over her stomach and reach for his hand.

This wasn't about her. This wasn't about him. This was about their baby. Lena wanted her baby to have as close a relationship with Konstantinos as she had with her own father. Every child deserved to be loved and wanted by both its parents and until barely twenty minutes ago she hadn't dared hope her child could be loved or wanted by its father. If forging that love and want meant swallowing her hurt then that was no price to pay.

His green eyes flickered as she wrapped her much smaller fingers around his and gently pulled his hand to her stomach, then used both her hands to flatten it at the area the movement felt strongest.

The roar between Konstantinos's ears was so loud it drowned out the drum of his heart.

Being so close to Lena when he'd only just backed himself away from the warmth of her floral scent, gazing into those stunning dark brown eyes that were like melted dark chocolate, had brought the night they'd shared together crashing back into his consciousness. Remembering not the physical aspect of it all but how it had run so much deeper, right down into his core, and the very fact that he *ached* to touch her again had been the very thing that had kept him rooted to the spot.

And now his hand was flat against the swelling of her stomach, her own hands pressed against it to hold it in place, and suddenly he felt it. Movement beneath the skin.

In an instant his heart ballooned to fill every crevice of his being as finally it sank into him that this was his child. *His* child.

His other hand pressed against Lena's stomach with no thought from his confounded brain, and he sank lower, suddenly needing to look at the swelling within which his child was growing.

An unexpected grunt of awed laughter escaped his throat when the next movement happened. Sheer impulse had him slide his hands to her waist and press a kiss to the spot his baby was most active… Not just his baby but Lena's baby. Their baby.

Fingertips dug gently into his skull. He closed his eyes at the sensation skittering over his skin before lifting his face to the woman who'd just given him the purest jolt of joy in his life.

The tenderness in Lena's eyes and the dreamy smile on her face only increased the swelling of his heart, but as he stared into those soft eyes, all the emotions consuming him began to alter. The thuds in his chest became heavier. The vim in his veins slowed to sludge. The scent of her warm body swirled into his senses and suddenly he became aware that his hands were clasped on her naked waist, that the smooth softness beneath them was her skin and as that awareness hit him, arousal thickened and he found his hands slipping around her waist to her back, his thighs rising to lift him and bring his mouth closer to the generous lips that had plagued his dreams all these months. As he closed in on her, the dreamy smile faded from her face. The tenderness in her eyes locked so tightly on his faded. There was a barely perceptible parting of her lips but it was enough for him to catch a hint of her warm, minty breath and for his senses to go into overload.

CHAPTER SIX

THE ROAR OF blood pounding in Lena's head was so loud it drowned out everything, including her ability to think. The expression in Konstantinos's hooded eyes when he'd lifted his gaze back to hers had made her heart throb and then burst into ripples, and the detachment she'd tried so desperately to impose on herself at his closeness and the sensation of his bare hands on her skin vanished. In the blink of an eye, her lungs soaked in the warm, masculine, citrusy scent of the man whose mouth was closing in on hers and locked it inside her. Awareness danced like fire over her skin and through her veins, fingers that had unthinkingly pressed into his hair falling to his shoulders. The mesmerising vampiric face tilted almost imperceptibly, and the warmth of his coffee-laced breath seeped into her moisture-flooded mouth a fraction of a second before their lips connected. Heat flushed through every part of her. Closing her eyes, her fingers reflexively tightened on his shoulders but the kiss never went beyond a fleeting caress of the lips. With an abruptness that came from nowhere, Konstantinos jerked away like he'd had a bucket of ice thrown over him. Coldness immediately filled the vacuum made by the loss of his body heat.

Her eyes flew open.

He'd reared back on his haunches, his expression as

tight as she'd ever seen it. 'Your phone,' he said in a tone that matched his expression.

Dazed at what had so nearly happened, she stared blankly at him before the ringing of her phone finally penetrated her brain.

It was her mum's ringtone.

Lena had never received a call from her mum that she didn't answer straight away, but there was no possibility of her even moving off the sofa to get it, not with Konstantinos staring at her with the look of a man who couldn't decide if he wanted to pounce on her and ravish her or plunge his teeth into her neck and suck all the life from her. His breaths were as ragged as the thuds of Lena's heart, right until he closed his eyes sharply and turned his face.

With a grace that confounded her, he rose to his feet and in a couple of strides lifted her phone from the counter above the freezer. He held it out to her wordlessly.

Still trying to pull herself out of the spell she'd been caught in, Lena straightened and took a deep breath before accepting the video call. Her mum's face filled the screen.

'There you are,' her mum said cheerfully in her native Swedish. 'I was starting to think you were ignoring...' She peered closer to the screen. 'Are you okay?'

'I'm great, thanks.' Lena twisted her angle so Konstantinos wasn't directly in her eyeline. 'It's just been a long day. How are you all?'

'All good here. The weather forecasters say we might have snow tonight.'

'Careful, you're starting to sound like a naturalised Brit.'

Her mum laughed. 'I miss the snow.'

'I know, and before I go to sleep tonight I'll do a snow chant for you.' Over more laughter, Lena asked, 'How's Heidi? Still recovering?' A moot question—her parents would have told her if Heidi's recovery from the chest infection that mercifully hadn't required hospitalisation had gone backwards in the two days since they'd last spoken. Lena had only agreed to leave England for Sweden after making her parents swear solemnly to never try to spare her worry about her sister's condition.

'She sent me to the library for audiobooks this morning.'

Ordinarily, Lena would have relaxed at this. Heidi asking for books always meant she was in a good place. With a heavy awareness of Konstantinos's attention fixed on her, there was zero chance of her relaxing into the conversation. It was hard enough thinking coherently with him sharing the same air. 'Definitely recovering well, then.'

Konstantinos had perched his backside on a tiny carved stool with a woodland scene etched on it. He was thankful it took his weight but it was so low he had to stretch his legs out, and space was so limited in the cabin that his feet were forced to rest next to Lena's. There was nowhere else for him to sit unless he sat himself beside Lena on the sofa and be forced to endure the heat of her body so close to his or, worse, sat on the bed covered in the same patchwork bedspread as the night they'd spent together. If he hadn't ordered food for them both, he would have left. A strong part of him thought he still should.

He could not believe how close he'd come to kissing her.

Close? Their lips had connected before her phone saved him. He'd come within a whisker of pulling her back into his arms so he could devour her properly before he'd come fully to his senses.

He could still feel the mark that brush of her lips had made against his.

Unwilling to dissect what the hell had gotten into him, he focused his attention on the video conversation being played out before him. He couldn't understand a word of what either woman was saying. He'd known Lena spoke good Swedish but had been unaware she had such fluency. One of the requirements of working at the Siopis Ice Hotel was competence in Swedish and English. Basic proficiency tests in both languages were conducted before candidates werc invited to interview. Lena's Swedish... There was something sexy in her fluency. To Konstantinos's ears, it was a musical language and the way her lips moved as she spoke and her tongue wrapped around the cadences...

He shot to his feet.

Damn this cabin for being so small. Damn this country for being so cold. If they were in one of the warmer countries he favoured he'd take himself outside and when she ended her call insist she join him out there. Then he wouldn't be stuck in a space hardly bigger than his childhood bedroom breathing in all the scents of Lena. This might be a different cabin to the one they'd conceived their baby in but she'd adorned it with the same soft furnishings. She even had the same battered old teddy bear in the centre of the two pillows and the same pictures hanging on the walls. He remembered being surprised that she'd chosen artwork more suited to a small child, simple watercolour paintings of two little girls, one of them paddling in the sea, one of them making a sandcastle, and one of them playing in the snow. There was something very familiar about the snow picture that he couldn't place, and he had no idea why he should look at paintings that only the hardest-hearted person wouldn't consider 'cute' and feel nausea roiling in his guts.

Gritting his teeth, he yanked open the two cupboards above the tiny area Lena used to fix herself hot drinks and heat food. No sign of coffee, not even that instant muck… What the hell was *camomile* tea? A method of torture? His Tuscan hotel had a camomile lawn. He loathed the smell of it, only kept it because it had become a feature of the hotel.

Another voice came onto the call, interrupting his attempts to distract himself. This one caught his attention because the new voice was so different and the way Lena was conversing had changed, too, and not just because she'd switched to English. He couldn't place just how Lena's voice was different but just as looking at the pictures hanging on her pine walls made his guts roil, the way she was speaking had the same effect. There was something laboured in the voice of the new woman speaking that added to the roiling, as if every carefully chosen word was an effort to make and so the words chosen were sparse and considered.

'We have a party of Americans booked in for tomorrow's opening night,' Lena was now telling her. 'They're celebrating a fortieth birthday and birthday boy's paying for them all to freeze for the night.'

'Think…they…will…last…night?'

'I'll place my bet once I've met them.'

'Who's…that…man?' the woman in the wheelchair asked. Konstantinos only knew she was in a wheelchair because a dread-like curiosity had made his legs take him to stand at the corner of the sofa to gaze over Lena's shoulder. Next to the wheelchair was what even Konstantinos's nonmedical knowledge knew was an oxygen tank.

Lena whipped her head around at him and beseeched him with her eyes to back off. He stepped back out of view of her camera lens.

'Just a friend,' she said, giving her attention back to the woman who looked so much like Lena that she had to be her sister.

Even though the angle Konstantinos had put himself at to keep out of the camera's range meant he didn't have a clear view, he could see the woman in the wheelchair's eyes light up.

'Don't look at me like that,' Lena scolded indignantly.

'About…time…you…had…friend.' The woman's speech might be laboured but Konstantinos heard the inverted quote marks she laced around the word *friend,* and, judging by Lena's splutter of laughter, she heard it, too.

'Your mind is filthy.'

The woman simply smiled beatifically.

'On that note, I'm going.'

The knowing smile broadened. The woman waved goodbye and then pursed her lips together.

'Love you, too,' Lena said, blowing her a kiss in return. 'Now, shoo.'

The screen on her phone went blank.

'Sorry about that,' she muttered after an awkward pause of silence, then added, 'That was my sister.'

'I guessed. She looks like you.' But a decade older than Lena's twenty-five years. 'What is wrong with her?'

Even though Lena's back was to him, he saw her tuck a lock of hair behind an ear. 'She was paralysed in a car accident six years ago.'

He said something in Greek Lena would put money on being a swear word. 'How old is she?'

'Twenty-six.'

He swore again.

The knock on the cabin door cut short a conversation Lena didn't want to have.

'I'll get it,' Konstantinos said.

She didn't argue. Her exhaustion was so great she suspected she might have trouble dragging herself off the sofa to crawl into her bed.

She didn't argue, either, when Konstantinos took charge, rooting through her cupboards for plates to serve their heat-sealed meals onto.

Sticking a cushion on her lap as a tray, she smiled her thanks when he handed her plate to her. She had a feeling the chef would cry if he saw how his usually immaculately presented food had been splattered on her plate.

'You know all the staff will be gossiping about us,' she said after they'd eaten in silence for a few minutes. At least, she'd tried to eat. It was difficult getting food down her throat with Konstantinos sitting across from her on the tiny table her mother had made for her and Heidi when they'd been little girls. She imagined it had been a long time since he'd eaten at anything but a formal dining table, never mind eating with his backside barely a foot from the floor and having to hover his plate close to his chest with one hand and so able to eat with only his fork with the other.

He stared at her meditatively as he swallowed his mouthful. While she'd managed barely a quarter of her dinner, he'd practically finished his. 'It will only get worse. It won't be long until everyone knows you're pregnant with my child.'

That tightened her throat even more.

The jaw with an abundance of black stubble tightened, too, and he said abruptly, 'What happened earlier was a mistake. I apologise.'

'Do you mean when you kissed me?'

He inclined his head.

'Do you have to keep insulting me?'

A thick black eyebrow rose.

'That's twice you've called me a mistake.'

'Lena, you are my employee.'

'Only for a few more months,' she muttered.

'We shall talk about that, but I meant—'

'What do you mean, *"We shall talk about that"*?' she interrupted, alarmed. 'You said you weren't going to sack me.'

'I'm not going to sack you but you cannot keep working here.'

'So you *are* going to sack me!'

'No!' Jaw clenched, he got to his feet and carried his plate to the sink. 'But you know as well as I do that you cannot have the baby here and I think it would be better—safer—for you and the baby if you left as soon as possible.'

'We're perfectly safe here.'

'For now, yes, but what if there are complications further along the line? The medical team and facilities here are excellent but they are not specialists in pregnancies. We need to start putting things into place now. Sven can take on your role until a permanent replacement can be appointed...' His eyes narrowed. 'You agree that you can't come back after the birth?'

She nodded miserably, not at the thought of giving up the job she loved—she'd long come to terms with that—

but at the realisation that all agency she had over her own life was being lost and placed into Konstantinos's hands.

'You don't agree?'

'No, I do agree. This is no place to raise a child.' This was a frozen tourist resort in the middle of nowhere; the only Siopis hotel without childcare facilities for its staff.

'Then why are you looking like that?' he asked.

'Because I'm now in your power and it's a scary place to be.'

'You are not in my power,' he dismissed.

'Of course I am.'

'If this is about earlier then I have already apologised.'

'You think this is about our *kiss*?' she asked in disbelief.

'I woke this morning unaware you were pregnant with my child. Hours later I felt it move. The emotion of the moment got the better of me. It won't happen again.'

'Yes, I know, it was just another mistake,' she said bitterly. 'You've made your feelings towards me crystal clear. You hate me.'

'I don't hate you. I hate that you kept our baby a secret from me.'

'Because of the power you hold over me! I was always going to tell you.'

'But only when you needed my money.'

'No, when you no longer had the power to leave me destitute. One snap of your fingers and you could have made me jobless and homeless.'

'You really believed that of me?'

'Look at the way you behaved the morning after we slept together. You didn't even have the courtesy to wish me a good morning, just straight out told me it was all a mistake and then...' She snapped her fingers in the same way he could have destroyed her. Could still destroy her. 'Gone.'

The pulse on the side of his clenched jaw throbbed. 'What would you rather I'd done? Pretend I was happy to wake in your bed?'

She'd been happy to wake next to him. So very happy.

'I do not lie, Lena,' he continued. 'I despise lies.'

'You didn't have to be so cold about it.'

He rubbed the back of his head and took another deep breath before saying, 'We both crossed a line that should never have been crossed. It was better to sever it immediately.'

'Well, you did just that. You spent the night making love to me, having sex with me, *making a mistake* with me, whatever you want to call it, and then you up and left as if I was nothing but a toy you'd played with and decided was faulty.'

His vampiric face contorted with disbelief.

Her lethargy gone, Lena stood and stomped to her teeny food area and barely resisted throwing her plate into the sink. Hands on her hips, she faced him, practically trapping him against the pine wall.

'That's *exactly* how you treated me, and you wonder why I was so scared to tell you about our baby, when you'd already made your disdain for me so clear? And then you came back five months later and made your loathing even more obvious. Until you learned about the baby you were cold and offhanded with me. I genuinely thought you were looking for a reason to sack me, and then this morning, *before* you knew about the baby, you were so keen to get away from me that you forgot your phone, so don't tell me that you only hate me for keeping our baby a secret from you. You already hated me.'

'Damn it, Lena…' He looked her square in the eyes. 'You are the only employee I have ever made this mistake with.'

She jabbed his chest. 'Stop calling me a mistake!'

He snatched her jabbing hand and held it tightly to his chest. She could feel the thumps of his heart beneath it. They matched the beats of her own thrashing heart. 'You *were* a mistake,' he snarled, green eyes swirling with dark emotion boring into her. 'It should never have happened and I have spent five months trying to forget it and forget you, and then I came back here and every time I look at you, it's all I can see. It's here in my head.' Leaning his vampiric face right into hers, he tapped the side of his skull for emphasis. 'Right here. I can't escape it. I can't escape *you*. I told you the truth the next morning that it was a mistake, and I was right. Only fools mix business with pleasure so that made me the fool who had to put the most incredible night of my life out of my mind and forget about it. God knows I've tried but I can't forget, and if I've been cold with you it's because sharing the same air as you—'

Lena's mouth suddenly attached itself to his. It came without thought or reason, her body taking full control for a swift, clumsy kiss that had, for one fleeting instant, felt as necessary as taking her next breath.

Konstantinos froze. A short beat later Lena froze, too, in horror at what she was doing, and reared away from him. Brain burning, frightened to look at him, heart racing and blood pumping frantically, she pulled her hand free from his and quickly edged away from him, already planning to lock herself in the bathroom until her mortification had passed when his large hand snatched at her wrist and he yanked her back to him.

An arm snaked tightly around her waist, crushing her against him and then his mouth came crashing down.

With a moan that seemed to come from the very core of her being, Lena melted into Konstantinos and the dark power of his kiss. Lips fused, tongues entwined, arms wrapped around each other, until every inch of their bodies that could be flush pressed together and every single tendril of emotion and pleasure she'd experienced in his arms roared back to life.

This…this was what had clung like a cloud to her all these months. The sheer headiness she'd found in the taste of his passionate kisses and the scent of his skin and the thrills of his touch. All of her senses responded to him, as if Konstantinos Siopis had been specially created for her sensory delectation, and being with him now, caught in the hot fever that had captured them that night in an explosion of hedonistic lust…oh, it was the most incredible feeling in the world.

Hot, sticky desire pulsed through Konstantinos, the arousal he'd kept under such tight control unleashed, urgent, scorching him. Pressing Lena against the wall, he devoured her mouth, her hot sweetness feeding his hunger, thrills ravaging him. Other than their devouring faces, not an inch of flesh touched through the thick layers they wore, but the heat from their crushed bodies was as consuming as if they were naked.

It was a heat like no other. The way he reacted to Lena was like with no other. For five months the night they'd spent together had been a living memory constantly springing free from the reinforced crate he kept jamming it into. He'd been unable to enjoy even the simple pleasure of a glass of wine without conjuring Lena's smile as she drank her own wine, unable to see the colour red without the image of unbuttoning her red blouse flashing into his mind. Damn it, even seeing the delivery of ice at one of his hotels had immediately made him think of her, which alone was enough for his loins to heat.

That was the worst part of it. It was impossible to think of her and the night they'd spent together without the accompanying tell-tale signs of arousal. Hundreds, often thousands, of miles of distance between them, differing time zones and climates and all it took was for him to close his eyes and he could feel her nails scraping over his naked back.

Breaths ragged and painful, he broke the fusion of their mouths and stared at her flushed, beautiful face with a heart that had swollen large enough to choke him. When he gazed into her desire-drugged eyes it came to him that much of the anger he'd been carrying since their night together had dissipated. Every part of him throbbed with desire but an invisible weight he'd barely noticed himself carrying had lifted.

'Please don't tell me that was a mistake,' she whispered, resting her head back against the wall.

His swollen heart clenched. 'That might have been my biggest mistake.'

She shook her head. 'Don't.'

With a groan, he rested his forehead to hers. 'Lena, I don't want there to be lies between us. There have been too many already.'

'I know. And I'm sorry.'

To his surprise, he believed her. He disentangled his arms so he could run his fingers through her hair and clasp the back of her head. 'I have spent all this time trying to forget our night together and now I learn you are having my baby, and I have to navigate a future where you are going to be in my life for the rest of my life and I don't even know how the hell to begin navigating it.'

She gave a wobbly smile. 'I don't know how to navigate it, either.'

He stared into her beautiful eyes and felt another clenching of his heart. 'I promise I will support you financially and in any other way I can, and be a father to our child as best I can, but that is as much as I can promise.'

She gave another wobbly smile and nodded. 'The only promise I want from you is the promise to always put our child first.'

The clenching in his chest tightened to a point. Resisting the growing urge to kiss her again, he bowed his head and stepped away from her completely, making his way to the cupboard he'd stored his outdoor clothing in. It was time to get out of this suffocating cabin and Lena's overwhelming presence. 'I give you my word.'

CHAPTER SEVEN

THE NEXT MORNING Lena ski-walked past Father Christmas ski-walking to his newly opened grotto, and grinned. The Siopis Ice Hotel didn't cater to children, but in December the snow and the atmosphere of the place turned many of their guests into big kids.

At the lodge she carefully removed her skis and placed them in the staff rack, then shook off the layer of snow that had fallen thick and fast during the slow journey from her cabin, and stepped inside. The warmth was welcome as was the brightness of the internal daylight-mimicking lights. She hoped the forecast of blizzards the next day proved wrong. There was nothing worse than making your way around the complex with zero visibility. Occasionally, the blizzards became bad enough that planes at the local airport couldn't land or take off.

As usual, the first thing she did once settled in her office was check their incoming and outgoing guests' flight status. No flights tomorrow, so if the predicted blizzard did hit, they wouldn't have to scramble for extra accommodation if those supposed to leave were trapped.

Busying herself firing off emails and messages to all the various teams involved in getting guests wherever they needed to be and ensuring everyone was prepared with the necessary bad weather contingency plans, it was the sudden plummet of Lena's stomach that alerted her to her office door being pushed open. She lifted her gaze to find Konstantinos stepping over the threshold.

The long, lean frame wrapped in the usual dapper dark suit and the darkly unattractive freshly shaved face that made her heart swell so greatly loomed over her desk before he sank into the visitor chair opposite her.

The greeting she'd found for everyone else she'd seen that morning refused to form for him. Her throat had closed too tightly.

His strong throat moved before he broke the silence. 'All okay?'

She nodded the lie she couldn't form verbally. Truth was, Lena was far from okay. Her emotions were all over the place. She couldn't make sense of any of it. Couldn't make sense of why, when Konstantinos had left her cabin so soon after the passion between them had erupted, she'd had to clamp her lips together to stop herself begging him to stay. Or make sense of why, during the long, dark night, she'd spent the many lonely hours fighting the yearning to call him, just to hear his voice.

She must be a masochist. That was the only explanation. Or her hormones were more bonkers than she'd given them credit for. Probably a combination of the two and all aggravated by that stupid, heavenly, passionate kiss, a kiss her cheeks kept flaming to remember that *she'd* instigated.

She was definitely a masochist. How else to explain why her reaction to a man angrily reeling off the reasons why sleeping with her had been a mistake was to stop him talking with a kiss?

It didn't matter that he'd pulled her back to him or that he'd been the one to envelop her in his arms and hold her so tightly while devouring her mouth. Compounding his mistake. If she hadn't made the first move, he wouldn't have made the second.

What was *wrong* with her? She'd made all the running the night they'd shared together, inviting him into her cabin, being openly dismayed when he said he should leave, angling her body closer to his, kissing him... It had all been *her*. She'd started it! He'd responded but she'd been the instigator, and she had no doubt that if she hadn't, nothing would have happened. Konstantinos would never have made the first move. And now she knew she couldn't even partially blame her actions that night on all the wine because she'd done it all again stone-cold sober.

For whatever reason, being close to Konstantinos seemed to cast a spell on her and make her act like a teenager with a crush. She accepted that she did have a crush on him—be a bit silly to deny something so obvious—but she wasn't a teenager, she was an adult, and it beggared belief that she could be mooning over a man who'd treated her like dirt after their one night together and might as well have spelt it out in neon lights that he wasn't interested in a relationship.

She shouldn't be interested in a relationship, either. She wasn't! She'd had no interest in relationships since the accident and chances were, if not for the baby, she wouldn't be entertaining any of these thoughts. But she *was* having his baby. A part of Konstantinos Siopis was growing inside her, so surely it would be more worrying if she wasn't entertaining relationship thoughts about the father of her child? Because didn't it make sense to at least try and see, for their baby's sake, if a relationship between them could work?

Oh, this was all so confusing.

It would be easier if he felt nothing for her. Even simple hate would be easier to deal with. It was his desire for her that added such toxicity to her confusion. Konstantinos had such detachment over his emotions that he found it easy to separate his desire from his head. Lena could only hope time would make that same detachment easy for her to find, too.

'I have rearranged my schedule,' he told her with that hateful vocal detachment. 'We shall stay here for another week. That will give us time to find a temporary replacement for you and get things in motion for a permanent replacement. I think Sven is well qualified to take the role temporarily—do you agree?'

'You want me to leave in a week?'

'We have already agreed that it is best you leave sooner rather than later.'

'I didn't think you meant that quickly.' She finally plucked up the courage to look him in the eye. Her heart flipped over to see the blaze roaring from them, completely belying his external aloofness, making it even harder for her to concentrate and get her words out. 'I don't have anywhere to go. My parents only have a sofa I can sleep on, which was fine when I wasn't pregnant, and my grandmother's cabin near Trollarudden isn't habitable. There's nowhere else for me to go.'

Konstantinos sounded out the unfamiliar word. 'Trollarudden?'

'Near Borlange?'

He shook his head. He'd never heard of it.

'It's hundreds of miles south from here.'

Everything was hundreds of miles south of here. 'In Sweden?'

'Yes. My mother's Swedish.'

'Ah.' That explained a lot.

'We spent our childhood summers at my grandmother's cabin here. My parents are teachers so had the same long holidays we had. Mormor—my grandmother—died when I was sixteen. My parents sold her house but we kept the cabin.' She grimaced. 'We always meant to make good use of it but the accident changed everything. I went to check it all over a couple of years ago and it's falling into ruin.'

'The accident…do you mean the one that paralysed your sister?'

She nodded.

'Do they know you're pregnant?'

'No.'

'Why not? I got the impression from your video call that you are a close family.'

'We are.' She sighed. 'I was going to tell them on my next visit home—I don't imagine I'll be able to hide it by then.'

'Why would you want to hide it from them?'

'I don't, I just thought it better to wait until nearer the birth. They're in no position to help me and they have enough to worry about with Heidi. She needs twenty-four-hour care. The last thing they needed was to spend nine months worrying about me, too.'

Though he would prefer not to look too closely at Lena's face and have to deal with the accompanying violent roll in his guts and the deepening of the awareness tormenting him just to share four walls with her, Konstantinos needed to see for himself if she was telling the truth or simply feeding him a line to make herself sound more in need of help than she actually was. He couldn't shake the nagging voice in the back of his mind that she'd deliberately seduced him for the sole reason of conceiving his child.

There was no need for her to play games. Deliberate conception or not, it made no difference to him if she had an army of family and friends offering their help; her child was his child. His responsibility. That made Lena's comfort and safety his responsibility, too.

Allowing himself to fully gaze into the dark brown eyes made his heart clench tightly. Too tightly. Made him remember the look on her flushed face last night when she'd suddenly pressed her lips to his.

Theos, she'd backed off as if she'd been scalded. *He'd* been the one to lose control of the situation. Him. What the hell had he been thinking, pulling her into his arms like that when he damned well knew to keep a physical distance between them?

He gritted his teeth in an ineffectual attempt to counter the throbs of awareness burning beneath his skin and lowered his stare to her desk. Lena had placed a miniature Christmas tree on it and wrapped tinsel around the framed photograph next to her monitor. He'd seen the photo before, only yesterday morning when he'd sat where Lena now sat, plotting his quick escape from this freezing hellhole. Those last minutes before he'd learned the secret she'd been hiding from him.

Twisting the photo round, he looked again at the two small girls—Lena and her sister—playing in the snow, and suddenly it came to him why the watercolour painting on her cabin wall had seemed so familiar. 'This is the photograph used to create the painting in your cabin?'

'Yes. My mother painted it. She often used photos as inspiration for her art.'

'Does she still paint?'

'Rarely.'

The sadness in her voice made him look back at her.

'Heidi's health issues are incredibly complex. She sustained such damage...' She trailed off with another deep sigh before her shoulders rose briskly and a note entered her voice to match. 'Mum and Dad share her care. They both reduced their work to part-time so one of them is always around for her. It doesn't leave much time for anything else.'

'Then why have you spent years here, thousands of miles from them, and not with them, helping with their burden?'

The anger that darkened and pinched her face was instantaneous. Pushing herself forward on the desk, she spoke with quiet venom. 'Heidi is not a *burden*. She is my sister and their daughter and we love her and would do anything for her, and I would thank you not to cast judgement on choices made that you know *nothing* about.'

'I wasn't making a judgement,' he refuted coolly. 'I was making an observation.'

'An observation cast like a judgement.'

He'd hit on a weak spot there, he thought. Was it guilt making her react so defensively?

At this thought, a pang of guilt punched through him. The evidence of Lena's love for her family and their love for her was everywhere. The photo of the two Weir girls playing in the snow was one of three photos in her office of her family. Her cabin was stuffed with family photos that he'd deliberately avoided looking at because it was easier to try and banish her from his mind if she was a caricature in his mind and not a flesh and blood woman with feelings.

He'd made his judgemental observation deliberately. With the intention of hurting her. And he'd succeeded.

Damn it, it wasn't Lena's fault he reacted so viscerally to her and that he was sitting in this confined office—*everywhere* in this hellscape was confined—fighting with every breath in his body not to pull her to him for a taste of her sweet headiness. He shouldn't punish her for his desire and his failure to control it.

'Do you want to be based near them when the baby comes?' he asked, making an effort to neuter the atmosphere he'd created. When her pinched features remained stony, he added, 'Everything is changing, Lena, and you will need a home. Given the choice, would you prefer to be close to your family or somewhere else?'

Holding his stare a moment longer, she drew her chest slowly off the desk and leaned back in her chair. Her expression now wary, she said, 'My choice would be to live close to my family.'

'Then I shall make it happen. Email me their address and I will get my people on it.'

'On it?'

'To find a suitable home for you and the baby close to your family. You get the final choice and the contracts will be made in your name. The home will be yours.'

Her mouth dropped open. 'That is… Are you sure?'

'Of course,' he dismissed. 'But I am not a miracle worker. It might take a month or two before you are able to move into it. I have a penthouse in London you can use until then.'

She shook her head as if clearing water from her ears but the wariness remained. 'That is very kind and generous of you.'

'I am a kind and generous man,' he said drolly.

She gave a sudden snort of laughter that made her shoulders shake and finally removed the last trace of her bristling anger.

Konstantinos had no idea why it made him feel so ridiculously pleased to hear that laughter again and why the softness returning to her eyes should ease the pressure that upsetting her had put on his chest, and then he remembered how hearing that laugh and seeing that softness during their celebratory meal had gone a long way into seducing him. It was a rare person who drew the humour out in him, a rarer person still who *got* it and by extension got him. Lena's gift that night—whether genuine or not—had been to make him feel that she'd looked beneath the ugly but wealthy exterior and seen the beating heart of the man, and that she'd liked what she'd seen. It had been an incredibly powerful aphrodisiac that had intoxicated him and drawn him into making the biggest mistake of his life because, unlike his usual dispassionate affairs, the remnants of their lovemaking had never left him.

'All I ask in return is that you spend Christmas with my family.'

The dark eyes that had widened with such passionate surprise at her first climax with him came close to popping out of her head. 'You've told your family about the baby?'

'Yes.' Like ripping a sticking plaster off in one go, he'd known it was best to get it over and done with and just tell them.

'How did they take it?'

'Very well.'

The wariness returned but this time underlined by fear rather than anger. 'You told them the circumstances?'

'Only that we are not in a relationship, but do not let that worry you. Family is everything to my parents and they want to welcome you into ours.'

'Really?

'To them, this is a blessing. They long ago gave up hope I would have children.' Only in the past few years had they stopped asking if he'd 'met' anyone. It had taken him a long time to control his anger at their bewilderment in his absolute refusal to even consider finding a partner. They'd been there. They knew the effect Theo's betrayal had had on him. 'They want to meet you. They are like children themselves when it comes to Christmas and it would bring them much joy to involve you in our celebrations of it. That isn't a problem for you, is it?' he added when Lena didn't respond. 'You couldn't have made plans to celebrate it with your family. You were supposed to be working the period here.'

'It's not a problem, no,' she said slowly. 'You've just taken me by surprise. I don't think I'd even considered that you had parents.'

'How else did you think I came to be here? Did you think I was grown on a Petri dish?'

The grin that spread over her face at this zinged through the air between them and injected another dangerous dose of warmth into his veins.

'I had wondered,' she said with a snigger. 'I take it this will be their first grandchild?'

'Their third.'

'I don't know why but I was always under the impression you were an only child,' she mused. 'How old are they?'

'My nephews? Seven and three.'

'That will be nice for our child. We have cousins from

my dad's side and it was always such a laugh when we got together as kids. We adored seeing them.'

'That will not happen for our child. I have not seen my brother in twelve years.'

That shocked her, he could see.

This was not a conversation Konstantinos wished to have but now it was here, he could see the necessity in telling her about it. Lena would discover the reasons for his estrangement from his brother at some point. Better to have it out in the open now. Better she understood, too, why she could never be more to him than his child's mother, and from the tempest of emotions thrashing through him just to sit across a desk from her, he knew he needed to remind himself, too, before the temptation to act on his emotions got the better of him again. Remind himself exactly why he would never commit himself to a woman again or trust their motives.

'His wife was supposed to be my wife.'

Her smooth brow creased. *'What...?'*

'My brother stole my fiancée from me.'

All the lightness on Lena's features vanished.

Keeping tight control of his own features, he said, 'I'd known Cassia all my life. She went to my school and worked in my parents' restaurant at weekends. I worshipped the ground she walked on but she never looked twice at me, not until I turned twenty.' He tapped his bent, overlong nose and added sardonically, 'None of the girls ever looked twice at me.'

The coldness that seeped into Lena's veins as he spoke sent the most horrible shiver coiling up her spine.

'She went to university but quit after a year and started working full-time for us. When she finally agreed to a date, I thought all my birthdays had come at once. She was my first lover. I hoped she would be my only lover. When she agreed to marry me, I thought I was the luckiest man alive. I was never ambitious until we got together. The family restaurant brought in enough money for us to have a decent life but in my eyes, Cassia was a princess, and princesses deserved the best of everything. I wanted to give her the world. I convinced my parents to take out a mortgage on the restaurant so I could buy my own. From that, I bought another and then another, and then I bought my first hotel. I wasn't rich like I am now, not by any means, but I worked hard and was turning over a decent profit. I believed Cassia and I would have the comfortable life we'd dreamed of with enough money to travel to exotic parts of the world and raise a family. What I didn't know was that while I was working hard to build our comfortable life, she'd started screwing my brother.'

Lena was finding it hard to breathe. She didn't know what was worse, what Konstantinos was revealing or the absolute dispassion in the way he was telling it. No, she did know what the worst part was—the fire in his eyes. The warnings being fired at her.

He was telling her all this for a reason.

'Two weeks before our wedding day she finally found the guts to tell me the truth. She didn't love me. She'd never loved me. She only agreed to that first date to make Theo jealous. It was my brother she really wanted. Not me.'

Lena covered her mouth in horror. She wished she could cover her ears, too. This was horrendous. Just horrendous. The kind of betrayal that must rip a man's heart out.

He grunted a laugh that landed on her ears like nails

on a chalkboard. 'And Theo wanted her, too. I knew he thought Cassia attractive—he was always joking about me punching above my weight with her—but I never dreamed he would act on it and betray me like that.'

'I'm so sorry,' she whispered hoarsely.

'What for? If they hadn't betrayed me I wouldn't have needed to find solace in my work. I wouldn't have built this empire.' He gave another of those awful laughs. 'I should have seen it coming. Theo is movie-star handsome. Why would the princess want the ugly brother when she could have the handsome prince?'

'You are not ugly,' she said vehemently, wishing she could teleport herself to Kos and scratch the eyes out of the two people who'd behaved so cruelly and caused such devastation.

Leaning over her desk, he eyeballed her. 'The mirror does not lie. If I wasn't rich, you wouldn't have looked twice at me. None of the women I've been intimate with would have.'

He shoved his chair back before she could even think of a response to his hurtful accusation. When he next looked at her, there was a gentler expression on his face. 'I am sorry if I sound bitter. I haven't spoken about Theo and Cassia in many years but it is only right you know about it, and hear it from me and not some gossip in Kos. Now you will have to excuse me—I have video calls to make. Tell Sven to join us in the meeting room in an hour so we can start on the transition process.'

He swept out of the office and closed the door behind him without looking back at her.

CHAPTER EIGHT

'I UNDERSTAND THERE is a blizzard and storm expected later today,' Konstantinos said as a form of greeting when he stepped into Lena's office the next morning.

Even though he hadn't told her to expect him this early, she greeted him with a cordial smile. 'There is a chance of it. It might miss us.'

He took a seat on the visitors' chair. 'Have you put the contingencies in place?'

'Yes.'

'It has been a few years since I've touched base on this. Explain them to me.'

She rolled her chair back until it touched the wall and then spoke in polite, professional detail about how they ensured guest and staff safety in extreme weather.

'Is Sven aware of the procedures?'

'All the staff are aware. It is part of our induction and we do ongoing training, too, to keep it fresh in people's minds.'

Now he remembered one of the things that had impressed him when he'd interviewed Lena for the general manager's role was her suggestion that the ongoing training be increased. She'd implemented it within days of starting the job.

'What time is he due?' In their meeting with Sven the

day before, one conducted in an atmosphere as cordial as the one they were having now, Konstantinos and Lena had discussed the transition process and Konstantinos's expectations of him for when he took over the role. The meeting had been cut short when Konstantinos needed to video call with his directors. He'd left Lena to arrange a time to continue it for that day.

'In two hours.'

'Good. That gives you time to look at the homes my people have shortlisted for you.'

Not by a flicker did she react in any way that could be construed as delight or pleasure, her features retaining their amiability, her tone remaining polite. 'That is wonderful, thank you, but I will have to look at them later— I'm due to give Jocasta her appraisal in ten minutes.'

'Should Sven not sit in on it so he can see how they're conducted?'

'We've already agreed he will sit in on Mikhail's appraisal at four.'

She didn't miss a trick. Of all his managers, she was by far the most thorough and conscientious. His hotel's loss was his baby's gain, a thought that gave him no satisfaction whatsoever. Konstantinos had felt out of sorts since he'd woken at what would have been the crack of dawn in any normal part of the world. His sleep had been abysmal, something he blamed Lena for.

Their conversation about his brother and Cassia's betrayal had had the desired effect. Any hint of emotional turbulence from Lena had been extinguished. She'd understood his unspoken message, that much was clear. What was not clear was why he was unable to get his own body to compute the message. Her body language was everything he wanted, not a hint of the expressive emotions that fed into his veins, not even during the meal they'd shared at the Brasserie last night when she'd acted as if she was dining with a business acquaintance. It was how she should have acted during their celebratory meal five months ago, he thought grimly. How *he* should have acted, too. And then he'd walked her back to her cabin like a gentleman should, the beats of his heart getting stronger the closer they'd gotten to it, his nerve endings tingling even as he mentally prepared the rebuffs he would make when she invited him inside, only to reach her door and be wished a brisk good-night.

'I shall sit in on Jocasta's appraisal,' he decided, folding his arms across his chest. He would have to deal with Lena for the rest of his life. Practice would make perfect his determination to rid himself of this physical infatuation he seemed to have developed for her.

If Lena was perturbed at this declaration, she didn't show it. 'In that case, I will have extra pastries brought in.'

He raised an eyebrow. 'You provide refreshments when you do appraisals?'

'I find it makes for a nicer atmosphere and allows them to relax.'

'An appraisal of your staff's work should be conducted professionally, not as if you're conducting a tea party.'

'It is conducted professionally, as you will discover when Jocasta gets here.'

'Professionally with pastries?'

'I prefer the carrot to the stick approach. It creates a feeling of openness.'

'That sounds like psychobabble.'

She shrugged. 'It's my way of working.'

'Because you dislike confrontation?'

'I dislike *unnecessary* confrontation,' she corrected,

the slightest hint of steel sounding in her calm voice. 'I have appraised a dozen staff since I took the role and sent the full reports to you. If you had a problem with them, you should have told me.'

She had him there, but he was saved from wondering too deeply why he was doing his best to pick fault with her—unnecessary fault at that, seeing as she'd no longer be his employee in four days—by a tap on the door.

Lena welcomed an early Jocasta inside, called out to her assistant for the refreshments to be brought in, and prayed for the strength not to punch Konstantinos in the face. She had the distinct impression he was deliberately trying to find fault with her, although to what end she couldn't begin to imagine.

She was doing her best. The message he'd given her when relating his brother and fiancée's betrayal had been received and understood. When he said he didn't do relationships and that she would only ever be the mother of his child to him, he meant it. Nothing more needed to be said about it, not by either of them. His accusation that she'd only slept with him because of his wealth sealed it. That he still had such a low opinion of her and that the most incredible night of her life was so diminished in his mind hurt immeasurably, but she couldn't defend herself because to do so would only dredge it all up again.

She wished he'd delivered his message when her time here in Sweden was done, not when she still had to suffer four days of his unceasing presence and had to pretend she felt nothing. She was proud, though, that when he'd walked her back to her chalet after their polite dinner together where they had made a tentative plan on how best to co-parent their child, she'd let herself in without giving in to the plaintive yearning to invite him inside; proud, too, that when he'd appeared in her office that morning she'd smothered the swirl of emotions playing havoc inside her to greet him with a smile.

Her crush needed to be kept under lock and key. The emotions Konstantinos created in her needed to be contained. It was the only way she could get through the next few days.

Lena had only just stepped out of the shower when her phone rang, a frantic Katya informing her that Niels, the night duty manager at The Igloo, had taken sick.

'Okay,' Lena said, 'let me make some calls. I'll have a replacement with you shortly. Any other problems I should know about?'

'No, but the way the snow's falling, it looks like the blizzard is coming our way after all.'

Looking out her window, she saw what Katya meant. Lena's hope as the day had gone on that heavy snow was the worst they would get looked to have been premature.

Five minutes later and she called Katya back to tell her she was on her way. Rachel, a currently off-shift duty manager, was going to take Niels's shift but, as Rachel had not yet had her dinner, Lena had offered to cover the first hour so Rachel could get some food in her. It also gave her an excellent excuse to message Konstantinos and get out of the meal with him she'd been unable to think of a spontaneous excuse to refuse.

Duty manager at Igloo sick. Need to cover so won't be able to make dinner.

She'd grab something to eat at the staff canteen on her way back, she thought as she quickly donned her layers and put her snowsuit on. Before setting out, she took the precaution of changing the batteries of both her head torch and her walkie-talkie. Out here, you could never be too careful.

Lena set off, her thoughts automatically taking her to Konstantinos.

She'd had no respite from him until she'd turned her computer off at six. The whole working day, he'd been there, tormenting her with his presence, filling her office and the corridors of the lodge with his citrusy cologne. Even his stubble had taunted her, steadily thickening as the day had gone on, reminding her of the pleasurable pain of it scratching against her skin.

The emotional distance she'd tried to impose had made no difference, she thought miserably as she carefully navigated her way through worsening visibility to the complex's main road. Konstantinos only had to walk into a room for flames to flicker inside her and her resolutions to flounder. Oh, she was *pathetic*.

Four more days and then she'd be out of here. He would install her in his London penthouse, a thirty-minute train ride from her family, and then off he'd pop to wherever was next on his itinerary and she'd get a couple of weeks respite from him. She'd have to suffer his presence over Christmas but it was only for a few days. After that, there was no reason to imagine she'd have to deal with him at all in person until the baby came. That would be more than enough time to get her stupid wayward feelings for him in order.

The falling snow was impenetrable but Konstantinos grimly held his steady course until The Igloo's reception appeared, not as a structure but as a hazy block of light.

Abandoning the snowmobile he'd had to fight the impulse not to ride at full speed, he bowed his head against the whiteout and crashed his way through the reception door.

The shock on Lena's face at his appearance would have been amusing if her reckless actions hadn't snuffed any humour out of him. He'd half expected to arrive here and find that she hadn't turned up, that she was lost in the blizzard.

'What are you doing here?' she asked.

He stamped more snow off his boots, uncaring of the pile of slush he was creating around him, and ripped his gloves off. 'The very question I wish to ask of you.'

Her message cancelling their dinner date had pinged into his phone while he was taking a bath. As he'd been taking a screen break, it had gone unread for forty minutes.

She looked around the horseshoe reception desk she was currently standing behind with a bemused expression. 'I'm covering for Niels until Rachel gets here. She's on her way.'

'So that's two reckless members of staff I pay wages to.'

That took her aback. 'What do you mean by that?'

'Going out in this abysmal weather is the height of recklessness.'

'Not as reckless as leaving The Igloo short staffed,' she countered calmly. 'Niels is ill. Besides, as we discussed just this morning, we're trained to cope with the weather.'

He jabbed a finger in the direction of the door. 'That is not *weather*. That is hell.'

'We're near the Arctic Circle. We get snow. We deal with it. That's what you pay us good money for.'

'That is more than snow.'

'Yes, it's a blizzard. It's unfortunate but, as I said, we deal with it.'

Her serenity was as infuriating as her irresponsible actions. After stomping over to the reception desk, he slammed his hands on it. 'Deal with it? Lena, you are five months pregnant.'

'And?'

'Don't be obtuse,' he snarled. 'I cannot believe you would endanger yourself and our child like this.'

The calm vanished. Angry colour staining her face, she slammed her hands down on the other side of the desk in imitation of him and leaned forward, bringing her face close to his. 'Excuse me, *buster*, but that is insulting poppycock. The snow wasn't as heavy as this when I set off, and even if it was, I've lived here for four years and can ski-walk the route with my eyes closed. I have never had the slightest weather-related accident here because I treat the weather conditions with respect and understand my own limits. I was well wrapped up and had taken every precaution—we *all* take every precaution. I'm not an invalid and my bump isn't big enough yet to cause me balance problems, and for you to even suggest I would endanger our child is so insulting it makes me want to be sick, so go and take your judgement and stick it where the sun doesn't shine!'

If the reception door hadn't opened and a person, so thickly covered in snow they could be mistaken for a yeti, thrown themselves inside, Konstantinos thought he might have exploded with rage.

'Sorry, Lena,' the woman said as she shook her hood off. 'It's *awful* out there. I couldn't see what I was doing to shake the snow off outside…' She suddenly clocked Konstantinos and squeaked, 'Mr Siopis!'

He nodded a terse greeting.

Glaring at Konstantinos before dragging a smile to her face for Rachel, Lena hurried over to her, thankful for the excuse to get away from him. That he had the nerve to criticise her for doing her job was beyond credulity.

'Here, let me help you out of that.' Konstantinos could jolly well freeze in his snowsuit for all she cared. 'Is it really that bad out there?'

'I couldn't see a thing. If we didn't have the guide ropes I'd have lost my way.'

She looked out the window. Rachel was not exaggerating. To think Konstantinos had made the journey on a snowmobile—she'd seen the glare of its lights barely a minute before he'd stormed inside—only ratcheted up her fury at his sanctimony and hypocrisy. He might own the place but he didn't know the landscape. He'd had none of the training she and all the other staff undertook. The idiot could easily have gotten lost or stuck in a snowdrift. She'd bet he didn't even have an emergency walkie-talkie on him.

'If I'd known it was going to get this bad I'd have told you to stay in your cabin and done the shift myself,' she said, trying hard not to let her fury at Konstantinos sound out in her words to Rachel.

'Well, I'm here now so you can go off if—'

'She is not going anywhere until the blizzard clears,' Konstantinos interrupted rudely, making Rachel blink with surprise and Lena openly glare at him again. It felt like she'd spent the whole day on the defensive against his subtle sniping and now he couldn't even be bothered to be subtle about it and she'd had enough. If he could be rude to her then she could be rude back. What was he going to do about it? Sack her?

'That might be hours away. It's getting late, I'm shattered, and I haven't eaten yet.' And nor had he, she thought with a pang that she immediately chided herself for. Let the overbearing hypocrite starve.

After storming to the door, Konstantinos yanked it open. Immediately, a gust of snow streamed inside with a howl before he slammed the door back shut.

'You want to go out in that?' he demanded.

Having now seen, heard, and felt just how bad things were out there, Lena blanched at the thought of ski-walking through such torrid conditions.

Maybe he had a point after all.

'Okay, you're right, it doesn't look like we're going anywhere soon,' she said with fake brightness, casting her gaze anywhere but at him as she sought a solution. Thinking aloud, she said, 'I guess we'll just have to stay here for the night. There's an ice room free—you can have that. I'm sure you'll enjoy the experience. I'll take the store room.'

'You are not sleeping in the store room,' he said flatly. 'How many ice rooms are free?'

'Only the one and I'm not sleeping in it.'

'You are not sleeping on a floor, Lena.'

'We've got loads of sleeping bags. I'll make a nest for myself. I'll be fine. Or… I know. I can sleep on a sofa in the lounge.' The Igloo had a number of permanent heated facilities reached via a network of ice tunnels.

'Do I have to remind you that you're pregnant?'

Ignoring the thump of Rachel's jaw dropping to the floor, Lena rounded on him. 'No, you don't, but there is no way I am sleeping in one of those ice rooms, not after the last time.'

'Keep a light on if you're worried about the dark.'

'I thought you were worried about me endangering the baby?'

'A pregnant woman checked in this morning. We know there is no risk to the baby, not if you keep warm.'

'It's not keeping warm that worries me! Do you have any idea how terrifying a panic attack is when you're on your own?'

A pulse throbbed on the side of his jaw. 'You never mentioned a panic attack before.'

'I saw your reaction to my confession of claustrophobia. That was enough. I am not sleeping in an ice room and you have no right to try and bully me into it when we both know you hate the cold so much you'd sooner eat a ready meal than spend the night in one yourself.'

'I'll sleep in one with you if it stops you from sleeping on a floor or on a sofa.'

Totally taken aback, she stared at him.

He folded his arms across his chest and glowered at her. 'No pregnant woman should sleep on a floor or a sofa let alone the mother of my child. This is the only solution.'

'But…' Konstantinos's offer was so unexpected that for a moment she couldn't even think of a but. 'You *hate* the cold.'

'It is a sacrifice I am willing to make for our baby's sake,' Konstantinos said, knowing even as he said it that this wasn't quite the truth. It was the thought of Lena lying uncomfortably, trying to sleep on a hard floor after another long day that made his stomach twist and his chest clench, reactions only slightly less acute than when he'd thought he'd have to tie her to a chair to stop her going out into the treacherous blizzard. If she had gone, it would have been to spite him, he was certain of it.

Why had he goaded her like he'd done? Sure, he'd been

angry with her for endangering herself and the baby by setting out in a blizzard...okay, he accepted Lena had set out when the conditions were better than they were now, and she was right that these conditions were perfectly normal to her and yes, there was the possibility he might have overreacted slightly to the situation...

A great sigh ripped its way through him.

It was his behaviour that had been faulty. Not Lena's. He'd commandeered a snowmobile he'd never driven before and set off in a blizzard in terrain that was alien to him. The fury that had driven him...it had not been normal anger. Not normal as he knew it. Fear had laced it. Fear for Lena.

He'd goaded her deliberately as punishment for frightening him. And to get a reaction.

Just as she'd understood the warning he'd given by relating Theo and Cassia's betrayal, now he understood where the bad temper he'd been carrying the entire day had come from. Lena had reacted to his warning in the exact way he'd hoped, by smothering any emotions so well they might well have been extinguished in their entirety, not even a glow in her eyes to hint at anything happening beneath her skin, nothing to indicate that the awareness that lay so heavily inside him for her was reciprocated; but instead of basking in relief that they could plan a cordial life as co-parents, he'd hated it. Hated the mask of calm serenity and professional politeness she wore around him.

What was it about this woman that provoked so many contradictory feelings in him? Why, seeing the stark abundance of emotions now shining in eyes that had been shuttered from him, did he feel like he wanted to fight through the blizzard to reach the moon and hand it to her as a gift?

A cough cut through the thickening silence.

They both blinked and turned their heads in unison.

Rachel was looking at them awkwardly. 'Shall I tell the staff we have extra guests for the night?'

Konstantinos turned back to Lena at the same moment she turned her stare back to him. Her shoulders rose slowly, colour heightening her cheeks before she gave a quick nod.

A surge of adrenaline he had no control over shot through him, making his heart pound and his pulse soar.

CHAPTER NINE

LENA HAD TO force the steak she'd ordered from the Ice Restaurant down her throat. Being a heated permanent structure with soft lighting and cosy booths, the twenty-four-hour restaurant wasn't strictly part of The Igloo; instead, it connected to it in the same way its reception and lounge did, via the ice tunnel network. This was handy in bad weather such as they were currently experiencing, allowing guests and staff to use the permanent facilities without having to step outside. Most found the experience of staying in The Igloo exhilarating. They'd paid a fortune to sleep in an arthouse freezer and were determined to get their money's worth. Lena had found it terrifying.

This time, though, she wasn't frightened because of the fear of claustrophobia crawling its way back through her but because she would be sharing a bed with Konstantinos. Her only saving grace was that it could not be construed in any way as romantic. The cold meant they would both be fully clothed and in separate sleeping bags. In reality, it would be more like a childhood sleepover. Those reasonings did nothing to stop the food she'd managed to eat from churning in her stomach.

It didn't help that they were practically cut off from the other diners in the cosy, private booth or that she was so painfully aware of Konstantinos's foot resting so close to hers beneath the table or that she couldn't think of a single thing to say. There were so many emotions zooming through her that her brain couldn't cope with speech, too. Their entire meal had been conducted in excruciatingly tense silence, the excited blizzard chatter of those dining around them only making the silence between them more profound.

It was while they were eating their desserts that an alert came through on Lena's phone: the local airport would remain closed until at least 6 a.m.

Without speaking, she passed her phone to Konstantinos so he could see the alert for himself. He read it expressionlessly before meeting her stare. Jaw clenching, his shoulders rose and his nostrils flared before he gave a tight smile that clearly said, 'so be it.'

What didn't need to be said, verbally or otherwise, was that any vestige of hope that the blizzard would die out sooner rather than later had been dispelled. There would be no returning to their individual cabins tonight.

All too quickly, the point was reached where they could drag it out no longer. They were the last people in the restaurant. Their dessert plates were empty, Konstantinos's second coffee and Lena's second hot chocolate had been drunk.

Even as she was thinking this, she still jumped when Konstantinos got abruptly to his feet. 'Come on. Let's do it.'

Taking a deep breath, she rose, too.

In silence they walked to the permanent heated changing rooms. Each ice room had its own designated changing room with a private bathroom and a locker to store possessions. Nothing could be taken into the ice room apart from the clothes on their backs. One of the American party from yesterday had ignored this instruction and been surprised to find his phone frozen solid to the ice bedside table he'd left it on overnight.

They stepped into their designated changing room. Their sleeping bags, pillows and a bag of toiletries had been placed on the bench that ran its short length. She felt Konstantinos's eyes dart to her and knew he'd picked up on the fact the sleeping bags they'd been given could be turned into a double, and it suddenly hit her fully that she would be spending the night sleeping beside the man she'd spent the past days desperately trying to turn her emotions away from and mentally dousing the awareness that vibrated through her just to look at him.

Those vibrations of awareness had ramped up during their excruciating meal and now, stuck within the tiny dimensions of the changing room, reached supersonic proportions.

Snatching up the bag of hotel-supplied toiletries, she backed quickly to the bathroom. She didn't care if he wanted to use it first. She had to get away from him and get her head together, even if only for a few minutes. 'You need to take your layers off,' she said, the first words she'd spoken since they'd ordered their desserts. 'It's best just to sleep in your thermals and socks. Oh, and a hat. Bring your gloves and scarf, too, just in case.'

'We are sleeping in a freezer,' Konstantinos pointed out, wondering if she'd just spent the past couple of hours dreaming up the best way to get revenge on him being an arse to her.

'The sleeping bags are designed to withstand temperatures of up to minus forty.' Her speech was rapid, her hand gripped tightly to the handle of the bathroom door. 'Honestly, it's easier for your body to regulate itself this way. You'll need to wear your snowsuit and boots to the room but put everything else in the locker...except your jumper. Lots of people swear by putting that in the foot of your sleeping bag so you've something warm to put on in the morning before you have to get out of your cocoon or if you do get too cold during the night.'

She disappeared into the bathroom.

Alone, Konstantinos blew out air that would likely be one of his last warm breaths of the night, clenched his hands into fists, and rolled his neck and shoulders.

It was only one night and all they were sharing was a mattress, he reminded himself. After three nights of terrible, broken sleep, hc was due a good one. The odds were he would fall asleep in minutes and when he woke, the blizzard would be over and so would the night. It would pass in a blink.

But even as he stripped his layers off as Lena had suggested—*was* she trying to induce hypothermia in him?—and repeated his mental pep talk, his thrumming body took delight in contradicting his thoughts, and when the handle of the bathroom turned ten minutes after she'd disappeared into it, the thick, heavy beats of his heart rippled.

She emerged smelling distinctly of toothpaste. Her gaze barely glanced him. She still wore her snowsuit but carried a neatly folded bundle of clothing, which she stashed in the locker. Maybe she wasn't trying to instigate hypothermia in him after all.

Once he'd finished in the bathroom and locked away anything that could freeze, Konstantinos gathered their sleeping bags and pillows and together they navigated the frozen tunnels decorated with tiny spheres of ice suspended from the ceiling to their designated room. The silence between them that had once again turned into a living entity was broken by Christmas carols playing out through cleverly concealed speakers and raucous voices and bursts of laughter that rang out as they neared the ice bar. Another tunnel and the door with their number on it greeted them.

The brightly lit ice vault they entered had clearly been inspired by Japanese culture. The perfectly curved walls were intricately carved into an arcade of cascading cherry blossom leading to a temple carved into the wall at the far end behind the king-sized ice bed, the mattress of which had already been laid with a thick insulating under-sheet and reindeer hides.

When the door closed, the silence was exactly as Lena had described it. Absolute. In an instant the frozen room shrank.

She pressed a switch by the door. The lights coming from the overhanging ice cherry blossom extinguished, leaving only the dim blue lights at the base of the tree trunks as faint illumination.

He looked at her sharply. 'Not too dark for you?'

She huddled her arms around herself, her gaze darting everywhere but at him as she shook her head. 'Neither of us will get any sleep if we keep the main light on.' Her voice barely rose above a whisper.

'If it gets too much, you tell me,' he ordered roughly; rough because he'd looked again at the bed and his insides had lurched and then bloomed like the carved blossom surrounding them to know that shortly they would lie side by side on it. 'Okay?'

He had to strain his ears to hear her whispered, 'Okay.'

He sucked in a frigid breath and decided to take the sticking plaster approach, stepping to the bed and laying the sleeping bags and pillows out. His heart thumped so hard his ribs were in danger of bruising.

Turning her back on him, she unzipped her snowsuit, then sat on the bed to remove her boots.

Konstantinos did the same, doing his best to tune out Lena's snowsuit sliding down her legs and off her feet, those same feet quickly slipping back into the boots, keeping his gaze averted when she hurried to the door to hang the snowsuit on a peg. Unfortunately, he wasn't quick enough to stop his eyes from darting to her when she hurried back to the bed. This time his heart thumped so hard he wouldn't have been surprised if it burst from his rib cage entircly.

She was rubbing her arms against the icy air. There was nothing sexy at all about what she was wearing. The cream thermal top and bottoms she wore covered her from neck to sock-covered foot. Under the blue glow of the barely there lights, though, her silhouette could have been sculpted from the same ice encasing them, and suddenly a memory flashed in his mind of when that same silhouette—with one obvious difference—had taken his breath away without any warning.

When Thom had recommended Lena as his replacement, Konstantinos had struggled to picture whom he was talking about. He employed thousands of staff worldwide. It was impossible to know each individual face. He went through the staff files to put a face to Lena's name and was surprised to discover that yes, she must have made an impression on some base level as he did vaguely recognise her, but then thought no more about it. A week later he'd flown in to conduct the interviews.

When Lena had entered the meeting room for her interview, the clouds that had been hiding the sun suddenly parted. Its rays had shone through the window and landed straight on her. Whatever trickery had taken place, for one brief moment his mind had interpreted Lena's silhouette as being cast in gold.

But it was when she'd smiled at him that his breath had been truly stolen, he now remembered, remembering, too, the way his blood had pumped when she'd slid into the chair across from his. Of course, he'd gotten those strange bodily happenings under firm control. So firm that he'd cast them from his memory. Cast from it, too, how his interview with Lena had gone on for three times as long as all the other interviews for no discernible reason whatsoever, and the extra special care he'd taken when shaving before their celebratory meal, and the strange way he'd reacted when he'd seen her for the first time dressed in something other than her staff uniform. The red blouse she'd worn and tight black trousers had not been in the least revealing but, *Theos*, they had made his blood pump hard.

All that had happened before they'd shared three bottles of wine and his subconscious had finally forced to the forefront of his mind that Lena Weir was the most beautiful woman he'd ever set eyes on.

How had he forgotten all that?

And now he had to fight to draw breath, unable to drag his stare away from the feminine beauty coming towards him. The generous swell of her unbound breasts jutted… he almost groaned as the memory of their taste danced on his tongue…beneath the fabric, hips gently swaying… And then her boots were off and she was on the bed and quickly lining her sleeping bag with the insulating sheet they'd each been provided with and sliding her legs into it, reaching for the zip at the bottom and—

Her eyes suddenly locked on to his.

A pulse of desire shot through him, so strong it stole whatever breath he had left.

Even under the dim lighting he could see the colour crawl over her cheeks, see the way her lips pulled in together before she whispered with a shiver, 'You're going to freeze if you don't get into your sleeping bag.'

Freeze? Even with the cloud of vapour that came with the exhale of the breath he'd finally managed to make, the last thing he felt right then was cold. One look at his groin and Lena would see for herself the heat of his arousal for her.

Somehow, he managed to pull himself upright and carry his snowsuit to hang beside hers.

When he turned back to face her, she was cocooned in her sleeping bag, only her cute nose and cheeks showing through.

Lena knew it was dangerous to peek at Konstantinos as his long legs carried him back to the bed, especially after she'd just caught him staring at her with that glint in his eyes that shot straight into her pelvis, but she was helpless to resist. One look was too much and she squeezed them tightly shut and quickly rolled over so her back would be to him, and tried desperately hard to get air into her lungs.

How could just looking at him cause such internal devastation? How could she explain the painful wrench of her heart and the aching throbs deep between her legs just to catch a glimpse of the soft black hair poking out at the neck of the black thermal top he wore?

The mattress dipped. She held her breath, squeezed her eyes even tighter, and gripped even harder to her biceps. She didn't know if she was holding herself so tightly because of the cold or as protection against him... No, she realised painfully, it was protection against herself. She would not act the role of hopeless, lust-riddled adolescent again.

Once he'd made himself comfortable, the silence in the room was complete. The only sounds Lena could hear clearly were the rapid beats of her heart and the short intakes of breath she managed to snatch.

She cocooned herself closer into her sleeping bag and wished she'd remembered to put her scarf on. She'd been in such a flux in the changing room that she'd thoughtlessly added it to the pile of layers she'd stuck in the locker. After her babbled words of advice to Konstantinos, she'd stupidly forgotten to bring a jumper, too. Her nose was cold.

Time passed. Not a single sound or movement came from the body lying beside her. She remembered waking between making love on their night together and watching him sleep through the light that still managed to filter in through the blackout blinds. She'd been fascinated. Her dad's snoring was so loud he was capable of waking the whole street up but Konstantinos slept without sound, only the deep rise and fall of his chest proving he was actually alive.

The urge to roll over and press herself as close as their individual sleeping bags would allow was unbearable.

Her brain wouldn't switch off. Her thoughts were spinning like a carousel. She could no longer keep her eyes closed. She wished desperately for Konstantinos to wake up and say something, anything to break the silence closing in on her. The longer the minutes ticked by, the more images of the past flickered in her vision, and the more the impenetrable dark shadowed walls closed in on her, and the deeper the muffled effect of the solid block of ice and snow they were encased in. The beats of her already erratic heart changed to a frighteningly ragged tempo, snatches of breath becoming almost impossible to find.

Despite his best efforts to relax his body so sleep would take him into oblivion, Konstantinos's best efforts were nowhere near good enough. He was aiming for the impossible. He was just too intensely aware of Lena huddled on the other side of the bed to relax, his senses attuned to her every breath and every tiny body adjustment. It was only now that he was lying within this ice vault that he truly understood what she meant about the silence being a silence like no other. Nothing penetrated the thick walls. It was just the two of them cocooned away from the world. Him and Lena.

It was the sharp gasping turn her breaths took that first alerted him to there being something wrong. If he was a dog his ears would have pricked up. He didn't need to be any animal other than human to sense the new form the tension that had laced her since she'd accepted they would have to share a bed for the night took.

And then came the faint hum of strained vocal cords. If they were anywhere but here, he wouldn't have heard it.

'Lena?' Alarmed, he rolled over. 'Are you okay?'

She didn't answer, just repeated the tune, but this time more clearly, enabling him to define the words of a song that made no sense at all. 'The big ship sails on the Alley Alley O...' A swallow. 'The Alley Alley O, the Alley Alley O.' Another swallow. 'The big ship sails on the Alley Alley O, on the last day of September.'

Instinct made him unzip his sleeping bag enough to free his arms so he could wrap them around her and spoon himself around her. She didn't resist. A hand poked out of the top of her sleeping bag and clawed for his. He caught it and held it tightly, pressing himself closer to her; all the while she sang another refrain of the strange childlike verse.

'Better?' he asked when the singing finally petered away.

When her answer came, it was a choked, 'Thank you.'

He squeezed her hand. She squeezed back.

'Is it always like that?' he asked quietly.

Lena shook her head. She hadn't had a panic attack since the last time she'd slept in The Igloo. That time she'd managed to slam the switch installed at the side of the bed and get some light into the room but the attack had continued for another fifteen minutes. This time its grip on her had lessened the moment Konstantinos spoke her name. The effect of his arms being wrapped around her and the clasp of his strong, comforting hand had soothed her more effectively than even her mother had been able to do when the panic attacks were at their height.

'Thank you,' she repeated. His arms tightened, his forehead pressing into the hood of her sleeping bag.

Lena's heart throbbed and tears filled her eyes. That Konstantinos was putting himself through what was for him personal torture just so she didn't have to sleep alone in her own version of it meant more than she could ever say. She wished she hadn't been so angry with his hypocritical sanctimony and then too full of fear that sharing a bed would see her betray her deep yearning for him to recognise it earlier. Having his arms around her and the strength of his body tight against her made her feel like a woman drowning in an ocean storm lifted onto a life boat and gently steered into calm waters.

'You must be cold,' she whispered once she'd kept the tears at bay. He'd disentangled himself from his warm cocoon to comfort her, and now her panic had subsided, other, far more dangerous, feelings were creeping through her, the beats of her heart thumping with that weighted raggedy sensation.

'It's okay,' he said, as if potential hypothermia was nothing, and suddenly she was filled with another emotion so powerful it knocked the breath out of her. Konstantinos had put his health at risk for her.

Overtaken by the need to look at him, she shifted just enough to roll onto her back without losing the solid strength of his lean body compressed against her and without releasing his hand. 'It's not okay. You'll get frostbite or something.'

He lifted his head. The dim blue lighting kept so much of his vampiric features hidden in shadows, but what she found in his hooded gaze made her pelvis throb and her heart swell so hard and so fast it crushed her lungs.

Unthinkingly, she let go of his hand and placed her fingers on his smooth neck. The shock of cold she found there melted her insides that little bit more. His skin was cold for her. Because he'd comforted her when she'd needed him. She swallowed hard. She didn't want to let him go. She wanted him to crawl into her sleeping bag and share the warmth his care had filled her with. 'Tinos, you're freezing.'

Konstantinos's heart clenched at the shortening of his name, the clench twisting painfully to see what was shining in Lena's eyes and know it was what she must be seeing in his own eyes.

He tried to draw in air.

Who was he trying to fool? The more he tried to fight

this combustible mix of emotions and desire that burned in his veins for Lena, the worse it got. The deeper it infected him. The more he wanted her. Wanted her like he'd never wanted anyone or anything.

Did he seriously think he could live his life with Lena Weir in it without waging a constant battle with himself?

Palming her cheek, he stared at her beautiful face, wondering how someone Aphrodite would envy could look at him and not be repulsed. Look at him with desire... No, more than desire. Like he meant something to her. Just as he was coming to see that she meant something to him...

Slowly, he brought his mouth down to hers.

CHAPTER TEN

THE TENDER MELDING of Konstantinos's lips against hers melted the last of the defences Lena had tried so hard to protect herself with.

There was nothing of the hard, scorched fury of the passionate kiss they'd shared in her cabin the other night but the emotion she could feel contained in it made her heart beat twice as hard and as fast.

He lifted his head again. His smile was crooked. 'Your nose is cold,' he said hoarsely, before pressing a kiss to the tip and sitting up. Working quickly, he unzipped the rest of his sleeping bag, then lay on his side to unzip Lena's. There was a shock of cold on the side of her body exposed to the frozen air but no time for it to properly penetrate her skin for Konstantinos immediately used his own body as cover to protect her from the chill, and got to work on opening their individual liners and zipping the two sleeping bags together.

By the time they were secured together tightly, he was shivering. When he groped for her hands, it was like being touched by blocks of ice.

'Burrow under,' she whispered urgently, pulling his hands together and holding them against her belly while rubbing them with her own, then wriggling down as low as she could in their newly created cocoon. As soon as he'd followed suit, his knees bent as much as the tightness of the conjoined sleeping bags would allow to accommodate his tall frame, she abandoned his hands and hooked her thigh over his hip, burrowed her face into his neck and breathed into his skin, wrapping her arms tightly around his waist and vigorously stroking his back, pressing every inch of herself that she could into him, doing everything she could to replace the warmth he'd lost for her.

The single-minded determination and care Lena was displaying as she used her whole body to bring warmth back into him touched Konstantinos immeasurably. His wealth and status meant people often tripped over themselves to ensure his every need was taken care of, but it was never out of concern for him as a man. Those people never saw him as anything but a billionaire with the power and contacts to be their meal ticket if they played their cards right. His lovers viewed him through the prism of his fat wallet. He couldn't even imagine Cassia in the long-ago days when she'd proclaimed to love him doing anything but lie there with the expectation that he do all the work needed to keep them warm.

Lena was having his child. She would spend the rest of her life without a single financial worry and she knew it. He was no potential meal ticket for her: the ticket had already been cashed. And yet, despite all this, despite there being no benefit to herself, she was trying her hardest to fight the cold for him.

Every stroke of her small hands over his back and shoulders and arms, every rub of her thighs and calves over his legs and hips, every hot breath blown onto his neck and jaw, spoke louder than words that he did mean something to her. A part of her genuinely cared for him. For *him*.

He didn't know if it was her tender ministrations or this astounding realisation that filled his chest with the final dose of heat needed to shake off the last of the chills, but it was Lena who'd filled it, and he roamed his hands over her body in turn, revelling in the softness of her contours through the clothing she wore, marvelling at the subtle changes to it since their night together, marvelling that he remembered every part of their night together so well that he could actually feel the changes pregnancy had made. Those changes only fed the desire that constantly burned for her. Clasping her peachy bottom, he rolled her onto her back, taking care not to squash her with his weight. Dim light poured through the opening his movements had created at the top of their tight nest, and he stared down at her in wonder.

Her hand moved to palm the back of his neck. It burned at her touch. 'That's better,' she whispered.

He had to swallow the lump that had formed in his throat. His face was barely inches above hers. 'Are you warm enough?'

Their private cocoon muffled their words, adding to the sensation that it was only the two of them in this whole wide world.

She smiled tremulously and razed her fingers through the hair at his nape. 'I am now.' And then she raised her face and kissed him.

Lena closed her eyes and sank into the slow, gentle fusion of their mouths. Her already overloaded senses greedily soaked in all the new sensations filling them, from Konstantinos's dark taste as the kiss deepened and he parted her lips with a push of his tongue, to the scratching of his stubble against her skin.

Something had shifted between them that night. And something had shifted in her, too. It had started when he'd held her so protectively during her panic attack and grown when she'd smothered his body to warm him, the awakening of a deep, primitive need to protect him just as he'd protected her.

And she knew he felt it, too. Whether the wall Konstantinos had built around himself to insulate him from pain in the wake of his brother and fiancée's betrayal was falling down because of the baby didn't matter. He was opening himself to *her*. It was there in his voice, in his every touch, and she responded to it like a moth to a flame. She was the moth and she'd carried his flame since the night they'd conceived their child.

With the tight enclosure they were trapped within preventing them from ripping off the barrier of their clothing, Lena could do nothing but hold him closely, wind her legs around his waist and drink in the ever-deepening kisses that sent sensation thrumming through her entire being and enveloped her in a cloud that contained only him.

How she'd adored touching him that night, exploring Konstantinos in a way she'd never done before; had never *wanted* to do before. And how she'd ached for *his* touch, a desperation to have his mouth and hands on every inch of her skin, opening herself to him in a way she'd never dreamed she was capable of. That burn was alive in her again, a burn to peel their layers off and get as physically close as it was possible to be, but as that was impossible, she would make the most of what they could share because right now this was as close to heaven as her delirious body was able to get.

Deeper still their kisses forged, an utter devouring of mouths and tongues, an assault of hands and fingers scraping and groping every inch of the other they could reach within the tight, tight confines. The weight of Konstantinos's arousal pressed tantalisingly against her flaming pelvis, sending such thrills through her that she could have wept for his possession.

'*Theos*, Lena, I want you so much,' he groaned into her mouth as he ground his erection against her, making her moan.

She clasped the back of his head and kissed him with all the passion she possessed and pressed her pelvis tighter against him, showing him with her body how badly she needed him. The burn inside her was fast turning into molten agony. 'Please,' she begged. 'Please.'

The beats of Konstantinos's heart had never pumped so hard. His blood had never felt so thick. Arousal had never felt like pain.

He didn't just want Lena. He needed her. Needed to be inside her, however impossible it seemed at that moment, because in that moment it felt as necessary as breathing.

The confinement of their wrappings against the freezing temperatures left little room for movement but enough for him to grip the waistband of her leggings. She lifted her bottom enough for him to yank them down to her thighs and then helped him yank his own past his hips, freeing his arousal to press heavily against the heat it so desperately needed to take possession of. The nails of one hand scratching into his hair, she grabbed his buttock with the other and writhed against him, her unashamed desire coming close to blowing his mind. It had been like that during their night together, a rabid hunger that had consumed them both.

Theos, he was trembling. She was trembling.

Aching to be inside her but with Lena's bunched clothing preventing their bodies from locking together in the way they both so desperately needed, he had to hold his erection and, with her plaintive urgings, guide himself into the slick heat. It was impossible to thrust the whole of himself inside her but it didn't matter. If this was all they could have then he would take it. All that mattered was this electrifying fusion of their bodies that zinged into his entire being.

'Oh, God,' she whispered breathlessly, her teeth razing over his cheek. 'Please, Tinos. Please.'

Sliding a hand behind her bottom, he gripped it tightly and began to move.

Tongues entwined, they found a slow rhythm that managed to give them both what they needed, their passionate kisses punctuated by gasps and moans of pleasure.

Lena was lost in a world of sensation. Lost in a world of Konstantinos and the slowly increasing pressure coiling so tightly inside her that came only from him. Only from him.

She was his, she thought dimly as the pressure built into a peak that exploded and had her crying out his name, sending her soaring on a kaleidoscope of sensation so intense the colours swirled together and white lights flickered behind her eyes.

This was like nothing Konstantinos had ever experienced. He didn't care that he couldn't be buried as deep inside Lena as it was possible to be; what they were sharing was beyond comprehension. And so he didn't try to understand, just closed his thoughts off to everything but

Lena, her scent, the taste of her mouth, and the exquisite pleasure of their bodies crushed together until his name spilled from her lips as a cry and her climax pulled him over the edge and into the abyss.

Lena's eyes fluttered open. The sleeping bag covered so much of her face that she was struggling to breathe. The darkness was as all encompassing as it had been before she'd drifted into that excuse for sleep but, other than the bit of her forehead exposed between where her hat rested on it and the sleeping bag started, she was as warm as she'd ever been. Cosily warm. How could she be anything else when she had Konstantinos pressed so snugly against her back and his arms wrapped around her?

She had no idea what the time was but instinct told her twilight—not that it existed here at this time of year— had long passed.

Reluctantly letting go of his arm, she pinched the top of the sleeping bag covering her mouth and nose, drew it down to her chin and inhaled the frigid air into her lungs.

His arms tightened around her. 'Are you okay?'

Konstantinos's sleepy voice made her chest expand. Putting her hand back on his arm, she gently squeezed. 'I'm fine. Go back to sleep.'

He shifted his head to rest his chin on her shoulder. 'You sure? If you have another panic attack coming, tell me. Let me help you.'

Oh, she could choke from the emotions filling her. 'Not another attack, I promise. I just needed air.'

He kissed her neck and slipped a hand beneath her top.

She groped for it, threading her fingers through his, and closed her eyes at the simple pleasure of his flesh against hers.

This was the most dangerous time. She knew it. She'd woken in the witching hours the night they'd conceived their child feeling like she'd woken in heaven, Konstantinos's hot mouth already urgent against hers, his possession of her almost savage in its intensity. She'd never have believed in those blissful moments that a few hours later he would look her in the eye and tell her it had been a mistake. She wanted desperately to believe that this time it would be different, that having a baby together made it different, but how could she trust that, especially with the warnings he'd given her barely forty-eight hours ago? What had happened that night hadn't been planned. A spell had been cast over them and she was terrified that when the bright lights that indicated daytime were switched on, the spell would be broken for him, just as it had been the last time.

'How long have you suffered with them?' he asked quietly, his chin still resting on her shoulder.

'I don't really suffer them anymore.'

'Then what was it you suffered earlier?' he asked in a dry, indulgent tone that made her smile and wish so hard for things she shouldn't wish for.

'It was my first one in four years.'

'So the last one was when you stayed the night in The Igloo for the first time?'

'Yes. I wouldn't have applied to work here if the attacks weren't under control. I didn't know I'd become claustrophobic. If I had, I wouldn't have stayed in The Igloo and the panic attack wouldn't have happened.'

'If you had them under control does that mean there was a time when they were out of control?'

Lena thought back to the time when having up to ten panic attacks a day was considered normal. Terrifying but normal. 'I don't know about out of control but they were pretty frequent.'

'Is it something you always suffered with?'

'No.'

'So when did they start?'

'Six years ago.'

'So around the time your sister had her accident?'

'Yes.'

If Konstantinos squeezed her any tighter he feared crushing her bones. He didn't understand why he felt the need to hold Lena so closely to him but, for that night, he accepted that whatever they were sharing was a spell of its own making.

With her hand resting on top of his, he made smooth circular motions over her belly. Earlier, after they'd straightened themselves up as best they could and he'd wrapped her into his arms, he'd put his hand to her belly like he was doing now and felt their baby move beneath his palm. He'd drifted off to sleep filled with emotions deep enough to choke him. 'What happened?'

She sighed and twisted in his arms so she lay on her back, and palmed his cheek. 'I was in the car with her.'

Ice spooled in his veins. 'When the accident happened?'

'Yes. It was my nineteenth birthday. We'd gone out with friends. Heidi wasn't a big drinker and offered to drive. We were driving back home when we were hit side-on by a drunk driver. We ended up upside down in a ditch.'

Konstantinos was glad she was no longer spooned against him or he feared he really would have crushed her bones at that.

Spreading his palm flat, he slid it round her back and

pressed his mouth to her forehead. 'What injuries did you suffer?'

'Nothing serious. The other car hit the driver's door. Heidi was… I thought…'

'What?' he encouraged gently, his chest filling with the ice crawling through his veins to guess what she struggled to say.

'I thought she was dead.' Lena blew out a choked puff of air and fought back tears as the terror she'd experienced when she'd begged and begged her unresponsive sister to wake up came back to her in full technicolour. 'I was so scared, Tinos. I couldn't get to my phone to call for help. It was pitch-black but I could smell blood and I knew it wasn't coming from me but from her, and I couldn't release my seat belt and get to my phone. I was hanging upside down and so disoriented and Heidi was upside down, too, like something out of a horror film, and she wasn't answering me and I could smell her blood and there was nothing I could do…and…'

Dimly aware she was on the verge of talking herself into another panic attack, Lena closed her eyes and moved her face closer to Konstantinos's neck so she could inhale his comforting scent. 'The big ship sails on the Alley Alley O,' she sang to herself, a technique her mother had read about and which, with the therapist's encouragement, had become the tool Lena had developed to control the attacks. 'On the last day of September.'

'How long were you there?' he asked into the silence.

She breathed in his musky scent again before answering. 'Only ten minutes or so—the accident was witnessed. But they were the longest minutes of my entire life. It felt like hours. The couple who witnessed it found us but by that stage I'd convinced myself I was going to die there, too, but I walked out of the hospital without a scratch on me.'

'Not physical scratches,' he murmured before kissing her forehead. 'But you were scarred in other ways.'

'Those scars are nothing. I'm healthy. I can walk. I can do everything for myself. I can feed myself and bathe myself. I can breathe unaided. I'm not prone to infections. I can have children. Heidi will never have any of that, and it makes me want to cry because she's the one who was always maternal, not me. When we were kids we played mummies and daddies and I always played the role of daddy because she insisted on being mummy. She always knew she wanted to marry and have a family whereas I was always indifferent. Children weren't even on my radar. Every hope and dream she ever had is dead and still she smiles and keeps cheerful and makes the best of each day, and she insists that I do, too. Remember you asked why I was here and not at home supporting my family?'

He gave a pained sigh. 'Lena, I am sorry. I should never have said that.'

'Believe me, it's nothing I haven't thought a thousand times. Why should I get to live my dream when Heidi lost *everything*? But she wanted me to go. Even when the panic attacks were still coming thick and fast she'd nag at me to go.'

'And your parents?'

'They wanted me to go, too. The three of them ganged up on me, the line of attack being that as Heidi had lost her health and her dreams, it was only right that I make the most of mine. It was Dad who spotted the advert for a receptionist here—he took it on himself to subscribe to a load of Swedish recruitment websites. Sweden was always my favourite place. I lived for the summers and Christmases we spent here. It was always my dream to live out here in the snow and ride huskies. He made me apply. They all did. They even had a leaving party for me. If Heidi could have jumped out of her wheelchair and helped me pack my suitcase, she would have done.'

'But you still feel guilt,' he guessed.

She took a long time to answer. 'It's always there. I can never shake it that while I'm living a full life, she's confined to a wheelchair and completely dependent.'

'Is that the real reason you haven't told your family about the baby? Are you afraid your news will hurt her?'

'I don't...' She swallowed. 'I hadn't thought of it like that. Maybe that's played a part in it.'

Remembering his trawl through the Ice Hotel staff's social media accounts and how Lena was mostly absent from the socialising that played such a big part in their off-the-clock lives, Konstantinos would guess it had played more than a part. He could understand her position as general manager would make her feel the need to remain above the wilder behaviour that sometimes gripped them, but she'd only had the role for five months. There was no indication she'd ever joined in the socialising in the way it was embraced by everyone else.

He'd trawled through those accounts seeking evidence that another man could be the father of her baby, he remembered with painful guilt.

'Tell me something else,' he said. 'Is Heidi the reason I'm your first lover since the accident? Am I wrong in assuming it was the accident that stopped you forming relationships?'

'I've only ever had one proper boyfriend,' she confessed. 'He ended it when he went off to uni a couple of months before the accident. Once the accident happened I didn't have the headspace to even think about relationships.'

'But you've been here for four years. You're beautiful. People are drawn to you. I can't imagine you've been single all this time by choice.'

'I've had offers for want of a better word but I was never interested.'

'Still pining for your first love?' For some reason he had to unlock his jaw to ask that.

'Lord, no.' For the first time since she'd started opening up to him, there was a lighter tone to her voice. 'James and I… I hate to admit this but I was really shallow in those days. The only thing I liked about him was his face. He was gorgeous. All the girls fancied him. I cried for a week after he ended it but really, that's because I was being dramatic. There was no real substance to my feelings for him. I just liked being seen with him.'

'If it's pretty faces you like, why end your celibacy with me?'

CHAPTER ELEVEN

FOR SOMEONE WHO was half Konstantinos's size and five months pregnant, Lena twisted round and pushed him flat on his back with a surprising agility.

'Now, you listen to me, Konstantinos Siopis,' she said fiercely, speaking right in his face. 'You are *not* ugly, and to put you right from what you accused me of the other day, I didn't sleep with you because you're rich or, just in case you're thinking it, because you're my boss, or even because of the wine I'd drunk. I slept with you because I couldn't not. You smiled at me... I'd never seen you smile before...and I felt it right in the place our baby's now growing.'

He gazed into the eyes glaring vehemently at him and felt something move in his heart.

Her face still hovering over his, she palmed his stubbled cheek. 'I have never felt *anything* like that before. You're not handsome, Tinos, but to my eyes you're beautiful. Every bit of you.'

He attempted humour to lighten the weight building in his chest. 'Even my nose?'

She kissed the tip. 'Every bit of you.'

'My brother broke it when I was eleven. That's why it bends.'

Something flashed in her eyes. 'Why did he do that?'

'We were fighting and he hit me. In fairness, I hit him first. The damage only became pronounced in my teenage years.' At the age of fourteen he'd suddenly shot up, growing six inches in the same number of months. His face had changed, too, becoming angular, his always too-long nose gaining prominence. It had taken Theo and Cassia's betrayal for him to understand that outer beauty often masked inner ugliness. That was when he'd stopped caring about his appearance. People could take him or leave him, and as his wealth had grown, people, especially women, had increasingly taken him.

Right now, here with Lena, he felt like he was with the first person who'd ever looked beneath the surface to see *him*.

'What were you fighting about?' she asked.

'I can't remember. We were always fighting in those days.'

'Sibling rivalry at its finest. Heidi and I hardly ever fought but I had friends who hated their siblings. Who's the oldest?'

'He is, by two years.'

'Strange,' she mused. 'It's usually the younger sibling who tries to outshine the older one and take what they have for themselves. He must have been incredibly jealous of you.'

He grunted a laugh. 'He had nothing to be jealous about. Theo's the one who had everything. He was movie-star handsome like your ex, and like your ex all the girls wanted him.' Those who'd befriended Konstantinos like Cassia had done so in the hope of getting closer to his brother. Even his parents had noticed the surge in young female applicants for the rare job vacancies in the family restaurant once Theo had started working there.

Her face tightened, that flash blazing in her eyes again. '*Exactly*. Tinos, he stole your fiancée. That's the cruellest thing a sibling can do. He stuck around to work in the family restaurant, didn't he?'

Fascinated at her obvious anger, he nodded.

The blaze continued to flash. 'I bet he hated your hard work and success taking the spotlight from him so he stole the one thing that meant something to you.'

'He fell in love with her.' Konstantinos was aware he was only defending his brother to provoke more of this reaction from Lena.

'I don't care. If he found himself developing feelings for her he should have stayed the hell away.'

Gazing into the face of the woman *he* should have stayed the hell away from, Konstantinos asked for the first time, not only aloud but to himself, 'What if he couldn't?'

Hadn't he been unable to keep away from Lena? For all the excuses he'd made, hadn't he flown back to Sweden seven months early because his craving to see her again had grown too strong to resist any longer?

'Oh, come on,' she said, oblivious to his new direction of thought. 'He was an adult, not an adolescent experiencing hormones for the first time. There is no excuse for what he did to you. None. They deserve each other and I hope their marriage is a living hell for them both.'

With amusement building amidst the weight in his chest, he slipped his hand back under her top. *Theos*, he loved Lena's skin, the soft texture, the way she shivered with obvious pleasure at his touch. Arousal spooled in his loins to imagine stripping her naked and making love to her with his hands and mouth, tasting every inch, licking the tips of her breasts in the way that had made her pant and plead and beg for more…

'I hate to disappoint you but my parents tell me they are happy,' he said, having to blink his concentration back to their conversation and not to the heady fantasies that had made him as stiff as a board.

'There's still time for karma to bite them on their butts,' she said stubbornly, even as she slipped her hand up his top and splayed her fingers through the hairs on his abdomen.

No one had ever taken his side without equivocation before. All these years, the ghost of Theo and Cassia had tainted every minute spent with his parents and extended family. He'd never expected anyone to take sides, least of all his parents, but expectation and want were two different things, and their love for their two sons and determination not to choose one over the other had festered like a wound. Konstantinos had been wronged. His life had been shattered. His trust had been destroyed. His dreams had gone up in smoke. And no one had taken his part, making every excuse under the damned sun to excuse the golden son's betrayal.

'Where does this fire come from?' he wondered idly as he continued to gaze at her, his mouth filling with moisture to imagine those lips currently set in an obstinate, furious line kissing fire over his skin. That this fury was on his behalf...

Her shadowed brow creased. 'I just think they treated you abysmally.'

Theos, she was beautiful.

Cupping her head, he pulled her down and kissed her, delighting when her obstinate lips sighed into his and returned the kiss with the same hunger consuming him.

With a soft moan into his mouth, she stretched her body half over his and slipped a thigh between his legs.

Twelve hours ago Konstantinos would have said it impossible that he would spend a night in The Igloo and wish for the morning not to come. And when Lena's hand slipped down his abdomen, then lower still and took his arousal in her hand with a groan and made a fist around it that made *him* groan, he closed his eyes and wished even harder for this night to go on forever.

'I've never ridden with huskies,' Konstantinos said. They were still huddled in their cocoon, Lena's face resting on the top of his chest, his hands making circular strokes over her back, her fingers making circular strokes around his nipple.

'What, never?' she asked in mock horror. 'You've owned this place forever and first you tell me you've never seen the Northern Lights and now you tell me you've never been on a husky ride?'

'Explain what I'm missing out on being dragged through snow in freezing temperatures?'

'The exhilaration of it all! You're out in the wilderness, your eyes are streaming because of the freshness of the air as it whips through your face —'

'The freshness of the air because it's so cold?'

She laughed. 'That's all part of the fun of it.'

'I will take your word for that.'

'Try it for yourself. You might surprise yourself and find you enjoy it.'

He gave a disbelieving grunt. She pinched his nipple. Before he could react in the way her body was already thrumming with anticipation for, there was a knock on the door.

Lena's deliriously happy mood plummeted.

The knock indicated that their night in The Igloo was officially over.

The door opened. It was always that way. The acoustics of The Igloo made it as impossible for sound to travel out of the individual rooms as it was for it to travel in. The knock was nothing but a polite courtesy.

Johan, the member of staff going from room to room with hot drinks, had clearly been prepped for who to expect in this particular one as he didn't even flicker to find the owner of the hotel and its general manager sharing the bed, or raise a brow that they'd zipped their sleeping bags together.

'Good morning,' he said cheerfully. 'Hot lingonberry juice?' A moment later the main lights were switched on.

So stark was the change in illumination that Lena had to wait for her eyes to adjust before she was able, working in tandem with Konstantinos, to sit upright.

Johan poured them both a mug of the steaming liquid and then carried their snowsuits over to them before leaving them to drink and get changed in privacy.

Cradling her mug in both hands, Lena found herself scared to look at Konstantinos even though their cocoon meant the sides of their bodies were still pressed tightly together.

With the knock of a door and the switch of a light, the spell had been broken.

Their whole night together, opening up to each other, making love, opening up even more, bringing each other to climax using only their hands, and then all the silly inconsequential chatter about everything and nothing that was neither silly nor inconsequential, the words an unceasing flow of reminiscences, potted histories, likes and dislikes with no question of wasting their precious time sleeping, and all that time holding each other, at one with each other, just them in the whole world...

And now it was over.

'What are you thinking?' he asked after the silence left in Johan's wake had grown to unbearable levels.

She swallowed and tried to keep the despondency from her voice. 'Nothing interesting.'

'Lena, look at me.'

If his order hadn't been so gently delivered, she would have ignored him.

What she found on his face made her heart throb.

Hooded eyes not leaving hers, he placed his empty mug beside him on the mattress and then rubbed his thumb along her cheekbone. 'That was no mistake,' he said quietly.

She tried to take in air. Afraid she would cry if she spoke, she bit her bottom lip.

His smile was crooked. It beamed straight into her swelling heart. 'Come back to my cabin with me.'

Now she wanted to wail like a child. 'I can't. I've got to work.'

'You need to sleep. Sven can cover for you—he'll be doing it for real in a few days. If need be, he can make any rearrangements to the rota.' Straightening her hat for her, he kissed the tip of her nose.

After a night spent in such confinement, the sheer size of Konstantinos's cabin was a stark relief to Lena. She rarely needed to enter the guest cabins and the last time she'd been in here, things had been so fraught between them that she hadn't appreciated how luxurious and inviting it was. The bed at the far end, behind the proper living area and proper dining area, was so large and filled with such plump pillows she took one look at it and felt the exhaustion of a night without sleep hit her.

He smoothed her hair off her face and cradled her cheeks. 'Shower and sleep?'

She nodded. Lethargy had gripped her so tightly her tongue felt too thick to speak.

Taking her hand, he led her into the bathroom. She gazed with longing at the huge rolltop bath but he shook his head. 'You'll fall asleep in it. Another time.'

Another time. She liked the sound of that.

She liked even more when he stripped all his clothes off then helped her strip off, too, liked more than that when he stood under the spray of the walk-in shower with her, and liked even more than that when he massaged shower gel over every inch of her skin and lathered shampoo into her hair. By the time he was finished, she was so relaxed she could have fallen asleep on her feet. Once they were dry and their teeth brushed, he got a huge, dry, fluffy towel, wrapped it around her, lifted her into his arms and carried her to bed.

The last thing she felt as she slipped into oblivion was Konstantinos's arms wrapping around her.

'Come on,' Lena cajoled. 'It's our last night here.'

'I'm not going outside,' Konstantinos said firmly. 'It's freezing out there.'

'It's always freezing out there.'

'And I only go out in it when it's strictly necessary.'

She didn't argue with him. No, she did better than that. Lena simply folded her arms under her breasts and stared at him with that look he was coming to recognise. It was the same look she'd given when they'd argued over which house would be more suitable for her and their child. He'd wanted the one in a plush gated community.

She'd wanted the one in the middle of nowhere. Both were a ten-minute drive from her parents' home town. Lena, he was coming to understand, loved the unpolluted night sky, which is what their latest standoff was about. The night sky—yes, he knew, it was currently always a night sky here—was cloudless, and Lena wanted them to leave the warmth of his cabin and stand in conditions colder than a freezer to look at it.

She'd won the standoff over the house, and, with a re-signed sigh, he admitted defeat over getting frostbite. If he didn't know better he would think Lena had him eating out of her hands.

Climbing off the bed he'd been trying to entice her into joining him on so he could make love to her again, Konstantinos hooked an arm around her waist and pulled her to him. 'If I do this, you will owe me.'

Her amazing dark brown eyes gleamed. 'If you stay outside with me for more than an hour, I will owe you *big* time.'

Gripping her bottom so he could press his arousal against her, he murmured, 'Can I take part payment now?'

She rose onto her toes, a hand sliding down his naked abdomen to take his throbbing excitement into her hand. With a gentle squeeze, she whispered into his ear, 'Nope. A full hour, Mr Siopis, and then we can come back in here and I will strip naked for you and let you do whatever you want.'

He groaned, then groaned even louder when she dropped his erection and skipped out of his hold and well out of arm's reach. Her gaze drifted down to his jutting arousal and she gave a mischievous smile. 'The cold outside will cure that for you.'

* * *

Okay, Konstantinos thought an hour later, huddled on one of the hotel's viewing benches, a ten-minute trek away from the lights of the main complex, Lena might have a point about the beauty of the night sky here. The moonless vast sky was alight with stars, high above them a long streak of hazy light with a high concentration of what looked like cloud interspersed with thousands of massed stars which she authoritatively told him was the Milky Way, explaining how Earth was located on one of its spiral arms and that was what enabled them to see its centre so clearly.

'See?' she said happily. '*That's* why I dragged you out here. It's only on nights like this that you can see it. There's too much light pollution for me to see it in England, but here...' She sighed.

'You will miss it?' Tomorrow they would fly to England. He'd further delayed his trip to Australia to help her settle into his London penthouse. The purchase of the house he was buying for her was set to be completed by the New Year.

'Very much. But I'll come back one day. When our baby's old enough... Look...' She pointed to their right, away from the Milky Way, to a cluster of stars shaped something like an hourglass. 'That's Orion.'

'How do you know so much about all this?' he marvelled.

'I have a phone app that tells me where all the stars and planets and constellations are. I've gotten to know the sky so well I rarely need to use it anymore.'

'What's the fascination?'

She pondered this before answering. 'Many things.

Knowing I'm looking at the same stars humans have been looking at for millennia, wondering which stars still even exist, wondering where in the billions of stars in the Milky Way life exists…' She looked at him and smiled. 'For me, it's endlessly fascinating. I've often said that if I make it to eighty, I want to be sent off in a spaceship and travel the universe.'

'There are already trips into space. You could do one of them.'

'You have to be a gazillionaire to afford that.'

'Lena, I *am* a gazillionaire.'

She sniggered and looked back up at the sky. 'If we're still together when I'm eighty, you can buy me a rocket that will take me farther than the stratosphere.' She pointed again at the Milky Way. 'I want to go there.'

He was glad she wasn't looking at him and so didn't see the shock on his face at her, *If we're still together when I'm eighty.*

Lena thought they were in a relationship?

A burn set off in his head as he racked his brain to think why she would think this. Had *he* led her to believe this?

Konstantinos tried to think calmly. They'd become lovers four nights ago. They'd spent every waking hour together since, working on the transition from Lena's management to Sven's by day, their evenings spent dining out in the complex's restaurants and making love, and making love some more. The passion and lust between them was strong, he did not deny that—he wouldn't want to deny that; he was having the most fantastic, hedonistic, fulfilling sex of his life; he simply could not get enough of her—but at no point in any of their myriad conversations had he even intimated that they were now in a relationship. He'd made it very clear that he did not do relationships, and he knew she understood this.

And then he remembered the *if* she'd preceded her words with. *If* we're still together when I'm eighty. *If.* That implied she understood what they were currently sharing had a natural end date. It had been a flippant comment. He was reading far too much into what had been a joke.

He didn't want to put an end date on what they currently had, was prepared to enjoy the ride for as long as it lasted, but one day it would end. He knew it. Lena knew it. And when it ended, they would raise their child with the utmost respect for each other and, who knew? Maybe when she reached eighty, he would buy her that spaceship as one good friend to the other.

Feeling more settled, he pulled her closer to him at the same moment she squealed and pointed with even more vigour at the sky. *'Look!'*

Konstantinos looked. Blinked to clear his gaze. Blinked again, and then realised there was nothing wrong with his vision. The spectacle unfolding before him was no illusion.

Before his eyes the sky lit up, an arc rising of the brightest green he'd ever seen. As it rose higher and higher, more colours emerged, purples, blues, pinks, reds, undulating and streaming, the colours billowing and shifting, circling them, flashing and swaying, the entire night sky ablaze in an ethereal magic that took his breath away.

He looked at Lena. The enchantment on her face, illuminated by the dazzling light show, was a wonder in itself. And then she turned her face to his, lips pulled into the widest smile, eyes filled with joy, and the clench of his heart told him the magic she contained was more dazzling than anything nature could throw at them.

CHAPTER TWELVE

KONSTANTINOS'S TWO-STOREY LONDON penthouse blew
Lena away. Never minding the panoramic skyline view,
the tall sash windows, the thick carpets her toes sank into,
and tasteful modern artwork throughout the three sprawl-
ing reception rooms and five humungous bedrooms; the
furnishings and adornments were exactly what she would
have chosen if money was no object.

Three days they'd been holed up in this penthouse.
She refused to be sad that tomorrow he would finally
fly off for his much-delayed trip to Australia, not when
he'd put himself under three days of sufferance from a
cold and stormy English winter. Not that they'd exposed
themselves to the weather. They'd been far too busy chris-
tening all the rooms of the penthouse to bother with the
outside world. Oh, it made her knees weak and her pelvis burn to remember the passion with which he always
made love to her. And it wasn't as if they'd be parted for
long. In ten days it would be Christmas. He would fly
back for her and together they would fly to Kos to spend
a few days with his parents. She didn't know what came
after that for them and right then, she didn't want to think
about it and spoil the happiness alive in her heart.

Tonight they were going out for dinner in an underground cavern she remembered reading about when it opened but which she'd had no idea was actually owned by Konstantinos. She'd known his empire was big, but not until they'd been idly talking about it while sharing a bath had she realised the extent of it. Many of the most famous restaurants around the world had Konstantinos Siopis as the silent owner. No wonder he hated ready meals so much! She wondered how many of them she'd get to visit with him. This meal was part night out and part unofficial appraisal, which was fine by her. His empire wouldn't run itself.

With the help of a personal dresser, who'd arrived at the penthouse with five assistants armed with enough designer clothing to satisfy an army of actresses at a showbiz award, Lena was dressed in the most exquisite long-sleeved deep green satin dress that flared gently at her waist and fell to midcalf. Beneath it, she wore black lace underwear and, for the first time in her life, sheer black thigh-high stockings. Lena was also the new proud possessor of a brand-new wardrobe of clothes, half of which were designed to accommodate her growing belly. She didn't dare think how much it had cost Konstantinos, nor how much it had cost him to chauffeur the UK's top stylist over as a surprise so she could have her hair professionally blow-dried. Since they'd become lovers, Konstantinos had treated her like a princess, and while it thrilled her to be spoilt, she couldn't shake from her mind that he'd treated Cassia like a princess, too. *In my eyes, Cassia was a princess and princesses deserved the best of everything...*

Lena was acutely aware that when Konstantinos spoke about the present, it was 'we,' and when he spoke about the future it was 'I,' and always in the abstract. With Cassia, he'd planned an entire future. With Lena, he'd mentioned nothing beyond Christmas.

She chided herself for thinking about what came next again when she'd already determined not to. The future would reveal itself in its own sweet time.

Sliding her feet into a pair of black heels she suspected she wouldn't feel safe wearing for much longer—her bump was still small but it wouldn't be for long—she reminded herself that she was having Konstantinos's child. He clearly had deep feelings for her. He clearly fancied the knickers off her. She had to remember he'd been single for over a decade for a reason and shake off the dread that rolled in her stomach whenever she thought about the woman who'd betrayed him with his own brother and broken his heart.

Konstantinos's restaurant in a quaint London suburb was nothing but an old stone barn on the outside. Appearances, as he knew very well, could be deceptive. Entering through a large oak door, to the left of the flagstone-floored hallway was a wide spiral staircase that led down to the cavern itself, a vast, dark room with discreet gold uplighting designed by his clever interior design team to give a 1930s Prohibition glamour vibe. Even the Christmas tree and sophisticated decorations matched the vibe.

They were shown to their table by the newly appointed maître d'. Not only did he trip over his own feet, he then pulled Lena's chair back with such force the leg hit the table and made the wineglasses wobble.

Konstantinos grimaced at the overly-fawning apology that followed. A maître d' was supposed be unflappable. The general manager of the restaurant had poached him from a restaurant in Mayfair. He had to wonder if the owner of that hotel had put up any kind of fight to keep him. On this performance, he'd have been glad to be rid of him.

He noticed Lena give the blundering idiot a reassuring wink as she took her seat.

'What did you do that for?' he asked as soon as they were alone.

She pulled an innocent face.

'Don't look at me like that. I saw you wink at him.'

'And?'

'Why would you reassure an idiot?'

'He's only acting like an idiot because you're here,' she replied sweetly.

'This restaurant is a favourite of celebrities and royalty,' he said, indicating the A-List Hollywood couple deep in conversation at the table closest to them. 'He should have control of himself at all times.'

She shrugged. 'Celebrities and royalty aren't his boss. You are. And you, Konstantinos Siopis, are terrifying.'

'You're exaggerating.'

'Am I...? Hmmm...?' Her generous mouth wiggled as she pretended to think before she gave another shrug. 'Nope. Not exaggerating. You're terrifying. When you interviewed me for Thom's job, I was so frightened I nearly put an adult nappy on, just in case.'

He laughed. 'You hid your fear well.'

Her eyes danced with amusement. 'Want to know how I did it?'

'Tell me.'

She leaned closer and dropped her voice. 'By imagining you naked.'

'You didn't?'

Her eyes gleamed. 'I totally did. And let me tell you, my imagination had *nothing* on reality.'

'What did your imagination get wrong?'

'I underestimated the muscularity and hairiness of your chest for a start.'

'And?' he prompted.

Her ankle rubbed against his calf and the gleam in her eyes deepened. 'I *totally* underestimated the size of your—'

'Are we ready to order?' A young waiter apparated at their side. Or seemed to apparate. Konstantinos was very tempted to tell him to apparate off.

Gritting his teeth to fight the arousal the beautiful woman now sitting with serene innocence opposite him had deliberately induced, he attempted a smile to prove he was not a terrifying ogre who reduced his staff to blundering messes.

From the widening of the waiter's eyes, his attempt was futile. Full credit to him, though; he laid their drinks down and took their order with the polite professionalism Konstantinos demanded of all his staff.

Alone again, Lena raised her glass of alcohol-free wine and gave a wide smile. 'Now, isn't this fun?'

His blood thick with desire, he soaked in the beauty no army of professionals could improve on. Even now, dressed to the nines and as ravishing as he'd ever seen her, he could only think that Lena looked her best wearing nothing at all.

By the time they made it back to the penthouse, Konstantinos was just about ready to explode. Lena had spent the entire evening torturing him. His idea of making the visit an unofficial appraisal of the restaurant had been forgotten the moment she rubbed her ankle against him. Her torture had been subtle. Anyone watching would have seen nothing but a beautiful woman gazing adoringly into her lover's eyes. What they wouldn't have seen was the way her arms pressed suggestively against her breasts, the way her gaze often drifted slowly up and down his chest as if she were mentally undressing him, how she licked her lips suggestively... They definitely wouldn't have seen the lascivious knowing in her eyes at the effects of her silent seduction. She'd known damned well what she was doing, and when they'd gotten back in his car and he'd pulled her to him, she'd calmly crossed her legs, held his hand firmly on her lap and refused to let it wander any farther.

'You're driving me crazy,' he'd muttered, to which she'd given that serene, innocent smile and said, 'Am I?'

He'd growled, envisaging the moment the door of his penthouse closed. And now that moment had arrived, but as soon as he tried to pull her into his arms, she skipped out of his reach with a throaty laugh and headed up the stairs.

Shrugging his suit jacket off and dropping it on the stairs, he reached the bedroom ripping his tie off... Only to find the room empty and the bathroom door closed.

Breathing deeply, he closed his eyes and tried to get a handle on the desire zinging so deeply in his veins.

Another deep breath and he undid the top three buttons of his shirt and pulled it over his head. He was just stepping out of his trousers, butt naked, when the bathroom door opened.

Mouth running dry, he straightened. His erection sprang back into a totem pole.

Her dress had been removed. But only her dress.

In a cloud of delicious, seductive perfume, breasts bouncing gently beneath the confines of the sheer black lace bra, hips swaying, she stalked towards him.

The extra inches of height her heels gave her meant when she stood before him, she almost reached his chin. Tilting her face up, she smiled. And then she pushed him onto the bed.

Lena had no idea what had gotten into her. She'd never set out to drive Konstantinos out of his mind. It had been seeing the darkening of his eyes when she'd teased him about how she'd imagined him naked that had started it; knowing that beneath the dapper dark suit arousal had pooled, and that she had caused it. It had been thrilling. Exciting. And it had turned her on as much as him.

Staring at him now, at the beautiful vampiric face contorted with his desire for her, her heart a pulsing ragged mess, her insides molten, she realised she loved him. That that was what this seduction was all about. She loved Konstantinos. Madly. Passionately. She wanted him. Madly. Passionately. She wanted to give him the same pleasure he took such pleasure in giving her. Worship him. Devour him. Make him hers forever...

She pounced.

Straddling his abdomen, she kissed him deeply, savagely, unleashing the last of the emotions she hadn't even realised she'd been hiding from them both. It was too late for self-preservation. Her heart belonged to him now.

Wrenching her mouth from his, Lena gazed into his hooded eyes, feeding on the hunger she found in them.

A noise like a groan came from his throat.

She kissed him again, harder. He returned it with equal ferocity. And then she wrenched her mouth away again and rubbed her cheek against the stubbled jaw before grazing her lips, tongue and teeth down his neck. There was not a single bit of Konstantinos she didn't love, she thought dreamily as she licked a brown nipple and felt him shudder. Her nails dragged through the thick hair on his chest and abdomen, the soft black hair the only part of him that was soft. Everything else was hard and yet so incredibly smooth, and she loved every part of it. Loved him, this complicated, sexy man with the beautiful green eyes and crooked smile and generous heart that had been encased in ice for far too long. Loved, loved, loved him. Loved eliciting one of his rare smiles. Loved eliciting one of his even rarer laughs. Loved the groans of pleasure coming from his mouth as she licked the velvet head of his erection and then ran her tongue down the long, thick length.

Lena had never been shy about showing her desire for him before, but this was a whole new level, Konstantinos thought hazily, his eyes flickering shut as she gripped the base and covered him with the whole of her mouth. This was nothing she hadn't done to him before, but... this was something else.

He moaned her name. *Theos*, this must be heaven.

The pace of her movements was strengthening. The rush of pleasure was intensifying. He was so close...

Too close. He wanted to touch her. Taste her... *Theos*, he could not get enough of her taste. Of her.

Lifting his head, he threaded his fingers through her silky hair and gently pulled her head back.

She looked at him with confused eyes drugged with desire. Her lips were shiny with the moisture her mouth had created. 'What's wrong?'

'Come here,' he said thickly. 'I need to kiss you.'

She crawled up his chest. As soon as their lips fused

together, he rolled her onto her back, then pinned her flat so he could get his fill of her, not just her scent and taste but the heat she exuded, the throaty moans that turned into gasps when he removed her bra and cupped her breasts, the cries of pleasure when he flicked his tongue over the cherry peaks. Her sensitivity to his touch never failed to thrill him, feed him. He wanted more. He wanted *everything*.

Lena had become a mass of nerve endings. Every part of her was on fire, Konstantinos's hands trailing scorch marks as he peeled her knickers off, the flames burning brighter when he flickered his tongue up to the delicate folds between her thighs and then teased it over the nub of her pleasure. And then he stopped teasing.

The molten heat inside her began to bubble at the pure pleasure he was endowing her with, each lap of his tongue driving her closer and closer to the release she craved, and all she could do was grip the nearest pillow tightly. 'God, yes,' she moaned, thrashing her head and arching her pelvis in fervent encouragement. 'Yes, Tinos, yes. Oh, yes.'

The heat was rising, her climax building, but just as she got the first sense of the telltale quickening, he cruelly moved his mouth away from where she so desperately wanted it to stay. Before she could protest, he was sliding over her and then he was sliding inside her, and her protest died into nothing as he filled her completely in one hard thrust.

There was no savouring. No slow, sensual buildup. Not tonight.

Lust-filled eyes fixed on hers, Konstantinos pushed her knees back and, his chest brushing against the tips of her breasts, pounded into her with a passionate savagery that fired her carnal responses as much as the ferocious concentration on his face. Her nerve endings caught fire and then she was crying out his name, begging him for more, more, more as the molten reached the brim, blood rushed in her veins, and suddenly she was drowning in wave upon wave upon wave of unadulterated bliss carried along by the roar of Konstantinos's own climax.

Lena had lain spooned in Konstantinos's arms for what felt like hours, unable to sleep, when their baby woke up and decided to have a party in her belly. Konstantinos must have felt it beneath the hand splayed on her stomach for he stroked it gently. She'd thought he was asleep.

She couldn't hide from her own thoughts anymore. The secret fears she'd tried so hard to keep locked away were flooding her, and now the greatest fear spilled out in a whispered, 'What happens between us after Christmas?'

She knew she wasn't imagining the tension that tautened his body.

Her words hung in the air for an impossible length of time, until his body relaxed and he rubbed his cheek affectionately into her hair. 'We will work something out.'

She kissed his arm and slowly breathed out her relief.

The wound from his brother and fiancée's betrayal cut so deep that she didn't know if Konstantinos would ever allow himself to love her, but she knew he had feelings for her that went beyond amazing sex. He showed it in so many ways, and, though she feared she was being foolish, she couldn't stop her heart expanding with hope that one day...

The swimming in Konstantinos's head alternated hot and cold, a mixture of strengthening emotions coursing through him. Slowly, much slower than it usually took, her breaths evened out. The hand holding his went limp.

Finally, Konstantinos felt able to move his head back and expel the longest breath of his life. Anger filled his next inhale, although whether it was directed at Lena or himself he couldn't determine.

He knew what her question meant.

He knew, too, what had felt so different about their lovemaking that night. It was what he'd felt from Lena that had been different. Raw emotion. She'd given the entirety of herself to him.

And now she wanted to know what came next for them.

There was no *them*. Not in the way she wanted. She should know that. She *did* know that.

He had told Lena, explicitly, that he did not do relationships. While he conceded that what they currently shared could be construed as a form of relationship, the fact remained that if not for their baby, neither of them would be in this bed. He was not prepared to commit himself to anyone and she knew it; the most he was prepared to do, and only because of the baby, was take things one day at a time, which was a hell of a lot more than he'd been prepared to do before. He didn't know how long that one day at a time would last. He didn't want to know.

He strongly suspected Lena wanted to know. She wanted to plan a future with him. He could feel it in his bones.

Future. A word that filled him with sulphur.

He'd done that whole future thing before and look how that had turned out. Betrayed. His trust destroyed. He would never put himself in that position again.

CHAPTER THIRTEEN

THERE WAS A heaviness in Lena's stomach from the moment she woke, a sick sense of dread. Konstantinos was leaving soon for Australia.

Clambering out of the empty bed, she pulled her kimono-style silk dressing gown on and went off in search of him.

She found him in the dining room, a variety of breakfast foods around him, reading something on his phone. He looked up as she entered and smiled.

'You should have woken me,' she accused, trying not to sound tearful.

'I didn't have the heart.' He shifted his chair back so she could sit on his lap. 'You were fast asleep. I was about to come and wake you.'

She sank onto his muscular thighs and kissed him. 'When do you need to leave?'

'In thirty minutes.'

She sighed and leaned her head back so their cheeks could press together. He was so freshly shaven that not even the slightest stubble grazed her skin.

He'd be back in a week, she reminded herself. That wasn't so long. It hadn't sounded long before. It had sounded short. Now her chest felt as if it had been injected with ice; Konstantinos flying to the other side of the world a stark reality.

She tried hard to hide her dejection. She didn't want his last memory to be of her mopey. 'All packed?'

'Yes. My cases have already been taken to the car. Are you still planning to visit your family later?'

She nodded. 'I'll wait until you've left and then get myself sorted.' They'd exchanged the same frequency of video calls and messaging, but her family was unaware she was already in England. She would tell them everything today.

'Call the concierge when you're ready. They will provide a car for you... You are sure you're familiar with how to use the concierge service?'

'Yep. Dial nine.'

He kissed her temple and tapped her thigh as a signal for her to get off his lap.

Sighing again, Lena slid into the chair beside his and surveyed the array of food spread out on the table. She had no appetite. While Konstantinos poured himself another of the strong Greek coffees he virtually overdosed on each morning, her tongue burned with the unspoken plea for him not to go.

'I have given some thought to what you asked me last night,' he said conversationally.

Her heart jolted.

Konstantinos had spent the morning drafting a speech in his head. He'd woken so early the sun—and that there actually was any sun was the only good thing about being in England in December—hadn't even attempted to rise. Leaving Lena sleeping, he'd worked out in his gym for an hour. By the time he'd finished, sweat had poured off him and the anger that had gripped him in the wake of her unwanted question and the implications he'd sensed underlying it had diminished enough for him to think rationally.

He didn't want to lose what they had. The sex was just too good to willingly give that up. He needed to strike a balance between making his feelings clear and not hurting her. Hurting her was the last thing he wanted to do. His prepared speech would do the trick, and allow him to fly to Australia without anything hanging over them.

'I should tell you now my post-Christmas schedule is incredibly busy and will be so until a few weeks before your due date. Once the baby is born then, naturally, things will change and I will work my schedule so that I'm away on business for shorter periods. This will leave me with more free time to be a father and give you the support you need.' This was something they had already discussed but he thought it worth reiterating.

'As you know, I am not a man prepared to commit to a relationship.' He stared at her intently, willing her to absorb what he was saying and not just hear it. 'But I am prepared to make a form of commitment to you. I appreciate that it isn't the full commitment I suspect you are hoping for, but it is a solution I think will suit us both very well without putting unnecessary obligations on each other, other than in respects to our child.'

Something flashed in her eyes but she didn't attempt to speak.

'I propose making you my official plus-one. When I attend functions that require a partner, I will fly you out to me. Obviously, this will have to be paused when the doctors deem you no longer safe to fly and until you are fully recovered from the birth. Once you are recovered, I will hire a nanny to travel with you. Also, I will provide you with a personal allowance, much more than the maintenance we've already spoken of.'

She merely raised an eyebrow and gave a sharp nod, silently encouraging him to continue.

Aware his time was limited, Konstantinos hit his stride. 'Being the mother of my child automatically makes you important to me.' This was something he needed to make clear. Lena was important to him and he wanted her to know it. 'We will be co-parents who share a bed for as long as the desire between us lasts. Once it comes to its natural end, we will simply be co-parents and, I am sure, great friends. We can decide then whether you will continue acting as my plus-one.'

Looking at him with thoughtful eyes, Lena poured herself a glass of orange juice and sipped from it before cradling it in her hands. 'Okay, let me make sure I'm clear on this.'

He looked at his watch. Fifteen minutes until he had to leave. 'Sure.'

'You will make pockets of time in your busy schedule to spend in the UK with me and the baby.'

'I would also like some of those pockets of time to be spent in Kos. It is my home. I want our child to know my parents and my heritage.'

'That's reasonable.'

Konstantinos relaxed.

'While you and I are lovers,' she continued summarising, 'those pockets of time will be spent together under the same roof, and when it comes to its natural end, you will collect our child and spend that quality time alone, possibly with me joining you for the odd day out or meal so our child can see his or her parents getting on fabulously well?'

He inclined his head.

'Have you thought about buying me a home in Kos? It might make things easier if we decide to part company as lovers while we're spending quality time there.'

Hadn't he known from the beginning how smart this woman was? 'That does make sense.'

'Doesn't it?' she agreed brightly. 'And, to clarify, while we are lovers, you will fly me out to wherever you are in the world when you need a plus-one, like a quasi-official escort, *and* give me an allowance as payment?'

About to agree that she'd described it all perfectly, her final two words took a moment to penetrate. 'I did not call it payment.'

'No.' She shook her head and gave him a look of such sweetness that a pulse began to throb in his head, a warning that something was off. 'My mistake. You're right. You didn't call it that.'

She had another sip of her juice, her velvet brown eyes continuing to appraise him thoughtfully.

Her silence unnerved him. Her whole demeanour did. The pulse in his head throbbed even harder. 'Your thoughts on my proposal?'

'Oh, it makes perfect sense,' she said musingly. 'If you're a complete psychopath.'

It was witnessing Konstantinos's jaw drop that tipped Lena over the edge.

She'd listened to him deliver what was clearly a prepared speech with something close to disbelief. She'd never expected a marriage proposal or anything even close to one, but this was something else. This was cold. Clinical. And deliberately so. If she wasn't carrying his child, he would be ending it right now, would already have ordered her bags be packed. And why? Because she'd asked for the impossible. For him to think beyond tomorrow. To think of *her* beyond tomorrow.

Throughout, her pride had whispered to her, telling her not to react, to keep calm, to thank him for his reasoned thoughts and then politely tell him that this wasn't something she could agree to, and end it herself.

Her pride could go to hell. And so could Konstantinos.

The hand she'd clenched so tightly around the glass, the hand she'd fought so hard to stop betraying her inner turmoil by trembling, took control of her and flung the remaining juice at him.

In a flash, he'd shoved his chair back and shot to his feet. 'What the hell, Lena?' he snarled. The juice had landed on his chest, soaked into his white shirt, splatters of it dripping off his neck and chin.

'What the hell, *Lena*?' she mimicked with a cry, slamming the glass on the table and giving it a good shove before shooting to her own feet. 'What do you think I am? Some kind of escort that you can fly out to you at your convenience?'

Swearing loudly, he swiped his chin with the back of his hand. 'Do not twist what I said. If my proposal is not to your liking, you only have to say no.'

She nearly snatched the glass back so she could throw it at him. 'No! I say no. Never. I will not prostitute myself for you.'

His furious face contorted. 'Prostitute yourself? How on earth did you come up with that?'

'Did you not hear yourself? You would have agreed to buy me anything I asked for, wouldn't you? And all in exchange for me keeping your bed warm as and when *you* decide, and with absolutely everything on your terms.

Well, forget it. I won't do it. If you can't respect me then you certainly don't get to sleep with me.'

'Of course I respect you! I offered you more than I have offered anyone!'

'Oh, forgotten about Cassia, have you? Forgotten all the plans you made with her?'

'That was different.'

'How?'

'You know how, but in any case, this has nothing to do with her.'

'It has everything to do with her and you know it. I am not Cassia, and I am insulted you think I'm anything like her.'

Outrage further darkened the features now leaning into her. 'I have *never* compared you to her.'

'You've compared every woman you've ever met with her!' she shouted back, stretching her neck so she could get into his face as much as he was getting into hers, close enough that every angry exhale he made landed on her skin like a blow. 'It's always in the back of your mind, isn't it? That we're only out for what we can get from you? The only thing I ever wanted from you, Tinos, was *you*.'

'I told you from the start that I don't do relationships.'

'We're having a baby!' she screamed, now completely divorced from the composure her pride had tried so hard to force on her.

'Yes, and that's the only reason we're even having this discussion.'

'Have you not considered for the slightest moment that it's the same for me? That you're not the only one who's backed away from relationships? You know I've been celibate for *years* but having our baby and being with you has forced me to look at why that was because I damned well didn't stay single consciously.'

The pulse on his jaw throbbed, a sign it sliced her heart to recognise. 'The guilt you still carry because you walked away without a physical scratch,' he said tightly. 'A family is the thing your sister most wanted.'

She laughed manically. 'See? You already knew the answer. In some ways, you already know me better than I know myself. I bet that terrifies you, doesn't it, that you've gotten close enough to understand me?'

She laughed again at the clenching of his pulsing jaw. He knew her but she knew him equally well, and it was that knowing that destroyed her. 'But yes, you're right, and I'm pretty sure the fact you were my boss and a heavily committed bachelor played some small part in my letting myself go with you because those things made you unobtainable. And if it wasn't for our baby there is no way I would have slept with you again no matter how badly I wanted to. God, Tinos, you would not believe how my heart would practically explode when a message from you pinged in my inbox, and then when I found I was pregnant with your child…'

It struck her then, the hopelessness of it all.

The anger draining from her, Lena cradled her belly and took a step back, her first step away from him.

'It changed everything for me,' she said simply. 'I was terrified of your reaction. You know that. But always there was this small part of me that dared to hope that once our baby was born and you were satisfied he or she was yours, that you and I could at least try, for the baby's sake. I knew it was a pipe dream but it was still there, but I know now that it is never going to happen. You won't let it happen. Your offer…' She shook her head and willed the tears she could feel burning the backs of her eyes to stay put just that bit longer. 'It isn't just a disrespectful insult to me but a disrespectful insult to *us* and everything we've found together. Our baby might have forced us together but what we've shared is all us, Tinos. You and me. You've made me the happiest I've ever been in my life and I know I've made you happy, too, and you're throwing us away. You gutless *coward*.'

Her *coward* was whispered but Konstantinos felt the impact of it as hard as if she'd shouted it laced with barbed wire. It only fired the fury that had run amok in his veins since she'd hurled the contents of her glass at him and thrown his offer in his face.

With slow deliberation, he looked at his watch and then looked back at her ashen face. 'It is time for me to leave,' he said with equally slow deliberation that contained all the bite of his anger. He did not think he had ever felt such loathing for another human being. That Lena, of all people, should twist his own words and actions and accuse him of disrespect when he had given her more damned respect than he'd ever given anyone, enraged him, and that she was now standing there with the air of a martyr only added fuel to this.

Her face pinched on itself but she raised her chin. 'Good.'

'I think it best my solicitor deal with you with regards to the house purchase.'

Contempt flashed in her eyes. 'I just bet you do.'

He glared at her with equal contempt.

Her chin remained risen. 'Have you an intermediary in mind for me to keep you informed about anything baby related?'

'Considering you never had any intention of me knowing about the baby until it was born, I am astounded you would think to ask.' Placing his phone in his pocket, he patted it. 'Message me. But only about the baby. I have no interest in anything else.'

Konstantinos left the penthouse with the burn of Lena's disdain still scorching his skin.

Lena gazed out her parents' kitchen window at the birds making themselves at home on the bird table her mum had made when Lena was still at school. She'd always loved their garden. Such happy memories. If she concentrated hard enough, she could see herself and Heidi practising their handstands and cartwheels, each determined to best the other. She supposed they'd had their own form of sibling rivalry after all.

Footsteps sounded behind her. A hand touched her shoulder; a kiss dropped into her hair. 'Are you okay, *älskling*?'

She pressed her head against her mum's. 'I will be.'

She had to be okay. For her baby's sake. It was for her baby's sake that she had forced herself to eat these past five days. It was for her baby's sake that she'd moved out of Konstantinos's penthouse and taken up her parents' and sister's heartfelt insistence that she stay with them. She hadn't had much choice when her dad returned from a mystery trip with a fold-up bed that must have cost more than a decent permanent bed, and rearranged the living room furniture to fit it in.

They knew everything. Once Konstantinos had gone, she'd dragged herself to the bedroom, pulled some clothes on, and got the concierge to arrange a driver to take her to her family. Her intention to only tell them about the baby without giving any details had been as good as her intention of never falling in love with Konstantinos. It had all spilled out. The only details she'd spared them had been of the actual conception itself. In many ways, it had been cathartic. In many others, reliving it all only made her despair grow. She'd handed her heart to a man who didn't want it.

Her family had been brilliant. She'd known all along that they would support her but what she hadn't comprehended was how much she *needed* their support. Their love. As for Heidi… The joy that had sparkled in her eyes when Lena had lifted her top for her to see the bump had put to rest her fears that this would be another kick in the teeth to a woman who had already lost so much.

She wished she had her sister's strength. She'd tried. Tried her hardest to save her tears until night came and the house fell silent with sleep. She was trying now, as she watched the birds feeding and the images of the two young girls practising their gymnastics continued to flicker before her filling eyes.

So much loss. So much pain.

'Mum?' she whispered.

'Yes, *älskling*?'

'I miss him.'

When the tears spilled out, she couldn't fight them, could only cling tightly to her mum and soak her jumper with her tears, praying her mum spoke the truth when she softly said time always healed.

Lena feared her heart had shattered into too many pieces to ever heal.

Konstantinos finished his Scotch. The temptation to pour himself another was strong but he resisted. He'd drunk more than he would usually consume in recent days. But not wine. For some reason the smell of wine currently turned his stomach. He'd put his hand over his glass to stop the waiter from pouring it during a meal with his senior Australian management team earlier that evening.

He'd only drunk more Scotch than usual because his chest felt so damn cold and hollow. He couldn't think what was wrong with him. Here he was, in the midst of a roasting Australian summer and he felt none of the usual benefits.

His phone buzzed. His heart thumped as it had done with every buzz since he'd landed here. He had no idea why that was, either.

He reached to his hotel suite's bedside table for it. A message from his mother. This time his heart clenched. She wanted to know what she should buy Lena for Christmas. Like most of their compatriots, the Siopis family exchanged gifts on New Year's Day but his mother had been researching how the Brits did it and learned they exchanged theirs, like a growing number of Greeks, on Christmas Day itself. His kind-hearted mother wanted Lena to enjoy some of her own traditions.

He sighed heavily and reached for the Scotch after all, took a drink and then relayed the message he should have told his parents days ago: that Lena wouldn't be joining them.

Why had he put it off?

Gutless coward.

He poured himself another drink, this time to drown the sound of Lena's contempt from his mind.

CHAPTER FOURTEEN

AFTER MIDNIGHT MASS with his parents, Konstantinos sat at the front terrace of the family restaurant that had been a part of his whole life and gazed up at the stars. How had he never seen them before? His formative years spent living in Kos's mountains, at a location where tourists flocked to watch the sunset, and not once had he lifted his eyes upward and seen what was above him. The night sky had simply been there.

He wondered if Lena was outside looking up, too.

He couldn't stop thinking about her. The harder he tried, the worse it got. A Lena-sized infection of the mind. And now it was officially Christmas Day and she was thousands of miles away, her silence as deep a chasm as the distance between them.

'What are you doing out here?' His father pulled up a chair beside him.

'Looking at the stars.'

They sat in comfortable silence for a long while. That was something Konstantinos had always appreciated about his father. He never felt the need to fill silences.

'Is something on your mind, son?'

He'd thought too soon.

He tried to smile. 'Nothing important.'

There was more silence, then, 'Is it that Lena?'

There was nothing malicious about his father's question but still he found himself bristling at her being referred to as *that* Lena.

Instead of answering, he asked a question of his own. 'Why did you and Mama take Theo's side?'

His father sighed. 'Tinos… We didn't take sides. We couldn't. You are both our sons.'

It was nothing he didn't already know. Nothing that, in truth, needed explaining. But it had only been since hearing Lena so vehemently take his part that he'd realised how deeply his parents' neutrality had affected him, that it bit to alternate Christmases and other significant events. That Theo and Cassia still enjoyed a close relationship with them.

His father gave another heavy sigh and reached for his hand to squeeze it. 'Theodoros behaved terribly to you. I have never condoned it. If you had asked me to choose between the two of you, I would have been duty bound to choose you, and I thank you for not forcing that choice on us. I know it has been hard for you, but Tinos, it is time to let it go.'

'Yes,' he agreed, surprising them both. 'It is.'

His father squeezed his hand again. 'Cassia was never right for you. She would have made you unhappy.'

'I know.'

That startled him. 'You do?'

'Yes. She is inherently selfish.' Lena had shown him that simply by being Lena. Lena didn't have a selfish bone in her body.

'She is,' his father agreed. 'That is why she is better for your brother. They cancel each other's selfishness out.'

A burst of unexpected laughter flew from Konstantinos's mouth but it died quickly in his throat, caught by a burst of something else, something that swelled in a wave and ripped through him before he could find the presence to clamp it down and smother it.

There was nothing he could do to stop the great sobs from racking him but cover his face in a futile attempt to stem the tears and admit the truth to himself.

The coldness in his chest the Australian heat had failed to cure was caused by him severing himself from the only pure sunshine of his life. Lena. She was *his* sun. His life had revolved around her since she'd walked into the meeting room for the interview and the sun's rays had beamed through the window and cast her in gold.

He'd been too blind to recognise it.

He loved her. God help him, he'd fallen in love with her, and he'd driven her away and hurt her and turned the love she had for him into contempt.

A meaty arm slipped around his back and pulled him into an embrace that only made his sobs louder.

'Whatever you have done to drive this Lena away, you can fix it,' his father said quietly once the sobs had quietened. 'I know you can.'

His father's steadfast faith in him brought no consolation. His father didn't know the depth of the pain he'd caused her.

He'd lost her. Lost his sun.

And it was all his own fault.

Lena was about to leave the hotel room when her phone rang.

'Did you forget one?' she asked, laughing. She'd not long finished a marathon early-morning video call with her family where they'd all opened their Christmas presents together, although this year she'd gotten them to open her presents for her. It was a tradition they'd formed when she'd first started working at the Ice Hotel. Her family had been disappointed when she'd told them they'd have to do the same this year—they'd thought that seeing as she was no longer working there, she'd be free to spend the day with them—but had understood the commitment she'd already made and wasn't willing to rescind, no matter the personal cost.

But there was no answer.

'Mum?'

Then she heard it. The sound of crying.

'Mum?' she repeated, alarmed. 'What's wrong? Is it Heidi?'

Her dad took the phone. 'Sorry, love, your mum's in shock. We all are.'

'What's happened?'

'Your mum checked her banking app—you know what she's like.' Lena did know. Her mum checked their bank account each morning like most people checked their social media feeds. It didn't surprise her in the least that she would do it on Christmas Day, too. 'Well…' Her dad cleared his throat. 'At some point since she checked it yesterday morning, we've had a million pounds deposited into it.'

'I'm sorry, what?'

'A million pounds.' He cleared his throat again. 'The crediting account was K Siopis. The reference was Merry Christmas.'

Lena walked from her hotel at the top of the winding, sweeping road that cut through the town until she found the name of the restaurant she was looking for. Having arrived late in the evening, the town had been alive with

Christmas lights and thrumming with people and groups of children singing Christmas carols. Now the town, as pretty by day as by night, lay silent.

She remembered Konstantinos telling her that you could open a door in the restaurant's kitchen and be in the family home, which his parents adamantly refused to move from. Now all she had to do was find the other entrance to it.

The main restaurant door was locked so she climbed the steps to its L-shaped terrace and stopped for a moment to admire the view. It truly was spectacular. No wonder the place was a Mecca for sunset worshippers. Laid out before her, as far as the eye could see, the Aegean Sea, gleaming under the brightening skies, as picture perfect as anything a landscape artist could compose, the few boats sailing on it mere daubs of white paint.

A peal of female laughter made her close her eyes to the vista. In truth, it hadn't been the view she'd paused for but a moment to gather herself before she saw him. So much hurt unbearably, but Konstantinos's leaving her to make her own arrangements to get here hurt the most. She had no way of knowing if she was too early or too late.

She followed the laughter around the terrace corner.

Two glamorous women, maybe a decade older than her mum, were standing by a huge plant pot, deep in expressive conversation, smoking. The shorter one spotted Lena first and immediately elbowed the other, who frowned and yelled out something to her she didn't understand.

Hesitantly, she inched farther forward. 'Excuse me,' she called, wishing she'd done a crash course in Greek. 'Speak English?'

The taller one's frown deepened. Her eyes dropped to

Lena's belly and then her eyebrows rose. With the same hesitation that Lena had spoken, she said, 'Lena?'

She nodded.

The woman's shock was so transparent that Lena instantly knew she'd made a massive mistake. She wasn't supposed to be here. But before she could apologise for intruding and go find somewhere private to lick her humiliated wounds, the woman crushed her cigarette underfoot, gabbled something urgently to the other woman then hurled herself at Lena.

In the blink of an eye, Lena found herself enveloped in a cloud of perfumed smoke, the welcome so profusive and heartfelt that tears stabbed the backs of her retinas.

'You came,' the woman finally said when she decided to let Lena breathe again. Rubbing the tops of Lena's arms, she smiled tremulously. 'You came.'

She blinked back the tears and nodded before quietly asking the woman she was certain was Konstantinos's mother, 'Am I still welcome?'

The woman's jaw dropped as if she'd been asked the most obtuse question in the world. 'Eh?' And then she gave her another powerful hug that answered more potently than mere words could that Lena was more than welcome in her home.

When she next released her, the other woman had reappeared on the terrace with two women of around Lena's age and four men. The tallest of the men stared at her as if she were a ghost.

She could have thrown up on the spot. Luckily, his mother clasped her hand tightly, and Lena clung to her for support as she was brought forward for introductions. Names were thrown at her. Arms were thrown around her...all but Konstantinos, who stood back wordlessly.

Konstantinos watched the scene unfold before him as if he was watching a movie. It didn't feel real. Lena had appeared like a mirage. If he blinked, she was sure to vanish.

But she didn't vanish, and when his mother dragged her inside, he followed with everyone else, then watched with that same observer feeling as another chair was taken into the dining room, where the Christmas bread already had pride of place on the table, placemats and cutlery rearranged to fit another place setting, heard the loud laughter when his mother produced a surprise packet of English Christmas Crackers and placed them around the table, too. He watched his family fuss around Lena, his aunt stroke her hair, his father hand her a drink, his cousin offer her an almond biscuit, the other cousin then take her hand and drag her off to see the Christmas tree that stood proudly in the living room.

His uncle came over to speak to him once everyone else had congregated in the living room. He recalled nothing of the conversation other than the panic that grabbed his chest when he looked again to where Lena had just been sitting and found she'd disappeared. It took a long time for the beats of his heart to regain any kind of regularity after she returned, her hand held by his mother, a necklace that hadn't been there before hung around her neck. From the way Lena kept pressing her hand to it, she was obviously enamoured.

'She doesn't bite,' his father said, standing beside him.
'What?'
'Lena. She doesn't bite.'
He tried to smile but couldn't make his mouth form anything. 'She isn't here to see me.' That much was clear.

Other than that first clash of eyes, she hadn't looked in his direction or gotten within three feet of him.

She was here, he knew, because she'd given her word. He still couldn't quite believe it.

'She's been here two hours and not looked at you once that I've noticed. No one avoids looking at someone for so long if they don't feel something for them.'

'She hates me.'

'Hate is a feeling. Your mother often hates me. Talk to her.'

He took a long breath and nodded.

His opportunity came shortly after, when his mother, aunt and one of his cousins bustled off back to the terrace to get another of their nicotine fixes and his father, uncle and grandfather went into the kitchen to check on the food. Konstantinos fixed his stare on Rena, his cousin currently practising her pidgin English on Lena. She noticed, murmured something he couldn't hear, and disappeared, leaving them alone.

*Theo*s, he could hardly breathe.

The beats of Lena's heart went into overdrive. She'd hoped the number of people crammed into the modest home meant she could avoid Konstantinos until it was polite for her to leave. She didn't want to make small talk with him. It was torture enough to share the same air as he did, knowing he hated her very existence.

She wished she could hate him. Wished she didn't feel so bereft without him. Wished she didn't long for him to pull her into his arms and tell her he was sorry, that he hadn't meant any of it, that he loved her.

She wished she could plug her ears from her thoughts.

He hovered before her.

Self-conscious, she crossed her legs and turned her

head to the door. If she willed it hard enough, someone would come in and save her.

'You came,' he said, unwittingly using the same words his mother had. The difference was his mother had been delighted to see her.

'I made a promise,' she said shortly. 'Although it's pretty clear they weren't expecting me. Thanks for letting me know you'd cancelled for me.'

'I didn't think you would still want to come.'

'Don't you mean you hoped? Well, don't worry, I won't outstay my welcome.'

'From the way they have all taken to you, you could never do that. If I'd known, I would have arranged all your transport and everything for you.'

'Christmas dinner is not baby related and so comes under the *not interested* category,' she stated acidly.

'About that.' She heard him take a deep breath and felt her insides shrivel. God, no, don't let him find more words to hurt her with. 'Lena—'

'Before I forget,' she interrupted. 'My parents say thank you for their Christmas present.'

There was a long pause. 'Please tell them it is my pleasure.'

She raised a shoulder. It was the only movement she was now capable of making. Her entire insides hadn't just shrivelled but clenched into a tight ball. That money would make a massive difference to their lives, especially to Heidi's. They'd be able to move, buy a much more spacious house where wheelchairs weren't prone to getting stuck.

A gong clanged out.

Konstantinos swore under his breath. It was his father's traditional Christmas method of announcing dinner was ready.

Lena had avoided his stare for the entire conversation.

Lena ate as much as she could of the roast lamb, spinach and cheese pie, and the vast array of vegetables and salads that accompanied it. She pulled her cracker with Konstantinos's grandfather and wore the paper hat that fell out of it and which all the Siopises seemed completely bemused by but followed suit with their own cracker hats. She ate her share of the sweet treats that followed. She tried to help with the clearing up but was shooed out of the dining room and banned from the kitchen. She sat with Konstantinos's cousins and helped them with the English they were determined to improve, and then she went back into the dining room for the traditional Siopis game of cards, a game she'd never heard of and which involved much shouting and swearing and accusations of cheating. She ate more of the never-ending stream of food brought out to the table. She exchanged amused looks with Konstantinos's mother when her father-in-law's head fell back mid-card game and he started snoring. And all the while, her insides clenched ever tighter and the pain in her heart became more than she could endure.

She didn't know it, but Grandfather's snoring was her means of escape. The uncle declared it time to get his father home and Lena used the distraction of all the kisses and embraces to quietly slip away with them.

Out in the cool, fresh air, she wrapped her jacket tighter around herself and took a moment to just breathe.

That had been the hardest day of her life. Every minute had been agony.

Never again. She couldn't. Couldn't be in a room with

Konstantinos and smile and laugh and pretend she was having a great time when the bleeding of her heart threatened to drown her.

She hid in the shadows until the uncle's car had passed and then set off. Ten minutes, that was all it would take to walk to the hotel. She would be safe then.

Safe from herself.

Safe from throwing herself at Konstantinos and begging him to come back to her.

Konstantinos spotted Lena's absence immediately.

'Where's Lena?' he called out sharply.

Everyone looked around, as if she could be hiding under a rug or behind a door.

Even as they searched the house calling her name, he knew she'd gone. She'd slipped out with his uncle and grandfather without saying goodbye. He yanked his phone out of his back pocket and called his uncle.

Why would she do that? That wasn't Lena. She would never just disappear without saying goodbye and thanking his parents for their hospitality. She just wouldn't.

His uncle finally answered.

'Is Lena with you?'

'No. Why?'

He disconnected the call and, for the first time since he'd left her in London, dialled Lena's number. It went straight to voice mail.

His phone rang. His uncle calling him back. He thrust the phone at his mother. 'You talk to him. I'm going to find her.'

There was no sign of her on the terrace.

He hurled himself down the steps and onto the street.

The Christmas lights were illuminating the town in their festive colours. Illuminating the street.

Which direction had she gone?

He tried to think calmly, no easy feat when panic had gripped him so completely.

Why the hell hadn't he forced her to talk earlier? No, why had he admitted defeat when the dinner gong had rung? *Theos*, all he'd needed to say were three little words. *I am sorry*. More than anything, those were the words he needed to say to her. He didn't think he'd find peace or sleep again until he'd said them.

There were no hotels to the right of the restaurant so she must have turned left, he determined, his legs already setting off as the thought formed. He knew she was staying at a hotel here; he'd overheard her telling Rena.

Upping his pace to a run, he flew up the winding road, rounding yet another bend until he spotted the figure in the distance, close to the town's giant Christmas tree.

'Lena!' he shouted. Tried to shout. It came out as a croak. Still running, closing in on her with every stride, he shouted her name again, louder, more audible this time. On his third attempt, she stopped.

Lena froze. For a moment she was too scared to turn around.

When she did turn, her tears blinded her from seeing clearly the tall figure rushing to her.

Rubbing her face with the palms of her hands, desperately trying to stem the flow of tears, she didn't give him a chance to have a go at her for her rudeness when he reached her, saying in a tearful rush, 'I'm so sorry, I didn't mean to skip out without saying goodbye.'

'Then why did you?' he asked with surprising gentleness.

'Why do you *think*?' she wailed, rubbing away more tears. 'I thought I could do it, okay? But like with everything else, I was wrong. I didn't know it would hurt so much. I'm sorry if I've embarrassed you and I'm really sorry if I've hurt your parents' feelings. I promise I'll apologise in person in the morning, just, please... I need to be alone. Please, Tinos, go back to your family. I'm fine.'

'Lena...'

'Just *go*,' she cried, losing all control. 'Please, Tinos, I can't see you. Don't you get that? It's just too soon. I should never have come here.'

Without waiting for a response, she stumbled off, barely able to put one foot in front of the other. They didn't want to cooperate. The whole of her body was screaming at her to turn back to him.

'Lena, you're not the one who needs to apologise.' There was a tremor in his voice that made her feet refuse to take another step. 'That's on me. It's all on me. I'm the one who should be sorry. I *am* sorry.'

Don't turn around, she pleaded to herself. *Walk away.*

'I've been trying to find the words since you turned up here. I thought I'd imagined you. I did not guess you would come. But I should have. You always do the right thing no matter the personal cost to yourself. It's why your family had to force you to leave your sister and forge a real life for yourself. If they hadn't, you would never have moved to Sweden. It's why you hid the pregnancy from me. You were protecting our baby as best you could despite knowing the longer it took for you to tell me, the angrier and more unreasonable I would be about it, and you knew that anger would be directed at you. It's why you hid your pregnancy from your family, too. You didn't want to add to your parents' worries until it was absolutely necessary or have your sister face the reality of another of her dreams never being realised. You always put everyone else's needs above your own.'

She heard the crunch of his footstep closing the small gap she'd created. When he next spoke, his voice was so close she could feel it breeze against her hair.

'You came here today for my family's sake. You knew you would see me. You knew it would hurt you, and still you came. For their sake. Strangers to you. If I wasn't already in love with you, that would have pushed me over the edge into it.'

Her breath caught in her throat.

She swayed as air swirled around her, and then hands rested gently on the tops of her arms. 'Please, Lena, look at me.'

For the first time since that one glance on the terrace all those hours ago, her eyes overrode her will and met his stare.

What she found there sent ripples through her heart. It was the same agony she knew was mirrored in her own eyes.

'I'm truly sorry, Lena. For everything. I'm sorry for my cruel proposal. I'm sorry for being a gutless coward. All these years I've let my brother's betrayal fester in me. Infect me. It cut too deep for me to realise his betrayal had actually done me a favour.'

He must have read the question in her eyes for the smallest smile pulled on his lips. 'I never loved Cassia. Not really. I loved the idea of her. I'd spent so many years infatuated with her that when we got together, I thought

I had to be in love with her. If I hadn't met you, I might have spent the rest of my life believing it.'

He lifted his hand and brushed his fingers over her cheekbones. She felt them tremble against her skin.

'But I did meet you. And my heart recognised you. I have fought it every inch of the way and I have hurt you. That kills me. My blindness. I pushed you away in the most cowardly way and it was deliberate. Deep down I knew you would never agree to that insulting proposal, and all I can say is if you give me another chance, I swear on our child's life that I will never push you away again. Not ever. I love you, Lena. I want to spend the rest of my life with you. You're the sun who lights my entire world and I can't go on without you.'

From spending the entire day avoiding his stare, Lena now found herself unable to tear her gaze from his. She didn't want to, anyway, not when such sincere, heartfelt emotion was contained in the green depths.

'Give me your hand,' he whispered.

It gave itself to him willingly.

He held it tightly to his chest. 'Do you feel that?' he asked in that same barely audible voice.

The strong beats of his heart thumped against her palm.

'This is yours to do with as you will. My heart and my life are entirely in your hands.'

Her own heart swelled like a balloon to fill every crevice in her chest, pumping blood that fizzed through veins that had feared they would never feel joy again. The fizz seeped into her skin and bones until every cell in her body was suffused with the warmth that came only from Tinos, and suddenly she could contain it no more. She was never certain if she threw her arms around his neck or if her arms threw themselves, but around his neck they went and all the agony they'd both lived in their time apart healed in the passionate urgency of their fused mouths.

Breaking apart, they stared at each other in wonder.

'I love you,' he said, his words sweeter than manuka honey.

'I love you more.'

'Not possible.'

Cupping her face in his hands, he pressed his forehead to hers. 'You will marry me, won't you?'

Lena laughed. She couldn't help it. 'Just try to stop me.'

A beaming smile broke out on the face she loved with all her heart and then he was squeezing her tightly, overwhelming relief pouring out as laughter from his mouth and into her hair, and as their dizzying happiness soared in the air like a cloud around them, their baby woke up and had a party in Lena's belly to celebrate.

EPILOGUE

STARS FILLED THE skies over Trollarudden. Lena, absorbed with the Christmas present her darling husband had gifted her with, stared through the powerful lens in rapture and astonishment. The *colours* she could see up there were…

'Hot chocolate?'

Moving her face away from the telescope, she beamed at Tinos and tilted her head for a kiss.

With a vampiric grin, he obliged, his green eyes flashing when he pulled back. She bit back her protest at this kiss, far too fleeting for her liking, when her mother emerged from the back door of the cabin Konstantinos had had rebuilt and extended that summer, carrying a snow-suited Phoebe in her arms. Right behind them came Heidi on her brand-new, all-weather wheelchair, followed by their dad carrying a tray full of mugs of steaming hot chocolate.

While everyone settled on the long bench with Lena, Heidi held her arms out for her niece. It never failed to make Lena's heart melt to see her sister's devotion to the youngest member of their family. Never failed to astound her with the progress Heidi had made this past year.

Lena had believed Heidi's recovery had long ago reached its limit. None of the Weirs had ever thought their beloved Heidi a burden but only once they'd moved into their new, gloriously spacious, wheelchair-friendly home did Heidi confess the guilt she'd felt at all they'd given up for her. Now, with both their parents having resigned their part-time teaching jobs, seeing their mother create pockets of time to fulfil the creative side she'd thought gone forever and their father dig his old golf clubs out of the garage, had lifted Heidi of the guilty burden none of them had known she carried.

But it was Phoebe who'd really proved the impetus for Heidi to throw herself even harder into her physiotherapy and, even with tears streaming down her face from the exertion of it all, strengthen her arms enough to safely hold the niece she was smitten with. Her devotion was entirely mutual and, wrapped in the sanctuary of her husband's loving arms, Lena watched her eight-month-old daughter place a mittened hand to Heidi's cheek with a contentment in her heart she'd never imagined it would be possible to feel.

Konstantinos's phone rang. Placing a kiss to his wife's temple, he disentangled his arms and accepted the video call from Kos.

His clearly inebriated parents filled the screen. Crowded around them were the rest of his family, and he carried the phone to Heidi and zoomed it in on his pride and joy, his baby daughter. Suddenly, his two nephews barged their way onto the screen to coo at the cousin they were as enamoured by as the rest of the Siopises. A fascinated Phoebe swiped for the phone in return.

Not even the glimpse of his brother in the background could dent Konstantinos's excellent mood. Over the summer they'd made, at Konstantinos's instigation, a rapprochement of sorts. He would never trust his brother and sister-in-law or form any kind of relationship with them outside family gatherings, but his anger and humiliation had evaporated. Lena's steadfast, passionate love had driven it away for good. Let their children be raised as cousins and their parents' loyalties no longer be torn.

Once the call was over, he sat back next to his wife, who was excitedly directing her mother's gaze through the telescope to Jupiter, and reached for her hand.

She leaned into him and tilted her head, smiling widely. 'I love you,' she mouthed.

With his heart as full as it was possible to be but mindful of their audience, he kissed her chastely.

Her fingers squeezed his, the nails digging into his skin a silent signal that when bedtime came, there would be nothing chaste about the kisses they shared.

Laughter filling his chest, Konstantinos cuddled her to him so her head nestled beneath his chin and his arms were wrapped around her, and stared up at the stars that could never match the beauty of the woman he would love and cherish for the rest of his life.

* * * * *

TWELVE NIGHTS IN
THE PRINCE'S BED

CLARE CONNELLY

MILLS & BOON

CHAPTER ONE

THIS WAS THEIR tenth shared birthday party, their tenth year as best friends, and despite what she'd lost in life Poppy Henderson looked out at the room filled with guests and felt grateful. What would her life have been like without Her Royal Highness Princess Eleanor Aetos and the whole Aetos family in it?

After her parents had died, she'd thought she'd never know this kind of contentment again. She'd thought she'd never know the love of family, the sense of belonging, but her parents' best friends, who just so happened to be the King and Queen of Stomland, had wrapped their arms around Poppy despite their own heavy sense of grief after the death of their oldest son, and never let go. They'd treated her like a daughter from the beginning, and their love had helped Poppy to heal. She was so grateful to them, there was nothing she wouldn't do for the King and Queen.

As for the royal children, Eleanor had become a sister to Poppy instantly and Eleanor's brother Adrastos...well, that relationship was a little harder to define. Up until she was twenty-one she would have described him as a brother of sorts, albeit five years older and a little serious and cool. But he'd been kind as well, and had never once acted as though he minded Poppy's intrusion into their family.

Of their own volition, her eyes drifted across the room,

finding him easily as they always did, and her heart kicked up a gear, her stomach tightening uncomfortably at just the sight of him. They'd barely spoken since that night, Ellie's and Poppy's twenty-first birthdays. Had it really been three years ago? Her skin flushed with memories she tried not to think about, the confusion of having someone she'd regarded almost as a brother draw her into his arms and kiss her until she was intimately aware of him as a man, a man she desired very, very much…

The memory she tried desperately to forget, because it was so incendiary and confusing she couldn't make sense of it. The way his hands had pulled her close that night, held her against his hard, taut body, his eyes challenging her for a moment before he'd dropped his head and his lips had met hers. Sparks of desire had ignited in Poppy's bloodstream and she'd finally *understood* what lust was. She'd lost herself in those moments, moments that had seemed to stretch and take over all of time for Poppy. He'd kissed her and she'd almost forgotten who and where she was, until a noise had broken through the spell and they'd pulled apart, each as shocked as the other, eyes locked as they'd tried to make sense of the madness that had overtaken them.

'That shouldn't have happened. I'm sorry.'

His apology had surprised her, because Adrastos wasn't the kind of man who made mistakes. He was never in the wrong—even the media had said as much: the papers were constantly running stories celebrating Adrastos's victories. Had the kiss been wrong? Reality had sliced through Poppy quickly enough and she'd remembered the truth of their situation, her loyalty to his parents, the fact they'd been raised since her parents' deaths almost as siblings. But *not* siblings, she hastily comforted herself.

Poppy stared at Adrastos now as if she were a starving person led to a banquet, while Adrastos was distracted enough for her to be able to take full advantage.

Where Eleanor had inherited her mother's blonde hair and slight figure, Adrastos was a throwback to his ancient ancestors, warriors shaped in the cradle of civilisation, with those broad shoulders and muscular arms honed by his pursuit of all sports, but particularly car racing and rowing—she remembered him waking early and taking to the Mediterranean, training with his crew until he was covered in perspiration. He would return to the palace smelling of sea salt and power.

Days after their kiss, it had been abundantly clear Adrastos had put it completely from his mind. He had been back to his usual tricks, pictured in the nation's papers with a beautiful actress from Germany. A week after that, it had been a Spanish model. Six weeks later, a world-famous Swiss athlete. Adrastos—a renowned bachelor—had simply got on with his life, just as it had been before The Kiss. So why couldn't Poppy get him out of her head even then? Why couldn't she date another guy? Try to find that same spark she'd felt when Adrastos had kissed her?

Locked in conversation with one of his cousins, Adrastos shifted slightly, his eyes moving quickly and landing directly on Poppy, almost as if he knew where she was standing, almost as if...

She put a stop to that thought, too. There was no way he'd been watching her.

Their eyes met and the same sparks that had ignited her bloodstream three years earlier were back, fierce and out of control.

On the night of her twenty-first birthday, quite out of nowhere, Poppy had been awakened with feelings she hadn't known existed. And she'd liked it. But ever since, that side of her had been dormant, unexplored, unknown. Her virginity was something she couldn't understand. It hadn't been a conscious choice. Before the kiss, she'd been busy at university, working very hard to live up to her parents' academic successes, and to make the royal couple proud. And afterwards? The thought of any other man turned her body to ice. It had been easy not to date, not to flirt, not to desire. But now, at twenty-four, in the same room as Adrastos, her body was charged with a billion tiny sparks, more energy than all the stars in the universe.

Perhaps it was the last disastrous date she'd attempted. A month earlier, she'd let Eleanor set her up with a friend of a friend. A man she'd liked. Enjoyed the company of. But when he'd tried to kiss her goodnight, she'd felt nausea rising in her chest and had known that if his lips touched hers, she'd have vomited over their shoes. Mortified, she'd recoiled, made an excuse and bolted inside her townhouse, feeling broken and stupid and wondering what the hell was wrong with her.

Like a sinkhole, Adrastos drew her attention back, and there it was: fizzing in her veins, a sense of certainty and need, a reckless desire to understand what had happened between them all those years ago, to understand why he had been able to flood her with desire where no one else had. Was she simply not a sexual person? Had she mistaken her reactions to Adrastos that night? Or would she feel the same way now, if they were to kiss once more…?

Swiping another champagne from a passing tray, she took three generous sips before clutching the glass a little too tightly in her hands and sashaying across the room, her pulse racing as she drew closer to Adrastos, her heart thumping so hard it jumped out of its usual position in her chest and lodged somewhere in the vicinity of her throat.

But surely this was too late? Three years? How many women had he been with since? Would he even remember?

And just as that question struck her in the face, Adrastos turned once more, their eyes locked, and the world stopped spinning. Poppy's mouth went dry and nothing else mattered. Spurred on by the fact it was her birthday, by just the right amount of champagne, and by the fact that earlier today she'd accepted a job in the Netherlands that would see her moving from Stomland and starting afresh, she inched forward, ever so slightly.

She had to know, to understand…to feel alive again… Her breath caught in the very back of her throat and when she spoke, the words tumbled out almost too fast.

'Do you have a moment, Your Highness?' The title might have seemed strange but even though they'd spent so much time together, certain formalities still tended to be observed, particularly when they were around others.

Adrastos's eyes narrowed almost imperceptibly, and Poppy's nerves were frayed, the possibility that he might say 'no' was real and suddenly very scary. But a moment later, he dipped his head, a curt expression on his face but agreement conveyed by the subtle gesture.

'What is it?' He took a small step away from the group he'd been standing with.

Poppy again squeezed the glass in her hand, surprised in the back of her mind that it didn't shatter completely. He was so handsome. So familiar and so completely strange all at once. Adrenalin made her aware of every vertebra in her back.

'Can we speak somewhere more private?'

His Adam's apple shifted but otherwise his face didn't move, didn't betray a single response to that question. After a beat, he nodded. 'There's a balcony. Do you have a coat?'

Poppy looked over her shoulder, waved indistinctly towards the makeshift cloakroom, over on the other side of the penthouse, with dozens of revellers in between.

'You may use mine,' he said, so Poppy's eyes skittered to his and she had to dig her fingernails into her palms to hold her resolve firm.

'I'm fine. This won't take long.' But even as she said it, she felt a little throb of excitement, the creaking open of a door to a world of possibilities she'd never before contemplated. She was being silly. Egged on by champagne and curiosity, by the fantasies that kiss had spawned when he'd taken a perfectly content yet inexperienced twenty-one-year-old and shown her just a glimpse of what her body was capable of feeling.

He didn't touch her, but as they cut through the room she felt his nearness like a caress and her whole body responded, goosebumps lifting, her stomach twisting with the realisation that she was about to be alone with him for the first time in years.

It was impossible to walk anywhere with Adrastos and not acknowledge the way people watched him. She saw heads turn, women appraise, men react with respect. A blade of doubt pushed its way into her thoughts, so she knew she had to do this quickly and get it over with.

At the doors to the balcony, he stopped abruptly, turning to look at her with an expression that could best be described as doubt, his eyes raking over her, almost as if he'd never seen her before, as if he wanted to say, 'Are you sure?'

In response to the unasked question, Poppy tilted her chin and held his gaze with a defiance she wasn't quite sure she felt.

A moment later, the Crown Prince opened the door, and a blast of ice-cold wind rushed in at the same time they stepped out, the gentle din of the party silenced the moment the door clicked shut behind them.

Poppy loved Stomland.

When she'd first come here, her heart had been broken, shattered by her parents' shocking deaths, and she'd recognised in the royal family kindred spirits—in many ways, but particularly in their shared state of grief, having lost their oldest son just months before her parents. They told Poppy, many times over the years, how her arrival had helped to mend their family, to make them feel a little closer to whole, and it was a sentiment Poppy shared.

'Well, Poppy?'

She almost flinched at the cool tone of his question. Before the kiss, they hadn't been close. Not like her and Ellie. They were best friends as well as sisters in spirit. Adrastos had always been a step removed, busy and important, carrying the weight of the world on his shoulders. But they'd at least been friendly. He'd been protective, just as he was with Ellie. She'd been in awe of him, intimidated by his overwhelming strength and masculinity, but there'd never been this kind of awkwardness, this skin-tingling awareness.

Now they were here, alone, the questions she wanted to ask seemed insurmountable to speak.

Silence fell, a silence in which Poppy was aware of absolutely everything. His breathing, the smell of the salt water, the sound of distant traffic, his aftershave, the cool night air, heavy with the promise of Christmas, just around the corner. They hadn't been this close, alone, since the kiss, and it was impossible not to feel ghost memories of that touch flicking over her skin. Was he thinking of it too?

'Poppy?' The sharpness to her name had her eyes darting to his, her heart racing. 'What did you want from me?'

It was a curious phrasing. Not, 'What do you want to discuss with me?' Somehow, his choice of words was so much more provocative. She took another gulp of champagne, eyes closed, letting it explode into her belly.

'I'm—' She opened her eyes, stared at him, and lost sense of everything. Whatever they'd been before her twenty-first and anything that had happened since didn't matter. The stars overhead seemed to wink down at them, giving Poppy their blessing, or, at the very least, their encouragement. Maybe it was a devilish idea, maybe she'd regret it, but tonight, Poppy was filled with a need that only Adrastos could meet. She didn't want to think about the consequences.

That kiss on the night of her twenty-first had been just a flash. A few passionate seconds she'd replayed over and over and over so many times the memory was in danger of getting static cracks through it from overuse. A fresh taste of Adrastos, a secret, forbidden kiss, just for this one night...

Time seemed to slow almost to a stop. She was conscious of the very atmosphere that wrapped around them, the cool winter's night, the sparkle of the stars overhead, the sound of the ocean lapping against boats in the distance, and then, Adrastos. All of him. Right there, within easy touching distance.

She licked her lower lip quickly, mouth dry, throat thick. His eyes dropped to her mouth and her heart accelerated so she thought it might hop out of her chest. It was now or never.

'What I want,' she said, slowly, but with steel underpinning those words, a challenge in each syllable, 'is for you to kiss me.' She moved closer, so her breath fanned his cheek. 'But this time,' she almost purred, 'I don't want you to stop.'

Adrastos felt the boundaries of his world tighten around his body, making it impossible to breathe, to think, to see anything besides this damned woman, this vexatious, tempting, beautiful woman. When had that happened? She'd been a teenager at first, just like his sister. The pair of them so silly, always giggling and whispering secrets. He'd looked on them both with fond indulgence. He'd never thought of Poppy as a *woman*, until her twenty-first birthday party, when he'd walked into the garden marquee that had been erected in the grounds of the palace and seen—not just a woman, but a deity. A goddess. Stunningly beautiful, untouchable and entirely transformed. Suddenly, all their conversations over the years, all their shared stories, everything he knew about Poppy, had shifted and morphed and he'd wanted to *really* know her, beyond the words they'd exchanged. He'd wanted her in a way that he hadn't even fully understood. He'd had plenty of experience with women, but he'd never wanted another human being in the way he wanted Poppy. It went way beyond sex. He'd seen her and wanted to make her his on some elemental level.

The need to possess her had terrified him. He'd spent the entire night trying to avoid her, to tamp down on those unwelcome feelings, and he'd almost succeeded. He'd almost won the war, but then she'd walked past him, quite distracted by a conversation with his mother, and Adrastos had fallen under her spell. Her fragrance, so sweet and sensual, had called to him, and when he'd found her alone, in the rose garden—one of her favourite spots—he'd known the war was far from over: it was no longer in his grasp to win.

If a waiter hadn't walked past that night and dropped a glass, rousing Adrastos to his sanity, he would have made love to Poppy then and there, amongst the roses.

But that had been three years ago. He'd run so hard from that night, that unfamiliar moment that had completely lacked Adrastos's trademark control, when he'd kissed a woman he'd been told to think of as his damned sister! He had no right desiring her. He had no right to kiss her. Any other woman, he thought with a grimace. Adrastos had made no effort to hide his lifestyle from the press. If anything, he'd relished that reputation.

Having been lauded as 'The Perfect Prince' since Nicholas's death, in one aspect of his life, at least, he didn't feel like a treacherous usurper. He couldn't change his traits, those inbuilt leadership instincts that did indeed make him an excellent prince. Nor could he change the fact that Nicholas had been, in many ways, unsuitable for the life for which he'd been born. He'd been quiet, academic, timid and naturally shy, every public outing a torture for the oldest sibling, where Adrastos cared so little for anyone's opinion of him that he'd not been bothered by any engagement whatsoever.

But he hated the comparisons.

He hated that at times there'd almost been a sense of joy at Adrastos's promotion to heir—never mind that it had come about through the death of his much-loved brother.

Was it any wonder he'd lashed out in the one area of his life that was beyond the control of anyone? While his parents desperately wanted him to settle down and marry, to have royal heirs of his own, Adrastos delighted in showing everyone they were wrong about him—at least a little. He wasn't The Perfect Prince. Not as perfect as Nicholas would have been, because surely Nicholas would have married by now, had he lived.

Poppy made a little noise, a husky exhalation, and she was pulling back, ever so slightly, so his gaze narrowed, his pulse grew louder in his ears and he knew he had seconds to act—or not act, which would be far smarter.

That night, he'd kissed her because he'd wanted her, and he'd pretended it had been just like with any of the women he met in bars or at parties. But this was Poppy. There were layers between them that complicated things. His parents viewed her as a daughter. She had no family besides *his* family. He couldn't take her to bed then forget about her. It was messy and Adrastos didn't do messy.

And yet, even just the thought of kissing her had his groin tightening, his arousal straining against the fabric of his trousers, so he was intimately aware of every inch of his manhood, the powerful need for Poppy compressing the walls of his world even further.

'Listen, Poppy...'

She lifted a finger, pressing it to his lips. 'I don't want to listen,' she murmured. 'I really, really don't want to talk about this. For three years I've wondered what the heck happened between us, and I've wondered why you stopped. I've never understood why all of a sudden we were kissing, and then we weren't, but I've had time to reflect on the whole kissing side of things and I liked it. So I want you to kiss me. Again.'

'And not to stop,' he growled, and despite his mind knowing this was an utterly *terrible* idea, that things were far more complicated than she believed, his hand lifted and pressed to her hip, holding her there, and his body was suddenly so close that they were pressed together.

'Not to stop,' she agreed with a small nod and a tilt of her head so her face was close to his and they were staring at each other. He felt as though he might tumble off the edge of the balcony if she kept looking at him like that.

'It was right to stop that night,' he said, as if he needed to grab a lifeline.

'Was it? Why?' There was an intensity to her question and he was reminded of how razor sharp her mind was, how impressive her intelligence. It was one of the first things he'd noticed about her, all those years ago, when she'd arrived in Stomland as a shell-shocked orphan and he'd felt an instant desire to protect her from any more harm. But even broken by the loss of her parents, she'd been insatiably curious and unabashed with her curiosity.

He compressed his lips and expelled a sharp breath. 'Because you're like a sister to me.'

She made a scoffing noise he regrettably found irresistible.

'A sister? Really?'

No, not really. He sighed again. 'Poppy—'

'Tell me you don't want to kiss me,' she challenged directly, and he was grateful for the darkness on the balcony, and the fact she wouldn't be able to see the tell-tale part of his anatomy that showed just how badly he wanted what she was suggesting. But then, whether by accident or design, she swayed forward, and brushed against his arousal. The moment they connected, her eyes widened and her lips parted on a soft exhalation. There was no longer any denying it. There was no longer a war to wage.

'It's a mistake,' he groaned, but he wasn't sure if she heard: the words were buried in the kiss, in the swift, urgent claiming of her mouth, in the beginning of something he wasn't sure he could control but that he could no longer fight. Hell, it was a mistake, but so was the kiss on Poppy's twenty-first. He'd simply have to live with the consequences in the morning. And in between now and then? He intended to enjoy every damned moment.

CHAPTER TWO

HE'D KISSED HER once before and it had rocked her world, shaken it to the very foundations, but this was something else. Something entirely different. She saw now that his first kiss had been *chaste*, if such a word could be applied to a moment that had switched everything on inside her and made her fully aware of her desires and needs as a woman. But this was different.

This was so raw, so real, so visceral. One hand came behind her back, pulling her hard against him, and his mouth took hers with a rush of desperate hunger, his lips separating hers, his tongue pushing into her mouth as if he wanted to taste every inch of her. She whimpered because it was so incredibly overwhelming, because she felt as if she were drowning, and there was no saviour in sight. She lifted her hand to the back of his head, tangling her fingers in his hair, making a small moaning sound that was swallowed by their kiss.

Desire flashed through her, heavy, hot, urgent, so now she didn't hear the ocean or see the stars, she felt only the tightening of her nipples against the fine lace of her bra, and the warmth between her legs, and the way her stomach was twisting, wanting, needing more.

She didn't ever want this kiss to end. She knew it would lead to complications, but his passion was a drug and she was high on it. Rational thought was no longer possible.

Pressing up onto the tips of her toes, so her breasts crushed against his chest, her body moulded to his, she felt the full force of his arousal and almost pulled back, because it was so confronting and real, such undeniable proof that he was awash with the same desire she was.

Something, somewhere, snapped through the waves of eroticism to steal Poppy's focus, and Adrastos was aware of it too. They both pulled away, staring at each other, chests heaving. Adrastos looked around, frowning.

It had been a flash of light. Lightning? The air smelled of salt and thunder; a storm had been forecast for the following day.

It had also been a wake-up call she desperately didn't want to hear; she couldn't have history repeat itself! The last time, they'd stopped because there'd been a sudden noise, and she'd always lamented that, and wondered what would have been if they'd kept exploring, kept kissing, kept tasting... Staring up at him, she knew the hammer was about to drop, that he would walk away from this and leave her and all her fantasies for the next few years would be fed by those wild, passionate moments of abandon.

'We shouldn't do this,' he said with a shake of his head, but he continued to hold her tight.

Disappointment seared Poppy.

'Anyone could walk out here and see.'

Her heart lifted. She felt as though she were on the fastest roller coaster in the world. His eyes pinned hers as if he was trying to wade through the madness, to find his way back to the shores of sanity. She held her breath, incapable of speaking, too scared to say anything that might shatter the moment.

'Come with me.'

The words were issued like a command, ringing with his

trademark authority, the same authority she'd been aware of when she'd first come to live at the palace in Stomland as a heartbroken fourteen-year-old. Eleanor had been a balm to her soul, but nineteen-year-old Adrastos, home for the weekend from military college, had been something else entirely. She'd quickly learned that the sun and moon revolved around him. Not just because he was the heir to this small, rich country, but because he had been born as a true king amongst men—second in line to the throne until his older brother's death, but Adrastos had always been possessed of qualities that made him rare and impressive. Confident, fiercely intelligent, unfairly handsome, educated, strong and athletic, he had been like some kind of god, and to be in the same room as him was to be aware of his gifts. She saw it again and again—the way people were awed by him, totally cast under his spell, just by being near him.

He drew her closer, hand on her back, guiding her across the balcony, every step taking them further away from the party, towards their own intimate celebration. It was a large penthouse, and they walked around the corner of the balcony before reaching a door. With one last, piercing look at Poppy's face, Adrastos pushed the door inwards and gently ushered her inside, the hand on the small of her back almost the only reason she could remain standing.

He flicked on the lights as he shut the door and locked it, offering privacy in what was a sumptuous bedroom. Poppy spun to face him now, dislodging his hand and jacket, which she'd worn loosely draped over her shoulders. It dropped to the ground without her realising it, because she couldn't quite believe what was happening.

A twenty-four-year-old virgin, in a bedroom with the Prince she'd secretly fantasised about for years...

Happy birthday, Poppy.

But this wasn't wise. It was a terrible idea. They'd both regret it.

Or would they? She wouldn't. She knew she wouldn't. In the same way she'd held those memories of their first encounter, sleeping with Adrastos would be another memory. A much, much better memory. And she'd no longer be a virgin... It was something that had niggled at the back of her mind for a long time. She was aware how out of step with her contemporaries she was. It hadn't been intentional. She'd honestly started to think she was just very non-sexual. Only, it turned out, Adrastos seemed to be the only man who could stir her to this kind of fever pitch. Why on earth would she even think about squandering that opportunity?

And if anyone found out?

Adrastos's family were all she had. They'd taken her in rather than letting her awful aunt raise her. Poppy had been so incredibly grateful that they'd fought for her, that they'd brought Poppy to live with them. They'd always gone out of their way to make sure Poppy felt welcome, but, at the end of the day, she wasn't their child. She wasn't really family. They needed Adrastos to follow through with his royal duties. His penchant for sleeping with anything in a skirt was a source of great pain for the King and Queen, and even to Eleanor. So if they learned Poppy had become one of his women? How could they fail to feel betrayed by that?

It would change everything.

Poppy couldn't lose them, too. She couldn't—wouldn't—do anything to upset them, to make them think she'd taken advantage of her place in their lives.

She prevaricated but whatever hesitations she had abruptly disappeared the moment Adrastos began to unbutton his shirt, slowly but determinedly, eyes on her the whole time so she felt as though he saw all the way through her, and she shivered.

Because she wanted him to see her. She wanted this.

It could never be more than this night. She wouldn't risk her place in his family by wanting more—she knew the boundaries. Honestly, Poppy didn't know if she'd survive losing the love of his parents and sister, not after all she'd already lost. Plus, she wasn't a total sadist. Wanting more than one night from Adrastos would be like wanting to sprout wings and fly. One day, he'd give up his bachelor lifestyle, but probably not for many, many years.

'Adrastos…' Her voice was a husky plea, an incantation of some ancient magic, a promise, a pledge.

He stopped unbuttoning his shirt, eyes meeting hers, and then he lifted his hand, holding it outwards. Poppy was just inches away. One single step closed the distance. She stared at his hand a moment, feeling the enormity of what he was asking, then put her own in it. A tremble ran the length of her spine at their connection. Her soul spun.

He was Ellie's brother.

She'd seen him as off-limits for years. To touch him now with freedom, to feel his warmth against her skin, set something going inside her that she almost couldn't bear. Her knees knocked and her stomach flipped.

'You do it.'

Another command.

At her look of uncertainty, he gestured to his shirt. Her veins were filled with a tsunami of blood. She took one more step, then, with fingers that weren't quite steady, began to unfasten the remaining buttons.

He smelled so good up close. Alpine and masculine, with whisky undertones making her belly do somersaults. She breathed in deeply, wanting more of him. She leaned closer, letting her face drift towards his now naked chest, inhaling his fragrance, her lips tingling with a desire to kiss and to taste.

He drew in a deep breath, so his chest moved, his skin just millimetres from her mouth now.

Poppy held back a groan, swallowing it in her mouth, swallowing hard. Reality seemed so far away, but if she was dreaming—again—then she didn't want to wake up.

Her hands pushed the shirt from his body completely, letting it fall to the floor, and her eyes sought his, trying to reconcile this version of Adrastos with the one she'd known for so many years. The heir to the throne, the 'older brother' figure.

'Are you sure about this?' she asked uncertainly, because she couldn't bear it if he changed his mind later. She needed to know. She needed a guarantee that this was going to happen.

'What do you think?' His eyes were hooded, his handsome face tanned, with a slight colouring to his cheekbones.

She lifted her slender shoulders in a half-shrug. 'I don't know.'

After all, how could she? Her experience with men was non-existent.

'You don't know if you're sure?'

'No.' She bit into her lower lip again. 'I know... I know what I want.'

And she did. God help her, she did.

His smile then was her undoing. Slow to spread and ever so sensual, it lit a thousand little fires beneath her skin.

'It's just...you're...you...'

His eyes flashed with something dark.

'Yes, and?' He moved closer to her, reaching for her strap

and sliding it down a little way so he could press a kiss to the naked flesh of her shoulder. Thought and sense fled.

What had she been trying to say?

What did she want from him?

She knew this night would mean nothing to Adrastos. His reputation preceded him, and, besides that, Poppy had taken a vested interest in the string of broken hearts he left in his wake. To a man like Adrastos, sex was nothing. She'd even heard him say as much, to his father of all people, when King Alexander had challenged his heir about his overactive love life.

'Why shouldn't I enjoy myself before signing my life away to serve this country?'

That was what tonight was.

Enjoyment.

Pleasure.

If Poppy overthought it, she'd be the one backing out, and she knew she didn't want to do that.

'But nothing,' she said after a beat. Then thought better of it. 'No one can find out about this.' She couldn't imagine how she'd ever be able to explain this to Ellie, or his parents.

His eyes narrowed, raking over her face, his lips tweaked into a slight frown. 'I wasn't planning on publicising it.'

'No,' she said, wondering why his quick agreement didn't fill her with the rush of relief it should have. 'I don't know how I'd face your parents, or your sister...'

'It's no one else's business.'

'I know.' She swallowed. She should really tell him about her lack of experience...but what if he changed his mind? What if...?

It didn't matter. She wasn't tricking him into taking her virginity. She just knew he'd have thoughts about that, that he'd feel betrayed if she didn't give him any kind of warning or preparation.

'I have to tell you something,' she said, but as an insurance policy she took a page out of his book, reaching around to the zip at the back of her dress and sliding it down slowly, her skin lifting in goosebumps as she anticipated what was to come next.

'Go on.' He crossed his arms over his naked chest, but his eyes devoured her body, watching as the silky fabric slipped lower, and lower again, revealing a lace bra and matching panties.

'I'm going to tell you,' she said with a nod, more to herself than to him. 'But you need to promise me it won't change anything.'

'I promise.'

She rolled her eyes again. 'You don't even know what I'm going to say.'

'No, but I'm telling you, right now, you could say anything on earth and it wouldn't change what I want to happen.'

His certainty was its own aphrodisiac.

'I'm waiting.'

She nodded, nerves firing through her belly now.

'Poppy?'

He moved closer, his warmth enveloping her, as his hands came around to her bra and unclasped it with effortless ease, reminding her how often he did this kind of thing. His mouth on her nipple caught her completely off guard and she cried out, tilting her head back instinctively to provide better access. His tongue encircled her areola and she whimpered because the feeling was so exquisite and sensual, heat pooled inside her and warmth slicked between her legs.

'Adrastos…' she groaned, and thought was no longer possible.

'Can what you want to tell me wait until afterwards? Because, frankly, I need this like you wouldn't believe.' Not you. *This*. And to emphasise his point, he ground his arousal against her sex, so she felt the rock-hard heat of him and whimpered, moving her hips to be closer to him, needing so much of what he promised. He dragged his mouth to her lips at the same time he lifted her, cupping her bottom and holding her right against his arousal so if it weren't for the barrier of their remaining clothes, he could have sunk inside her, taking her and pleasuring her as she'd been dreaming about all these long years.

He pushed her back against the wall of the room, holding her there with his body, his mouth ravishing hers, his hands roaming her skin, feeling her, touching her, driving her crazy with his perfect, sublime nearness. But it wasn't enough. Maybe that was the point? She didn't have enough experience to know but she guessed this was a kind of foreplay—to make her want when she couldn't have, to fill her body with lust and desire until she was trembling and then take her just as she was about to lose her mind?

'Adrastos, please,' she cried out, her head hitting the wall as she tilted it back and stared at the ceiling, need bursting through her. In response, he repositioned himself so his arousal was pressed right against her sex, hard and strong even through his clothes, and he ground himself there as if they were actually together, so she was spinning out of control, pleasure making her eyes fill with stars.

'You are so sexy,' he said, and, even in her desire-addled state, she wondered why he sounded a little angry about that. 'So goddamned sexy.'

Sexy? And here Poppy had always thought herself lacking any kind of sex appeal whatsoever... 'I want you,' she said, simply, a sentence she'd thought many times in her head and never been able to speak aloud. Until now.

'Let's see about that,' he growled, catching her behind her bottom and carrying her once more, away from the wall and towards the bed, which he placed her in the middle of and brought his body over hers, staring down into her eyes. His hands found the elastic of her thong and slid it down her legs. He moved quickly and yet it was so sensual, his touch thorough and the air against her body cool. She shivered all over, earning a smile from Adrastos.

'Even better.' His eyes roamed her body with possessive heat, lingering on her breasts, her flat stomach, the apex of hair at the top of her thighs, admiration something she knew she wasn't imagining in his features.

Perhaps she should have expected it, given his last statement, and yet his touch against her sex was totally foreign to Poppy so she startled, jerking to a half-sitting position. His face shifted, focussing on her for a moment before he returned his attention to her womanhood, pressing a finger inside, and the totally unfamiliar sensation made her pulse riot and her body explode.

'Adrastos!' Now his name was a cry into the air, rent with passion. He moved his head upwards, pressing a sharp kiss against her lips, lingering there, his tongue striking hers.

'Shh,' he commanded into her mouth, with the hint of a laugh in the single sound. 'You are so loud, someone is bound to come and investigate.'

She wasn't sure she cared, in that moment. What mattered beyond this?

He pressed another finger into her, filling her so she arched her back and moaned, the pleasure so different, so full, so utterly indescribable.

'You are so wet,' he muttered and, for a moment, Poppy

wondered if there was something wrong with that. She wished she had more experience, that she knew a little more about what they were doing and what Adrastos would want. 'So perfectly wet,' he said with a shake of his head. Not a bad thing, then.

He moved his mouth back to her breasts, flicking one then the other with his tongue as his fingers moved inside her, the rhythm in sync so she was facing multiple wildfires throughout her body, all of them burning out of control.

He drew his mouth lower, to her stomach, and then removed his hands from her breasts, pushing her legs apart and holding them wide, so she was momentarily bereft, because his touch was so perfect and she ached to feel him in her.

Only, he wasn't finished. The mouth that had driven her so wild by licking and sucking on her nipples pressed to her sex now, his tongue striking at her so she cried his name, pleasure saturating the syllables. She'd never imagined this could feel so...so...

'Oh, oh, oh...' she moaned as waves of pleasure built within her. His hands massaged her thighs and his tongue struck at her until she was crying out faster and faster, filling the room with the audible proof of her passion and then her release. She shook all over, trembling from head to toe as a new, terrifying and overpowering knowledge seeped into her body.

'Holy Mother of God,' she said with a shake of her head, breathing almost impossible, as he looked up at her, his expression one of utmost intensity. He stood with slow purpose, his hands unfastening his belt and removing it, placing it on the edge of the bed before he returned to his trousers, undoing the button first, then the zip. He moved at normal speed but to Poppy it was excruciatingly slow, because she wanted to feel, and she wanted to see. Sitting up when she was able, she wriggled to the edge of the bed and took over, her eyes hooked to his as she pushed his trousers down and then hooked her hands into the waistband of his briefs.

Desire exploded in her veins.

He was so beautiful. She was terrified of what was about to happen, but also absolutely sure it was what she wanted, no matter the consequences.

She pushed his underpants down, then realised she hadn't thought this through. His arousal was at her eye height and she had no idea what to do with that, only she felt she wanted things she didn't know enough about. She didn't want to disappoint him, and so, instead of leaning forward and taking him into her mouth, she lifted a hand to his shaft, wrapping her fingers around him and swallowing past a sudden lump in her throat. Because he was big. Not just big. Huge.

It startled her back to reality quicker than anything could.

He swore, the curse filling the room, and when she jerked her face to his, she saw that his eyes were closed, his skin pale, his lips compressed.

Had she done something wrong? She dropped her hand away quickly. 'You don't like to be touched?'

His eyes blinked open, fixing directly on her. 'Like it?' he repeated through clenched teeth. 'You think I didn't like that?'

'I… I'm not sure.'

He frowned slowly.

'Then let me be clear: I did. I do. But in the interest of honesty, if you touch me like that, I'm going to come, so don't do it again.'

She trembled, an unknown, unfamiliar power moving through her.

'Because I want *you*.'

More power, more pleasure, but also the shifting of certainty, doubts returning, and, thankfully, a hint of sanity. Urgency. She had to tell him that she'd never done this before.

'I want that as well,' she said after a pause, and, despite his warning, she lifted a hand to his base and wrapped her fingers around him, smiling at the sound of air hissing between his teeth.

'Poppy.' Her name held a warning.

'Adrastos,' she replied in kind, growing bold, moving her hand up and down his length, smiling at his ragged breath and the bead of liquid that pearled his tip. She might have been a twenty-four-year-old virgin, but instincts were stronger than experience, it turned out. Curiosity had her leaning forward, her heart racing with nerves as she pressed her lips to his arousal and tasted his essence, groaning as it hit her mouth.

He swore again, and this time pulled away from her, out of her reach, hands on hips, dark eyes glittering with emotions she didn't understand.

'That's enough.'

She was being pulled from one direction to the next. Had she done something wrong?

Or was it that he'd enjoyed it too much?

She wished she understood.

'That's enough,' he growled, moving back to the bed and quickly coming down over her. He was rough, she was smooth. He was hard, she was soft. His chest hairs brushed against her breasts, and the tip of his arousal, which she'd just taken into her mouth, was now at the entrance to her womanhood. They were seconds away from something she'd always wanted. Something she wanted with *him*, and no one else.

But she had no idea what it would be like for him, what

he'd think if he realised she was a virgin. Despite the fact she wanted him with the power of a thousand suns, she wasn't going to risk breaching a moral wall she suspected he would value.

'I need to tell you something *now*, Adrastos.'

He made another noise, a hiss, as he pushed on his elbows and stared down at her, eyes piercing her, face flushed, lips parted.

But he waited, hitched at her sex, body held perfectly immovable.

Nerves flooded her, and desire was making it hard to think straight—harder still to do what she knew she needed to.

'I'm—'

'Damn it, Poppy, are you sure this conversation cannot wait until afterwards?'

Maybe this wasn't really a big deal. Maybe he wouldn't notice. Maybe, maybe, maybe…

'Poppy?'

He was right there, and it felt so good, so natural, so right, she simply nodded, surrendered, gave herself to what was about to happen and hoped for the best. What else could she do?

But she was didn't want him to stop and when he thrust into her, it was as though her whole body were exploding with bright white light. Pain at first, searing, sharp, overpowering, so she stilled, eyes wide, locked to his, lips pale from how hard she was compressing them, and her own sensations were so strong that she almost didn't see the expression on his face, almost didn't read the shock and incredulity in his eyes.

But then, pain receded as quickly as it had come, leaving a new sort of awareness, of being full of someone else, of having him so deep inside her, of being pleasured from the inside out.

'Poppy.' His voice was strangled, deep, a warning in the depths of his tone, but a warning to whom and about what?

'Please,' she said again, arching her hips instinctively, so he groaned, his own expression held tight now, his eyes pushing into hers and the rest of him completely still. 'Please,' she repeated, knowing she wanted this desperately.

He swore then, dipping his head forward, shielding his face from hers. Was it over? Was he going to end this? Then, he moved, pulling halfway out of her and pushing back in, rolling his hips, lifting his face to watch her, studying her, reading her and seeing what brought her pleasure, what she responded to, so Poppy closed her eyes and drifted away on a growing wave of sensuality.

Adrastos had never had a problem with stamina before. He prided himself on being able to pleasure a woman multiple times before finally succumbing to his own release, but Poppy was so tight, and her inexperience made her responses so completely innate. It wasn't just that she felt good, it was that she was in awe of how good she felt, shocked by her body's ability to respond to a man. Her eyes were wide, her skin dewy with sweat, her body trembling all over. It was the single most incredible experience of his life even when, in the back of his mind, an anger was building that he couldn't fathom nor explain.

Only he knew every reservation he'd had about this, every fibre of conscience, had been right. Poppy was not like the women he usually took to bed. Not only was she considered a part of his family, she had, until a moment ago, been a goddamned virgin.

Anger charged through him, taking over his need for release, so even as he moved inside Poppy and watched her fall apart for perhaps the first time in her life, he knew he would not succumb to his own yearning, aching need to finish.

He waited for her cries to soften, for her breathing to come back to normal, for her muscles to stop convulsing around him, and when she blinked up at him with eyes that were slightly sheened with tears, he felt an ocean of regret build inside his chest.

A lack of confidence had never been Adrastos's problem, and yet…living your life in someone else's shoes, as he'd been forced to, meant you second-guessed yourself a lot. The comparisons were inevitable. How Nicholas had been, how he'd lived, what he would have been like if he'd still been here today. One thing was for sure: he would never have given into temptation with a woman his parents viewed as a daughter. This was his *family*, for God's sake, and his family had already been through enough.

Adrastos pulled out of her quickly, as though he'd been burned, the faint smear of colour on his still rock-hard arousal all the evidence he needed that what he'd felt had indeed been the physical barrier of her innocence.

Silence sparked in the room, charged with his fury, so the air seemed to almost dance with electricity. Poppy lay there, her breasts shifting as she struggled to properly regain her breath, as she made sense of the feelings that were wracking her inexperienced body, so Adrastos had to turn away from her, to do his best to control his own breathing, to will his arousal into submission, and, most importantly, to stop himself from saying something he'd regret.

Because while he was angry at Poppy, it would be wrong to take that anger out on her in this moment. Whatever else this night had been, it was her birthday, and he'd unwittingly become her first lover.

He groaned, the magnitude of that inescapable. The kiss had been bad enough! But this bound them in a way, and always would. What the hell had he done? Panic was a surging tide, threatening to drown him. Adrastos wanted to shout into the room, to issue a denial, to take it all back. He would *never* be bound to anyone, especially not Poppy. It was the one small beacon of independence he held. His life, his right to date whom he wanted, his sexual freedom. Having sex with a virgin carried more meaning than the simple act of two people coming together—and knowing he'd been Poppy's first? What had he done? What had she let him do?

'Adrastos?' Her voice was soft and sweet, tremulous. 'Look at me.'

He closed his eyes hard, so little cracks formed at the edges of his face, then turned, his expression now stiff, his face bearing a mask of cool indifference even when inside he was a torrent of feelings. 'You were a virgin.'

He didn't need her to confirm it, but it felt somehow important to speak those words aloud.

Her eyes darted around the room and then she nodded, once. Her cheeks were stained pink.

'You're twenty-four.'

'I know that,' she whispered, not meeting his eyes.

He tried to control his anger. After all, it wasn't directed at Poppy—not all of it, anyway. Virgin or not, he shouldn't have brought her here, shouldn't have agreed to kiss her and 'not stop'.

'Why did you proposition me?' he demanded, remembering belatedly that she'd instigated this. He'd had no idea of her inexperience, but Poppy had known. And she'd goaded him into being her first!

'I—just—'

'You just what?' His words cracked around the room, frustration evident in the resounding bite of his syllables.

'I just wanted—'

'Sex? To lose your virginity?' he accused, jacking his thumb towards the wall behind her. 'Well, there are about two dozen men out there who would have happily obliged. Why the hell did you choose me?'

'It wasn't— I just wanted—'

The night Nicholas had died, Adrastos had felt terrifyingly out of control, and he'd hated it. His world had crumbled and Adrastos hadn't held any power to stop that, to change it. Afterwards, he'd done everything he could to retain a grip on his life. He never let himself feel more than he wanted, never lost himself in sentiment or emotion, except for two times in his adult life: in the rose garden on Poppy's twenty-first birthday, and now. Even with his family, he'd pulled back just enough to protect himself from any more loss.

He'd worked hard to call the shots in every aspect of his life. But he hadn't been in control from the moment Poppy had approached him at the party, and that sense of powerlessness was bringing back subconscious echoes of how he'd felt when Nicholas had died, making him react stronger, harder, out of a fierce need for self-preservation.

'It's not a big deal, is it?'

The soft question had his head pounding as if it might explode. He jerked away from her, needing space to cool down, reaching for his boxer shorts and dragging them on his body. Her flimsy underwear lay at his feet and he scooped the thong up swiftly and tossed it in the direction of the bed.

'Get dressed.' The words were curt, and he had his back turned to her—more self-preservation—so didn't see the way her face paled and lower lip trembled.

'Why won't you look at me?' she whispered, a moment later, and so he had to steel himself to do exactly that, turning as he roughly buttoned up his shirt, then wishing he hadn't when the sight of her made Adrastos feel as though he'd been punched right in the middle of his chest.

She was dressed in her bra and pants, but her hair was tumbled and loose and her lips bruised from his kisses, her body so beautiful and fragile. His damned arousal jerked and he wanted to run. To literally run a marathon, to get this frantic, desperate energy out of his system.

He tried to regain control, to be reasonable, to take the edge off his anger, but he felt powerless and used. Yes, he felt used. She'd wanted to lose her virginity, she'd chosen him, to hell with the consequences. To hell with how that could potentially have affected his family.

'This was a mistake,' he said firmly. 'You are like a daughter to my parents, a sister to my sister.'

She tilted her chin with unexpected defiance. 'But not a sister to you.'

He felt nauseous. 'God, Poppy. You *should* be like a sister to me. After your parents died, my parents all but adopted you. You are their goddaughter. They raised you since you were fourteen.'

She closed her eyes. 'Thank you for the biographical information but I'm aware of all that already.'

He ground his teeth. 'This isn't the time for sarcasm.'

'I'm sorry, I've never done this before. How should I be acting?'

'Apologetically,' he muttered.

'You want me to apologise?'

'You know this shouldn't have happened.'

'You came in here very willingly…'

His eyes flashed with frustration. 'I had no idea you

were a virgin. How the hell could I have known? You're twenty-four!'

'Yeah, well, we don't all live the way you live, Your Highness,' she snapped.

Her attitude was only making his anger worse. He didn't want to be reminded of his lifestyle in that moment. Strangely, it felt inappropriate to bring the shadow of other women into this room, now. 'Fine, but surely you've had boyfriends?'

The pink in her cheeks deepened.

'Poppy? You've had boyfriends, haven't you?' But Adrastos already knew the answer to that. He frowned, staring at her without seeing, as he realised the truth. Not once had a man been mentioned in connection to Poppy. He'd met a few of Eleanor's boyfriends, but never had Poppy brought someone home. Not once had her mother called him excitedly about some guy Poppy was dating, as she had for some of Ellie's men.

'So what?' she muttered, and something in the region of his heart splintered, something sharp and painful. Suddenly, Poppy was fourteen again, her cheeks tear-stained as she sat sobbing in the library, when he'd known he'd move heaven and earth to stop Poppy from ever feeling like that again, when he'd felt some strange sense of imperative to remove that pain from her life. They shared that grief—Poppy was better at expressing it, but it was inside Adrastos too, growing as a tree, wild and out of control at times.

'You should have told me,' he finished, his anger evaporating on a wave, leaving only a sense of sick disappointment in himself, and a sense that this was all going to get much worse.

'I meant to.'

He closed his eyes, remembering her insistence that she

wanted to tell him something and the way it hadn't seemed anywhere near as important as losing himself in her.

He swore then, a short curse filling the air like an explosion. 'You should have just said it. I deserved to know.'

'And you'd have stopped.'

Anger whipped again. 'Excuse me?'

'You would have stopped what we were doing.'

'So you *chose* not to tell me, to trick me, into being your first?'

She blanched. Perhaps she hadn't consciously realised what she was doing, but that was what it amounted to.

'You had no right.' He pushed home his point. 'Of course I would have stopped. That would have been the right thing to do. Damn it, Poppy. This was—a mistake.'

'I don't want you to feel that,' she said quietly. 'I—I don't want to be something you regret.'

'It's a little late for that.'

He glared at her and now, fully dressed, if somewhat dishevelled-looking, he stalked to the internal door of the room, wrenched it open and strode out, slamming it behind him with a dull thud.

He had to get the hell away from her, to go for that run, to hope like hell he could push this from his mind. The one saving grace was that nobody knew what they'd done.

CHAPTER THREE

'Oh, crap... Oh, crap.' She pushed her mahogany-brown hair back from her eyes and blinked several times to focus on the screen of her phone as words swam before her over-tired eyes.

The taste of champagne rose in her throat and Poppy winced as she remembered how many glasses she'd consumed in rapid succession after rejoining the party, in an attempt to blot out the events that had transpired.

She stared at Ellie's text and prayed to any god who'd listen that somehow Poppy had misunderstood.

Please tell me nothing actually happened between you and Adrastos?

Memories sliced through Poppy and, despite the argument that had come after, all she felt was the rush of desire and awareness, of tingling, sensual heat as she felt again the sensations that had twisted inside her as Adrastos had kissed her, held her, touched her and finally made her his. Heat coloured Poppy's cheeks and slicked between her legs.

But why would Ellie even ask? Was it possible she'd said something after glass number however many of champagne?

She swiped out of the message and into another, this one

from Ellie and Adrastos's mother—Poppy's godmother—Her Majesty Queen Clementine Aetos.

Darling? Call me when you get this. We need to talk.

Panic drummed through her. No one knew what had happened. No one. Unless Adrastos had said something?

To his parents? Not bloody likely. With a growing sense of trepidation and flashes of memories and experience garnered over years of living adjacent to the royal family, she thought of the microscope that was trained on Adrastos's life by a well-meaning but nonetheless outrageously invasive public. His every move was reported on, the tantalising speculation surrounding each of his brief, high-profile relationships something with which Poppy was all too familiar.

But this was different.

He hadn't taken Poppy to a movie premiere or dancing at a nightclub. Their dalliance was a secret, it had taken place behind closed doors and, afterwards, Poppy had gone back to the party and pretended nothing had happened. Adrastos had left by the time she'd emerged.

So what had happened in the eight or so hours since she'd come home and flopped into bed, and now?

With fingers that were shaking, she loaded a browser on her phone and typed first her name, then deleted it and typed Adrastos's instead.

And grimaced.

Sure enough, several of the trashier papers were already running the story, salivating at Poppy's connection to the royal family, so her heart was beating so hard in her chest it was like a heavy, metallic drum. Adrenalin filled her veins.

The first photo was benign enough—it showed Adrastos in the corridor outside the bedroom. While there was little scope to misinterpret what he'd just been doing—that he had dressed in haste was clear—it didn't necessarily implicate Poppy. And though she was hungry to understand the rest of the story, she couldn't help but idle on that image a moment, to stare at his face—thunderclouds would barely describe the emotion on his symmetrical features.

Swallowing, she quickly scrolled down and then saw the truly damaging image: a photo of Poppy on the balcony, cinched in against Adrastos and being kissed as though... She trembled. Was that really what it had been like? Just looking at the photo almost seared her with passion and urgency.

She dropped her phone like a hot potato.

'Darling Poppy...'

Clementine's voice was soft, and Poppy knew the Queen well enough to be able to perfectly picture the expression her face would bear.

'I find myself in a very difficult position.'

Poppy closed her eyes on the squirming sense of guilt. She had ignored several more calls from Eleanor and the royal courtiers but when the Queen herself began to ring, Poppy found it impossible not to answer. She didn't know what she'd say, but figured she would work it out as the conversation progressed. Only now, she was uncharacteristically lost for words.

'When your parents passed away, I was determined to bring you home with us. I was determined to raise you as my own, to love you as they did. I knew I could never replace your own dear mother, but I was desperate that you would know a mother's love, that you would know how adored and wanted you were.'

Tears filled Poppy's eyes.

'It is what I know your mother would have done for my children, had we—had anything happened to us.'

Poppy bit down on her lower lip.

'You have been a part of our family for a long time and I am grateful every day for that.'

A lump formed in Poppy's throat. She felt lower than low.

'But that means you *know* us better than anyone else.'

Ice spread through Poppy. *Us.* It was one tiny word, one of the smallest in existence, but its weight was hefty, for it made Poppy instantly feel like an outsider. She grimaced, pressed her back against the wall and tried to breathe in and feel strong.

'Adrastos is a good man, and he will be an excellent king, but there can be no misunderstanding where his priorities are in his personal life.'

Clementine's voice, though still soft, was also heavy; it carried a sadness that Poppy had heard before, usually when some Adrastos scandal or other had landed him in the papers. It didn't matter though what Adrastos did in his personal life. He was so roguishly charming that even his pathological inability to commit was looked on with fondness by the public. Only within the palace did it cause serious, ground-shaking despair. And now Poppy was a part of that narrative.

'Your Majesty,' she said, reverting to Clementine's title. It felt appropriate, in the circumstances. Guilt was searing her. She knew what the family thought of Adrastos's philandering. Having slept with him somehow made Poppy complicit in that. She couldn't bear for them to think she didn't take their worries seriously, that she didn't *understand* why they held such concerns. 'I wish I knew what to say...'

Clementine sighed. 'He's gone too far this time. And at your birthday party. At *Ellie's* party!'

'The photos are misleading,' she murmured, trying to pull on all her legal training to connect the dots. What did the evidence show? What could be proven? But Poppy had never been a good liar, she'd never felt comfortable with any elimination of the truth, no matter how small, and lying to Clementine felt particularly wrong. And yet, the situation was so complicated. Wasn't it sometimes better to blur the lines, just a little, if doing so was harmless and the result eased another person's suffering? 'We thought we were alone.'

'You thought you were alone, but Adrastos should have known better,' Clementine huffed. 'He has lived this life long enough to know there are very few places where privacy is assured.'

Poppy's eyes narrowed. She conjured an image of Adrastos, seeing him as he was: strong, indomitable, a force of pure energy and courage, and imagined how little Clementine's criticism would upset someone like him. Only it wasn't fair. None of this was Adrastos's fault. He'd simply done exactly what she'd asked.

'Oh, Poppy.' Clementine sighed. 'I cannot help wondering how and why this happened. You *know* what he is like. The King is beside himself. The idea of Adrastos involving *you* in his lifestyle, the idea of him treating *you* like the others...'

Poppy made a chortled sound of disbelief. She had worried she might be exiled and, instead, the Queen was simply *worrying* about Poppy. Worrying because of Adrastos's reputation. Well, she wasn't wrong, and yet an unexpected protective instinct licked through her, and she thought of the time in the library, many years ago, when Adrastos had found Poppy crying and promised her that everything would be okay. She'd felt his protectiveness and his protection and those feelings moved through her again now, only it was Adrastos she wanted to protect and defend.

'It's not like that,' she mumbled, speaking almost without thinking. 'I promise, it's different.'

Clementine was so quiet, and that silence should have given Poppy time to think, to reflect on the words that were forming in her mouth, but all she could think about was how much she wanted to spare Adrastos from his parents' criticism. After all, she'd seduced Adrastos. The whole thing had been *her* idea. True, he'd gone along *very* willingly, but he wouldn't have touched her with a ten-foot bargepole if he'd known about her innocence—a point he'd made blindingly clear immediately afterwards.

Poppy winced.

'Generally, the palace doesn't comment on Adrastos's... business,' Clementine said with obvious distaste. 'But you are our goddaughter, and everyone knows it. Anders would like to discuss the best way forward, the best damage control, if you will.'

When Clementine referred to the King's private secretary, Poppy knew it was a really big deal. Anders didn't get involved in anything beneath his pay grade.

Suddenly, Poppy felt that she was in way over her head. It was all too much.

'I'm just so disappointed, Poppy, in both of you, if I'm honest. How can our family proceed after this?'

Poppy felt the world crumbling beneath her, she felt the reality she was facing. Clementine might have been angrier at Adrastos, she might have pitied Poppy her stupidity in having a one-night stand with him, but, when push came to shove, he was their son and heir to the throne and if things became awkward it was Poppy who'd face exile from the family, not Adrastos. She couldn't lose them! This family was all she had.

It was vital to find a way through this that spared the

King and Queen from feeling awkwardness, from having to make the difficult decision to cut Poppy from their family's lives.

'He should have known you, of all people, were off limits, but he cannot help himself, it seems. I am so disappointed,' she repeated. 'And you know what he is like! You know better!'

Poppy flinched. None of this was meant to be in the public sphere. It had been her personal moment, a personal triumph. She'd lost her virginity and now the whole world knew about it. Not that she'd been innocent, but that she'd been taken to bed by the great philanderer Adrastos Aetos.

'You do know better, don't you, darling? I have tried to raise you as your mother would have, to instil sense and reason, to guide you. I wouldn't have thought...' The Queen trailed off, lost in thought, and Poppy cringed, feeling as though she'd badly let down her godmother.

Clementine sighed, rallied, began to speak once more, a different tack this time, no less effective. 'You've worked so hard, Poppy, but what about your professional credibility?' the Queen murmured. 'You were so eager to establish yourself all on your own, without our help and contacts, without any connection to us. Surely you can see how damaging this will be to your reputation?'

'It's not the nineteenth century,' Poppy couldn't help pointing out. 'My private life is still my own. I cannot see that it will have any impact on my work.'

'That's naïve,' Clementine said gently, with sad affection. 'And idealistic. Of course it *shouldn't* impact your work, but it will. Events like this have a habit of taking over, of becoming all that a person is known for. Your professional successes will be mentioned as an afterthought to this. You must have known how many ripples in the pond would come from spending the night with Adrastos?'

Poppy felt as though she might vomit, and it had nothing to do with all the champagne she'd drunk after sleeping with Adrastos. The picture Queen Clementine painted was suitably dire, and, unfortunately, not entirely inaccurate. Poppy was well respected in her role as a human rights lawyer but none of her achievements would ever be mentioned before this piece of gossip. There would be whispers behind her back for a long time to come now her night with Adrastos was public knowledge.

Unless…

She sat up straighter, stared at the wall, an idea coming to her quite out of nowhere. It seemed crazy at first, but as she held the idea in the front of her mind and examined it from all angles, she realised it wasn't crazy so much as the only way through this that might preserve her professional reputation, save Adrastos from his parents' wrath, and also make it possible to maintain the status quo within the family—something that meant more to her than she could ever put into words.

'Your Majesty, there's something I have to tell you…'

Poppy moved with greater dexterity than she'd been capable of summoning half an hour earlier. She changed into a pair of jeans, a turtleneck skivvy and a faux fur jacket, dashed some bright lipstick into place and finger-combed her hair over one shoulder, before donning dark sunglasses and pulling open the front door of her house with one mission in mind: she had to speak to Adrastos.

But as soon as the door opened, she was blinded—by the startling winter sun first, then the flashes of a thousand cameras.

'Oh, my God.'

She dipped her head forward, pulling the door shut quickly and moving through the pack, numb and terrified at the same time. Why hadn't she anticipated this? Because she'd been a bundle of nerves and emotions since waking. Everything had happened so fast, like a snowball caught in an avalanche, and Poppy hadn't dared take time to stop and think about whether or not this course of action was wise: it was the only solution, so she'd had to pursue it.

'Poppy, is it true you're secretly engaged to the Prince?'

'Poppy, how do you feel about him? Is it love?'

'Poppy, Poppy, Poppy!'

She walked quickly, fingernails digging into her palms, but the photographers followed her as a swarm of bees might ambush a picnic, so she was regretting her decision to have this conversation face to face. Only she *had* to see Adrastos. She was a tumble of feelings and nerves, and while seeing him might make it worse, it would also, she thought with crossed fingers, make it somehow better.

Paparazzi engulfed her until she reached her car, parked on the narrow street of Stomland's capital that she'd called home ever since moving out of the palace to attend university. Her parents had left her an inheritance and on her eighteenth birthday it had matured, enabling her to buy the charming, historic townhouse in a little mews location. While the King and Queen hadn't wanted Poppy to move out, it had felt important to Poppy to repay their generosity with a sign of independence.

Or was it that, deep down, she'd been afraid to wear out her welcome?

They'd always made her feel like a part of the family, but she wasn't, not really, and that idea kept scrolling through her mind as she slipped into the driver's seat and started the engine.

Still the photographers snapped away and she couldn't help wondering why. Surely they had whatever image they would need by now?

With a look of exasperation, she pulled out from the kerb and began to drive to the home she knew Adrastos lived in, but had never personally been to, with a growing sense of trepidation and disbelief. Was she really going to ask him to do this?

When Nicholas had died, Adrastos had wanted, more than anything, to find a way to turn time backwards, to go back into the past and see Nicholas again, to be able firstly to fix him, and, failing that, to be able to *tell* him everything he felt, everything he thought. As boys, they'd been competitive: separated by only thirteen months, one the heir, the other a backup, they'd been pitted against each other without their realising it at first.

It didn't help that Adrastos had been bigger and stronger. He'd walked from a younger age than Nicholas had, he'd run, jumped, talked younger. He'd been faster. More confident and charming, and, though he hadn't been consciously aware of it, Adrastos had enjoyed the competition, for he'd always won.

But when Nicholas had died, Adrastos had regretted having competed with him. He'd regretted taking every opportunity to show his superiority. He'd wanted to rewind his life and do it differently, better. A complex, heavy thought for a teenager to have, nonetheless, it had been clear as anything in Adrastos's mind.

And now, staring at the front page of the newspaper, he felt that same desperate, foolish longing. He wanted to go back in time and undo it all. What the hell had he been thinking?

She'd propositioned him, sure, but he was older, wiser, clearly more experienced. So why the hell hadn't he just flat out refused? Why had he gone outside with her? Breathed her in? Kissed her. Held her body against his?

He groaned, dropping his head forward with a sinking feeling in his gut.

Nobody dared question his lifestyle choices publicly. He was aware of his parents' feelings, aware of the headache it gave the courtiers who ran—or attempted to run—their lives, but no one had been brave, or stupid, enough to directly criticise him for his almost pathological need to enjoy a woman's company.

That, he suspected, was about to change. Poppy was no ordinary woman. There was no way his parents would let this infraction go without some dialogue.

And worse, what would it do to their family?

It was almost Christmas, a time of year when they came together and ate around the table *en famille*, Poppy included. Were they all to ignore the elephant in the room?

Not for the first time, he fantasised about not going, but even Adrastos couldn't do that. Not to his parents, who had buried their oldest child, who existed in a strange half-life, here in the present even as they were simply going through the motions, waiting to be joined with Nicholas again.

Adrastos grunted, stood, paced his living room then paused as a noise alerted him to something beyond his door.

The paparazzi scrum outside her own apartment was nothing compared to the assembly of photographers waiting at Adrastos's. However, at least there was a security presence here to keep them at bay. Adrastos had four military guards on his front steps, as well as a dozen security cameras set up on the façade of his beautiful residence. Poppy hadn't been able to park anywhere near his home, so she walked the last of the way, on the opposite side of the street until the last possible moment to avoid the attention of the paparazzi and then, with her head down, across the street and straight into the lion's den.

It was fortunate for Poppy that one of the security guards saw her first, putting an arm around her shoulders and leading her up the steps and to the front door before shepherding her inside swiftly, but not before the clicking of cameras had almost deafened her.

She looked around just as Adrastos stalked into the tiled, double-height foyer, and the logical, calm-sounding explanation she'd concocted on the drive across town burst into flames on the periphery of her mind as everything went blank except the sheer euphoria and electrical charge of seeing him again.

Her pulse went crazy, her mouth dry, her fingers began to tingle and her stomach twisted and tightened until she could hardly breathe.

'Adrastos.' His name was barely audible, a throaty, emotional noise from the depths of her gut.

'You shouldn't have come,' he grunted, evidently feeling none of the temptation at seeing Poppy again that she was managing being confronted by Adrastos.

She tried to control her nerves, to calm her rapidly firing pulse, but she was awash with sensation. It was about a thousand times worse than her first trial, when she'd had to stand up and argue in front of a judge.

'We have to talk.'

His jaw moved as though he were grinding his teeth. Contemplating rejecting her?

'It's important.'

'I have not changed my mind about last night, Poppy. It was a mistake. One of the worst of my life. Talking about it will not alter that.'

She flinched. Okay, she hadn't expected him to be jumping for joy about it all, but to refer to it in such bald terms made something in the region of her heart ache unbearably.

'I don't want to talk about last night,' she answered after a brief, painful pause.

His brows lifted. 'I cannot imagine we have anything else to discuss.'

Poppy rolled her eyes, an expression that he evidently hadn't expected, because his gaze narrowed and surprise briefly flitted in the depths of his pupils. 'You know that's not true.'

Perhaps he did, because a moment later, with a look of resignation, he gestured towards the doorway that led from the foyer into what appeared to be a living area.

'Fine. Let's talk, then.'

But he didn't move, and in order to step in the direction he'd gestured, Poppy had to therefore walk past Adrastos, and even passing within two inches of his tall, masculine frame had her pulse skittering wildly, memories slamming into her so she gasped and quickly looked away, digging her nails into her palms and willing her brain to engage, to take over, so other parts of her body didn't start calling the shots.

I want you to kiss me, and this time, I want you to not stop.

Had she really said that to him? She was in awe of her bravery, and stupidity. All of this was her fault. And now she'd gone and made it all so much worse…by doing the only thing she could think of that would ultimately fix it.

Poppy had come here to talk, but, having never been in

Adrastos's house, she couldn't help the curiosity that flooded her as she stepped into his living room and looked around. The décor was similar to the palace, only a little less intricate, more modern. There was a distinct lack of personal touches—no photographs or artwork on the walls, no candles or flowers. It was like a five-star hotel, she thought with a small frown, the kind of place one could walk into and out of without a thought.

'Have you spoken to anyone today?' She turned slowly to face him, her mouth parched once more as he rolled up the buttoned shirt sleeves to reveal tanned, toned forearms.

'I have,' he said with a dip of his head. 'The prime minister, about a trade deal with Argentina, my valet too.'

She fought the urge to roll her eyes again. 'I mean about last night.' Then, with an embarrassed whisper, 'About us.'

'No, Poppy,' he drawled. 'That has not been on the top of my priority list.'

'Your mother hasn't called you?'

He frowned. 'Not yet.'

'She will,' Poppy muttered.

'I take it she has called you?'

'Her, Eleanor, Anders,' she said, tapping her fingers to enumerate the list as she mentioned each name. 'I'm surprised the King himself didn't beat a path to my door to find out what the heck we were thinking.'

'I would struggle to give an explanation to that question,' he said grimly.

'Me too.' She pressed her teeth into her lower lip. 'But we did sleep together, and there are photos that make it pretty obvious. We can't change what happened, so we have to manage the consequences.'

'Consequences?' His brows shot up and he stared at her with pale skin, a look on his face that Poppy didn't understand. He swore then, moved closer, wrapped one hand around her forearm. 'You're not telling me you're pregnant?'

Poppy's heart did a funny little skip and she immediately envisaged the children they could have—their children—and an emptiness opened up in the centre of her being. A real family. Her own family. She quickly shook her head. 'Surely you know it's way too soon for that?'

'Of course,' he muttered, closing his eyes. 'I am not an idiot. And yet last night, I acted like one, well and truly. I cannot believe I was so stupid, so ignorant.'

She lifted a finger and pressed it to his lips. 'I'm on the pill,' she said gently, shocked to realise she almost wished that weren't the case. 'I have been for years.'

'But you're not sexually active.'

She didn't correct the tense he'd used. 'That's not the only reason people go on contraception,' she said with a lift of her shoulders. 'You can rest assured, the chances of me having conceived your baby are very, very slim.'

'But not impossible.'

She wrinkled her nose. 'Well, no, but very unlikely.'

His Adam's apple jerked as he swallowed. 'Is this what you wanted to discuss?'

'No. Until you mentioned it, the idea of a pregnancy hadn't even occurred to me.'

'Then what can I do for you, Poppy?'

He stepped backwards, withdrawing from her, removing himself incrementally until he was unfamiliar and strange, cold and detached.

She furrowed her brow. 'Don't be mad.'

He didn't visibly react, but she felt a shock wave move from him to her. 'About?'

Poppy wrung her hands in front of her chest. 'So I spoke to your mother this morning, and let's just say she was beside herself. She was angry at you, disappointed with me, worried for both of us, and she raised some very valid points about my career. You know how grateful I am to your family, how much I hate the idea of hurting them...'

His nostrils flared. 'What you and I do privately is of no concern to them, or anyone.'

'Do you really believe that?'

His eyes held hers for a long time and Poppy's concentration was failing, everything was fading, the world beyond them, the physical items in his home, even the air grew thin, as she felt only the insane connection between herself and Adrastos and an almost magnetic desire to act on it.

'I believe it's how it should be,' he conceded after a beat.

'So do I. But unfortunately, reality is different. We made a mess, Adrastos, and we have to clean it up.'

'And you have some brilliant idea for how to do this?'

'Well, I don't know if it's brilliant,' she said with a lift of her shoulders. 'In fact, on the drive over here, I kept thinking how *stupid* it is, but, getting to the point: I've already told your mother, the die is cast, and there's nothing for it but to carry on now.'

'You've told my mother what, exactly?'

Poppy sucked in a deep breath, tasting him on the tip of her tongue, wanting him, needing him. 'She hated the idea of me being just another one of your women,' she said, not noticing the way he stiffened. 'And I hated the idea of her thinking that too. So I told her... I told her...' Poppy groaned, then tilted her head back, staring up at the ceiling.

'You told her what?' he repeated, but with more urgency.

'That we're secretly dating,' she whispered. And then she waited for Adrastos to react.

CHAPTER FOUR

LIKE THE EYE of an epic storm, seconds passed in silence, and yet there was an undercurrent of pulsing, of raw, untameable energy, and then, Adrastos spoke, his voice controlled, but the kind of control that somehow sent Poppy's nerves into a state of abandon.

'You did what?'

'Hear me out,' she said, closing her eyes because it was impossible to look at him and see rejection on his face. She felt as though she'd dug an incredibly deep hole and he was the only person who could help her out of it. Until that moment, it hadn't really occurred to Poppy that he might not agree to. 'You must know how your parents feel about your, erm…'

She forced herself to blink in his general vicinity then, an unspoken plea on her face.

But Adrastos didn't help her out. He stood like a totem pole, massive and unyielding, arms crossed over his broad chest, eyes boring into her.

'Lifestyle,' she finished after a beat. 'Your habits with women are well documented. They hate it, but they know better than to try to convey that to you, for fear you'll resent their interference so much you'll increase your, erm…activities.'

He barely reacted, but in his jaw, a muscle flexed.

'You are the heir to the throne. They want you to settle down.'

'You do not need to interpret my parents' feelings for me, Poppy. Whether they have expressed their wishes to me is beside the point: obviously they would rather I was married by now, with the obligatory minimum of two children.'

She pushed aside the strange, barbed feeling tightening at her chest.

'Sleeping with me was…' She hesitated. 'Well, they're annoyed.'

'So?'

She flinched. 'You might feel that way, but I sure as heck don't. I love your parents and the last thing I want to do is repay their generosity and kindness by disrespecting them, by disappointing them.' Her voice crackled with feeling.

'Again, Poppy, what you and I do in our personal lives…'

'That's not true. They're a part of my personal life. Eleanor is my *best friend*. Sleeping with you was…' But she couldn't say it was a mistake. She couldn't say she regretted it. 'I wish no one had found out, but they did, and the only thing we can do to fix this is pretend it wasn't just a meaningless one-night stand,' she mumbled. 'A one-night stand *is* disrespectful. But a secret relationship?'

'I do not get involved in relationships. My parents know this better than anyone.'

'This isn't a real relationship,' she pointed out caustically, rubbing her fingertips to her temple, pushing aside the question she had. *Why didn't he get involved in relationships?* 'We'll pretend we're dating, that we like each other, but that we're taking it slowly because of the family situation. Can't you see that it makes everything better? Jeopardising my relationship with your family for a one-night stand is stupid and unthinking, but for a relationship…'

'Why did you do it, then?' he pushed. 'You knew all this last night,' he pointed out.

'I also told you expressly that no one could find out.'

He rocked back on his heels a little. 'That's hard to control, when you choose to sleep with someone like me.'

'I see that now.'

He sighed heavily. 'I'm sorry, Poppy, but I have no interest in pretending to date you.'

Her stomach dropped to her toes. 'Well, then, you'll have to call your mother and tell her the truth,' Poppy said with a lift of her shoulders. 'Tell her your oversized libido couldn't pass up the opportunity to take my virginity,' she added with an extra shrug.

He glared at her. 'You are well aware I had no knowledge of that.'

'It doesn't change anything.'

He opened his mouth then closed it, rubbed a hand across his jaw. 'Have you thought about the timing of this? It's Christmas. We're about to spend almost two weeks at the palace, as we do every year.'

'I've thought of nothing else.' She groaned. 'But can't you see how much less awkward this will be, for everyone?'

His eyes were mocking. 'Really? You don't think there is an inherent awkwardness to us carrying on a faux relationship under my parents' watchful gaze? As for my sister, she will want all the details. Are you really prepared to lie to them?'

She shook her head and, to her chagrin, tears moistened her eyes. 'No. Yes. I hate the idea, of course. I hate it. But my back was against a wall,' she said honestly, before remembering the truth of that sentence, the way he had held her with her back against the wall, grinding his arousal into her.

But they both pictured that moment, she knew it. The air between them seemed to spark.

'Your mother was so…disappointed. I had to tell her something.'

'And what next, Poppy? Do we get fake engaged? Fake married?'

'No,' she almost shouted. 'God, no. We'll break up.' Poppy drew a deep breath. 'I've accepted a promotion, Adrastos, at The Hague. It's a huge opportunity for me. I leave early January.'

She waited for him to respond, but all he did was narrow his gaze slightly. Poppy swallowed. 'When the dust has settled on all this, we'll explain that I'm leaving, and given the geographical difficulties of a long distance relationship, we've decided we're better as…friends.' She faltered, because she hadn't thought of him as a friend for a very long time, probably not ever. 'They'll be a little disappointed, but not compared to how they'd feel if you immediately go back to sleeping with anything with a pulse.'

'You've really thought it all out, haven't you?'

'Not really,' she said with a humourless laugh. 'I acted without thinking it through at all, but I believe my instincts are right. This is the only way to save them from embarrassment, to avoid a ridiculous amount of scandal, and to save face in front of them. Don't you agree?'

He stared at her for a long time, and Poppy found it impossible to know what he was thinking. But finally, he took two steps towards her, hands on hips, eyes now challenging rather than mocking.

'You are asking me to do this, for you,' he said quietly.

'For your parents—'

He shook his head. 'I am used to what my parents think of me. I would not be doing this to change that. But I understand why *you* need us to do this.'

She bit down on her lip, hating that a single tear fell from her eyes, hating that he saw her vulnerabilities as clearly as if they were writ across her breasts.

'So you agree?'

'Perhaps.'

A feeling like hope fluttered in her chest, but there was something else, too. A rush of adrenalin. A charge of fear. 'Perhaps?'

'You should be sure about what you are asking of me.' He moved a step closer, then surprised Poppy by reaching out and pressing his fingers to her chin, tilting her face so their eyes met squarely. 'You should be clear about what I would expect in return.'

Poppy's pulse went crazy. She couldn't speak for several moments and when she finally did, the words were trembly and weak.

'What would you expect?'

His smile was more of a smirk: damn him for even making that look sexy!

'My parents will only believe this if we are convincing. I would not agree to pretend to date you and then have them discover it was a lie. If we do it, it must seem real.'

'Obviously,' she snapped.

'At the palace, you will sleep in my room. In my bed.'

Her lips parted on a rush of surprise. 'I—can't see that that's necessary.'

Another smirk. 'You are so quick to point out that my parents know what I'm like. Do you really think they'd believe anything less?'

He had a very valid point. Damn it, why hadn't Poppy thought of that?

'But we can't—I'm not—suggesting we, erm—'

Nearer he came, closing the distance between them completely. 'Sleep together again?' he murmured, the words warm against her cheek.

'Right,' she said, uneasily, because her pulse was now just a tsunami in her veins and her knees were trembling.

'I cannot promise you that,' he said quietly.

She shivered, adrenalin making her body shake. 'You said it was a mistake,' she reminded him, shaking her head. Even when she desperately, desperately yearned for him, on some instinctive level, she knew that to give into that desire would be an absolute nightmare.

'Some mistakes are pleasurable to repeat.' And he kissed her, with as much intensity as their first kiss, more perhaps, because so much had happened since then, and her whole body responded with an arc of fierce, bright electricity and a burst of something like light that came from the depths of her soul and flared outwards. She wanted to cry and laugh and scream and melt into a puddle of pleasure at his feet, but all she could do was kiss him back, and wrap her hands around his neck and hold him closer to her, lift her body, press it against him, her breasts squashed to his chest, her hips so close to his manhood, her mind wishing away their clothes so that they could rediscover what they'd shared last night.

His tongue moved with devastating effect, rolling hers, teasing, his mouth punishing and proclaiming her as his even before she could understand what he was doing. She was exploding from every pore of her body; she was awash with sensations and then, into his mouth, she was begging for him. She didn't care. She needed him. It made no sense, but nothing about this did. Just like last night, she was overpowered by something so much bigger than her; she just hoped Adrastos could help her make sense of it all.

He pulled away and she stared up at him, bewildered,

still flooded with an electrical current, body jolting, waiting for his hands to lift her shirt, to remove her clothes then his—but he stepped away from her instead, and his features bore a mask of cool reserve.

'There is no sense pretending you do not want to sleep with me, Poppy. We both know that is a lie.'

She gasped. Had he kissed her just to prove a point? God, and she'd let him. She'd let her objections go so quickly and easily.

She was trembling from anger now, and yes, desire too. 'Are you saying you'll only do this if I agree to…have sex with you?'

To his credit, he blanched. 'Do you honestly think I am desperate enough to deliver such an ultimatum?'

It wasn't the time to be reminded of his prowess with women.

'So?' she said crossly. 'What, then?'

'You will sleep in my bed. This is not negotiable. I will not agree to lie to my parents and then have that lie found out. We all have our boundaries: that is mine.'

She had to respect his position on that, particularly as she'd forced him into the lie.

'But you should realise that sex is a very real possibility of the situation you've orchestrated. If you have an issue with that, you should work out a way to extricate yourself now. Otherwise…' his eyes met hers, held, and a shiver ran the length of her spine '… I suggest you sit back and enjoy the ride.'

While Adrastos had earned a reputation as a playboy prince, he was also revered and respected for both his work ethic and nous, and with good reason. At nineteen, he'd been catapulted into the position of heir to the throne but his interest in good governance and social policies predated it. From almost as soon as he could remember, Adrastos had been fascinated by the way things worked, and, more importantly, by how he could make them better.

His position of authority simply gave him a vehicle for change, and he was not slow in using it.

However, as he pored over a report he would usually have devoured in a single hour, he found his concentration wandering, his focus bizarrely absent.

Or perhaps it wasn't so bizarre, he thought, leaning back in his broad leather chair and rubbing his palm over the back of his neck.

After all, the experience of making love to Poppy was still fresh in his mind, and though he'd done an admirable job of acting in control earlier that day, when she'd come to his home, Adrastos had kept a grip of his own desire with a maximum of effort.

When that tear had rolled down her cheek, he'd felt the same instincts that had overcome him as a teenager, when she'd arrived heartbroken and grief-stricken. He'd wanted to fix everything for her because he'd hated to see her in pain. He'd told himself it was because he knew loss and wished someone had been able to make it better for him, but now, he wasn't so sure. Maybe it was just… Poppy? Maybe there was something about her that inspired that protective streak?

He expelled a frustrated sigh, because it went way beyond wanting to protect her.

Last night had been about pure need, plain and simple. But Poppy?

Sure, he'd wanted her. That was impossible to deny. But he could have had just about any single woman at that party— that wasn't arrogance speaking, so much as experience. And any woman would have been less complicated than this. Instead, her breathless little entreaty for him to kiss her and not stop had weaved through him, rebuilt him as a new man, a man who wanted, more than anything, to be with Poppy. He'd known she was forbidden. Hell, he'd had three years to regret that one damned kiss, to be thankful as anything he hadn't allowed it to go further. That should have been the salient lesson, the reminder that stopped him from acting on his desire.

Instead, he'd let one part of his anatomy do the talking.

Since Nicholas's death, Adrastos had had to walk in his brother's shadow—even when the papers feted and adored Adrastos and made comparisons praising him without, perhaps, realising that there was implied insult to Nicholas in those lines of adulation. Adrastos hated it. He had been happy enough to compete with Nicholas in life, but now, it wasn't fair, it wasn't right.

And yet he'd stepped up, taken on Nicholas's role, borne the survivor guilt that plagued him constantly, become what was expected of him, except in this one small regard: he was not going to be the dutiful heir and marry some available princess hand-selected for him by a royal courtier. He was not going to roll over completely and fall into line with what everyone wanted.

At first, sleeping with women, flirting with them, seducing them, had been a way to forget about Nick. To forget about love and loss and the powerlessness of an individual when faced with terminal illness. After Nicholas died, Adrastos had felt bad, all the time, except when he had sex. It was, therefore, an easy equation.

But then, he began to crave the criticism and disapproval, even when it was only something he glimpsed in his parents' faces, even when they tried so damned hard not to say what they were thinking.

He relished failing them, because he knew Nick never would have.

Nick would have married years ago. Someone appropriate and suitable. It was a small, stupid way to honour his brother's memory, to allow his brother to 'win' in their unspoken competition, but it was nonetheless important to Adrastos.

And now he'd unwittingly found himself in a relationship, albeit a pretend one, with the kind of woman his parents would be desperate for him to marry. He groaned audibly. Their break-up would be the ultimate disappointment, which should have satisfied him on some level. But he didn't feel satisfied. He didn't feel anything except numb.

He was regretting his acquiescence; he was regretting everything, but Adrastos was a man of his word, and he'd given that word to Poppy.

He'd made his bed, and now he had to lie in it. He wouldn't be alone though. Poppy had made sure of that. No wonder he couldn't focus on the report in front of him.

'I just can't believe this. How did it happen?'

Poppy grimaced. Lying to her best friend was the absolute worst, but it was a necessary evil. She'd looked at this from a thousand different angles before calling Eleanor, trying to see if there was any other way, if she could back out of the fib she'd unthinkingly told the Queen, but there was no solution at hand. If Eleanor, of all people, knew the truth, she'd be livid—at both of them. Poppy couldn't bear to let Ellie down.

'We just got talking one afternoon…'

'But you know what he's like, Pops.' Ellie groaned. 'You *know.*'

'People change,' she said, but she was cold to the centre of her being.

'You're really dating him?'

'We're getting to know each other. It's not serious—'

'But you're spending Christmas together.'

'Well…' Poppy bit into her lip until it hurt. 'I always spend Christmas with you.'

'And so does Adrastos, but this is different.'

Poppy felt lower than low. Yet, how could she tell Ellie the truth? Who knew how the Princess would react to the news that, instead of being in a relationship with Adrastos, Poppy had actually just lost her virginity to him in a super-sexy one-night stand? Hardly the kind of news a best friend would want to hear.

'Do you mind?'

The silence that followed Poppy's question was the longest of her life.

'It's weird,' Ellie admitted after a minute. 'You're my best friend and he's my brother. The thought of the two of you is hard to get used to. But it's more than that, Pops.'

Poppy waited, nerves stretching.

'I love Adrastos. It's just…he's different to you. He's…'

'More experienced,' Poppy said.

'I don't want you to get hurt,' Ellie urged.

'I promise you, I won't.'

There was no scope for her to be hurt because this wasn't a real relationship. He was faking it and so was she, more or less.

'Maybe he'll be different with you,' Ellie said, but her own voice showed ambivalence. 'Just…be careful. He's a great guy, but I've never seen him with a woman he hasn't treated as expendable. And you're most definitely not that.'

'We're taking it slow. I promise.'

Poppy disconnected the call with a tremor of anxiety. Taking it slow? Hardly. They were going to be sharing a room in the palace, doing their level best to convince his parents they were madly in love. This could be a recipe for disaster.

* * *

After her parents' deaths, this palace had become a salvation to Poppy. It was a place where she was loved and safe and, for four years of her life, it had been her home, day in, day out. Despite that, a kaleidoscope of butterflies took over her tummy as she went through the gates now—because for the first time, she was in the same car as Adrastos, their arrival carefully planned to ring with truth.

The act they'd discussed almost academically was about to begin and Poppy knew she had to give the performance of a lifetime.

With Adrastos.

Pretending that he was her lover!

Just the idea of that made her pulse race and her stomach twist. How could she possibly convince the people who knew her best?

But how could she not? Ever since those photos had run in the papers, more and more stories had been printed, each more fanciful than the next, the speculation quite wild, the interviews incredibly invasive. Because Poppy had refused to hold any media events herself—naturally—there'd been interviews with whomever the less scrupulous tabloids could drench up, from old school 'friends', to lecturers at university, never mind if Poppy had never been in their class. But with each article to run, Poppy became gladder they'd agreed to do this, to give some flesh to the fact they'd slept together. His family would be disappointed when they broke up, but at least they wouldn't think that either Poppy or Adrastos had been so stupid as to fall into bed together, to hell with how that would impact anyone else.

'Ready?' His voice was deep and gruff and made her already oversensitive nerves tremble. She turned to him slowly, her pulse all over the place, her heart twisting painfully. Their eyes met and she was tumbling through the cotton candy of her memories, straight back to that night, when he'd pulled her against him and kissed her until she saw stars.

'Adrastos?' Her eyes were huge, her skin pale.

He skimmed her face for several beats, his lips pressed together, then made a noise that sounded like encouragement.

But Poppy was suddenly shy.

'That night…'

'Which night?'

But he knew. Of course he did. 'At my party.'

'Ah. The night we had sex?'

He was being deliberately brazen. Her cheeks flooded with colour. 'Please don't talk like that here.'

'We're supposed to be dating. You don't think your boyfriend should mention S-E-X around you?'

Her cheeks grew hotter. 'You're *not* my boyfriend,' she hissed, even though they were alone.

He lifted a hand in mock surrender. 'This was your idea.'

'Yes, and I'm already regretting it,' she muttered, closing her eyes and inhaling deeply, for strength.

'What about the other night?' he asked, suddenly serious.

'I didn't… I don't know if I thought that was going to happen. But what I really wanted, what I really wanted to *know*,' she corrected, 'is why you kissed me the other time.'

'Which other time?'

Her heart stammered. He hadn't forgotten. She *knew* he hadn't forgotten because she'd mentioned it again at her twenty-fourth birthday. 'You know which night.'

'Yes,' he agreed after a moment, eyes dropping heavily to her lips.

'You followed me to the rose garden. You pulled me against you and you…you kissed me. Why?'

Without intending it, Poppy had leaned forward, her body so close to Adrastos's their faces were only an inch apart.

'Why do you think, Poppy?'

'I don't know. I've wondered ever since. Was it because I'm a woman and you're, well, you? Had you been drinking? Were you bored?'

His lips tugged to the side. 'Perhaps it was all of those reasons.'

Poppy's eyes dropped to the console between them, her brows knitted together. She didn't want him to read the disappointment in her face. She couldn't make sense of it herself.

'That was a mistake too.'

She needed to change the subject before she said something stupid, like how much she'd liked being kissed by him, how much she'd liked sleeping with him, how no other man had ever made her feel even a hint of what he did. 'I hate the idea of this.'

His eyes roamed her face and, while it felt as though he was looking right into her soul, she had no idea what he was thinking or feeling. 'It will be over soon.'

'I'm so angry at whoever took those photos.'

'It's not their fault.'

'Then whose fault is it?' she demanded, disagreeing with him entirely.

'Mine.'

'Yours?'

'Of course.'

'Why? You didn't sell those pictures to the tabloids.'

'But I erred, Poppy. I was indiscreet. I should not have kissed you like that, there, of all places.'

'You couldn't have known—'

'Yes, I could. Don't forget, I've had a lifetime of having my every move monitored. I shouldn't have let this happen.'

Poppy's lips pulled to the side. Perhaps he was right. Unlike Poppy, Adrastos had bags of experience with living a very public life. 'Then why did you?'

His eyes probed hers, his features a mask of iron. 'Does that matter now? The point is, I should have been more guarded. Kissing you in the first place was a bad idea, but to do so at a party—it's unforgivable.'

Her heart twisted.

There was some logic to what he was saying but Poppy hated hearing him describe the kiss in that way.

'I asked you…'

'And I could have said no.'

The palace staff were waiting by the doors. Poppy's stomach was in knots. 'Forget about it. Let's just…get this over with.'

He put a hand on her thigh, and she almost jumped out of her skin. 'Poppy.' His voice held a warning. 'You can't look like a deer in the headlights every time we touch.'

She stared at his hand, tanned, large, strong, commanding, and remembered the way it had felt for him to touch her body, to slide his fingers inside her, to pleasure her so skilfully, and felt as if the air were being dragged from her lungs.

He was right. She had to make this more natural, but that was hard to contemplate when he was capable of setting her on fire with the lightest of touches.

He lifted his hand to her chin, tilting her face towards his and, just like the deer in headlights he'd accused her of being, she stayed perfectly still, incapable of movement.

'Are you about to kiss me?'

His eyes showed surprise. 'Yes.'

'Why?'

'You need to relax.'

'I don't think kissing you will relax me.'

'Let's see,' he murmured, moving closer, his lips brushing hers, so Poppy's eyes flared wider and she looked at him for one terrified moment before her eyes swept shut and she found herself leaning further forward, inviting the kiss. For the benefit of whoever might be watching, she told herself reassuringly as her lips parted and she held her breath.

It was a totally different kiss from any they'd shared before. On previous occasions, his mouth had taken hers as if driven by the fires of passion, but now, he kissed her slowly, gently, tentatively, a kiss of idle exploration and inquiry, a kiss that unfurled desire in her belly like a snake stretching on a hot rock, rather than a torrent of lava, but desire was there, nonetheless. As his tongue flicked hers, she moaned, leaning further forward, hands lifting to his shirt, fingers bunching the fabric together, mind in tangles as she tried to cling to reality, to remember that this was fake, even as her body's response was very, very real.

He pulled away, eyes glinting with purpose as they met hers and held. 'Are you ready?'

Was she imagining the throaty quality to his voice? The huskiness?

'I think so.'

He nodded his head once, the implied approval doing something to Poppy's heart.

She tried not to take it as anything other than it was, a gesture of agreement, but her insides trembled and she experienced a little burst of something a bit like a shooting star in the cavity of her chest, an unfamiliar sensation of pleasure lightening her heart.

'Yes, I'm ready,' she said breathily. 'Let's go.'

CHAPTER FIVE

USUALLY POPPY SAT beside Eleanor at the dinner table, with the King and Queen at either end. When Adrastos was in the palace he took one end, and Queen Clementine moved to sit opposite Ellie and Poppy. Tonight, Adrastos had been placed beside Poppy, Eleanor and Clementine opposite, and a watchful King Alexander at the head.

Watchful because he didn't believe their relationship was real? Or because he didn't trust Adrastos not to hurt Poppy?

Poppy flicked a glance at her best friend, guilt assaulting her in waves whenever she contemplated the lie they were telling. But Eleanor had no idea: she was as happy as always, her love for Christmas evident in the joy she showed at this time of year, on a snowy Christmas night in the stunning royal Palace.

Champagne glasses were brought to the table, filled with ice-cold, fizzing liquid. Poppy took a quick sip of hers, even before a toast could be made, because she needed something to calm her fractured nerves.

She replaced it quickly, tilted her face and caught Adrastos watching her, his expression unreadable, but somewhere near 'thunder' on the scale of faces and moods. She lifted a brow, questioningly, and he winced out a smile—the kind of smile that would freeze ice.

Suddenly, it occurred to her that pulling this off would

be harder than she'd realised. He'd said they'd need to be convincing, but he was acting as if he were heading in for a root canal.

'Well.' Alexander's voice broke the awkward silence. 'Here we are. Family.'

Poppy's eyes shifted now to Queen Clementine, whose smile was bittersweet, and then to the empty chair at the head of the table, where, in an alternate reality, Nicholas would have sat. His absence was, as always, everywhere.

'To family,' Clementine echoed.

'And new beginnings,' Eleanor drawled with a single arched brow. Poppy's heart pumped fast.

'Yes.' Clementine turned to the supposedly happy couple.

But there was a hint of doubt in her voice, a look of worry around her eyes, as if she had major reservations about this too. Poppy sipped her champagne again. They'd decided to play out this ruse and so they had to make it a success. Beneath the table, she pressed her hand to Adrastos's thigh and, despite what he'd said in the car only an hour earlier, it was he who flinched at her touch, his powerful leg reacting to the simple, meaningless contact. She squeezed his thigh, hard, and shot him a warning look.

She was trying to show that she was in control, but when he placed his hand over hers, then laced their fingers together, any possibility of being in control fell by the wayside. How could anyone *ever* control this absolute torrent of sensation?

Awareness made her skin prickle; she turned away from him quickly, cheeks warm, reaching for her champagne with gratitude and taking several quick gulps. Beneath the table, Adrastos squeezed her hand but she refused to look at him again.

Though she'd eaten at this table many times, something

had changed, and now Poppy saw it almost as an outsider, noticing the elaborate decorations that ran down the centre, the palace staff posted like sentries around the room, making genuine conversation difficult. She'd never felt that before, but the speculation from recent days had reminded her of just how highly watched this family was—and now, Poppy.

She knew from Eleanor how oppressive that could be, but Eleanor was highly adept at living her own life regardless of the press intrusion. And for the most part, as second in line to the throne and someone who had kept a low profile, there wasn't much interest in her. Unlike Adrastos, who'd made an art form of his bachelor ways.

Alexander and Clementine did most of the talking, reminding Poppy of how wonderful it had been to come to this place, where for all they were royal, they were so *normal*, reminding her of her own parents, of what real family should be like. The grief they'd endured, when Nicholas had died, had seemed to make family time even more important to the King and Queen.

Except, Adrastos had fought that.

He'd pulled away when they'd drawn closer.

Poppy had noticed, and she'd wondered, but now something had shifted and the curiosity she felt was no longer a background hum, so much as a rattling at the very front of her brain, demanding answers.

Why had he pulled away?

Why had they let him?

'Poppy?' She blinked, looking at Eleanor first and then Adrastos, who had said her name and was looking at her with a smile that didn't quite reach his eyes, his arm along the back of her chair in a perfect imitation of relaxed intimacy. It made her shiver a little, because it was fake, but for a moment she let herself imagine what it would be like if this were real.

If Adrastos were actually her boyfriend. If *she* were his girlfriend.

It was a treacherous thought, the reality so far removed from a real relationship, she couldn't even go there.

'I'm sorry, did I miss something?'

'My parents were asking if you'd like to join us at the hospital tomorrow.'

Poppy's eyes were huge. It was a visit the royal family made on the day after Christmas every year, to a children's hospital in the city. They spent hours meeting with families, children, doctors, handing out small gifts to each child on the ward.

It wasn't something Poppy had ever attended.

'Given the publicity surrounding your relationship,' Clementine said gently, 'it makes sense. It's well known that you're very much a part of our family, and, as you're now dating, the public will anticipate your attendance.'

'Oh.' A lump formed in her throat. Lying to his family was bad enough, but having to go around as his girlfriend in public? She shook her head slowly. Why hadn't she foreseen this? 'I understand what you're saying, but I don't think so.'

'Why not?' This was Adrastos, his fingers moving from the back of her chair to her shoulder, brushing her flesh slowly, rhythmically, so warmth spread through her, making thought difficult.

Poppy bit down on her lip, thinking quickly, knowing she had to control the narrative. 'We had no intention of our relationship becoming so public so soon. We wanted to take things slowly, you see. We're mindful of how complicated things are, given my relationship with your family.' She didn't look at Adrastos, but she was pleased with the way her explanation was sounding—so rational and measured. 'The story's out there now, but I don't think we need to further fan the flames. You should all carry on as normal, and I'll do the same.'

'But it's not normal,' Eleanor said with a lift of her shoulders. 'The whole world knows you're an item. So what harm could come from spending time together publicly? You've done nothing wrong.'

Hadn't they?

'Poppy's right.' It was Adrastos, and his support was like steel in her backbone. She felt it flood her and breathed out, relaxing. 'There will be other hospital visits, other festive seasons. We do not need to rush anything.'

Poppy's breath hitched in her throat at the ease with which he lied—and the convincing nature of it. He made it sound as if it were a foregone conclusion that they would still be together this time next year, and the one after that. She almost believed him! She caught the surprised, happy look that Clementine and Eleanor exchanged and almost died with mortification. This was a terrible lie she'd been caught up in—a necessity of circumstance. It didn't make it any easier to sit across from these people and deceive them.

'The offer is there, should you change your mind, Poppy darling. You know we think of you as one of our own.'

She could only hope that was still the case when all this was over.

Nothing in the palace had ever been off limits to Poppy. From the minute she'd arrived, she'd been welcomed with open arms and told to think of the place quite as her own home. Eleanor had taken her under her wing and together they'd explored every nook and cranny, running through the beautiful, ancient, elegant corridors, some with parquetry floors, some with marble, all with high ceilings, gold vaulted, and enormous floral arrangements on every single piece of furniture. The palace itself dated back to the twelfth century, the oldest parts of it having been refurbished in the rococo style hundreds of years ago, so they were incredibly ornate and breathtaking.

There were only two areas she'd avoided, and not because anyone had ever said as much, but because Eleanor had avoided them and Poppy had understood. They'd never gone anywhere near Nicholas's room, nor had they approached Adrastos's.

The former because it was too hard for Eleanor, who'd only been thirteen when her oldest brother had died. The latter because he was someone who seemed to demand, without ever saying as much, that his privacy be respected.

They'd been girls when Poppy had arrived—just fourteen—and Adrastos a man of nineteen. He was intimidating and frightening, silent, strong, brooding and powerful. Even Eleanor had been a little afraid of him.

He's not like Nicholas. Nicholas was gentle and soft. I could tell him what I wanted to do and he would always go along with it, never mind that I was so much younger. Adrastos is...scary.

Silently, Poppy had disagreed. He wasn't scary, so much as intimidating. There was a vital difference. Scary implied something negative, whereas to Poppy it had always seemed that Adrastos was simply too much of everything. Too smart, too powerful, too strong, too athletic, too handsome by a mile, and so it was difficult to be oneself around him.

And so it was that despite having spent years living in the palace, after dinner, Adrastos guided her to a part of it that was wholly unfamiliar, through a wide set of double doors she'd never crossed, into a corridor with one door on either side.

'My office,' he explained, waving a hand to the left. 'And my room.' His eyes held hers for a moment too long, as though he was hesitating or working out what else he could say, then he pushed the door inwards and stood just inside, waiting for Poppy.

Her nerves were stretched, her heart racing, blood washing through her ears as loud and urgent as the ocean on a stormy night, but Adrastos was watching her, and waiting, and she didn't feel as though she could simply hover on the threshold.

'This is weird,' she said on an apologetic half-smile, thinking longingly of her own room, just down from Ellie's, the familiar view over the rose garden.

'A little.' He dipped his head forward in agreement, still waiting, so she sucked in a breath and pushed forward, step after step, into his room, looking first at Adrastos and then quickly away when their eyes met and she felt as if she were losing her footing.

His room was big, and she expelled a breath of relief. More than spacious enough for the two of them.

She took a few more steps, towards the bed, then froze. The bed.

It was right there. Huge. Reminding her of another bed, in a faraway penthouse.

She spun abruptly, almost bumping into Adrastos, who was so close she could have reached out and touched him. Her heart was in overdrive.

'I—'

What?

What could she say in that moment? Everything was spinning completely out of control.

'I think they believed us.'

'It would not occur to any of them that we would lie. Not about this.'

That was an indictment, if ever she'd heard one. 'I hate that we're doing this.'

'There is no sense discussing that now. We've made our choice.'

So final. So simple. Could he really be so clear-cut about something so complicated? Perhaps that was a secret to his strength: no ambivalence. Poppy, perhaps through her legal training, saw everything through every facet.

Adrastos moved away from Poppy, towards a door. 'There's a bathroom there, a kitchen, a lounge. Obviously you should feel free to call staff for anything you require.'

Poppy wrinkled her nose. She rarely availed herself of the palace servants. Though she'd come to live here and been treated as one of the family, she knew she *wasn't* actually an Aetos, and hadn't wanted to ever seem to be taking things for granted.

'Do you mind if I make a tea?'

'Not at all. So long as you don't mind if I have something a little stronger,' he responded with a tight smile.

She toyed with her hands. 'Of course not.'

They stared at each other for several beats.

'I was—'

'Do you—?'

They spoke at the same time, so Poppy lifted a hand to her throat and pulled a face. 'Please. What were you saying?'

He gestured to the door of the kitchen, and Poppy was relieved to move that way, relieved to have something practical to focus on, instead of the inherent discomfort afforded by this circumstance.

'You did well tonight,' he said, and she had no idea if it

was what he'd intended to say or not but, either way, the praise warmed her heart.

'So did you.'

The kitchen was luxurious and well appointed, but not enormous—like something in a five-star hotel, she thought, moving behind the bar and filling the kettle. Adrastos went to a liquor cabinet and removed a bottle with a label Poppy didn't recognise, pouring a generous measure into a crystal glass before turning to face her, bracing his hip on the edge of the counter.

She made a tea, watching as the water darkened, then lifted her gaze to him, uncertainty holding her silent, but curiosity finally pushed her to speak. 'How come you're the way you are?'

He pulled a face, perhaps intentionally misunderstanding her. 'Tall? Dark? Handsome?'

Her lips tugged to one side in an unconscious sign of amusement. 'All of the above,' she agreed with a little wrinkle of her brow. 'But that's not what I meant.'

'No? Then what are you asking?'

She sighed. 'With women,' she blurted out, catching her by surprise. 'How come you don't date?'

His eyes were locked to hers but there was nothing in them. No hint of feeling, no suggestion of an explanation. He was so good at hiding his innermost thoughts! 'Does it matter?'

She pulled a face. 'I'm not sure.'

'Then let me tell you: it doesn't.'

'I'm curious, though.'

'Why?'

'Because you're old enough to be married,' she pointed out. 'And it's certainly expected of you.'

'Eleanor will marry.'

Poppy tilted her head to the side, considering that. 'Are you saying you don't see it as your role to marry and have heirs?'

'Not necessarily. However, should I fail in that area, Eleanor's children may inherit the throne. I do not consider it my birthright, nor do I consider my children the sole heirs to the responsibility.'

Poppy's lips parted, her mind swimming. She hadn't expected such frankness, but his answers were deeply unsatisfying, for everything he said only made her want to know more.

He was a riddle, complex and ever changing.

And then, he was moving towards her, pacing slowly, yet there didn't seem to be enough time to brace for his nearness.

'I am much more interested in your relationship history, or lack thereof,' he said with a gentleness to his voice that might have been a reproach.

She shook her head, unable to think anything approaching straight because of his proximity. 'I—there's nothing to tell.'

'I beg to differ. A twenty-four-year-old virgin is not exactly commonplace.'

She frowned. 'Gee, thanks.'

He shrugged. 'It's the truth. Would you prefer me to lie?'

'I would prefer not to talk about it.'

'Are you embarrassed? Ashamed?'

'No, and definitely not.'

'I am glad to hear it.'

'But it's personal.'

'You tricked me into taking your virginity.'

'I did not trick you!'

His nostrils flared but otherwise he didn't react. 'We were

both there. You had a chance to tell me; you didn't.' She couldn't refute that. He was right; they both knew what had happened that night. 'Don't I deserve some explanation?'

She closed her eyes and he moved closer, his body so strong and warm, and even though it was his questions filling her with uncertainty, he was also the antidote to that, so she wanted to lean against him and draw strength and courage from his powerful frame.

'Damn it, Adrastos,' she groaned, blinking up at him.

As if he understood what she needed, he closed every last skerrick of distance between them, his eyes half mocking, half sensual, when they held hers.

She chewed on her lower lip, shaking her head. 'It's not a big deal. I've just never had sex before.'

Standing so close, he now lifted a hand to tuck some hair behind her ear, the touch gentle and light, before falling to her shoulder. She almost jumped at the contact. 'You went to a co-ed school. Then university. You have a job, in an office, with, I presume, other people. You have lived away from the palace since you were eighteen years old. There has been no shortage of opportunities, and I am sure no shortage of willing and available men throwing themselves at your feet...'

'If they were, I didn't notice.'

'Oh, come on. You're not seriously saying you've never noticed how men look at you?'

Her pulse throbbed heavily in her veins. 'What are you talking about? You've never seen me with men.'

'But I've seen *you*, and I am a man. I know that any red-blooded male would find it hard to be around you and not wonder...'

'Don't say that.' She squeezed her eyes shut against his

compliment. It wasn't, couldn't be, true. Not of him, and not of anyone. 'I know you don't feel that way.'

'I understand that you're inexperienced but you were there the other night, weren't you? You saw the effect you have on me.'

'I thought it was a mistake?'

'It was a mistake to act on my attraction but that doesn't change how I felt.'

She shook her head, sipping her tea quickly, and burning her tongue. 'Damn it.' Her voice shook a little. She placed her tea down quickly. 'Just…stop.'

'I can't understand why this is an issue.'

'Because I'm not—I don't—I mean, I've been asked out. I'm just…'

His eyes had an intensity that made her realise he was paying very close attention, not just to her words but to what she wasn't saying as well. He moved his hand lower, down her arm, to her wrist. Goosebumps trailed in the wake of his touch.

'You've been asked out, and?'

And any of the dates she'd gone on had been abysmal failures, because she'd treated them almost like job interviews. It had been of little interest to her before her twenty-first, but after that kiss, something had shifted inside Poppy, had been completely closed off, so she couldn't think of a man without remembering the way Adrastos had made her feel.

'I've been busy, Adrastos,' she said, unevenly. 'Law school, my job—'

'Not so busy you couldn't date.'

'We weren't all born to be playboy princes,' she said with an attempt at dismissive humour she immediately regretted, because she knew he hated the moniker the press had given him. He wasn't a playboy. He was intelligent and focussed on his role as Prince; he just happened to see a lot of women in his downtime.

'Somewhere between my lifestyle and yours there is a happy medium,' he said, his voice gruff, so she couldn't help but tilt her face towards his, to see him better. Then wished she hadn't when their eyes locked and she felt that powerful, zapping connection.

Her heart stammered and she swallowed unevenly.

'When I kissed you,' he said slowly, moving his hand to the small of her back and pressing her forward lightly, so their bodies were melded. He smelled of cologne and Scotch. Her stomach rolled.

'Which time?' she asked, aiming for tart and instead sounding breathless.

'At your twenty-first birthday.' He moved his other hand to her cheek, his thumb brushing the corner of her mouth. She closed her eyes on an uneven breath.

'Yes?'

'Was that your first kiss?'

Her eyes flew open. She should have been prepared for the question. Mortification at her inexperience was making her toes crawl.

'Answer me,' he demanded, moving his thumb further over her lower lip, tracing the outline, and a thousand fireworks ignited in her bloodstream. She was mesmerised, quite possibly hypnotised by him. In that moment, she would have answered him anything, *given* him anything.

'Yes,' she muttered, gaze held locked to his.

'Am I the only man to ever kiss you, Poppy?'

Slowly, careful not to dislodge his thumb, because she liked being this close to him, loved being touched by him so intimately, she shifted her head once, in something like a nod. So what if he knew the truth? Did it really matter?

She couldn't interpret the emotions that swirled in the depths of his eyes, the colour shifting, his expression changing infinitesimally, but she felt a burst of something like restlessness, of need, something unfamiliar wrestling inside her.

'Poppy.' He said her name slowly, as though it were a thing of great wonder, and then, slowly, giving her plenty of time to anticipate his intention, and even more time to move if she wanted to, he lowered his head, his eyes probing hers with confusion and disbelief, until his hand fell away from her mouth a short moment before his lips claimed that space. The only man who'd ever kissed her and he kissed her now as though he wanted to read her, to understand her, with his mouth alone. Poppy whimpered as the beast inside her thrashed and turned and her body grew white-hot and she wanted, more than anything, to growl or cry. She couldn't understand why she felt the way she did, but the energy bursting through her veins was strong enough to power a small country.

She mumbled his name into Adrastos's mouth, and then he lifted her, placing her on the edge of the kitchen bench and standing between her legs, making him a better height to explore her mouth, his hands on her hips at first then falling behind her, bringing her forward, all the while he kissed her and she wanted to surrender completely, to lie back then and there and have him take her once more.

He was the only man she'd ever kissed. The only man she'd ever made love to, but the same could not be said for Adrastos. He slept with women all the time. None of this meant anything to him. He was very, very skilled at turning women's bones to mush, just like this. It was an art form for him, going through the motions, not special, not unique.

It was meaningless. Just as the other night had been.

If Poppy hadn't been a virgin, if someone hadn't snapped photos and sold them for a nice little pay day, they wouldn't be doing this.

He was just making the most of the situation, of having her there, and she was going along with it because she had no experience and even less self-control.

With a sharp groan, she pulled away from him, wiping her mouth with the back of her hand as though by erasing his kiss she could jolt herself out of the sensual fog.

'I'm not going to sleep with you just because we're sharing a room,' she said bravely, eyes clouded with uncertainty, but she tilted her chin to make that point.

Adrastos was also confused, she could see, but he rallied faster, concealing his emotions with far greater ease. 'That wasn't sex, Poppy, it was a kiss.'

Heat bloomed in her cheeks. What a perfect comment to make Poppy feel every bit as gauche and inexperienced as she was.

'Yes, well, I don't want you to do either,' she lied. 'Would you please step aside so I can get down?'

She couldn't meet his eyes.

The last thing she was expecting was Adrastos's gentle touch as he moved his hands back to her hips and lifted her off the bench, bringing her against his body until her feet were back on the kitchen floor.

The wild beast inside Poppy had stilled, was watching, waiting to see what would happen next.

'What is it?'

Of course he could tell something was wrong. One minute she'd been kissing him back as though her life depended on it and the next she was barely able to look at him.

'Nothing.' She shook her head. How could she explain

her strange, amorphous jealousy? Of the women he'd been with, of his confidence with women, of his skill...

At her birthday party, she'd wanted him in spite of all those things, perhaps because of them, but the intimacy of their new arrangement had bred a wariness in Poppy, and a warning, too. It would be impossible to relegate this experience with Adrastos to 'just another guy', as he would easily do with her, because she had no point of comparison, no other experience.

In Poppy's work, she dealt with injustice every day, she worked with people who'd been in situations of inherent unfairness and power imbalance, which made it easy for Poppy to identify that here. The idea of wanting him with her whole soul, and knowing that, for Adrastos, Poppy was just someone to keep his bed warm because they had to share a room, made it all the more imperative for Poppy to draw and maintain some boundaries, or else she'd lose herself in this entirely.

'I'm going to bed.' Her glare was an attempt at a warning, and nothing that could be construed as an invitation. 'Goodnight.'

CHAPTER SIX

SHE HAD SLEPT like a log, despite the tumult of the day and that moment in the kitchen. She'd passed out almost as soon as her head had hit the pillow, but then, at some point, she'd become aware of Adrastos beside her, and then Poppy had been wide awake, the beast in her chest doing laps, pacing around, desperate for Poppy to *do something*.

'Do you need a sleeping tablet?'

His voice broke through the silence and she flipped her head towards his without thinking—an act that brought their faces within a couple of inches. In the silver light of the night, his features were shadowed and somehow more impressive.

'Why?'

'You have been tossing and turning for hours. Are you always such an animated sleeper?'

'I wouldn't know,' she responded, squeezing her eyes shut in a very poor facsimile of sleep.

He sighed then was silent, his breathing rhythmic once more. Poppy turned onto her side and stared at the windows. Adrastos did not have a view of the rose gardens, like Eleanor and Poppy. His room overlooked the other side of the palace, a wooded area that was wild and ancient. As a boy, he used to go hunting in there, with his father and brother. Poppy knew this because Eleanor had told her with a sniff of disapproval as they'd researched animal welfare groups online and planned all the ways in which they'd outlaw hunting if ever they had the opportunity. They had been sixteen and idealistic.

In the darkness, Poppy could see the enormous trees silhouetted against the night sky, and her eyes chased the tops of the trees for a long time, her heart twisting, her mind gnarled and overactive, her every breath making her aware of the other occupant of this bed, his breaths, his nearness...

She groaned softly, then flipped onto her back, tapping her fingers on her stomach.

'I can't sleep,' she whispered, so quietly that if he was still asleep, he wouldn't have heard.

But his response was immediate. 'Evidently.'

'It's your fault. Everything's different. I feel weird.'

Another sigh.

'You are the one who suggested this.'

'I know.'

She frowned, looking at him again. Was he annoyed at her about that? She'd acted on instinct, terrified of losing this family that had taken her in when she'd been at her lowest ebb. But that had completely changed his life—at least for the next twelve nights. How did he feel about that?

'Turn onto your side.'

She hesitated. 'Why?'

'Because if you don't sleep, I won't be able to either and I have a full schedule tomorrow. Roll over.'

'What are you going to do?' she asked, but as she spoke she did as he'd said, flipping onto one side.

The bed dipped as he moved closer. Her heart almost gave out. 'Close your eyes.' His tone was hoarse. A moment later, his finger pressed to the centre of her back, pausing there a moment before moving in a slow, steady figure of eight. A shuddered breath fell from between her lips.

'Oh.'

'Keep your eyes closed.'

She did as he said, but with every swish of his finger, something shifted inside her, a growing bundle of awareness and need, so she wondered if she should tell him that his attempt to lull her was having quite the opposite effect. He was so sexy. So incredibly sexy. From the first moment she'd seen him, she'd been overpowered by his appeal, and it hit her now right between her solar plexus, so she had to fight an urge to roll over and face him, to pull him down to the mattress.

It was the last thought Poppy had before falling fast asleep, Adrastos's soothing touch at her back continuing for a long time afterwards, his hands roaming her body on autopilot until finally he realised what he was doing and stood, staring down at the sleeping woman with consternation before slipping from the room, needing space to clear his mind.

Poppy had come into his house as a fourteen-year-old and since then she'd been a regular fixture. Regular enough that any decent man would have considered her basically a sister.

But he'd never felt that for Poppy, he realised, as he stepped into the kitchen and leaned against the fridge. He'd fought those feelings tooth and nail, even as his family had embraced her and made her an unofficial member of their clan. He'd wondered, at the time, if it was loyalty to Nick, as though everyone else was trying to replace the boy who'd been lost with a stray girl, but that didn't quite seem right. He'd held her at arm's length, and now he wondered if *this* was why. Maybe he'd always known their chemistry had the power to burn him to the core. Maybe he'd always wanted to reserve the right to explore this...

He bit back a groan of his own because no matter how he felt about Poppy, to his family she was one of theirs. He shouldn't let this go any further. They both had to make it through their relationship pretence unscathed, emerging as 'friends' when she left the country, so his family would accept the break-up with a small degree of disappointment and move on.

But hell, if he didn't want to kiss her awake and make her his. He didn't know why she'd pulled back in the kitchen. It was as though something had flicked off inside her, and the wild, whimpering woman who had been dissolving into a puddle in his arms became instead a frightened animal. And just as he would with such a creature, he'd backed off immediately, knowing that space was needed to calm her down. His own desire though had been to lean forward and kiss her back to fever pitch, which he knew he could have done easily. Which he knew he could do now.

Just knowing that he was the only man to ever stir those feelings in her spoke to some kind of ancient, male part of his soul, a part he should probably have been ashamed of. Whatever had happened between them in the kitchen, Poppy was running from it. Out of fear? Lack of experience? Nervousness?

He moved to the bench where she'd sat and pressed a finger against it. Heat travelled from his fingertips to his shoulder then spread through his chest. He closed his eyes and breathed in; his lips almost tingled with the memories of kissing her, and then he frowned, because he couldn't remember the last time he'd given a woman this much space in his head, if ever.

For Adrastos, the end of this pretence, and Poppy's departure from Stomland, couldn't come soon enough.

Poppy couldn't help herself. The day after Christmas, while the royal family was at the hospital, she found herself watching the coverage on the national station, and when the reporters approached the Aetos family outside the hospital, almost all the questions were about Adrastos's love life. It was quite remarkable how he tolerated the invasive remarks without flinching, answering with a practised deflection, turning attention back to the hospital whenever he could. It was a masterclass in PR.

Nonetheless, it was apparent to Poppy that her own life was going to be altered by this.

Even after their purported break-up, there'd probably continue to be a level of interest surrounding her that might even make it difficult to tackle her work in the usual way. Should she at least make contact with the HR department of her law firm, to explain the situation?

To explain *what*? she thought with a grimace. To broaden this bloody lie? To more people?

She was under no obligation to disclose personal details to her work. Surely they'd have seen the reports like every other person in the world. It wouldn't impact her job performance—she wouldn't let it—so there was no problem there. But she didn't relish the idea of going about her business with a paparazzi entourage.

Surely it would only take a week or so, after they broke up, before the press bored of her. The interest would be in Adrastos, and his next quarry. He wouldn't be single long. Then that woman would become the object of their scrutiny.

Just the thought made Poppy's heart drop to her toes. She turned off the TV and wandered through the palace, not to

Adrastos's room, but to her own. She needed a little space and clarity, and somehow the familiar outlook of the rose garden would, she hoped, calm her fluttering mind and erratic, fast-moving pulse.

It was like stepping back in time. Six weeks ago she'd been here, but she felt *different* from that Poppy. More awakened and alive. On the night of her twenty-fourth birthday, something had happened to her, and even though they were living a lie, she wasn't sure if she would change anything about this adventure. Because it was an adventure to pretend to be Adrastos's girlfriend. As if riding on a roller coaster, she felt as though she were zipping in one direction after the other the entire time, never sure what to expect.

But this was the room that centred her. She had been coming here for a decade—it was a home to Poppy. She moved to the windowsill, staring out at the beautiful garden, memories shifting through her mind.

It was lucky she'd been at the palace for a week already, on that first trip, before Adrastos had come back from military college. In that one week, she'd had a chance to fall in love with Eleanor, Clementine and Alexander. The latter had proven a balm to her broken heart with all the stories he'd told of her parents, almost making them come back to life for a grieving Poppy. Clementine had held her tight each evening, as Poppy had drunk a sweetened milk, and Eleanor had become her best friend almost instantly. They'd been so similar, like sisters separated at birth, they always joked.

They'd settled into a routine that was everything Poppy had needed. For the first time since her parents' deaths, she'd felt as though she could breathe again.

And then, just like that, Adrastos had returned.

She'd known he was coming, because his arrival had been spoken of, but she'd presumed in the older brother she'd find another family member like the three she'd come to know and love. Instead, Adrastos had exploded like a tropical storm, so powerful and big, so different, instantly changing the atmosphere, charging it with an electrical current.

He was unlike anyone Poppy had ever met.

Her brow furrowed.

She'd been awestruck, yes, but it was something else. Something more.

Without her knowledge or consent, so much of her mind had begun to focus on him. She began to wonder about him, to think about him even when he wasn't around. She was too self-conscious to ask Eleanor the million questions burning through her, and, in fact, instinctively knew she should hide her feelings from her friend. It felt illicit to fantasise about her best friend's brother, but she couldn't stop.

He never came back for long.

'He's always busy,' Clementine had said one day, a wistful smile on her beautiful face.

Poppy had felt the same wistfulness in her heart.

From that first visit onwards, she was on tenterhooks, waiting for him. Listening for him.

Those brief flashes of time, in which Adrastos would arrive and become a complete centre of gravity. When he wasn't at the palace, there was no shortage of information online about Prince Adrastos. It was a double-edged sword to search his name because so many of the stories made her heart sink.

For as long as she'd known of Adrastos, there'd been speculation about his love life. Speculation about his girlfriends, whether this one might be 'the one', whether a royal engagement was in the offing. At the time, she'd told herself that the sense of irritation she felt about those stories was because she knew how important it was to Clementine and

Alexander that Adrastos settle down. She told herself it was loyalty to them, and their wishes. But what if, even then, it had been more? What if even as a teenager, that overwhelming awe she'd felt for Adrastos was actually something far more mature?

She sighed heavily, turned away from the window and the rose garden and strode out of her room, back into the wide, marbled corridor, in the direction of the suite she was sharing with Adrastos.

She'd manoeuvred this; all of it. Not intentionally: she would have died rather than have the whole world know something so intimate as the fact she'd slept with Adrastos. But if Poppy hadn't approached Adrastos at the party, it wouldn't have happened. If she hadn't dug her way out of Clementine's disapproval by making up a pretend relationship, then this situation would have been avoided. But she'd done both those things, and now she had to act her heart out to convince everyone this was the real deal. For the sake of her relationship with the entire family, they had to pull this off.

CHAPTER SEVEN

'Oh!'

She started as he entered, so it occurred to Adrastos, belatedly, that he should probably have knocked. While technically it was his room, they weren't really a couple, and it was natural that Poppy should expect some privacy during this twelve-day sojourn.

Not that it had been anything like a sojourn, and it had only just begun.

Exhaustion seeped through Adrastos—an unfamiliar emotion for a man who could run on air.

'Did I disturb you?' he asked, unable to stop his eyes from slowly roaming her body, from the top of her darkly shining hair to her slender shoulders and generous breasts, lower to her neat waist and curved hips, slim legs, dainty feet. His gut tightened in unwelcome response. She wore a pair of jeans and a long-sleeved T-shirt, fitted and a little too short, so it revealed just the smallest hint of midriff, reminding him of how soft her skin had been, like a rose petal. That did very little to help the tightening of his body.

'I wasn't expecting you,' she said with a murmur, putting down an iPad and turning to face him. 'I was just catching up on some work.'

That interested him—Poppy worked hard, she always had. And now, she'd earned a promotion that would take her to the place where human rights law was, largely, written. She had every right to be proud of that.

He moved past Poppy even as his body was doing its best to drag him to her, into the kitchen, where he opened the fridge and removed a bottle of mineral water. He held one in her direction.

She shook her head. 'I have tea, thank you.'

'I thought you were on holiday?'

'I am, technically. But my to-do list is about this high.' She waved one hand way above her head. 'I figured I could get a jump on it during my spare time. How was the hospital?'

The conversation change was swift and frustrating, because he found he had more questions about her work, her life. He was curious as to how she filled her days, now that it was abundantly clear she had no social life.

'Fine,' he said, frowning. 'Difficult.' The admission surprised Adrastos. It was something he hadn't ever remarked even to his parents, despite the fact they did this every year.

Poppy's face crumpled a little with a soft sympathy. She was very beautiful. As a teenager, there'd been something unsettling about her. Those huge brown eyes, so big they could almost have been digitally enhanced, full, curving lips, and a watchful nature that had made him feel uncomfortable and somehow wrong—a feeling Adrastos had never otherwise felt. As she'd grown up, her face had changed. She'd grown into her features, but the watchfulness was still there, that same sense that Poppy saw far more than anyone else, that she processed everything carefully before passing judgment.

'It must bring back a lot of memories.'

He tightened his grip on the mineral water. A perfect image of Nicholas, smiling, came to Adrastos and his throat was suddenly lined with razor blades. 'I've made plans for us tonight.'

She blinked at him, the answer obviously the last thing she was expecting.

'Oh.' She looked down at her iPad, face averted for far longer than it took to press the off button, so he knew she was taking a moment to conceal her emotions. Frustration chomped through him.

'Unless that's a problem?' His tone was sharper than he'd intended, but he didn't like how clearly she understood him, nor how quickly he'd confided in her. Even that one word—*difficult*—had been too much.

'I—well, why?'

'Why?'

'Why should we go out? Isn't the point of this to convince your parents and sister we're the real deal?'

'And ask yourself this: would I really expect any girlfriend of mine to sit around the palace for twelve days straight, without a little fun thrown in?'

'But I'm not any girlfriend,' Poppy pointed out. 'I'm like family to your family. I don't mind if we stay here the whole time.'

'Well, I do. It doesn't ring true and my parents will see that.'

She pulled her lips to the side, considering that.

'So where would we go?'

'Does it matter?'

She scrunched her face. 'I'm a planner.'

'So much of a planner that you've hesitated your way out of a sex life?'

She flinched and he regretted the comment—which hadn't been intended cruelly. He was simply struggling—

still—to understand how she'd missed such an important part of her development.

'You don't know what you're talking about.'

'So enlighten me.'

'No.'

He arched a brow. 'You do realise that by turning yourself into a challenge, you're making me want to win?'

He saw the way she shivered, her eyes almost pleading with his. 'There's nothing to win. My love life is none of your business.'

Frustration arced through him, but it wasn't necessary to push this now. They had more than enough time together to explore the matter at his leisure. 'Can you be ready in an hour?'

Poppy stared at him with obvious consternation. 'Are you serious?'

'Of course.'

She hesitated, and he could see that she was torn between agreeing and fighting. Eventually, common sense won out.

'Fine,' she murmured. 'But only in the service of this ruse.'

He moved closer to Poppy, eyes sparking with hers, relishing this chance to be close to her, even just for a moment. 'Exactly as it should be, *deliciae*.'

He pressed a kiss to the tip of her nose, then, unsatisfied with such a pointless, insufficient contact, yanked Poppy hard against his body and took her mouth, claiming it with all the desperate, angry, sad, needy emotions that had been pummelling him all day. Suddenly, he saw the chasm of pain in his chest, saw it as it always was: a part of him. But he saw an antidote, a solution: Poppy. When he kissed her, that pain became almost bearable, and for a moment, he forgot. Forgot that he was only the spare. That none of this should have been his. Forgot that he was walking through life in another man's shoes, forgot the survivor guilt that dogged him mercilessly, so that he was simply a man, making love to a woman.

'Adrastos,' she groaned into his mouth, lifting one leg and wrapping it around his hips, desperately trying to be closer to him so he felt her groan deep in his soul because what he wanted, more than anything, was to strip her naked and finish what they'd started last night. He pushed his hands into her hair, pulling it from the messy bun she'd scraped it into, drawing her head back so he could kiss her more, so he could devour her, kissing her until she was almost whimpering and she was grinding her hips in a rhythm that spoke of hunger and need, wanting him to take her, offering herself to him as much now as she had that night.

It terrified him, how much he wanted her. How much he wanted to forget her part in his family, how much he wanted to remove her from his family so she was just *his*. Was this what had stopped her last night? Had she also felt some kind of shock at the strength of their connection?

As though he'd been burned, he pulled away from her quickly, doing his best to assume a cynical expression. 'You definitely look the part now.'

Her eyes were hooded, her face flushed, her lips swollen from where he'd been sucking and pressing them, her body trembling, her nipples taut through the flimsy cotton of her shirt. He took in the picture of her and committed it to memory because she was the most beautiful and sexy woman he'd ever seen. But her eyes blinked in confusion and then hurt and shame and he felt the strangest feeling in the pit of his stomach, his own sense of remorse.

He spun away from her only so he could move to the door. 'One hour, Poppy. I'll be back soon.'

He left the room without another word. He was too busy replaying what had just happened and wondering if he would ever be able to be alone with Poppy without losing control completely.

She'd chosen a dress that was conservative and simple, and yet somehow, perhaps because of the way Adrastos had kissed her not an hour earlier, Poppy felt distinctly…sexy. She stared at her reflection with a deep frown, her eyes taking in the image she saw in the mirror with more than a little uncertainty. She'd gone to extra effort tonight, some feminine pride insisting she really looked the part of Adrastos's girlfriend.

The dress was beautiful—bought for a film premiere a couple of years ago and stored here at the palace, with all of her most exquisite clothing. It was burgundy in colour, with a halter neck that showed off Poppy's toned arms, fitted all the way to the knees, and cinched at the waist with a belt in a matching material but with a slight pattern. The shoes were black and sky-high—fortunately, Poppy was comfortable in heels. For jewellery, Poppy had chosen a pair of pearl earrings that Clementine had given her for her sixteenth birthday.

'Your mother was with me when I got these,' Clementine had offered at the time, with a sad smile. 'In Western Australia, we visited the most exquisite pearl property on the north coast. It was a wonderful holiday, for all of us. We both bought a pair, you know. I don't know where your mother's went, but I thought you should have these. I hope you like them, Poppy darling. I know she'd be thrilled for you to wear them.'

Poppy did wear them, but only rarely, because they were so special to her, she couldn't bear to think of anything happening to them. But when she needed a little extra kick of confidence, to feel that her mother *and* fairy godmother were watching over her, the earrings were a must. And tonight definitely constituted a night for extra confidence.

Ten minutes before the hour was up, when Poppy conceded that yes, she was ready, a knock sounded at the door. Well, that was better than having him barge in. She crossed the room a little unsteadily.

This was all for show, she reminded herself, pulling the door inwards, the sharp barb she'd prepared freezing when she saw Eleanor on the other side.

'Ellie!' The relief was enormous. She threw her arms around her best friend and almost cried with relief.

Ellie laughed. 'Goodness, are you okay?'

'Yes, I'm fine. I just—I'm glad to see you.'

Eleanor pulled back a little, studying Poppy thoughtfully. 'I understand you have a date with my brother.'

Poppy bit down on her lower lip, nodding. Oh, how she hated the necessity of this lie.

'Well, that's fine, but first of all, come with me.'

'Oh.' Poppy looked over her shoulder. 'He'll be here any minute—'

'Yes, I know. I heard him making the arrangements and, believe me when I tell you, it will do Adrastos the world of good to be kept waiting.' Eleanor winked. *'Trust me,'* she said, conspiratorially. 'This is for his own good—and yours too.'

Poppy *did* trust Eleanor, and when it came to matters of the heart, there was no questioning who had more experience. 'Okay.' Poppy smiled almost her first real smile all day. 'Where are we going?'

Ten minutes later, they were ensconced in the family's favourite living room, with a beautiful Christmas tree twinkling in the flames cast by the fire, a glass of ice-cold champagne in each woman's hand, and the awkwardness of the last few days erased completely by the old, familiar routines that they'd spent a decade establishing.

They talked about Poppy's next case, and Eleanor's love life, and skirted around the issue of the hospital visit, which Poppy knew was always difficult for Eleanor as well, just as Adrastos had admitted it was for him. They talked non-stop, so that before Poppy realised it half an hour had passed and she'd finished her champagne. Eleanor had just left the room to top up their glasses when Adrastos stalked in, expression like thunder.

'I thought I asked you to wait in my room?'

Poppy's eyes flared wide and she was immediately enraged by his tone. 'Do you really think you have any right to speak to me like that, Your Highness?' she asked in a hushed whisper, standing and moving towards him with more than a spark of anger.

'We had a deal, remember?'

'No, we had a "date".' She used air quotation marks with some enjoyment. 'And you didn't do me the decency of consulting me before making plans, so you could have had no idea if I was already busy or not,' she pointed out. 'And I was.' The champagne had gone just a little to her head already.

'What plans?' he asked, and then, as if seeing her for the first time, he devoured her with his eyes, in that slow yet impatient way he had, as if he needed to visually inspect every single inch of her.

'That would be me,' Eleanor called from across the room, her smile the exact kind one sibling could reserve for the other, the smile of someone who was enjoying needling an older brother just a little too much.

Adrastos glowered.

'I'm sorry, Adrastos. Blame me. I've hardly seen Poppy since you arrived.'

'We all had lunch together earlier,' Adrastos pointed out, somehow extinguishing his temper—or the appearance of it—almost immediately.

'I mean, *just* Poppy and me.'

A muscle jerked in his jaw. 'I see. Have you had enough time together?'

'No,' Eleanor responded quickly, even as Poppy was already moving to collect her handbag. 'Now I'd like to spend time with both of you. Please, take a seat.'

Poppy laughed softly. 'Ellie, you're making it sound like an interview.'

'I'm curious,' she said with a lift of her shoulders. 'Indulge me.'

Poppy threw Adrastos a look, wanting him to whisk them away, but his features now bore a mask of resignation. He moved to a small sofa, took a seat then gestured with his head for Poppy to take the space beside him. Only it was *not* a large sofa at all and Adrastos, with his bulky macho warrior's frame, took up considerably more than half of it, meaning it was almost impossible to imagine being able to squeeze herself into the seat without touching him.

But the alternative was to choose a different seat and, given that they were trying to convince Eleanor their relationship was the real deal, Poppy had no option but to go and sit beside Adrastos. She perched her bottom on the edge of the cushions. Adrastos leaned forward, pressing a kiss to her exposed shoulder, whispering so that only she could hear, 'Relax.'

Not likely.

And made almost impossible when he brought an arm to

her shoulders and pulled her back a little, positioning her against his body, his arm draped with casual possession around, his fingers grazing the top of her breast so her whole body was an electrical live wire. She drew in a shuddering breath and turned to face him. Eleanor was distracted by the music, changing from an upbeat Christmas song to a slower classic, so Poppy took advantage of that and leaned towards Adrastos, whispering, 'What are you doing?'

'You want to play games? I'm going to play them right back.'

His smile was wolfish and Poppy's body lifted with goosebumps. She didn't doubt him. 'What games?'

'Keeping me waiting?'

She bit down on her lip, eyes shifting betrayingly to Eleanor.

'Ah,' he murmured, moving his lips closer to her shoulder. 'Let me guess. It was my sister's idea.'

Loyalty kept Poppy quiet. She sniffed slightly and looked away, but Adrastos was not an easy man to ignore.

He moved his body so it almost engulfed hers, so big and broad was he, and Poppy couldn't breathe without tasting him and smelling him and feeling him in every single one of her senses.

'So.' Eleanor looked up from her phone and took a seat opposite, looking relaxed except for the glint in her eye. 'Tell me about this.' She gestured from one to the other.

'I—' Poppy faltered, her heart dropping. Oh, how she hated lying! To anyone, but especially Eleanor. Why, oh, why had she ever thought a fake relationship was a good idea?

'This?' Adrastos repeated, moving his fingers ever so slightly, so Poppy couldn't help but be aware of the building of tension, the frisson of awareness rocketing through

her. 'It's a relationship, Eleanor. You might have heard of
the concept? When two people decide they'd like to get to
know one another better, in a romantic sense, and commit
to going on a series of dates?'

'I know you're more than familiar with the concept,' Eleanor volleyed back witheringly, with no idea of how hurtful that observation would have been to Poppy were this
relationship genuine. 'I mean, specifically, you two. How
did it happen?'

He sighed. 'Is this a "protective best friend" thing? Do
you need me to assure you I'm not going to hurt Poppy?'

'That would be good,' Eleanor agreed with an overly
sweet smile as a palace staffer appeared with a trolley of
drinks and food.

'Ellie,' Poppy interjected, but again, Adrastos spoke
sooner, once they were alone.

'I have no intention of hurting Poppy.'

'I suppose that's something.'

'What more would you like, little sister?'

'I want to understand how two people who almost seem
to have made an art form of *avoiding* one another have decided to date.'

'People grow and change,' Poppy said carefully. 'We're
just dating. It's not serious.'

'It's serious,' Eleanor disagreed. 'When you both come
and stay here. When you go out on dates looking like this.'
Ellie gestured to Poppy.

'What do I look like?'

'Beautiful, of course,' Eleanor supplied quickly. 'But you
also look...'

'Yes?' Adrastos's voice held more than a hint of warning.

'Like you're being groomed for a specific role.'

Poppy's eyes widened. 'What do you mean?'

'You look like a princess-in-waiting, Pops. I know you might not be taking this seriously yet, but you should be aware that everyone else will be.'

'Everyone else will have to wait for an official announcement before they start ordering their wedding attire,' Adrastos said quietly.

Poppy wanted to shake him. There was no 'waiting for an announcement'. There would be no announcement, no wedding.

'Maybe she's right.' Poppy turned in the seat, so she was facing only Adrastos, and suddenly it was just the two of them in the room. She lifted a hand to his chest, pressing it there, fingers splayed wide, mind racing. 'Maybe this is too public. Too much, too soon.'

'It's not.'

'But what if it is?'

He pressed a hand over hers and moved his face closer to hers. 'Because I've anticipated that. There will be very little press intrusion into our night, Poppy. You must relax.'

But how could she? Everything seemed to be spinning completely out of control. As if he understood that she was on the precipice of a panic attack, he leaned forward and kissed her slowly, gently, keeping her hand between them, his own hand stroking hers, just as his mouth moved over hers. 'Relax,' he murmured, and she pulled back a little, somehow dredging up a smile, and it was not a smile for Eleanor's benefit, but one that came to her naturally.

'Okay.' She realised Ellie wasn't the only Aetos she trusted. He reached across and took the champagne flute from her spare hand, placing it on his side table, then turned to face his sister. Eleanor was watching them with unashamed interest.

'We're going to leave now, Eleanor.'

The Princess was very still for a moment and then finally nodded. 'I can see that.'

Poppy wondered at the tone in her best friend's voice. There was something there she didn't like. Sadness?

'Do you want to come with us?' Poppy heard herself offer, so the hand of Adrastos's that was holding hers squeezed a little tighter.

Eleanor laughed and shook her head, suddenly herself again. 'I can just imagine how my big brother would enjoy that. No, thank you. I'll be your third wheel another time. Go, have fun.' She turned to Adrastos. 'Take care of her.'

'I intend to.'

CHAPTER EIGHT

THE CAR PULLED out from the palace and, as expected, flash-bulbs erupted. Despite his having made the arrangements to assure the utmost secrecy, the palace was being watched even more closely than normal in light of the 'news' of Adrastos's latest fling. Of their own volition, his eyes slid across to Poppy, in the seat beside him, her lips compressed, her hands clasped tight in her lap.

'This is not supposed to feel like torture.'

'It doesn't,' she reacted quickly, apology in the little grimace she offered him. 'It's just...a little overwhelming.'

His hands tightened on the wheel.

Of course it would seem overwhelming to Poppy. She had no experience with dating anyone, let alone someone who brought this level of scrutiny. In the rear-vision mirror, he saw a motorbike give chase and expelled a rough sound of impatience, then quickly muted it when he noticed Poppy's flinch.

'You get used to it.' It was a throwaway comment he immediately regretted, because it somehow implied he wanted *her* to get used to it, which might almost suggest he wanted her to stick around, beyond the terms of their fake relationship, and of course he didn't. Adrastos couldn't wait to get through this and find a satisfying way to 'end it' for his family's benefit, so he could get back to his real life.

And go back to only seeing Poppy a couple of times a year, he tacked on mentally, for good measure, the vow an important one to make to himself.

Poppy turned in the seat, angling to face him, and all he could focus on was her slender thighs, exposed by the way her dress had crept up as she'd taken her seat. 'Do you?'

Her eyes pinned him in place earnestly. He forced himself to keep his attention on the road. 'Eventually.' The word was given as a grudging concession to the fact it had taken him quite some time to accept this level of scrutiny. And he certainly didn't enjoy it.

'Do you mind?'

'I accept it comes with the position.'

She frowned. 'But you don't like it?'

'Who would like it?' He responded quickly, turning the car down a side street, away from the embassies that were in the suburbs closest to the palace, leading them to a fashionable precinct with streets of restaurants.

'Lots of people, I suppose,' she said with a lift of those incredible shoulders. He really should have used a chauffeur but, for some reason, he'd railed against that. With Poppy, he wanted to be completely in charge. He wanted to call the shots, to run the show. He wanted to be answerable for everything that happened between them. Besides, it was harder to speak frankly with the presence of staff, and he liked being honest and open with her. As she was basically a member of his family, he could trust her implicitly. 'Celebrity has become a level of attainment in and of itself.'

He grunted his agreement with that, but it was something Adrastos had never personally felt. 'There are many good things about the position of privilege I occupy. Having my every waking move dissected by the press is not one of them.'

'Of course not.'

'You must have experienced this with Eleanor.'

'It's different. She isn't followed like you are.'

'For that, I am supremely grateful.'

'She lives a mostly normal life,' Poppy continued thoughtfully. 'I mean, there are photographers. There's interest in her, of course. She's adored. And reported on. But not to this extent. When we were at university, we were just like any other eighteen-year-olds.'

'I'm sure there are a great many secrets you could tell me about my sister,' he said, surprising them both with a grin.

Poppy blinked, a study in wide-eyed innocence. 'You must know I could never tell you anything that Ellie had told me in confidence.'

The fact she thought he'd even ask was one of the strongest indictments of his character he'd ever known. He focussed on the road. 'I would never ask you to.'

She breathed out. 'Sorry. I'm nervous.'

'You don't have to be. I'm not really a big bad wolf.'

'Aren't you?' she asked, then pressed a hand to her lips. 'I'm sorry again. That just came out. Sometimes, when I'm with you, I find it just far too easy to say the wrong thing.'

'Why is it the wrong thing, if it's what you really think?'

'Well, we can have many thoughts,' she said after a beat. 'But not all of them reflect how we truly feel.'

'A fascinating comment, Poppy. I'm tempted to analyse that further and ask how you really feel about me.'

He turned to face her, but Poppy had grown pale. He was pushing her too far, teasing her. Reaching out, he curved his fingers over her knee and she startled. Yes, he was glad no chauffeur was around to witness this.

'Hey.' If they weren't being followed by a pesky photographer on a bike, he'd have been tempted to pull over and kiss all these nerves away. 'I promise, this is going to be fun. I know this isn't real, but, for tonight, let's pretend we're actually dating. I think we could both enjoy that, hmm?'

That was the problem! If Poppy wasn't very, very careful, the lines between reality and make-believe would get woefully blurred and she'd wake up half in danger of believing that Adrastos actually cared for her.

With a heart rate that wouldn't slow, she waited as Adrastos pulled the car into the sweeping drive of a five-star hotel in the city centre. She'd heard of it, but never been.

'A hotel?'

'The bar,' he said with a nod. 'Come with me.' He stepped out of his side of the car at the same time a hotel valet opened the door to hers. It was only as she exited that Poppy became aware of the security presence—four men emerging from a car behind them—and then, several motorbikes with paparazzi. But Adrastos was right there, a reassuring arm around her waist drawing her close to his side so she forgot about everything and everyone and was conscious only of how well she fitted against him, of how warm and masculine he was, how hard and strong. His arm was like a clamp, his body a brick wall, and she was water, melting and liquid, filling in the gaps.

Once they stepped into the foyer, the paparazzi disappeared—no one followed them inside except for his security guards, who travelled up in the lift with them. Even then, Poppy was barely aware of their presence, because once inside the lift Adrastos seemed so much bigger and stronger, his body wrapping around her, if not physically, at least in terms of presence.

The doors pinged open and the security guards stepped out, two on either side, forming a passage for them to exit.

But instead of leaving, Adrastos turned his body, shielding Poppy from the view of the bar.

'Adrastos?' She blinked up at him, her mouth as dry as the desert. He was looking at her in a way that was now familiar to Poppy. She bit down on her lip, blinking up at him. 'You're going to kiss me again, aren't you?'

'Yes.'

'Why?'

'You look to need it.'

'I'm not sure if that's true.'

'But, Poppy, haven't we established I'm the expert on all things kissing?'

She rolled her eyes. 'You know, your ego is—' She didn't get a chance to finish the sentence. He kissed her and she smiled, because he was right. She had needed it, and being kissed by him like this, being held by him, was enough to burn her soul to the ground in the best possible way.

The bar was so super exclusive that paparazzi access was forbidden, and the clientele was high-profile enough to assure a degree of anonymity. Though, no, Poppy reflected, leaning back in their booth seat. Anonymity was not quite the right word. Adrastos could never truly be anonymous. He was recognisable to anyone in the world who didn't live under a rock, and even here, in a bar crammed full of billionaires, celebrities and nobility, there was Adrastos, a wholly different species.

Poppy tried not to focus on how many women ogled him.

Nor to think about how many of these women he'd ogled back. Or more.

But it was impossible to blot those thoughts, impossible not to reflect on how active his love life had been, nor to think about how active it would be again after this.

So even though they sat in a private booth with exquisite views over the city, and Adrastos did an excellent job of acting as though she were the only woman in the entire world, Poppy couldn't help folding a little in on herself as the night went on.

He ordered a beer and she a champagne, and her nerves eased slightly, but it just took the passing by of one glamorous woman for Poppy to be reminded of the fact she didn't belong here. She wasn't a part of Adrastos's world.

'Tell me about your work,' he commanded, fingers trailing her shoulder then drawing circles, reminding her of the way he'd eased her to sleep the night before. She shivered, a tingle of pleasure, of warmth and awareness, then cleared her throat, trying to focus.

'My work can be a depressing topic.'

He dipped his head. 'Yet you do it anyway.'

'Someone's got to.'

'Why you?'

'You think I should be doing something else?'

He narrowed his gaze. 'I didn't say that.'

'I always wanted to practise law. I wasn't sure until I started studying what I'd specialise in, but the truth is human rights are so important and as we make our way through the twenty-first century, I'm shocked by the erosion of rights in so many parts of the world. It makes my skin crawl to think how some people live.'

'So you're driven by a desire to fix the world?' he asked, voice light, even when his eyes were stripping away her layers, peeling right into the centre of her being.

'It's sure not the salary,' she said with a wry grimace.

He lifted a brow.

'I'm employed by a not-for-profit organisation. If I was looking to make my fortune, I'd have gone into commercial litigation, but working for oligarchs who want to make themselves richer by selling boats to other billionaires isn't how I see myself spending my days.'

'And you work long hours,' he said, neatly bringing the conversation back to what she suspected he really wanted to discuss—her lack of a sex life.

She sipped her champagne. 'Yes.' She did. Not because she always had to, but because it was one way to avoid entanglements. 'I like to be good at what I do.'

'Why do I suspect you're excellent at it?'

Her eyes widened. 'I don't know,' she said with a shake of her head.

'Poppy?'

She stared at him; she was drowning.

'There must be a reason,' he said after a beat, his meaning clear despite the apparent change of subject. 'Someone broke your heart?'

She took another sip of her champagne, almost choking. 'No. Never. Really, I'm very boring, Adrastos.'

He bit back whatever he'd been about to say. 'That's not how I would describe you.'

Beneath the table, she pressed a hand to his thigh. 'Really, you don't have to do this.'

'Do what?'

'Flatter me.' She blinked away from him, chagrined by this conversation. '*Pretend*, when it's just the two of us.'

'Didn't we agree we'd both pretend tonight?'

'Yes, but the flattery, it's just not necessary. I know the kind of women you're usually with. I know I'm not like them.'

His eyes skimmed her face. 'You're interested in the women I date?'

She rolled her eyes and hoped her demurral would sound

convincing. 'No.' She ignored his sceptical look. 'I just mean I've seen stuff. Stories. Over the years. I know you date a certain type of woman, and I'm not it.'

'In what way?'

She shook her head. 'We shouldn't do this.'

'Why not? I'm interested in what you think of my love life.'

'Well, for a start, I wouldn't call it a love life so much as a sex life,' she responded quickly, then wished she hadn't when she felt him pull back a little.

'Don't stop,' he said, reaching for his beer and having a drink.

His eyes narrowed, and he moved closer, so their bodies were touching beneath the table and Poppy was grateful for the linen cloth, because if any guest did decide to take a photo with their phone, the image would be every bit as intimate as the photos taken on the night of her birthday, if not more so.

'Not that I give this matter much thought,' she said a little unevenly, her body surging with attraction so she was far too aware of him on a cellular level to think clearly.

'Too busy saving the world?'

'Something like that,' she lied. Of course she'd thought about his hectic sex life—how could she not, when she knew it was a source of pain for Eleanor and Clementine? Loyalty had made her cross with Adrastos. She went to pull her legs away from him, but beneath the table, his hand curved over her thigh, holding her still.

'Why did you want to sleep with me?'

The question caught something in Poppy's throat. Her eyes flew to Adrastos's and she tried desperately to think of an answer.

'Don't lie to me,' he said quietly. 'I want to understand.'

She opened her mouth then slammed it shut. She supposed it wasn't an unreasonable question. After all, she'd somewhat blindsided him with her virginity. 'I didn't plan for that to happen,' she muttered.

'No, but once it did, you could have pulled back.'

'You were there. You know how you made me feel.'

'You let me kiss you, when no other man has come close.'

Poppy hadn't intended to talk to Adrastos about this, but sitting so close, touching beneath the table, she was hypnotised by him, just as always.

'I've thought about that, over the years,' she said, softly, her lashes dark fans against her soft, milky skin, her attention focussed on the past so she didn't notice the intensity of Adrastos's stare. 'I mean, I'm so out of step.' She shrugged self-consciously. 'Ellie, our other friends, they all went through the normal teenage stuff, and I just…didn't. I never had a crush,' she said breathlessly, ignoring the feeling beneath her ribs, the heat emanating from Adrastos, the pulsing in the back of her brain making her wonder if maybe that wasn't true, if maybe she'd had a crush on him all along. She pushed the thought aside because it was too difficult to contemplate and things between them were complicated enough. 'I knew I wanted to study law. I needed good grades, so I studied hard.' Her eyes moved to Adrastos thoughtfully. 'My parents praised me for my grades, you know. They were so proud of me; I didn't want to let them down. It's silly, isn't it? I mean, they aren't here any more, but I still felt—'

'It's not silly,' he demurred. 'Not to me.'

Her eyes met his and something strange crackled in the air between them. Was he quick to agree because of his own feelings of loss and grief?

'But it was more than just being studious.' She inhaled

softly, tried to find the words for her thoughts, then shook her head. 'You're going to think it's childish.'

'Try me.'

'Well, I was fourteen when they—when I lost them—and my view of their relationship, of all relationships, is I suppose a little stuck in time. When they died, I saw them as these most perfect people, as a perfect couple. They were so happy, so in love. I'm sure that there were times they argued, that there was more nuance to their relationship. As I've got older, I've learned that all relationships take work, that people can't always be perfect and happy and life isn't completely rosy. But what I saw then? It was like a fairy tale.' She sighed again. 'And I guess, somewhere in the back of my mind, I unconsciously decided that that's what all relationships *should* be like.' She lifted her shoulders. 'That if you can't love someone as my parents loved each other, what's the point?'

He frowned, but at least he didn't criticise that thought, nor did he argue with her.

'I imagine your parents didn't love each other like that right from the start,' he pointed out after a brief, thoughtful pause. 'That kind of connection grows with time. Did it occur to you that in order to share that love, you'd need to start with a date? A friendship that will grow over weeks and months?'

'Speaking from experience?' She couldn't help probing.

His smile was tight, almost dismissive. 'We're talking about you right now.'

She lifted her eyes to his and blinked away, almost too embarrassed to say anything else. But having started down the path of baring her soul, she wasn't inclined now to stop. 'It's more than just wanting a perfect relationship,' she said, pulling her lips to the side, lost in thought. 'There's also a question of…chemistry.'

He lifted a brow.

'You know, I guess I just haven't felt it that often.' She didn't want to admit she'd never felt it with anyone but him. 'Even as a teenager.'

Perhaps he had questions. In fact, she was sure he did. But Adrastos, always in control, bided his time. 'That sounds like the opposite of my teenage experience,' he said with a half-grimace, so she couldn't help responding with a smile.

'When hormones ruled your every move?'

'I would like to think I still showed them who was boss, but that would be a lie,' he said with a shake of his head. 'I think I could have found chemistry with a lamp post…'

She laughed, even as a warning bell sounded in her mind. His words reinforced why she had to keep her focus about this, why she had to remember that, for Adrastos, she was just like any other woman.

And for you? a voice in her head demanded, even as Poppy shied away from answering the question.

'I'm curious, though, Poppy,' he said, leaning closer and almost kissing the words against the flesh just beneath her ear. It was so sensitive, she trembled. 'You still haven't answered my question. Why did you decide to sleep with me?'

Her eyes flared wide and her heart twisted in on itself. 'I—' She bit down on her lower lip. 'Wanted to,' she said, after a beat.

'To lose your virginity,' he murmured, lifting his head just far enough so their eyes could meet. 'And you thought someone like me, someone who sees sex as an inconsequential act, would be the easiest solution?'

It wasn't accurate, not really. She hadn't expected that night to mean anything to him, but that wasn't why she'd chosen Adrastos, and having him believe that sat strangely in her gut. And yet, she didn't correct him. Some ancient self-preservation technique had her shrugging, almost as if in agreement.

'I don't know if I really thought it through,' she said, finally, brushing the subject away with an overbright smile. 'It happened and, unlike you, I don't regret it.'

CHAPTER NINE

BUT HE DIDN'T regret it either. He could think something was a mistake without wishing it hadn't happened. It was a technicality, but an important one, and yet Adrastos didn't correct Poppy. As with all things Poppy, her answers had only given him more questions, but he was in no rush to push the subject tonight. Again he thought of an animal in the forest, of not wanting to frighten her into bolting.

There was something about her, a fragility that was almost at odds with her success as a lawyer and her outward confidence.

When she was fourteen, he'd wanted to protect her, and those instincts were still a part of him. It was why he'd gone with her at the party when she'd approached him. He hadn't known then that she was about to proposition him, but he'd seen urgency in her eyes, and recognised that she was coming to him, just to him, that she needed him.

And why had he slept with her? He wondered, as he showered that night, lathering his body until it was covered in white suds then standing beneath the stream of water until his hair was plastered over his brow. He was no virgin, but a man with more than enough experience under his belt to control his libido—or so he'd thought.

Frustration twisted in his gut.

He felt like a stranger to himself.

Where usually Adrastos could understand his own motives, his reasons for acting, in this regard, he drew a blank. After all, he'd leapt at the chance to take her to bed. Whether she was a virgin or not was beside the point. Sex with Poppy was still...layered. Complicated. Made so by her relationships with his family, her place *within* his family.

He groaned, pressing his head forward, against the tiles. The water was so loud in his ears—or was that his own pulse?—that at first he didn't hear the knocking on the door, but it grew louder, and he switched the water off impatiently.

'Yes?'

'Are you okay, Adrastos?'

His body responded instantly. Naked and wet, his groin tightened at the sound of Poppy's voice, and his heart thudded heavily against his ribs.

'Why?'

'You've...um...been in there a while, and you just groaned as though you'd stubbed your toe.'

He couldn't help smiling, but it was a smile of irritation and impatience. Whatever desire had flooded his body and thrown rational thought away on the night of Poppy's party, it was still a part of him, dictating and controlling him, so before he could think it through he switched the water back on and turned towards the door.

'If you are concerned about my welfare, you are very welcome to come in and check on me.'

Having thrown down the challenge, he had no real expectation of her taking it up. Poppy had very wisely put a stop to things whenever he'd kissed her, but he stood still, waiting, for several long, tense seconds, hope swelling in his chest until he realised that of *course* she wasn't going to walk into the bathroom as he showered. He reached behind his back for the tap just as the door creaked open and her familiar, beautiful face peeped around the door.

Not her body, which she kept firmly anchored on the other side, as though she were afraid of stepping into the abyss. But her face was enough. Her eyes, huge and round, stared at him, locked to his at first, before dropping to his lips, which she hungrily studied, then falling lower, flashing, almost, to his cock, lingering there, so he grew hard and hungry beneath her inspection, then lower again, sweeping over his legs until she closed her eyes and stayed right where she was, head peering around the crack in the door, elegant neck aching to be touched.

He groaned at the futility of this, of the frustration. 'Well?' His voice, though, was pleasingly level. 'Are you going to come in, *deliciae*?'

Her eyes flared open, locking to his once more, and he felt her indecision and uncertainty like a sledgehammer. A curse filled his mind, reverberated around his skull, as he contemplated his next move. Only Adrastos wasn't sure that this was a time for thinking.

With Poppy, he didn't think. And maybe that was just how it had to be between the two of them? Instincts alone had brought them together—his, on the night of her twenty-first, then hers three years later. And his when he'd thrown caution to the wind and ignored what he *should* have done, what he'd known was right, and done what he'd simply, desperately wanted. Poppy's when she'd concocted this plan to save hurting his family's feelings or making things difficult for Adrastos.

Their instincts had guided them and maybe their lot in life was to act first, regret later, but he couldn't be sure.

Out of nowhere, he remembered what she'd said only hours earlier: *'Unlike you, I don't regret it.'*

Moving without thinking, he stepped from the shower, and Poppy stayed where she was, just a head, until he opened the bathroom door wider, eyes probing, challenging, warning her to stop him now if she wanted to.

But to his delight and relief, once the door was open, and their bodies close, it was Poppy who moved first, melding to him as she pushed up onto the tips of her toes and tilted her head back so they could kiss. He was naked and wet and she fitted against him so perfectly, her body so soft and sweet, reminding him of something he'd felt the first night they'd kissed, years earlier.

There had been so much passion in that kiss but there had also been a strange, eerie sort of peace, like the stars in the desert sky in the very middle of the night. Clarity. Ancient wisdom. He'd felt as though he was every single version of himself that he was ever destined to be, distilled into one omniscient moment.

A strange way to feel as he'd simultaneously delighted in the mastery of his body over another's, but that was the effect Poppy had had on him, and he felt it again now. He was conscious of nothing. Not the still-running water behind them, not the loud pounding of his heart, not the ticking of the clock in his suite, not the palace, not his family, nothing.

'I have wanted to do that all night,' she said, pulling back a little and blinking up at him, surprised by the admission, or perhaps by the passion that had ignited the second they'd touched. But Adrastos couldn't bear the thought of Poppy pulling away from him again. He couldn't kiss her and catch fire and not give into it.

'I kissed you earlier.'

'But there were people everywhere,' she replied breathlessly. 'Watching. Possibly recording…'

He should have been glad for her awareness of that because Adrastos, despite his years of living in the public eye, hadn't had the fortitude to think of their surrounds for even a moment.

'I want you,' he said, rather than analyse why he'd been incapable of being more discreet.

Her eyes were shuttered from him then, hiding whatever she was feeling, and her skin went from flushed to pale, so he had no idea what he'd said or done to make her prevaricate, but he felt her uncertainty suddenly and wanted to release a deep, guttural growl.

'Poppy, listen to me.' He caught her face in his hands, held it steady, stared deep into her eyes. 'You have no experience with men. I don't know why you doubt the truth of my words, why you think I would say I want you if I didn't, but please stop. I want *you*. Here and now, I ache for you in a way I will never be able to put into words.'

Her lips parted and something shifted in her features. Confusion, wonderment, and something else. Uncertainty? But it was gone, in an instant. She smiled at him, a bright smile that he wasn't sure he'd ever seen on her face, certainly not directed at him, and then lifted her brows. 'Well, then, Your Highness, what exactly are you waiting for?'

He growled as he swept down and picked her up, carrying her against his wet frame, right back into the shower— more than big enough to comfortably accommodate the two of them—and kissing her hungrily as he stripped her out of her beautiful dress, growing darker and wetter by the minute as the shower drenched it.

It was harder to strip from her body than it should have been. The fabric clung to her wet skin, and he felt utterly thwarted and quite mad with longing by the time it finally dropped to the tiles beneath them and she stepped out of it, revealing a simple pair of briefs and a strapless bra.

Such utilitarian underwear, really, as though she'd chosen it with no thought of him seeing it, and yet it was somehow the sexiest fabric he'd ever seen. Nonetheless, he discarded it quickly too, seeking her nakedness, needing her to be as bare-skinned as he was.

The first time they'd made love had been her first time ever, and Adrastos hadn't even found his own release. That was something he intended to rectify. In fact, there was much he wanted to change about what that experience had been.

Poppy had deserved so much more than that for her first time, he realised with a growing sense of anger. How had she ever thought a one-night stand would be enough? She deserved to have been seduced properly, kissed until she was mindless, built to a fever state then made love to again and again until her body was so awash with sensations that she could barely stand.

Suddenly, he saw the gift she'd given him, the responsibility, and wanted to live up to it. He wanted to be not just her first but her best, for ever, so that no man who came after him in her life could ever equal the pleasure Adrastos had given her.

The thought evoked something strange and primal in his chest, a feeling that stirred almost barbaric instincts to life. It was normal to feel jealous, imagining other men with your lover. At least, he imagined it was: Adrastos had never been a particularly jealous man.

He didn't want to think about Poppy's next lover or lovers.

With a dark sound deep in his throat, he kissed her harder, more hungrily, as he lifted her and pressed her slim body against the tiles, standing between her hips, holding her easily at his waist, his arousal hard and throbbing for her, so he was almost mindless with desire. Wet and slippery made this somehow more hedonistic and elemental.

He moved his mouth to her breasts, revelling in the feel of them in his palms, his mouth, his stubbled jaw dragging across them until he knew every inch of her. The sounds she made, her little cries, were driving him wild, making it almost impossible to resist driving into her then and there.

But Adrastos wanted to slow this down, to make it last. He wanted to make this a night to remember. He wanted to give Poppy the sort of pleasure she should have understood by now, to show her everything her body could sense and feel. He wanted...everything.

With a guttural noise of impatience, he knelt down, hands on her hips pinning her to the wall as he pressed his mouth to her sex, tasting, teasing, listening to her cries of pleasure, feeling the wobble in her legs as she struggled to support herself and, finally, her shuddering release as she moaned his name over and over. Water doused him, doused them, but nothing could wash away his intensely urgent need for her. As he stood, their eyes met and the air between them seemed to light up with sparks, her mouth was parted and her gaze seemed to be pleading with him in some way.

He understood, without words. Her fear, her surprise, her desire to feel *more*. He snapped off the water and grabbed Poppy in one motion, lifting her against his chest, pausing only briefly to grab a huge black towel from the rack. At the foot of his bed, he placed Poppy down and dried her, but even that was a temptation and torment. She was so beautiful. He shifted his gaze to her face, staring at her, and something shifted in his gut, or his chest, or his throat, making it harder to breathe, to think, for his heart to pump blood through his body.

'You turned into a woman overnight.'

Her smile was slow, and wry. 'Not quite overnight. You just missed a lot of time here.'

He had. He'd been busy for a long time. Busy with the military, in which he held several command positions, busy with policy work for the government committees he served on. Busy staying away? From his family, from their expectations, from Nicholas's absence. From Poppy, too?

He kissed her rather than dwell on that: why should he want to avoid Poppy? She spent so much time with Eleanor, it wasn't as though her presence in the palace was a problem for him. Particularly not when she made his parents so happy.

'I noticed at your twenty-first,' he admitted. 'I came home and, all of a sudden, you were all grown up, and so very, very tempting.'

Her eyes closed and he had a familiar sense, a misgiving; she'd reacted like that before, to something else he'd said, only he couldn't quite remember. It was as if she didn't want to hear the compliment, or didn't believe it.

'Stop talking,' she said with a rueful shake of her head, an attempt at a joke, and he let it go, because it suited him fine not to talk. Adrastos wasn't one for conversing while making love. Not usually, anyway. He'd never bought into the 'spending the night' concept either. For him, it was sex, and that was that.

Better to avoid entanglements, raised hopes, better to leave before anyone could ask him to stay.

'Your wish is my command.'

'Isn't it meant to be the other way around?'

'We can take turns.'

'I like the sound of that. Only...' Her lips pulled to the side. 'I don't really know what to do.'

He moved closer, so close that his mouth brushed hers

as he spoke. 'You're already doing it.' And then, he pulled her with him back to the bed, his body so hard, his need so great, he couldn't think straight, he couldn't do anything except allow his body the freedom to touch every inch of her, to be in this moment feeling, pleasuring, giving, receiving...

Poppy felt different the next morning. Physically different. She was stretched and sore and her nerves buzzed and hummed with new pleasures rendered and experienced, with the feeling that Adrastos had made her his so utterly and completely she wasn't sure how she'd ever think of herself as her own person again.

That thought had her sitting upright, her face draining of colour, and her eyes seeking him on the other side of the bed. She was relieved that he wasn't there, even when her heart gave a funny little clutch and her lips tugged downwards. But the truth was, seeing Adrastos now would be too much.

She needed time and space to give some perspective to what they'd shared.

Or, she thought, her frown deepening, she needed to talk to someone, to her very best friend in the whole world, who always helped Poppy know what she wanted when Poppy was lost. But how could Poppy turn to Eleanor at a time like this? What would she say?

She dismissed the idea completely.

This was her ruse, and the last thing she wanted was to involved Ellie in any of it.

But that strange sense of doom, of danger, lurked on the edge of Poppy's mind. She felt as though she were walking through a field of snakes, burrowed deep in their holes but likely to emerge at any point and strike. She felt danger prodding her and yet she couldn't explain it.

This was temporary. They both knew what this was: a

pretend relationship. The sex was by the by. Poppy was attracted to Adrastos. It was clear Adrastos felt the same, but Poppy wasn't naïve enough to think that she was special to him in any way. If Poppy hadn't been here, Adrastos would have found another woman to be with. That was who he was. It was who he'd always be.

She shook her head, wondering why that knowledge, a piece of certainty she'd held for a long time, suddenly made her throat feel as though it were filled with sharp rocks. Why should she care that Adrastos was a serial bed-hopper?

It wasn't her business.

And this was just sex.

Her heart gave that strange twist again and she dropped her head forward, staring at the crisp white coverlet of his bed. Where was he? Poppy told herself again that she was glad he wasn't here, but, deep down, Adrastos might have been the only person on the face of the earth who could have helped calm her fluttering nerves—by kissing them right out of her head—and he was nowhere to be seen.

He hadn't intentionally avoided her, and yet giving both of them space had seemed wise after last night. He couldn't think of it without a growing sense of disquiet. It hadn't been 'just sex', for the pure reason, he reassured himself, that neither of them had been able to leave again afterwards. Sharing a bed, naked, limbs entwined, they'd fallen asleep with Poppy's head on his chest, his hand curved around her back, fingers possessively splayed over her hip, and when he'd woken several hours later, it had been because Poppy was kissing his chest, still half asleep, in the early hours of the morning. He suspected she hadn't even been aware of what she was doing, but Adrastos had kissed her back, waking her up the rest of the way, until they'd come together in a frantic, desperate joining, as if neither had known the other's body for years, not hours.

He'd been too wired to go back to sleep after that. He'd waited for Poppy to slip into dreams, then pushed back the covers and strode out of the room, pausing only to grab some clothes on his way to his office, where he greeted the dawn, staring out at the forest, admiring it for its ancient trees and wisdom, for the fierce danger that lurked beneath the beautiful, almost serene-seeming surface.

It was the kind of forest that made up postcards of this region, so picturesque and pretty, but there were many threats amongst those broad, round trunks. Predators, the weather, the lack of cell service so if you didn't know exactly what you were doing and became lost, there was no easy rescue. Adrastos had been told, as a young boy, never to go into the forest alone, which of course had only made him determined to do exactly that. But he was no fool: he understood the dangers and so he respected them. He took precautions each time, testing his strength as one grew and developed a muscle, until he was confident he could walk amongst those trees like any of the predators who owned the woods.

Just as he was confident he could control what was happening with Poppy. True, it was different from his usual relationships, for many reasons, not least because he knew her and, worse, she knew him. Really knew him—in the way you couldn't avoid having knowledge of a person when you'd been in their home and immersed in their family. She saw facets of him he liked to keep all to himself.

But that was also to his advantage, because she understood what he was like. She'd seen his attitude to relationships, she'd heard his parents and sister bemoan his inability to settle down, she knew that after their very gentle, respectful 'break-up', he'd go back to his normal life, and she'd go back to hers, and they'd return to seeing each other a few times a year, when palace life brought them home at the same time.

It was a thought he held like a talisman, but, much like his early walks into the forest, he sensed danger in the idea, because he was no fool. Sleeping with Poppy was different and new, and he would need to train himself to treat her like any of his other lovers; he'd need a different kind of strength to simply walk away from her and stay away.

Adrastos, fortunately, never failed once he'd set his mind to something and, in this, he was determined.

CHAPTER TEN

SHE FELT INEXPLICABLY SHY! Poppy knew these people, loved them, and yet sitting at the table, beside Adrastos, she found her tongue was tied in knots and her fingers quivering so she had to hold them in her lap. She was nervous and over-come, a jangle of feelings, of awareness. She felt, she re-alised, as the waiters brought out plates ladened with local delicacies, as though she were on a first date. With Adras-tos, and his whole family.

She could barely look at the man, for goodness' sake! After the intimacy of the night before, after the way he'd made her feel, after the way *he'd* felt, she reminded herself with a deep crimson blush spreading over her cheeks, she was unprepared for how to go from that level of sensual connection to this, to normal life, to pretending they were just themselves, and yet not themselves, because Poppy and Adrastos had never been *this*. A couple. A pretend couple.

She sipped her water, barely listening to the conversation swirling around her, barely conscious of anything, except at one point, when Adrastos physically stiffened beside her, so that his tension was impossible to ignore. Poppy sat up straighter and tuned into what was being said.

The King was speaking—with obvious pride—shaking his head at how naturally Adrastos had handled a trade ne-gotiation. 'They can be difficult to work with, you know.

I've never found it easy, at least. But you, of course, had them eating out of the palm of your hand. You will have to teach me how you did that.' Alexander's eyes crinkled at the corners and Clementine added some noises of congratulation. Adrastos's face was ash beneath his tanned complexion, and when he thanked them, it was in a voice that was almost completely devoid of emotion.

Poppy skimmed his face, trying to understand, but then he turned to Poppy and her pulse almost throttled her, and her body flooded with warmth and need and all thoughts of understanding Adrastos fled from her mind.

The festive season in the palace was beautiful and wondrous and usually Poppy adored it, but she found it hard to focus on the little traditions this year, on enjoying the quintessentially local food. In fact, she could barely taste anything!

Somehow, she made it through the main course, and then dessert, but afterwards, when Clementine suggested they adjourn to the drawing room, where the family traditionally listened to classical music and drank something very similar to gin but made from berries grown only in Stomland, Poppy made her excuses.

'I have a bit of a headache,' she murmured apologetically excusing herself, barely able to meet anyone's eyes, least of all Adrastos's. Would he be annoyed with her? Or secretly relieved if she left, so he could also stop pretending?

'I'll come with you.' His voice was low, gruff.

'Oh, no, no,' she said, far too quickly, and had to force a smile to avoid arousing suspicion. 'That's not necessary,' she added with a lift of her shoulders. 'I'll be okay. I just need an early night.' She turned back to the King and Queen, curtseying without thinking about it—a small gesture that was always observed, regardless of how close they were.

'Are you sure you're okay?' Ellie asked. 'You look pale.'

'I'm fine,' she stressed, reaching out and squeezing her friend's hand, but not before the sting of tears threatened at the backs of her eyes. She couldn't bear the solicitous enquiry. Not when she was lying her butt off to these people, her makeshift family.

It wasn't the lie though, she realised, when she was safely back in Adrastos's suite, having a cup of tea on the balcony, wrapped up in a thick, woollen blanket. It was the intimacy they'd shared last night. Not sex. Intimacy. True, life-changing closeness and connection. It was more than just physical desire. Somehow, being with him like that had kickstarted a response inside Poppy that had intensified as the day went on. It was as if he'd become a part of her soul, and with every breath his hold on her spread, until he became all she could think about.

'How are you feeling?'

She should have expected his return—surely she didn't think he'd just let her run away to his room with the complaint of a headache and not come to check on her? And yet surprise was on her features when, not fifteen minutes later, Adrastos stepped onto the balcony and frowned, because snow was in the air and Poppy had chosen here, of all places, to drink tea?

'Fine.' But her smile was stretched and her gaze frustratingly skittish, just as it had been over dinner, so he wanted to kiss her more than ever. It seemed to be the simplest way to make her relax, to simply exist and not overthink, to bring her back into the light, but it was also a way of delaying, of running, and Adrastos had never tolerated cowardice.

'No headache?'

She pulled a face. 'Brain ache, more like.'

'Explain.' He crossed his arms over his chest, mainly to stop himself from reaching for her, from bringing her to stand against his chest. He wanted to comfort her, but something held him back, something vital that he didn't fully comprehend, yet respected nonetheless.

'I just hate lying to them.' She wrinkled her nose and lifted a hand as if to forestall his possible response to that. 'I know, I know. It was all my idea. My stupid, stupid idea.'

His nostrils flared with the force of his sigh. '*Deliciae*, as you pointed out, we had very limited options once those photos were printed.'

'Yes, but I know you would have just faced the music without flinching.'

'Far less frightening for me to do so.'

She blinked up at him.

'They're my family,' he said, gently, crouching down then, ignoring his better instincts and putting a hand on her knee. 'And while I know they love you as if you were their biological child, it's understandable that you would feel less secure in that love. You didn't want to lose them, as you lost your own parents, and so you did the one thing you could think of to make that unlikely.'

A tear rolled down her cheek and he bit back a curse.

'You will never lose them, Poppy. Our stupidity on that night aside, you are their daughter.'

She shook her head, as if to clear his words from the sky.

'It's untenable,' she whispered. 'After this is over, how do we go back?' Huge, haunted eyes looked at him, but she wasn't really looking at Adrastos, so much as desperately hoping to find strength in his frame, a strength he wasn't sure he could give but knew she needed.

So he forced himself to convey it, to show absolute certainty even when he didn't completely feel it. 'We simply go back,' he said with a shrug. 'It's not complicated.'

Her eyes skimmed his face thoughtfully, as though she was analysing that from every angle. 'I want to believe that.'

'You have no experience,' he reminded her.

'But you do.'

He dipped his head, not wanting to think about former lovers. For the first time in his life, he felt an unusual sense of remorse, a wish that he'd known fewer women, a wish to erase them from his memories so there was room only for Poppy.

'So this is normal,' she said with a slow shift of her head. 'You can turn this on and off, like a tap?'

The directness of her question caught him off guard. It wasn't accurate at all. 'It's more that I can enjoy an experience for what it is, be grateful for it, and then move on,' he said after a moment, glad that his voice sounded so measured and reasonable. 'I am grateful for this experience with you, Poppy, even though it is far more complication than I would usually entertain in my personal life.'

'Why?' she asked, eyes locked to his as she sipped her tea. All night at dinner, she'd avoided looking at him, so he'd wanted to reach out and draw her chin towards him, to force their eyes to meet, so he could understand why she was so quiet. But now, in the delicate silver of the moonlight, she wouldn't stop looking at him, so he felt almost too seen, far too visible.

'Do I really need to answer that?' he said with a shake of his head. 'You were here last night, weren't you?'

Poppy's eyes widened and her cheeks flushed with that telltale crimson, showing embarrassment. It was so innocent and adorable. He balled the hand by his side into a fist, a way of holding his control.

'I meant,' she murmured softly, 'why do you avoid complications in your personal life?'

The question shouldn't have surprised him. He'd opened the door to it, by mentioning his usual prerequisite for relationships. But he floundered for words, strangely uncertain as to how to respond. Ordinarily, he'd have given some dismissive response, a non-answer, but with Poppy, the truth hummed and zipped through his veins, fairly bursting to be spoken.

He stood up, hoping that physical space might squash that instinct, but Poppy stood too, moving to his side, one hand on his shoulder, the blanket dropping a bit, revealing the delicate blue cardigan she'd worn at dinner. His hand had brushed her back as they'd taken their seats and he'd felt how soft the wool was, even as he'd fantasised about removing it later, because her skin was so much softer and he yearned to touch her, to feel her.

'You think that's unusual?' He volleyed back a question to buy some time.

She considered that. He really liked how thoughtful Poppy was. She didn't just blurt out whatever occurred to her, but rather took time to form her thoughts and express them well. Her inner lawyer, or perhaps what had drawn her to study law in the first place?

'Your whole life is unusual,' she said slowly. 'The way you were raised, the expectations on you since birth—'

'Not quite since birth,' he said with a shake of his head, then wished he hadn't interrupted, because his response gave far too much away. The darkness inside Adrastos that he preferred to keep all to himself.

'Since birth.' Poppy was firm. 'The expectations changed, after Nicholas died,' she murmured, 'but you were still raised with very clear ideas about who and what you needed to be.'

'Was I?' She was right, and he couldn't say how he felt about that, only that he *felt* a lot.

'Of course. As a young boy, an adolescent, you were Nicholas's spare, a backup. No one thought you'd ever be called upon to rule, and, as such, you were required to mute yourself, as much as possible, to allow Nicholas to excel.'

He made a grunting noise. 'Is this your interpretation, or has my sister been filling your head with this nonsense?'

Poppy's eyes held his for a long time, before flitting away, focussing on the moon across the wild woods. 'I don't think I'm wrong,' she said, eventually. 'Except you're not someone who is easy to mute.' The smile that touched her lips did funny things to Adrastos's gut.

'It must have been hard for Nicholas, to grow up in your shadow, despite the fact he was the older brother.'

'Poppy—' Loyalty, and his ever-present survivor guilt, had Adrastos's stomach churning. 'Can we save the psychoanalysing for another time? Say, never?'

Her smile was wistful now. 'Is it why you avoid relationships, Adrastos? Is it because you felt hurt by your parents? By them always wanting you to be different? Or is it something else?'

'Why does there have to be a reason?' He was pushed into a corner and lashed out rather than look at the horrorshow reality she presented him with. 'Can it not simply be that I like sex?' His voice was far too loud. She flinched a little, but held her ground, and he fought hard to bring himself back under control. 'I like sex,' he repeated, and Poppy's eyes widened, so only an idiot would fail to realise that he was hurting her, and only a heartless bastard wouldn't care, but Adrastos was certainly, in that moment, the latter.

'I sleep with women because I enjoy it. Lots of women. And one day, if Eleanor fails to marry and produce happy little heirs to placate the palace, then I will do my inherited duty and marry someone suitable and set about impregnating her. Is that what you want to hear, Poppy?' His gaze narrowed. 'Unless, of course, you happened to conceive my child on our first night together, in which case, we might as well make everyone happy and just get married.'

She gasped, took a step back, and he could see he'd gone way too far, that he'd lashed out intentionally to hurt her and, instead, he'd said things that were cruel and unnecessary.

'I'm on the pill,' she reminded him. 'So you can relax. Neither of us has to go through with a marriage that we'd both hate.'

He scowled, glad to hear her describe it that way, glad to hear her say that, because they would both hate to be married. So why did it feel as if all the gravity in the world had changed and was now pressing down on his chest, making it hard to breathe, difficult to see straight?

'Wonderful.' He grunted, his mood darkening by the minute.

'And with that,' she said, quiet dignity dripping from the icy words, 'I'm off to bed.'

He expelled an angry sigh rather than answer her, and a moment later, Adrastos was on his own, just as he liked to be, just as he always would be, if he had his way.

Poppy slept poorly. Worse than poorly, she barely slept at all. The entire night was spent clinging to her side of the bed, trying to keep her wits about her, out of a fear that her body might forget she was cross with Adrastos and her hand would stray to his side, would touch him, would pull him to her, would beg him silently to make love to her, to kiss her and tell her everything was okay.

But she didn't, and nor did Adrastos. At some point around dawn, she felt him move, the weight of the mattress changing as he pushed up and then strode towards the door of the bedroom. Poppy squeezed her eyes shut, feigning sleep. Evidently, Adrastos had no interest in continuing their conversation from last night; he slipped from the room without a word.

Good, Poppy thought to herself, rolling onto her back and staring at the ceiling.

She had a lot to think about.

Their conversation last night had given her no shortage of mulling points, including his insistence that this was normal. He'd experienced this sort of thing before. Poppy wasn't special.

She rolled onto her other side and now she allowed her hand the liberties she couldn't take in the night, reaching out and running her fingertips over his still-warm pillow, feeling the indent, as a sting in the backs of her eyes threatened tears. But Poppy wouldn't cry. She couldn't. To cry would be to acknowledge something far too dangerous to herself: it would be to admit how much she cared about Adrastos.

Which was a disaster.

What she needed was her best friend and a proper distraction. Reaching for her phone, not minding that it was still early, she texted Eleanor.

Can we spend the day together?

The response was almost immediate.

I thought you'd never ask.

There was a little love-heart emoji for good measure.

Whatever else happened, Poppy would always have Eleanor—her very best friend in the world. Poppy had to push Adrastos way out of her mind, and a day with Eleanor was just what she needed.

Unfortunately, Eleanor had suggested a shopping trip into the city, one of their favourite pastimes, particularly at this time of year, when they selected the gowns each would wear to the New Year's Eve banquet at the palace. Where they'd usually been able to slip out with a degree of privacy, that was not possible now, and, to Poppy's chagrin, the paparazzi scrum tailing them from boutique to boutique all seemed to want to harangue *her*.

'Poppy, is it love?'

'When's the wedding?'

'Princess Eleanor, will you be a bridesmaid?'

Eleanor squeezed Poppy's hand at that last question, keeping a blank face where Poppy was sure her abject horror must be quite visible on hers. They gave up after only forty minutes of trying on dresses, with Eleanor instructing the final boutique, 'Please send these six to the palace. We'll make our selections and send the rest back.'

Poppy was too shell-shocked to say a thing.

In the car, being chauffeur-driven back to the palace, Poppy turned to Eleanor. She hadn't realised how badly she was shaking until Eleanor reached out and put a steadying hand on Poppy's. 'It will be okay. This will die down.'

Poppy nodded, but Eleanor was wrong. At least, in theory she was wrong. If Poppy were actually dating Adrastos, then the media attention would only intensify. There'd be an engagement, and a wedding, and then pregnancies, all to navigate in the spotlight of this sort of media circus. How could he ever be expected to fall in love when this was his life?

'That was intense,' Eleanor said, perhaps just to fill the silence, or maybe to justify the sense of fear both women were feeling. 'I didn't expect it. I thought it would be like normal.' She grimaced, removing her hand. 'But this isn't normal,' she whispered, her own voice quivering a little. 'Poppy, what's going on with you guys?'

A lump formed in Poppy's throat. The outright question made it almost impossible to answer, because lying to Ellie was her worst nightmare. But she'd made this awful, awful web and had no choice but to stick with it. Just for a little while longer, she mentally added. The original plan had been to stay at the palace for the full twelve days, but she could leave early. Plead work deadlines and escape back to her own home. That wouldn't change anything about the faux relationship, nor their 'amicable break-up', but it might just spare her sanity.

'What do you mean?' she asked, not bothering to try to smile.

'Adrastos has never been with a woman for more than a week.'

He hadn't been with Poppy for more than a week really, she thought with a grimace.

'He's certainly never brought a woman home for Christmas.'

'That's not what he's done,' she said with a shake of her head.

'Nonsense,' Eleanor dismissed. 'You're dating. You're sleeping in his room. If things were as casual as you seem to want to insist, then why not stay in your own room and simply spend time together?'

Heat flooded Poppy's cheeks. How could she answer that

delicately? Because the only silver lining in this whole debacle was getting to share Adrastos's bed.

'You know what he's like,' Ellie said gently. 'Which means you must see that this is very serious to him?'

Guilt was an awful, toxic taste in Poppy's mouth. She shook her head, wanting to deny it with the truth, feeling suffocated by the car's heating, by Eleanor's nearness, by the lie she'd told with the best of intentions that was now eating her alive.

'It can't be serious,' she blurted out, finally, latching onto a way out. 'Do you remember the promotion my name was put forward for?'

Eleanor nodded.

'I got it,' Poppy admitted. 'I only heard on the day of our birthday party, and I was going to tell you straight away, but all this…' She gestured to herself, implying the relationship. 'There's been so much going on. The thing is, I'm leaving in the new year,' she said, so glad she could finally say something that was completely honest. 'And Adrastos must remain here.'

'Oh, Pops.' Ellie's eyes were moist. 'I can't believe it. The timing—could it be any worse?'

Actually, it couldn't be better. Suddenly, Poppy was desperate for the escape route offered by her new job.

'But long distance? It's not so far away. He can come and see you—'

'Adrastos has his hands full here. Besides—' Poppy worked hard to keep her voice light '—you know what your brother's like. I'm sure he'll replace me quickly enough.'

Eleanor's eyes narrowed. 'And that's okay with you?'

Poppy squeezed her own eyes shut. 'What do you think?' She sighed. 'I'm trying not to think about that.' More honesty! 'I'm just living in the moment, enjoying it while it lasts. Your brother is very special. I care about him, Eleanor. But this doesn't have a future. I wish no one had ever found out about us.' Speaking so frankly and openly was a balm Poppy badly needed. She was trying to simply enjoy things with Adrastos without getting ahead of herself. She was living in the moment. And she cared about him, a great deal. If only their one night together had remained their secret!

But what then?

It would have been the end of it. Adrastos certainly hadn't been going to chase Poppy up and ask for a repeat performance. If those photos hadn't been printed, they'd have been awkward acquaintances, instead of…instead of what?

She turned away from Eleanor, staring out of the window at the city as it passed them by, a blur of ancient grey buildings, falling white snow and the most beautiful Christmas lights still strung from one side of the street to the other.

Christmas was over, and now Poppy had to focus on the new year, and on the new version of herself. Once she left Stomland, she had to put Adrastos behind her, and never think of him again.

It was the only way she could move on with her life, as he surely would, the second he was at liberty to do so.

CHAPTER ELEVEN

IT HADN'T BEEN easy to analyse his mood that day. The remnants of irritation remained—had tortured him most of the night, and had lingered in the afternoon. And then he'd seen her stepping out of the limousine in the rather grand private turning circle.

From his vantage point on the second floor, where he'd been staring out of the window almost without seeing, all his energy became focussed on Poppy as she stood with innate elegance from the back seat the moment the door was opened, her slim body looking so vulnerable. He couldn't see her face, but a moment later, Eleanor came around to Poppy's side, putting her hands on Poppy's shoulders, squeezing, then pressing her forehead to Poppy's and smiling. Eleanor was…crying? And so was Poppy. Something in his chest split. A moment later, Eleanor wrapped Poppy into a huge hug and held her tight.

It was a hug Poppy needed. He could tell by the way her body sagged into it, from the way she rested her cheek on Eleanor's shoulder and closed her eyes, and suddenly, the thought of Poppy needing a hug and him not being there to offer it seemed all kinds of wrong.

He paced out of the office quickly, took the wide marble staircase, then turned into the tiled hallway just as Poppy and Eleanor entered.

He stopped walking. Stared at Poppy as she stared back, and Eleanor looked from one to the other—but he didn't even notice his sister. Every fibre of his being was focussed on Poppy and her tear-streaked face.

'What's happened?' he demanded, pushing his body, lengthening his stride to reach her more quickly.

'Nothing,' she demurred, dashing at her cheeks and offering a weak smile.

'Don't say that. What is it?' Exasperation made his voice louder than he'd intended and out of nowhere, he remembered last night. The way he'd lost his temper with her. But it hadn't been Poppy he was annoyed with, not at all. He'd felt threatened, he realised now, by her questions and how honest he'd wanted to be with her. He turned to his sister. 'Eleanor, would you excuse us?'

Eleanor looked at Poppy then nodded, reaching out and touching Poppy's cheek. 'I love you.'

A moment later Eleanor was gone and all Adrastos wanted was to scoop Poppy up into that hug he knew she needed. But standing right in front of her, it wasn't so easy.

'I—' she started.

'You're upset,' he said at the same time.

'Yes.'

'Because of last night?'

Her eyes shuttered, her glance falling to a huge vase across the corridor, stuffed full of festive flowers. 'Partly.'

He nodded slowly. At least she wasn't denying it. 'Will you come with me, so we can speak more privately?'

Some of the women he'd dated might have demurred, in the hope he'd beg, but Poppy was not like other women. She simply nodded. 'I think that's a good idea.'

He was relieved but also, suddenly, inexplicably nervous. He wracked his brain for where they could go—not his room, where the bed would distract them both, and memories of last night would be fresh in their minds. And not away from the palace, where photographers would be hungry for images of them.

Then, inspiration struck. 'Give me five minutes,' he said. 'Don't—Just don't go anywhere.'

The woods to the west of the palace were the only place Poppy had been told unequivocally never to go, and so she hadn't. Even though she knew Adrastos would go in with hunting parties, even though she knew they were simply woods, the warning given to her most sternly by Queen Clementine when Poppy was just a teenager had rung in Poppy's ears ever since.

So even though Adrastos was with her, as they neared the edge of the forest she stopped walking, hesitating, looking from the thick trunks to Adrastos then back again.

'It's quite safe. I'm with you.'

She bit down on her lip, wishing that those simple words didn't offer so much comfort.

She took a step forward, and another, and then she was enveloped—there was no other word to describe it—by the ancient wood, the smell of pine needles, the soft, fresh snow underfoot.

'Tell me why you are upset.'

It was a simple commandment, but also incredibly complex to answer.

'I—' She lifted her gaze to his. 'I didn't like arguing with you last night.'

His expression gave nothing away, but when he turned to look at her, she was sure she saw something like anguish in his eyes. 'We didn't argue,' he said throatily. 'I lost my temper, and I am very sorry for that.'

The apology was unexpected. Then again, why should it have been? He had been wrong, and he was confessing to that. Adrastos was nothing if not moralistic, and when he erred, he fixed things.

'Thank you,' she said, simply.

'It's not enough,' he said with a shake of his head. 'I lost my temper and you deserve to know why. The problem is, I'm not good at talking about any of this.'

She stopped walking, held out a hand. 'It's quite safe,' she said with a hint of a smile. 'I told you, I'm with you.'

His eyes widened and then he offered a smile back, the repeating of his own reassurance like an incantation, the bringing of a spell.

'You came so close to the truth of it all, Poppy. I wasn't expecting that. But I should have. You're so perceptive.' He lifted a hand, cupping her cheek.

'About Nicholas?' she prompted gently.

His face was grave; he continued walking—perhaps he found it easier to talk as he walked, rather than under the full glare of her watchfulness. Poppy fell into step beside him, reaching for his hand as the physical embodiment of her promise: *I'm with you.*

'We were competitive as boys. There were just thirteen months between us, you know, and I was always big for my age. We looked almost like twins. But we were not alike in any other way.' He shoved his other hand deep in his coat pocket, looked around, studied the lower branches of a tree they were passing. 'We were competitive, but it was never really a competition. While Nicholas was studious, book-ish, he was also gentle and sensitive. He didn't like sports, he didn't like camping, hunting, any of the things our father valued. He would much prefer to read than run.'

'Whereas you were always the opposite,' she said quietly.

'I remember how strong you were, how big, how athletic, that first Christmas we spent together.'

'Do you?'

She blinked away, feeling as though she'd revealed something important, something she should have kept to herself, though she didn't know why. Sniffing, she added, 'Objectively speaking, you were a very sporty person.'

'Objectively speaking,' he repeated with a small lift of his lips. 'After Nick got sick, and grew weak, I felt this…awful sense of self-loathing. I cannot explain how much I hated my own selfish, stupid desire to beat him at all things. It had never been a fair competition. I had been born with skills he didn't possess and didn't have any interest in. I prayed to any god who might listen to let him live. I promised I would never gloat over him again, that I would never delight in my similarities to our father where Nick had so many differences.'

Poppy listened without speaking but, inside, her heart was breaking for the young man Adrastos had been.

'And then he died.' Such a small sentence to encompass an enormous amount of hurt. 'I hadn't realised how much I loved him until he was gone. Our competition was just a pretence to be together, to be a part of the same thing. I wonder if it was the same for him. I hope so—I can't think why else he would have kept agreeing to race me.'

He turned to face Poppy.

'No one ever asked me to mute myself for him, though, God, how I wish they had. I wish I hadn't been so arrogant, so desperate to prove my superiority at every turn.'

He shook his head angrily.

'And then he died, and life moved on. I became the heir, the sole focus of the media's attention.' He stopped talking, stopped walking, just simply stared into space. 'I was no longer in competition with Nicholas, but he was everywhere around me. Every article written about me carried within it a silent comparison to my late brother. And oftentimes, unfavourable to him, as if he wouldn't have been able to do the things I was doing. I was ashamed of my successes. Ashamed of any of the media attention I received. I hated it. I wanted them all to shut up and write about Nick instead. To write how much he'd loved reading, how many languages he spoke, how thoughtful and clever he was, how philosophical. These were things I couldn't see value in as a child—but I had been a child! What excuse did these journalists have? Couldn't they understand how special he'd been?'

Poppy couldn't help it. She moved to him and lifted up onto her tiptoes just so she could place a kiss against his lips, just so she could show him what she couldn't say: how special he was. How much she understood and cared for him.

'You are special too, Adrastos.'

He shook his head, his frustration evident.

'I wanted, more than anything, for them to hate me,' he said, simply. 'I wanted the papers to write, *Prince Adrastos is the worst thing to happen to Stomland. If only Prince Nicholas were still here.*'

Poppy frowned, as something like a flame flickered in the back of her mind.

'You wanted their disapproval.'

'I wanted them to realise that Nick would have been a great heir. That he should still be here.'

'And so, while you couldn't change the skills you have that make you perfect for this role, you could ensure you didn't fulfil anyone's expectations when it came to relationships. Marriage. Babies.'

His eyes flared dark when they met hers.

'You've deliberately avoided relationships,' she said quietly, as it all suddenly became so abundantly clear, 'because you want people to disapprove of you.'

'I have no doubt that Nicholas would have been married years ago,' he said quietly.

'Oh, Adrastos.' Poppy shook her head. 'Poor Adrastos,' she repeated. 'Even then, no one blamed you for your love life. If anything, it simply adds a roguish charm to your persona.'

A muscle jerked in the base of his jaw.

'And as you pointed out last night, you have decades before you need to marry.' The words were wooden in Poppy's mouth. She pulled away from Adrastos, scanning the woods, which were dark courtesy of the thick canopy of branches.

'The thing is,' she said, slowly, 'I only met your brother once, when I was much younger. I don't remember him very well. But through your parents, and Ellie, and now you, I really do feel as though I have a sense of the man he was. I know he wouldn't want you torturing yourself like this.'

Adrastos's face was drawn.

'You're right. He kept competing with you. He must have known he couldn't win half of the things you fought over, but he came back, to be beaten, to be eclipsed. I think he adored you. I think he probably worshipped you a bit. Don't you understand,' she added gently, 'that he would want you to live your life without this guilt?'

He cleared his throat, shook his head a little.

'You don't need to atone for anything.'

'Don't I?'

'Of course not. You couldn't have saved him. He had leukaemia and he died. It's tragic and awful but none of that is your fault. Adrastos, listen to me,' she said, urgently. 'I need to tell you—' But she shook her head, because it was so hard to put her own feelings into words, so she sought instead to offer general advice. 'You are a wonderful person, and you deserve to be happy. Truly happy. You deserve a partner, someone you can love.' Her voice cracked. 'I saw that with my parents, and I've seen it with your parents. You deserve that. You're seeking to prove something no one will ever believe. That you're not a suitable heir to the throne. But you are. Single or not, you will be an excellent king. So why keep fighting that? I beg you…please, stop pushing women away in the hope you'll get some bad press. It won't bring him back.'

'I could say the same to you,' he said, after a moment. 'You have also made an art form of pushing away relationships. Our reasons are different, but the result is the same. You're seeking perfection and, in doing so, you've closed yourself off to the possibility of happiness.'

Poppy's heart twisted. He was right, yet he was wrong. It wasn't just about ignoring other possibilities. It was that there was only one possibility she wanted to consider.

She nodded in the hope it might appear that she agreed with him, but the realisation of how much she felt for Adrastos was detonating inside her chest, making it hard to breathe.

'I have never discussed this with anyone,' Adrastos said quietly. 'I appreciate how ungrateful it must make me sound. But you kept asking, and I simply felt—' He frowned. 'When I saw you today, I couldn't bear the thought of having upset you. I needed you to understand…'

She jerked her face to his then looked away.

'I *was* upset last night,' she agreed quietly. 'I didn't like how it felt to know that we'd argued, but it was more than that today.'

'Why? What happened?' It was as if he hadn't just bared his soul to her. Prince Adrastos was back, all mind-blowing control and power.

'It's nothing important,' she said, quietly. 'There was a paparazzi mob following Ellie and me. It was…frightening.'

She shuddered. 'It made me very glad this is all fake,' she added for good measure, pleased that she could speak those words with such apparent honesty even when she now knew she wanted, more than anything, for this to be real. 'Because being tailed like that for too long would seriously suck.'

He didn't say anything, and Poppy didn't look at him. The air between them felt thick and heavy and Poppy's heart was hurting, but she didn't take the words back, even when she desperately wanted to.

'And then, in the car, Ellie had some questions, about us.'

'I see.'

'I told her the truth. Not the whole truth,' she clarified. 'But about the job in the Hague, and I explained why you and I would be breaking up soon. It felt…like a weight was lifted off my shoulders to finally be able to say something honest to her, and to know that there's light at the end of the tunnel.' Even to her own ears, the words sounded flat.

The air around them seemed to crackle and Poppy held her breath, waiting, wondering, how he would reply.

After a moment, Adrastos freed his hand from hers then brought it around her shoulders, drawing her body close to his side. 'Tell me about the promotion,' he invited. 'I'd like to hear what you'll be up to.'

It was an impressive opportunity for someone so young. Long after their walk in the woods, Adrastos had been thinking about Poppy's work, about the Hague, about the role she'd accepted on the day of her twenty-fourth birthday. He was happy for her. More than that, he was proud of her.

But what right did he have to be proud? Poppy had achieved this all on her own, just as she'd always wanted, without letters of support from his parents, without the connections they could offer. He'd watched her working, seen her succeed from the sidelines and, yes, he realised now, he'd always felt proud.

· Actually, if anything, he'd been in awe of her.

So why was there a corresponding sense of something dark spreading through his body, like anger and rage, all wrapped up in one? A feeling that he was being forced to walk a path he didn't want, that he was bound and on a track that wasn't his own?

It was different from the way he'd felt when Nick had died. Then, he'd recognised his anger and sense of impotence but at least he'd known why he felt those things. For Adrastos, this was harder. Nobody was dying. There was no grief to grapple with, and yet he was experiencing…the strangest weight bearing down on him. All day, and all night. Every night that passed, with Poppy in his bed, the weight became worse. They made love, and his body rejoiced in hers, his ego exploding at her obvious pleasure and delight, the euphoria he was able to give her and show her, the awakening of her body's senses. This was all *good*. So why didn't he feel that?

Nothing about it made any sense.

At the start of their Christmas visit, he'd just wanted this whole ruse to be over. He'd hoped they might fall back into bed once or twice, but he hadn't been prepared to lose sleep over it. It was only a fortnight, a little less, and afterwards, his life could resume its usual rhythms. A buoying thought, except he couldn't marry what he wanted now with how he'd felt then. Rather than wishing this visit to be over, he found himself contemplating the end of their arrangement with a distinct lack of relief.

And on the night of the famed New Year's Banquet, he wished he could understand the darkness creeping through his thoughts, the weight in his mind. He wished he understood himself better.

CHAPTER TWELVE

'You look…'

Beautiful? Stunning? Perfect? All so insufficient for the vision Poppy made as she stepped into the living room, dressed for the ball.

'Too much?' she asked, running a hand down the front of the red gown.

He shook his head, frowning, still unable to speak. The dress had a fitted bodice and sleeves that fell just beneath her shoulders, at the very top of her slender arms, so his fingers tingled with a need to reach out and touch that creamy, perfect skin, never mind that he'd spent all night touching, that he'd touched until he knew her inch by inch, could recreate her body in the dark. The dress hugged her torso like a second skin, to just a few inches beneath her breasts, where it suddenly flared into a frothy but somehow incredibly elegant skirt, so swishy and…lovely.

'Adrastos? Please? One of the courtiers sent it over. I had chosen something far more…normal… I don't want it to look…'

He shook his head. 'Don't even think about changing.'

Her eyes showed doubt though, and he cursed himself for not reacting better. He'd been sideswiped by the vision she made. Ordinarily, he liked her hair down, loose in waves around her shoulders. He particularly liked it when it formed curtains on either side of her face as she straddled him, staring down into his eyes with an expression of wonderment…but tonight, it had been styled into a loose, sensual bun with tendrils loose about the face. Her neck was bare, and suddenly, Adrastos wanted her to wear something as beautiful as she was, something stunning and frosted like the snow falling outside their windows.

'I want you to wear this dress,' he said gruffly, closing the distance between them and lifting his hands to her hips, holding her there, feeling her familiar warmth through the fabric, 'until later tonight, when I will remove it from you.'

Her eyes widened, then a dimple formed in one cheek as she smiled shyly. 'Next year, you mean.'

He grinned back—it was the easiest thing in the world to do. 'Of course.'

'I just realised our "relationship" will span two years of your life—that's probably a first.'

She was right, but he didn't like hearing her say that. He didn't like the reminder of how he'd lived his life before.

The thought brought him up short. Before? Before Poppy? Before this week? Nothing had changed, he reminded himself forcibly. Sure, this woman he'd been encouraged to think of as a little sister had turned into something else entirely, but that didn't mean *he* was any different.

'You need a necklace,' he said after a beat. 'Let me arrange one for you.'

'Arrange one for me?' she repeated incredulously. 'That's okay. I…think the dress is over the top enough.'

He considered that. 'There are jewels available in the vault. Come, have a look.'

Poppy hesitated a moment, eyes huge in her face, and then she nodded. 'Let's go and see.'

* * *

She had no intention of wearing any of the jewels from the vault, but she'd be lying if she said she wasn't excited to peep inside. The vault was a place that had inspired great games of imagination for Ellie and Poppy as teenagers—a place they knew they weren't allowed, *ever*, because it stored some of the rarest, most valuable jewels in the country, possibly the world. But Adrastos, as heir to the throne, and not being a teenager, Poppy thought with a smile, simply had to appear at the heavily fortified door and he was waved through. And then, through another door, and another, and finally, a suited man met them in a room with some gentle lighting above a line of wooden cabinets. In the centre of the room, though, there was a glass case, and within it stood crowns and tiaras, at least a dozen.

Poppy stopped walking and stared. 'Ellie should be here,' she said with a smile at Adrastos, and her heart skipped a beat, just as it always did now, whenever she looked at him. How could she go back to the way things were before? How would they interact after this?

Where usually certainty sat inside Poppy's chest there was only doubt now, a big chasm of not knowing. She didn't like it.

'I'm actually quite pleased she's not,' he drawled.

'Is there anything particular you would like to look at, Your Highness?'

Adrastos turned to Poppy, stared at her for so long her skin prickled all over and heat flooded her cheeks.

'Diamonds. A choker, I think.'

'Very good, Your Highness.'

'Adrastos.' Poppy shook her head. 'I wanted to see the vault, but I can't possibly wear—'

The man in the suit approached, holding a velvet board

with a single necklace in the centre of it. A diamond choker, just as Adrastos had specified, and quite possibly one of the most beautiful things Poppy had ever seen.

'This was a gift for Her Majesty Queen Marguerite, in the late nineteenth century. The diamonds were initially the property of Queen Elizabeth the First of England. They were refashioned into a necklace as a gift for Her Majesty. Queen Clementine has worn this necklace only once before, to a state dinner. It is a beautiful item.'

Poppy couldn't look away from the thing. It was so much more than beautiful. Delicate, shiny, exquisite, and with the kind of history that made Poppy almost want to pass out. Imagine wearing at her throat diamonds that had once belonged to the famed Elizabethan Queen, a woman who'd known Shakespeare and was recognisable the world over?

She shook her head quickly. 'I can't wear it.'

'Why not?' Adrastos asked, reaching out and lifting the necklace without any of the awe that Poppy felt. Why should he be awed? To Adrastos, this was all normal. It had not been his birthright, and yet he'd assumed that role with the same effortlessness he brought to everything. He couldn't understand how, to Poppy, this was just a step too far. Their game of make-believe was getting harder to understand, the rules no longer clear, the parameters shifting so wildly.

'You know why not,' she whispered meaningfully, glaring at him.

'Please, give us a moment.' he murmured towards the palace jeweller, who bowed and left immediately.

'Adrastos, I wanted to see the vault, but not because I thought I would actually wear anything from here. These things are beautiful, but it's not my place to wear them.'

'Why not?'

'You seriously can't see the problem in this?'

'No.'

'If I wear that—' she gestured to the necklace, then couldn't resist reaching out to touch it '—someone is going to recognise it as one of the palace jewels. An article will run about me wearing it. People will believe that we are way more serious than we're pretending to be. And this is all just pretend,' she said, needing desperately to remind herself of that. 'If I wear that, your parents, your sister, are going to see it and they might think, they'll hope...'

'Yes, they'll hope,' he agreed, but with obvious irritation. 'It's just a necklace.'

'You know better than that. These jewels are all about symbolism, and the symbolism of me wearing one tonight would be too much. We're lying to everyone,' she said with a catch in her throat. 'I don't want to make this worse than it already is.'

He frowned, but evidently thought better of arguing. 'It's your decision,' he said, quietly.

A short while later, as they made their way to the grand foyer that provided the entrance to the ballroom where the banquet would be held, Poppy hesitated. She felt as though it were almost impossible to breathe, as though she could hardly speak, but she knew she needed to say something. Uneasiness was creeping into her veins, a darkness she couldn't explain but knew she somehow needed to.

'Adrastos, listen, about tonight.' She stopped walking, reaching for his wrist to hold him back with her. There would be people in the foyer. They had only a few steps to go before they were absorbed by the evening. 'I think we should be careful, with how we behave.'

'Meaning?'

She gnawed on her lower lip. 'In six days, I'm leaving the country. We've done what we set out to do. Your parents don't think we had some reckless one-night stand. They're not mad at us. But I don't want to give them false hope. I don't want them to think we actually have a future.' Her voice wobbled a little. Damn it, her emotions were all over the place. She forced a smile. 'It just makes sense.'

'Would you like me to stand over on the other side of the room? To ignore you all night?'

Was he annoyed? She couldn't tell. He sounded calm enough but there was a flicker of something in his voice that confused Poppy. 'Not exactly, no. But you shouldn't...'

'Shouldn't what?' he asked, eyes skimming her face, and Poppy drew a blank. Shouldn't look at her as if he wanted to peel the dress from her body? Shouldn't ask her to dance? Shouldn't stand with her and talk until she smiled, or laughed?

'I don't know,' she gave up with a shrug. 'Just...be careful.'

'Poppy, the whole world believes we are dating. To be seen together at the ball is going to reinforce that belief.' He lifted a hand, gently touched her cheek. 'Are you regretting this?'

She pulled a face. 'I regret lying to your mother,' she said, then wrinkled her brow. Because that wasn't quite accurate. She hated lying, but this week had been one of the best of her life. She would never take it back. 'I just don't want anyone to get hurt.'

He nodded slowly. 'Fortunately for you, I don't think anyone in the world has any confidence that I can make a relationship work. We'll part ways in six days' time, and all the world will know it's just Adrastos being Adrastos.'

He smiled, but it didn't reach his eyes. Poppy wanted to kiss him, but she knew that if she did all the tension and doubt in the middle of her chest would burst into something else and she might actually break down and cry.

'In which case, let's go, Your Highness.'

But his last statement sat with Poppy all night, tightening around her throat almost as if she'd worn the necklace and the necklace had been a noose. She felt it and, despite lifting her hand to her throat and pressing her fingers to the flesh there, she couldn't loosen it, couldn't make herself relax, make her breathing grow easier. She was exhausted as the night went on—not from making small talk with people but from being close to Adrastos and trying to get everything *right*. How to play the part of his girlfriend without allowing it to appear as though either had a serious wish for *more*?

Why did that matter so much to her? Why did she want to rail against the genuine expectation that their relationship might somehow seem permanent? That was obviously a risk they'd taken right from the beginning of all this, so why did it bother her so much now?

Because of the parameters shifting, she reminded herself, sipping a champagne just before midnight.

'Come with me.' Adrastos appeared out of nowhere, catching her hand, pulling her with him. She frowned, looked around, but everyone was far too merry and involved in their own conversations to care too much about Adrastos and Poppy. He pulled her through the edge of the crowd and towards a set of large glass doors that opened onto a terrace.

Just like that first night, Poppy's birthday, it was cold. Colder, in fact, tonight, with snow falling in swirls around them, and Adrastos shrugged out of his jacket and wrapped it around Poppy's shoulders. The hum of the party was behind them; here, they were alone.

'What are we doing?' she asked, her heart lifting, her stomach squeezing.

'Celebrating the new year.'

'Isn't that what the party is for?'

'Given our conversation before the ball, I thought you might not appreciate being kissed in the middle of the room.'

This was so ridiculous. Shouldn't she have insisted he kiss her in front of everyone? Wasn't that the point of a fake relationship? She shook her head slowly, a sigh strangled in her throat. It was almost impossible to wrestle with her emotions. All night she'd been trying, and all night feelings had stormed through her. Now she was alone with Adrastos, emotions were taking over.

'Poppy?'

'I'm sorry. I was just thinking how strange this all is.'

'In what way?'

'We're doing this to convince everyone we're a couple and yet I'm insisting we don't do anything couifiey. I don't know... I've lost sight of everything.'

He moved closer, his body warm and big, his strength wrapping around her, making Poppy's heart lift.

'What have you lost sight of?'

She shook her head. She wanted to explain, to put into words how she was feeling, but she didn't have the words to properly answer him.

'We'll part ways in six days' time, and all the world will know it's just Adrastos being Adrastos.'

But then it dawned on her. Poppy didn't want to part ways in six days' time. She didn't want to leave Adrastos. Not then, not ever.

She pulled away from him, moving down the terrace a little, the din of the party just background noise to the frantic nature of her thoughts. This was a fake relationship, but why? What about it was fake? Not the way they talked to each other, not the way they slept together, not the way they just...clicked.

Everything about Adrastos was *right* for Poppy. It was all *real*. She gasped, lifting a hand to her lips and turning to stare at him as her heart went *kerthunk* in her chest for another reason altogether now. Relief that finally Poppy was listening. Finally, she understood.

She loved Adrastos.

Not fake love.

Real, all-consuming love. From the tip of her head to the bottom of her toes. *Love*. For all of him. The warrior, the ruler, and the broken, grieving brother. She loved this man, every angle, every facet, every part.

'Adrastos...'

His name was a whisper on the breeze, barely audible, but with that one word, she might as well have been pledging herself to him for life. Her heart cracked, because Adrastos didn't want that. He'd made that clear. He'd told her why he avoided relationships, he'd told her he didn't even care about producing the required royal heir. But that was *before*. What if his parameters had changed too? What if the easy, rule-bound fake relationship they'd established in the beginning had morphed into something else for Adrastos too? What if he loved her back?

Hope was a soaring light within her, brighter than the snow was cold.

Inside, the countdown to midnight began, a chorus of voices, happy and joyous, with no idea that, outside, Poppy was walking a tightrope, happily ever after on one side and desperate loneliness the other. For though she'd been alone before Adrastos, it was only now, in contrast to the way she'd begun to feel when they were together, that she would know loneliness.

'*Ten—nine—*'

Adrastos lifted a finger, crooked it towards himself.

'*Eight—seven—*'

And despite her fear and the doubts tumbling through her like detritus in a hurricane, Poppy travelled forward, one step, and then another—

'*Six—five—*'

He smelled so good, like citrus and pine needles, so masculine and so familiar, so she knew she'd never be able to walk in a forest again nor pass by an orchard in the summer without thinking of Adrastos, without wanting him.

'*Four—three—*'

His hand came around her back, fingers splayed wide, pushing her forward. Their bodies melded, so perfect, so right, so blissful. His mouth lowered and the air around them sizzled and popped.

'*Two—*'

Poppy held her breath, her toes curled in her elegant shoes.

'*One!*'

His lips claimed hers, slowly, gently, perfectly, so the sting in her eyes gave way and a tear rolled delicately down one cheek as she tilted her head back, giving him access to all of her, kissing him back with the desperate certainty that she couldn't wait another six days for the axe to drop. This either had to be their last night together, or it had to be a true beginning: a new year, and the start of something new for both of them—a real relationship.

Cheers and crying and clapping came from inside and the strains of 'Auld Lang Syne' filled the air. Adrastos lifted his head, looking down at Poppy, eyes so beautiful and all seeing, a frown forming as he recognised the tear and lifted his finger to smudge it away.

'Happy New Year, Poppy.'

Her breath caught in her throat. She wanted to say it back, but other words were more urgent, more pressing, and instead she found herself just nodding, jerking her head.

'Adrastos—' His name now flooded her body with a powerful, drugging need. He was her other half. The perfect love. Just as her parents had felt that happiness and completeness, she'd felt it too. Here, with Adrastos. He was a part of her. But was she a part of him? Her parents' love had been a fairy tale because it was mutual. If Adrastos didn't love her back, then everything she felt might as well have been a torture device.

'Let's go upstairs.'

To his suite. She stared at him, the floor feeling uneven beneath her feet. But the idea of disappearing into that apartment was anathema to Poppy. It was another part of the pretence, and yet it was where their relationship had begun to feel truly real for her. Before she crossed that threshold once more, she had to know: was his apartment a stage set, or the backdrop to their real-life romance?

'I—Not just yet. I need to—' She bit into her lower lip, frustrated with herself. 'We need to talk.'

He was quiet, waiting for her. Not so much a 'we need to talk' as Poppy needing to talk to Adrastos. To ask him something important.

But how could she? Prior to the night they'd slept together, she'd had no experience with men in the bedroom, and she had even less experience with the emotional side of a relationship, with the vocabulary required to discuss feelings.

Just be honest.

Oh, how ironic, given that this was all supposedly fake.

'This is hard,' she said on a sigh.

'You can tell me anything, Poppy. You can say anything.'

Sure she could. But what would it change between them? Anything? Everything?

'I'm starting to have doubts about this,' she said, quietly. 'About the agreement we made, about what's meant to be the clear-cut nature of our "relationship". Things have become more complicated than we anticipated.'

His expression gave nothing away. The air pulsed with nervousness, tension, anxiety, but was it all from Poppy? Or did Adrastos have some sense of what was coming?

She took a deep breath. She had to do this. Didn't she? Or could she just pretend everything was normal? Stick out the next six days and then leave as planned? She was about to throw a grenade into both their lives, didn't it bear thinking about, at least for a moment? The weight grew heavier, the feeling of something being wrapped around her throat, and the words responsible, choking her from within, refused to budge.

'It doesn't matter,' she said after a beat, cursing herself for not being brave enough, while simultaneously thanking her lucky stars she'd averted a definite disaster. 'I think I'm just tired.'

His lips tugged downward and his brows knitted together, but a moment later her hand was in his and he was leading her to their room, not through the party but along the terrace and into a different entrance, so no one else could see the paleness of her face.

CHAPTER THIRTEEN

ADRASTOS HAD LITTLE time for indirectness. He appreciated the importance of discretion at times, particularly with regards to diplomatic discussions, but in his personal life, he always spoke clearly.

It was why he could be confident that he'd never hurt a woman with false expectations. Even if his reputation hadn't preceded him, Adrastos was frank about his situation *before* getting into bed with a woman. It was an easy enough conversation to have: a short discussion of his desire to stay single, to keep things 'light' and temporary, an aversion to future planning, to discussing anything overly personal.

These were rules he'd broken again and again with Poppy, but only because they had the broader protection of their 'fake' relationship and her upcoming departure to enforce invisible, important boundaries.

He didn't need to avoid personal conversations because they'd defined what they were doing at the start of this. She'd created the need for a ruse, and at first he'd been hesitant, but actually it was…a lot of fun. He'd enjoyed himself. He almost felt sorry that she was leaving in six days, which was exactly why he was craving the end to this.

He needed the simplicity of life pre-Poppy, the order that came from knowing he was alone, all by himself, and always would be. Perhaps it wasn't fair to put such expectations on Eleanor—maybe she would want to avoid marriage too? But somehow, he doubted it. It felt right that she should provide the royal heirs Nicholas couldn't, a way of sharing out Nick's responsibilities between both siblings.

He fell asleep that night with Poppy beside him and a determination about what the future held that didn't quite fit in his gut, but that he knew he had to stick to. Adrastos had spent a long time carving out a very specific life for himself: it was the only way he knew how to live. Nonetheless, perhaps it wouldn't hurt to clarify things with Poppy again.

Last night, he could have sworn she'd been about to say something. Something important. He didn't know for sure it was about him, about their future, but just in case she was starting to feel something silly, like that she might want more from him, it was probably a good idea to remind her that Adrastos wasn't the man she was looking for. In the morning, he'd make sure she understood his limitations. It felt important.

He turned onto his side, stared at the wall, and put aside thoughts of his own future, the life he'd made for himself, to imagine Poppy's life after this. To imagine Poppy and her career, her future bright and glittering, so beautiful and fascinating, compassionate, smart, loyal, kind. He imagined her leaving the palace, leaving him, and the people she would meet, the opportunity she'd have to replace him, and told himself he was glad: she deserved the happiness she sought, the perfect relationship her parents had shown her.

Adrastos would always be glad, though, that they'd shared this experience. Something had changed within him, and he suspected, he hoped, it was the same for Poppy too.

Poppy woke with a start as the dawn light broke across the forest, bathing the trees in shades of purple and silver, ghostly and ancient against the winter's sky. She stared at them without seeing, the beating of a drum sounding in her ears, before wrenching her gaze towards Adrastos, who lay sleeping, half dressed, in the bed beside her.

She had to tell him.

Every moment, every breath she took, without being honest with him was like a form of torture. She would have no peace, no relief, unless she did this.

With shaking fingers and a frazzled mind, Poppy slipped out of bed and into the bathroom, where she showered quickly then changed silently into a pale lemon jumper and a floor-length skirt. She finger-combed her hair over one shoulder then paced the foot of the bed, lost in thought, until Adrastos shifted, eyes on her, so she wondered how long he'd been watching her for.

'It's early,' she murmured, flinching as she looked towards the window.

'I can see that. What's going on?'

She stopped pacing and stared at him, her heart thumping hard into her ribs. 'We need to talk.'

He frowned. 'Yes, we do.'

Hope soared in her chest. Was it possible he felt the same after all? She dug her nails into her palms. It was cowardly, but she was glad to be able to say, 'You go first.'

He sat up a little straighter, skimming his eyes over her face then focussing on her gaze, so her stomach twisted. When he looked at her, Poppy felt as though he saw right into her soul.

'I've enjoyed doing this, Poppy. Pretending to be your boyfriend has been more fun than I thought it would be,' he said, with no idea how faint that praise was. 'I think you are a very special young woman. I'm looking forward to seeing what your future holds.'

Your future, not ours. Seeing, not being a part of.

She nodded jerkily, awkwardly. The hope in her chest ebbed.

'You are wonderful,' he said quietly. 'And you should be happy. I hope, after this, you find yourself more willing to take a chance on a relationship. I think you'll make some guy incredibly happy one day, Poppy, and I hope he'll make you happy too.'

It was the absolute worst thing he could say, though of course he didn't know that. But for Poppy, it felt as though he'd grabbed a knife and slid the blade between her ribs. She spun away from him on a sharp, deep breath, her eyes filling with stars.

'My job makes me happy,' she said, stiffly.

'You are a passionate, loving woman.' He spoke with his quiet, trademark authority. Poppy squeezed her eyes shut. 'You cannot—should not—continue to ignore that side of yourself.'

But how could he speak like this? So dispassionately? Without a hint of jealousy? When Poppy allowed herself the sadistic indulgence of imagining Adrastos with whichever woman would come after herself, she wanted to curl up in the foetal position and rock in the corner. Yet here he was, so blithely wishing her well with whomever she decided to sleep with next. Of all the insults!

And when they supposedly had five more days together!

Well, that was a hard no. Poppy couldn't do this. She was strong and determined but she wasn't so filled with self-loathing that she'd subject herself to this level of emotional torture.

'I am, however, glad we have some more time together before you leave.'

Again, so calm. So reasonable. He could speak of her departure without even a hint of emotion. How deluded had she been to think, to hope, that he might actually care for her? That her feelings could be reciprocated?

Poppy could only be relieved that she hadn't blurted out how she felt. That would be her secret, held close to her chest, something she never intended to tell another soul.

'Actually...' Her voice wobbled. She cleared her throat. 'That's what I wanted to talk to you about.'

She turned, faced him, did her best to breathe normally, to keep her features relaxed when inside she was a tangle of feelings and nerves. But this would be over soon. She'd say what she had to say, pack her bag and leave, and never look back.

Except she *would* look back because this place was her home away from home and his family was her family. But she couldn't think about that now, or she'd cry at the hopelessness of it all. Maybe it had been hopeless from that first kiss, from the moment they slept together. Maybe it always would have ended this way. She'd lied about the nature of their relationship to avoid hurting other people, but in the process she'd put herself right in the firing line.

Had it all been a mistake after all, just as he'd said?

Poppy had thought herself not a good liar. She hated dishonesty and always had. Yet, looking across the room at her fake boyfriend, she found her next fib came easily enough— a form of salvation. 'My supervisor emailed to ask if I could start sooner. They're desperate for staff to cover this case.'

He frowned. 'It's the holidays.'

She shrugged. 'The bad guys don't really care that much...'

He was quiet a moment. 'I presume you can email back and say no?'

'I could,' she said breathlessly, wishing her heart wasn't

in such an awful state. 'But I won't. They need me, and I can't—I don't see why—isn't this a good thing?' she insisted with quiet strength, when she could think of nothing else to say. He stared at her without answering. 'This gets you off the hook earlier. I'll tell your parents about the job, and about us—how it makes sense to end things given I'm going to be in the Hague for the next three years at least.'

'Three years,' he responded, sitting up straighter, something briefly sparking between them before his expression returned to neutral. 'You didn't mention that.'

'I'm going into a division that takes on long-term investigations. My project is forecast to take three years. I'm supervising a team of twenty— I have to be committed.'

'You didn't mention this,' he repeated.

'Is it relevant?'

He stared at her as though she were speaking in a foreign language. Poppy's chest hurt. She needed to end this.

'I'll leave this morning,' she said quietly. 'And be on a flight out this afternoon, ready to start tomorrow. It's the way it has to be.'

'This makes no sense. You always spend the holidays here, the whole holidays.'

She blinked away from him, turning once more to the woods and craving instead the familiar view from her own room of the rose garden. There was too much of him in this space, this view. Too much masculine, wild, elemental power. 'This year is different.' Which was putting it mildly.

'Are you saying that remaining here any longer will jeopardise your job?'

She turned slowly, her heart breaking. 'I'm saying I've been asked to go sooner, and I intend to. Adrastos, think about it: if we weren't in a fake relationship, if we weren't pretending to be a couple, would you really care? Do you even really notice when I'm here and when I'm not?' She took in a deep breath. 'Of course not. Think of this as a get-out-of-jail-early card. I'm leaving, and in a few hours' time you'll be free to resume your life as though none of this ever happened. Isn't that good news?'

'Oh, Poppy, I'm so torn. Of course I'm proud of you, and happy for you, but I'm also—'

Poppy braced herself for what Clementine would say next, and the older woman's gaze flitted to King Alexander, who sat in an armchair, watching both.

'We're disappointed,' he said into the void. 'We love you, and naturally we hoped you and Adrastos might progress from dating to something more serious. We cannot think of anyone we would rather welcome into the family as a daughter-in-law, nor anyone better suited to the requirements of the role.'

Poppy's face drained of colour. 'I'm very sorry if you thought there was any potential for that. This job is important to me. Adrastos always knew I'd be leaving after the holidays.' She offered a tight smile. 'We would have preferred to keep our relationship private, but once those photos were printed—'

'Yes.' Clementine winced. 'Pesky invasive shutterbugs.'

'The important thing to understand,' Poppy continued with the lines she'd rehearsed, 'is that Adrastos and I have the deepest respect for one another. We're…friends, and always will be. But that's all.'

Poppy left the room a moment later, eyes closed, lungs hurting with the force of her breathing, but Clementine was right behind her.

'Poppy, my darling girl, just wait a moment.'

Poppy stopped walking, forced a smile, then turned.

'I just need to know one thing before you leave.'

Poppy nodded, thinking longingly of the limousine that would spirit her away from the palace.

'If you love Adrastos as I think you do, then why can't you find a way to make this work?'

Poppy stared at the Queen, pain lancing her. 'Your Majesty...' she murmured, shaking her head.

Clementine waited with the appearance of kindly patience.

'I care for Adrastos deeply, but we're not in love.' She spoke truthfully. After all, that was a mutual state, and her love was entirely one-sided.

The Queen's voice was soft. 'I've seen the two of you together. I've seen the changes in him, in just these few days. You're good for him, and I think he's good for you, too. Why on earth would you both let that go?'

'My job—'

'Is a vocation, and I understand, with you, it is also a calling, but this is your *life*, my darling. I swore at your mother's funeral that I would stand in her stead, that I would love and advise you as I would my own daughter, and I hope I've always done so. I hope you know how I feel about you. But this is a mistake, and I cannot let you go without expressing that.'

Poppy's tummy squeezed. 'With respect, you're mistaken. Adrastos and I are not as well suited as you think.' She reached out and squeezed Clementine's hand. 'Please, don't worry about either of us. I'm looking forward to the challenges of my job,' she murmured, truthfully, 'and Adrastos will probably have forgotten all about me by nightfall,' she added, lifting her eyes heavenward in an attempt at humour that she was very far from feeling.

* * *

Adrastos was so deep into the woods, another man might have feared he'd never get out, but not Adrastos. He had every faith in his abilities, but, failing that, he wasn't sure he particularly cared. He stood in the centre of the woods and stared up at the leaden sky, at the snow that was falling around him, and pushed himself not to think, not to listen. He didn't want to hear the car pull out from the palace, he didn't want to think about Poppy ensconced in the back seat, being driven—where, exactly? To her apartment to pack more things? Or straight on to the airport? He didn't want to think about her flight taking off, about her physically being in another country. He didn't want to think about all the things he'd so blithely rolled off to her that morning— her life post Adrastos. His hopes for her future.

They were all genuine, but this morning, they'd also been somewhat academic. Easier to discuss because the reality of that life had been at least five days away, five days Adrastos had intended to spend buried inside Poppy, holding her, making her laugh and burrowing deep into her secrets to understand every single part of her. He'd thought they had *time*, five days. It might not have seemed like much, but when you spent your time as intensely as they did, five days had seemed like almost enough.

Almost?

He ground his teeth, pushed on, deeper into the forest, through trees that grew thick and gnarled with age.

It had to have been enough. It would have been enough. But instead, she'd thrown her departure at him like a bomb and simply...left. Disappeared.

He would also leave tonight. He didn't want to be here without her. He didn't particularly want to face his parents or sister, or the void Poppy would leave—another absence in their lives, like Nicholas's. He ground his teeth, walked faster, harder, uncaring for the snow that began to fall heavier, his footsteps that became buried. He had waypoints to navigate this forest and knew he'd be safe. Safer here, he suspected, than out there, where he had to deal with the fallout of their pretence—without Poppy by his side. She'd never be there again.

CHAPTER FOURTEEN

BUT IT WAS no use. She was here too, in his home in the capital, in the kitchen, palms curved around a teacup as she begged him to go along with her ill-conceived ruse. She was in the air, in his mind, her fragrance lingering in some of his clothes, her touch like a phantom against his skin, so if he closed his eyes and imagined hard enough maybe, just maybe she would appear?

She didn't. He went to bed that night and woke reaching for her, his mind not cooperating with reality, making him forget, so he woke with the happiness of a man who got to reach out and grab hold of a woman with the power to make the world shimmer gold.

Reality though banged into him at the moment his fingertips scraped empty, cold sheets, an unrumpled side of the bed, Poppy's absence.

The fib had given Poppy some breathing space. She would leave the country on the sixth, as planned, and until then she could hide away in her apartment, licking her wounds, bracing herself for the magnitude of work required of her, for the post-Adrastos life she had to step into.

There was a lot to do, in any event. She had found someone to lease her apartment, so she busied herself with packing up personal items, boxing some for storage and others to ship to her new home. She didn't like to think about that. Beyond Adrastos, there was a lot in Stomland she would miss like crazy, chiefly, Ellie, and the King and Queen.

When she'd been put forward for this promotion, Poppy had consoled herself that she would come back often to see the family, that she'd take all her vacations here, so it would almost be as though she hadn't left. But the palace was tainted now, a poisoned chalice. How could she go there? She'd half be hoping to see Adrastos and half desperately hoping he was anywhere else.

Poppy squeezed her eyes shut as another wave of tears crashed down her cheeks. It had been like this for the three days since leaving the palace. She would be busily doing something, like an automaton, working away, and then a memory or feeling would spark and she'd be crying, paralysed and unable to do anything until the grief began to recede. Sometimes that took ten minutes, other times, hours. Poppy was not in control, she just had to let the feelings wash over her.

She'd never wanted her own mother so badly as she did now.

As night fell, Poppy, a captive to her apartment, knew one thing that would make her feel better. A go-to she always employed whenever life got on top of her.

Poppy was a runner, and she needed now to pound the pavement, to feel strong and powerful and in charge of *something* in her life. She changed into workout gear, switched off the lights to the house then peered out. Paparazzi hadn't been there for days. She pulled the door shut, nodded at one of her neighbours without stopping to speak and then ran, hard and fast, until her legs burned and her breath hurt, and she was so sore and tired that it was almost impossible to think.

Running was her salvation, but she suspected she'd have to basically circumnavigate the globe before she felt anything remotely like herself again.

He stared at the photo as though it had magic abilities. As though if he looked long and hard enough he could actually understand if it had legitimately been taken only the day before, or if this was a trick by the tabloids, designed to drive clicks and make sales. Maybe this was an old photo of Poppy? Because why would she still be here, in Stomland, when she'd told him she was leaving earlier? Why would she be a ten-minute drive away when he'd been torturing himself imagining the miles between himself and her? Why would she be alone in her apartment when she could have been in his bed at the palace, or, better yet, his bed here?

Why, why, why?

Cursing, he grabbed his keys, and without stopping to think through the wisdom of this, or to consider that maybe she'd lied because she needed space, space he shouldn't invade, he ran out of his front door and into the car that was always waiting for him.

'Take me to Poppy's,' he barked as a flash ignited through his window and he ground his teeth.

To hell with the press; he didn't care. All he cared about in that moment was seeing Poppy and getting some answers. No, that wasn't completely true. He cared, almost more than that, about kissing her until she agreed not to leave. This became his sole objective.

Poppy read Eleanor's text just a moment before a knock sounded at her door.

I thought you were leaving!?

She didn't have a chance to write back though. Moving through her home, phone in hand, she paused at the door, peeked through the hole and then pressed her back to the door in a complete fear response.

Adrastos!

Oh, no!

Oh, yes! Her body rejoiced, yearned to throw open the door and wrap her arms around him, but her mind, her sore, battered heart, knew that seeing him again would be a disaster.

'Damn it, Poppy, I can see the shadow of your feet beneath the door. I can *hear* you. Open the door before someone comes and takes a damned photo.'

Well, there he made a pretty decent point.

But there was no time to strengthen herself, no time to build a wall of defence around her fragile self. She opened the door and Adrastos breezed in then slammed it shut behind himself.

And then he stood.

And he stared.

And he stood, so still it was as if he'd turned to stone, and he stared, for so long Poppy felt as though he must see deep inside her, past her flesh and blood and bones and tissue and right into her soul.

She tried to move. She wanted to. But her feet were as stone-like as his body, so she also stood, and stared and ached, and needed, and longed for the way she'd been able to reach out and touch him whenever she'd wanted, for a few brief days. But it had left a lifetime of memories and she knew she'd never *not* want to reach out to him.

'You're still here.'

She opened her mouth, belatedly remembering Ellie's text, too. 'How did you know?'

'Is that really what matters?'

'It's just, Ellie...she messaged me too...'

'There's a photo of you running. The papers said it was taken last night, but I didn't believe it. After all, you told me you'd been asked to start your new job early. You told me you were leaving. I thought you'd left.'

It wasn't like Adrastos to babble, and he wasn't exactly babbling, but nor was he speaking with any conciseness.

'You said you were leaving.'

Her heart felt as though it had been speared by a thousand arrows. 'I am leaving,' she responded quietly, then expelled a soft breath. 'On the sixth, as planned.'

He nodded once, a sharp jerk of his head, but his eyes narrowed and his face showed confusion. 'Then why did you lie to me?'

'Apparently, that's what I do now,' she said, glad that her feet finally got the memo and carried her away from him, towards her living room. But Adrastos caught her at the wrist, spinning her back to face him.

She closed her eyes, his touch so incendiary her body began to tremble.

'Why did you lie to me?'

This time, a glib response wasn't going to cut it. She shook her head, words failing her, tears—so much a part of her now—shimmering on her lashes. 'I needed to leave.'

He frowned. 'Was it really so awful?'

She closed her eyes.

'I thought you enjoyed being with me. I thought you liked what we were doing. If that was not the case, you could simply have told me so. I'm a grown man, Poppy, I could have handled the truth.'

She wanted to repeat that famous movie line to him, because she didn't really think he could handle the truth in this instance, not the honest to God truth anyway.

'This was easier.'

'Easier?' he repeated, his jaw moving as he stared down at her. 'For whom?'

She blinked up at him, confusion warring with anger. 'I cannot understand why you are behaving like this,' she said after a minute. 'Is it your ego that's hurt? Your pride wounded? You cannot believe any woman would want to leave you sooner than you were ready to let her go? Is that it?'

'I cannot understand why you lied,' he contradicted. 'I cannot understand why you would choose to hide out in your apartment here rather than just be honest with me—'

'Oh, go to hell,' she snapped, anger winning, confusion something she could analyse and interpret later.

'I beg your pardon?'

She wrenched her arm free, rubbing her wrist to erase the warmth of his touch.

'Go to hell, Your Highness,' she corrected, storming into the living room and looking around.

Her fingers itched to grab something and throw it, an impulse that truly shocked Poppy, who was not, and never had been, prone to violence.

'Stop right there,' he growled, standing in the door to the room, arms crossed over his broad chest, so she realised she had actually picked up a ceramic vase. Her eyes were like flames, pure heat.

'We are having this conversation and then I am leaving. But first, I want to understand what happened that morning. No, what happened the night before,' he corrected. 'At the ball. We went outside, you wanted to talk to me, then you changed your mind. And don't say it was about the job: I know now that's not the case.'

She ground her teeth together.

'There is no point to any of this,' she said angrily, slamming the vase back on the side table and moving to a window. 'You told me what you want—I just gave you your wish a few days earlier.'

'At no point did I say I wanted us to end things then and there.'

'No, but you did want it to end. You wanted to get back to your life, for me to move on with mine, to find someone who'd "make me happy",' she muttered. 'Do you have any idea how that felt? To hear *you* of all people calmly elucidating your wish-list for me? How inappropriate I consider it for you, the man I lost my virginity to, to be openly plotting my next relationship?'

Silence arced between them, as fierce as electricity.

'I was not—'

'Yes, damn it!' She rounded on him. 'You were.'

'Well, so what?' he said, not moving a muscle. 'Is there something wrong with me expressing a wish for you to be happy?'

'With *someone else*,' she reminded him contemptuously.

'And this is why you left?' he demanded. 'Because you didn't want me to talk about our futures? About what life would be like after this came to an end?'

Poppy's heart, already so broken, no longer seemed to exist. In her chest, where it had once been the centre of her body's functioning, was just a black, inky void.

'I want you to go now.' She stared at him, and all the love she felt morphed into something closer to hatred. She despised him. She despised the way he lived his life, even though, in a calmer moment, she might have conceded that she could understand it. But now, she was hurting and breaking, falling apart at the seams, and she just wanted him to go away again. This was a torment, the prolonging of an agony she'd thought she'd already navigated. She'd thought she'd seen him for the last time and had stepped into her post-Adrastos life. She didn't much like it, but at least she'd taken those first few steps and survived.

'I need you to go,' she amended softly, eyes huge in her face.

He swore, shook his head. 'This makes no sense.'

Of course it didn't make any sense to Adrastos. His heart wasn't on the line. His heart wasn't anywhere near the playing field.

'I don't understand.'

She nodded slowly. 'I know that.'

'I want to understand.'

She toyed with her necklace, a fine chain she'd bought herself when she graduated university. It reminded her of another necklace, one far grander, that Adrastos had wanted her to wear.

But how could she explain any of this to him?

'Our relationship did what it was supposed to. There was no point prolonging it, and so I came home.'

'That's very logical, except for one point: you lied to me. If it was all so simple, why not tell me that at the time?'

She blanched. She couldn't answer that.

'Tell me the truth. Why did you run away from me?'

Poppy groaned. 'Please, Adrastos, if you care about me at all, you'll just let it go and leave me in peace.'

He drew himself up to his full height, inhaled so his chest puffed out, then spoke quietly, in a measured tone, that was somehow at odds with the emotions swirling in his eyes. 'Let me be clear: you want me to walk out of that door and have that be the end of it? You want me to leave, and let you leave for your new job, and we will never speak of this again? Is that what you wish?'

No, her insides screamed, but Poppy nodded, her voice quivering. 'Please.'

He glared at her, his nostrils flaring, and she held her breath, until finally he spun on his heel, stalked towards the door, yanked it open and left, just as she'd asked him to, and this time she was pretty sure it would be for good.

The car drove him through the streets he knew so well, black body, black windows, as black as his mood, and with each mile he travelled he felt as though his head were getting closer and closer to exploding from the ravaging, pounding of his blood, he felt as though his skin were being stretched and his mood becoming apocalyptically awful until he leaned forward and said to his security guy, 'Take me back.'

The words emerged as a growl, or maybe even a threat. Adrastos didn't care. He sat back in his seat, stared out of the window and tried to shape his feelings into order, and then from that order to form words to explain them to someone else. By the time he'd arrived back at Poppy's, he still wasn't sure what was driving him, and he sure as hell didn't know how to relay that to Poppy, but he wasn't just going to disappear from her life.

'I told you to go away,' she said, through tears, so many tears, so he pushed the door shut and this time did exactly what he'd wanted to before: he wrapped her in his arms, pulled her against his chest and just…held her there. He held her while she sobbed and he stroked her hair gently and whatever words he'd wanted to say still wouldn't come out but it didn't matter because she was crying and he had it within his power to make her feel better just by being there.

And he wanted to be there.

He wanted to *always* be there, whenever she needed him, and whenever she didn't. He wanted to watch her soar, but also to be there when she didn't, or thought she couldn't.

He just wanted…her.

'Poppy, I don't want to leave.'

She sobbed. That strange ache in his chest spiralled and he realised now what was hurting—his heart. His heart hurt.

In a way it hadn't done for years, if ever.

'I get it. I understand now. I understand why you left. Why you lied to me. I understand why everything I said to you was possibly the worst thing in the world. I understand now what I didn't then because I understand us better.'

'You're not making any sense,' she whispered.

'Yes, I am. For the first time in years, possibly.' He caught her face, tilted it to him, because he needed to see her and, more importantly, he needed her to see him, to see the truth in his eyes.

'I have spent most of my adult life running from relationships, running from the very idea of a relationship, but maybe that's because I had already met my perfect other half and I just needed to be brave enough to realise that? Poppy, you are a part of me,' he said when she stared at him in shock. 'You are inside me, all of me, you are the very *best* part of me.'

'But you said—'

'I said whatever I needed to in order to make it seem as though I was completely in control of things, as if nothing between us had changed.' He grimaced. 'Believe me when I tell you: I would never have been able to let you go without a fight. Not now, not on the sixth, not in a year, not ever. You are my love, my heart, my everything.' He kissed the tip of her nose, gently, achingly. 'If you left because you feel the same way, if you left because you wanted something you thought I'd never offer, then let me say this: I am offering you my everything and my all, I am offering you the rest of my life, lived with you.'

Her sob now sounded different.

And a smile broke through, then grew wider, and then she was laughing, crying, shaking her head, a beautiful, perfect, emotional woman, the holder of his heart, the keeper of his future.

How could he have ever thought he wouldn't want this?

Because he'd never been with someone like Poppy.

Maybe it was even why he'd resisted relationships. Maybe his subconscious had known there would never be another woman who could mean to him what Poppy did? Maybe it was all for this moment, this perfect, stolen moment.

'But my job, Adrastos. I can't—how can we make this work?' Her smile slipped and the sun went behind a cloud. He would do whatever it took to make her smile again.

'You've worked hard to earn that promotion. I'm not asking you to give it up.'

'But you're here. You can't leave.'

'I can travel. You can travel. We can make this work. Can't we?'

She blinked at him.

'Do we have any other choice?' he pushed, because, now that he'd finally realised how he felt, he couldn't imagine a world without Poppy in it.

'No.' She laughed again. 'I guess we don't.' Then another sound. 'But there's something else: I've rented out my place. Someone's moving in next week.'

'That is not a problem so much as a godsend. You'll stay with me, of course, when you come back.'

Her lips parted. 'Adrastos—you don't have to do that.'

'I don't want to spend another day apart from you. For your job, I'll make do, but when you are here, in Stomland, it will be in my home, my bed, my life, with me. Okay?'

Her heart stammered and she nodded, finding it almost impossible to believe this twist in her reality. 'Am I dreaming?'

He kissed her softly, slowly. 'No, Poppy, you're not asleep. We're both, finally, fully awake.'

* * * * *

COMING SOON!

We really hope you enjoyed reading this book. If you're looking for more romance be sure to head to the shops when new books are available on

Thursday 9th November

To see which titles are coming soon, please visit

millsandboon.co.uk/nextmonth

MILLS & BOON

MILLS & BOON ®

Coming next month

A BILLION-DOLLAR HEIR FOR CHRISTMAS
Caitlin Crews

'What exactly are you trying to say to me?'

Tiago sighed, as if Lillie was being dense. And he hated himself for that, too, when she stiffened. 'This cannot be an affair, Lillie. No matter what happened between us in Spain. Do you not understand? I will have to marry you.'

Her eyes went wide. Her face paled, and not, his ego could not help but note, in the transformative joy a man in his position might have expected to see after a proposal. 'Marry me? Marry *you?* Are you mad? On the strength of one night?'

'On the strength of your pregnancy. Because the Villela heir must be legitimate.' He looked at her as if he had never seen her before and would never see her again, or maybe it was simply that he did not wish to say the thing he knew he must. But that was life, was it not? Forever forcing himself to do what was necessary, what was right. Never what he wanted. So he took a deep breath. 'We will marry. Quickly. And once that happens, I will never touch you again.'

Continue reading
A BILLION-DOLLAR HEIR FOR CHRISTMAS
Caitlin Crews

Available next month
www.millsandboon.co.uk

LET'S TALK

Romance

For exclusive extracts, competitions
and special offers, find us online:

 MillsandBoon

 @MillsandBoon

 @MillsandBoonUK

 @MillsandBoonUK

Get in touch on 01413 063 232

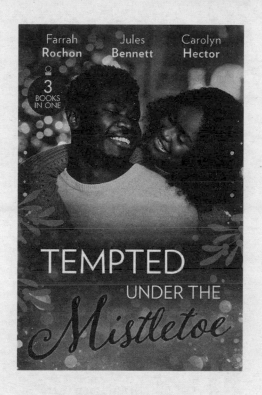

MILLS & BOON

THE HEART OF ROMANCE

A ROMANCE FOR EVERY READER

MODERN — Prepare to be swept off your feet by sophisticated, sexy and seductive heroes, in some of the world's most glamourous and romantic locations, where power and passion collide.

HISTORICAL — Escape with historical heroes from time gone by. Whether your passion is for wicked Regency Rakes, muscled Vikings or rugged Highlanders, awaken the romance of the past.

MEDICAL — Set your pulse racing with dedicated, delectable doctors in the high-pressure world of medicine, where emotions run high and passion, comfort and love are the best medicine.

True Love — Celebrate true love with tender stories of heartfelt romance, from the rush of falling in love to the joy a new baby can bring, and a focus on the emotional heart of a relationship.

Desire — Indulge in secrets and scandal, intense drama and sizzling hot action with heroes who have it all: wealth, status, good looks…everything but the right woman.

HEROES — The excitement of a gripping thriller, with intense romance at its heart. Resourceful, true-to-life women and strong, fearless men face danger and desire - a killer combination!

To see which titles are coming soon, please visit

millsandboon.co.uk/nextmonth